Demons Force

Cassandra Morphy

Copyright 2020, 2023 Cassandra Morphy
Published by Crowbarland Books

Chapter One
The Invasion, Live and In Color

A single red light could be seen on the back of the camera. Its bright illumination fell upon the overweight and overworked cameraman sitting behind it. This single source of light made the man the only crew member that Samantha Sanderson could see from her place behind the anchor desk. This made the place a lot lonelier than she liked. But it was her responsibility to be there. To be part of the newsmakers and media, for the betterment of her and her group.

Sami was part of a secret society, one that no one outside of the group knew about. There were members of the group dedicated to making it stay that way. Their job was finding and killing anyone that knew the secret, and those members that let the secret fall into the wrong hands. After all, it was easier to create new members than keep the old ones in line through other means. The secret society had been created just months after the failed terrorist attacks on September 11th, though it had nothing to do with the events. Or, at least, not that any of the society knew about.

Sami was still reeling from the loss of their founder and leader barely a month earlier, as many of their group were. What made it that much more difficult to handle was the fact that no one had been able to figure out just how she had died. Natalie was still young, barely past 47. And yet she just passed out in the middle of an important meeting, one signaling their eleventh anniversary. Some in the group started thinking that the anniversary was related to her sudden death. But no one wanted to admit what that would mean to the group if that were true.

Still, she tried to put thoughts of that loss, and the possible ramifications, out of her mind as she focused on the last news item of the day. As usual for the last story, it was just a simple fluff piece. This was when most of their viewers were thoroughly depressed from the devastation they had been forced to report on and would need a little humor to lighten things up. This time, it was related to yet another prediction for the end of the world falling false.

"Our last story of the night takes a little more humorous bend than those we've reported on so far this hour. Today is December 21st, 2012. For those of you that aren't familiar with that date, it was the day that the Mayan calendar was set to end. Supposedly, this would signal the start of a new era, or, as some would say, the end of the world. As it is only an hour before midnight here on the west coast, I think it's pretty safe to say that that prediction, like so many that have come before it, will not be coming to pass. This, of course, will, unfortunately, mean that you will have to be going to work on Monday, just like any other Monday that has come before us. Sorry about that."

Stifled laughter came to her from behind the camera, more so than what the one cameraman could provide. It was her only indication that there were still other people back there. That they were still working the sound and light systems, where such controls couldn't be manned from the control room. Sami smiled at the humor, properly landed on the only audience she could hear from. She winked into the camera. It was her typical signal to the rest of her group that she was still loyal. That she still worked for their benefit from the relative comfort of her place in life. Most of the money she made went straight to the group. And it was a lot of money, despite being only a regional celebrity. The money was dedicated to growing their numbers and establishing themselves intrinsically in the folds of society. They were working towards the day that they could rise up, taking over the nation, and then the world. As it was so right for them to do.

The laughter died quickly, though. Quicker than Sami had been expecting. She glanced up at the clock, which was ticking down the last few seconds of the hour. "And with that, we end our broadcast," she said. "As always, I am Samantha Sanders--." Her voice cut off, as a sharp pain inserted itself into her neck from behind. Barely a split second later, she could no longer breathe. She could no longer pull air through her throat.

Screams filled the large room. The screams of several people as they ran from her. They ran from the blackened area of the room. Sami wanted to run with them. To run from whatever it was that they were running from, though she didn't know what that was. She tried to turn around. To look behind her. To try to see where that pain was coming from. The room started to dim, though it was already quite dark, with the spotlights almost blinding her. Blackness rose up to greet her, just as the sharp pain receded. She fell forward, dropping down onto the anchor desk. Her head fell just so that she was able to look behind her. Back towards a very familiar figure looming up behind her.

Sami didn't think much of the fact that she was standing behind herself. Even as the long instrument of death, the spike that had ended her life, morphed into an exact replica of her own hand. All she thought about as the light faded from her eyes was "What is this going to mean for the hulandan society?"

###

Semi was blinded as she stepped forth from the portal. It took only moments for her eyes to adjust. She had been prepared for it. She had known what to expect when she arrived on Earth from Hell. She had once lived there, back when she was still human. That was quite a long time ago, though. So long, in fact, that the world had changed quite a bit in the years since. She thought she was prepared for that. She had tried to get as much information from the other Earth born demons in the months leading up to the great departure. Then again, given where she had arrived, there was little that she would have done differently had she known what was happening.

"This, of course, will, unfortunately, mean that you will have to be going to work on Monday, just like any other Monday that has come before us. Sorry about that." The words came to her from the light in front of her. The laughter those words had conjured died quickly when the people in the room had spotted her, standing there in all her glory. She was still wearing her battle armor, as if prepared to invade Heaven itself, though that hadn't been their intent. No, mostly she just hadn't wanted to leave it behind, back in Hell. She had no intention of returning there.

Once her eyes adjusted to the world around her, the room she had found herself in, she saw the source of the voice. The woman sat right in front of her, not three feet away from her. As the portal closed behind her, the wall that had been there before fell into view. With the portal gone, she was sealed into the world. It blocked off any path of escape that she might have considered, back when she was just a lowly human.

Semi glared down at the woman in front of her. The woman was oblivious to her presence there. This gave her a few precious seconds to eye her attire, the jewelry that hung over her body, and her face. The styles of the world had obviously changed quite a bit in the intervening years. Even so, it was clear to Semi that this woman, whoever she was, was well off. She had money and status, both of which she would need to establish herself in that world, now that she was stuck there. Despite the audience in front of her, the forms she could easily make out in the shadows that fell across the far side of the room, she went to work.

She squeezed her hand, causing the dagger that was hidden in her gauntlet to slip free. It slipped forward into a locked position, perfectly lined up with the rest of her hand. With a quick thrust, Semi plunged the dagger into the back of the woman's neck. The woman let out a couple of gurgling sounds, but showed no other signs of having noticed the weapon ending her life. As the dagger fed on the woman's life's blood, Semi started to change. She shrunk almost a foot, though her previous stature was grand to begin with. This dropped her down to a more reasonable height, though still taller than she had been back when she was human. Her long, black locks, long since crusted over with the sweat, blood, and tears of her fallen enemies, became soft again, turning blond like that of the woman's. She felt more than saw her eyes turn from the harsh, golden hues to the cornflower blue that had gotten the woman far in life. As her face took on the form of the woman, Semi pulled the dagger free. She knew that her transformation into the perfect copy of her most recent victim was now complete.

With the dagger no longer holding the woman in place, she slid forward. Her face fell onto the desk that stood in front of her. The woman's eyes stared over at Semi, an accusation and a question locked in them as the life drained from them. The screams of the other people in the room barely registered to Semi as she started to strip the woman, pulling free the clothing and jewelry that would now be hers. Once she got the woman out of the strange undergarments she wore, she let the body slide down beneath the desk. It was no longer good for anything but incriminating her.

After getting dressed in the recently deceased woman's clothing, leaving her own battle armor on the floor next to the body, she pulled the chair that the woman had been sitting on towards her. Semi was taken aback when the chair rolled forward, coming towards her more freely and much quieter than she had been expecting. Still, she paid it little mind as she slid into it, rolling forward back into the position she had found the woman in. Once there, she picked up the papers that had become strewn across the desk. They were stained red in the blood of the woman. She started trying to make sense of them, trying to figure out just what role she would now take in the world at large.

She didn't notice the red light in front of her, still blinking. Nor would she have known what that meant to her and her fellow demons as, one by one, they entered the world. Each would take on the identity of someone near them when they arrived, trying to blend into the world around them. This new world that would become their own. Little did she know that her actions that day would make such a disguise almost impossible to maintain.

The camera stayed on the demon for almost an hour as she poked around the room and generally tried to acquaint herself with this new world that she found herself in. It was so much more different from the one she grew up in centuries earlier. It wasn't exactly riveting tv, but no one was in the control room to turn off the feed. Still, other broadcasters picked up the feed, showing this strange creature to everyone around the world. At the end of that extra hour of broadcasting, the feed cut away, replaced by the presidential seal. There was no introduction by reporters, no segue between the demon and what was to follow, as the president addressed the world on what was happening.

Camera flashes hit the man from every angle as he focused on the papers in his hands. The podium before him went a long way to hide the subtle shaking from the crowd. His nerves were long shot. He had been in closed door meetings with his advisers for much of the hour, though none of them had known what to say. Even as he stared down at his prepared statement, he could barely believe what he was about to tell the public.

"My fellow Americans. As we all have seen here tonight, we are not alone in the universe. My closest advisors are busy at work analyzing the broadcast that is coming out of Seattle right now. While some of you may have missed the creature's arrival, it seemed that she came through… a kind of portal.

"I've been told that this creature is not alone. That others of its… of her ilk had come through as well. I am happy to report that these portals, while spread out over a wide area, were as of yet limited to the Pacific Northwest. Specifically, to Washington and parts of northern Oregon. The portals all opened simultaneously and closed shortly after they opened. There is no reason to believe that such an event would happen again. However, we will be vigilant about any signs that would suggest such an event had occurred in the future.

"Now, as we speak, we have a strategic attack force lined up to take the creature into custody."

He looked over at one of the men that was standing on the stage next to him. The man was older, edging towards his sixties, and balding. The black suit that he wore hid much of his form. The earpiece in his ear suggested that he was a member of secret service. However, the president knew better.

The president waited before continuing with his speech, holding for a signal that was about to follow. He would have liked to have waited until after the attack on the creature to start his speech. But the people needed reassurance that everything was in order. He would make sure that they got that reassurance that night.

Once the man nodded towards the president, he continued. Thankfully, he wouldn't need the added speech that he had stuffed into his pocket.

"And she has just been apprehended."

The crowd cheered those six words. The president smiled, taking in the cheers, the adulation of those assembled, waiting for it to abate naturally. If anything was going to go wrong, it would be then, with the creature just getting pulled into custody. He had been assured that they were quite capable of handling someone, something, like her.

"While we still don't know what these creatures are, where they came from, or how many have come through, I have tasked a new organization to discover just that. I present to you Agent Herbert Branch, head of the Homeland Protection Services."

The president motioned towards the balding man, before leading the crowd in another round of applause. He stepped away from the podium, giving Herb the floor to talk about his plans for the efforts to chase down and apprehend, or kill, all of these creatures.

Herb just stood there, shocked as he stared at the president. It was clear that he hadn't been expecting the move. But the president was just glad that the spotlights weren't on him anymore.

Chapter Two
Ten Months Later a Body Was Found

The black crown vic made its way through the parked cars, getting as close as possible to the yellow tape that marked off the area. Hank knew that anyone looking on would be impressed by his maneuvering of the car through the tight gaps, though that wasn't why he did it. He just wanted to be lazy, and it helped to have the car close at hand, the HPS insignia emblazoned on the hood. Just the sight of that symbol, the heralding cry of their organization, was enough to open doors that would normally be shut hard. At least when it came to a federal agency hoarding in on a local crime scene.

Even with his advanced driving skills, he could only get the car so close. This left a good dozen or so paces between where he was forced to park and where the local cops were standing. It had been mostly luck that they were in the area when they got the call. There had been a report of an incident just three towns over that turned out to be little more than a rumor, barely even a false report. The supposed demon had been a human with implants to make it look like he had horns. Ever since the demons had invaded, his little two man team had been run ragged by their organization, the Homeland Protection Services. With Seattle being the epicenter of the invasion, and, coincidentally, the location that their group had moved to after the incident in New York, it was their organization that had been tasked to keep the demons in line. It wouldn't have been so bad if they had gotten the increased personnel that they had requested months ago. But with the post turning into little more than a babysitting gig, not many were wanting it.

As he turned off the engine, Hank nodded over to his partner, Jack, sitting in the passenger seat. They had been working together for over a decade, long before the demons had even shown up. They knew each other well enough as not to need words. This had a tendency to unnerve the locals a little, as the mystery behind their organization was as deep, and twice as broad, as those surrounding the MIB, the Illuminati, and the supposed alliance between the Abominable Snowman, Bigfoot, and the Loch Ness Monster. The air of mystery had its place, helping out at times. It got in the way just as often, mostly when it came to their social life. Hank thanked his lucky stars every day that he had met Blanche when he did.

In almost coordinated unison, the two agents stepped out of their car. Each pulled out identical sunglasses, putting them on in one fluid, well-practiced motion. The practice made them look like twins, despite the fact that Hank was a good six inches taller than Jack and they weren't the least bit related.

"Alright," someone called out near the crime scene. "Wrap it up."

"Think we missed all the action?" Jack asked. Despite being with the organization for almost twelve years, Jack was the least experienced among them. He had come in during the incident from a somewhat unsavory, but mostly civilian, life. Hank still found it refreshing, if not slightly annoying, that he could be so naïve at times. Often, he thought it was his only redeeming quality. He just didn't let that fact show when he could avoid it.

"The body was only reported a couple of hours ago," Hank said. "There's no way they'd be done so quickly." He started leading the way, weaving in and out of the crisscrossing cars that had blocked the last few feet of their drive up to the scene. They came to the yellow tape while the assembled masses of officers and detectives started to pack up their equipment.

The tape flowed outward, crossing the entire width of the street and wrapping around a tree on the left and a stop sign on the right. Hank followed the flow of yellow into the distance, where it met with a telephone pole and a mailbox. The intersection was just a T-junction with the cross street on the right coming to an end. It was packed with the blue uniformed officers, the detectives in their cheap suits, and three CSI specialists in their t-shirts, proudly showing their department across the back. Jack gave him his usual puppy dog eyes, his usual plea for them to trade in their signature black suits for something more laid back like the t-shirts. Hank didn't bother reminding him that they would often need to blend in more than the t-shirts would have allowed.

Everyone was swarming around as they packed up everything they had already pulled out to document and mark the scene. The crowd was so thick that Hank still couldn't make out the body that was supposedly in the middle of all of that. He knew it was there, from the report that had gone over the radio and the follow-up request from Herb himself, the director of the HPS and Hank's direct supervisor. The only good side of having so few agents in the organization was the short chain of command. As the two men approached, the crowd seemed to part, letting them in, almost embracing them, as they entered the crime scene. Jack pulled up the yellow tape, stretching it against the tension built up within it. Three of the uniformed officers left just as they entered, as if the area was already at capacity and they needed to leave in order to obey the fire code.

As the crowd broke around them, like so much water on the rocks of the shore, one man came into view. His imposing glare on the others left little doubt that he was the man in charge there. Or, at least, he had been, before Hank and Jack had arrived. Hank set his sights on the man and walked through the crowd, knowing they would part around him with little prodding on his part. He felt more than saw Jack's continued presence in his wake, the comradery between them almost palpable when surrounded by the local police force.

"You're the Demon Force, right?" the man asked, when they got close enough to be heard at a normal volume over the bustling happening all around them.

Hank flinched at the term, as if their mandate had been limited to this one aspect of the unexplainable that had taken over the shadows of their world over the past twelve years, rather than the entirety of it. He had to admit that, since the invasion, the demons had been dominating their attention. But there were still missions that had nothing to do with them. Still people that need saving from less recognizable forces that are still running amuck in their world.

"Yes, we're the HPS," Hank corrected, through his teeth. He eyed a CSI tech that came unusually close to him before scurrying off, her toolbox clutched securely in her hands as if she was afraid that they would take it from her.

"I figured, on account of that insignia on the hood of your car," he said. Hank rolled his eyes as the man revealed just how stupid his original question really was. "Anyway, you think a demon did this?" he asked. The man nodded over to the body, not five feet from where they were standing. As he did, the crowd seemed to part, like the fog lifting, revealing the body in all its morbid glory.

"No," Hank said. He shook his head, as he looked down at Jared.

He was immediately recognizable for Hank, despite his contorted visage. Tire marks could be seen in the black blood that spread out from his body, glistening in the sunlight from above, shining off the darker shade of the asphalt beneath it. His left arm, the source of much of the blood, was broken in three places, his skin stretched out where the tire ran over it. There was swelling all along his forehead, enough that it should have made identifying the body difficult. His legs were bent back underneath him, with bones poking out at obscene places. The body was not a pretty sight, and as Jack started to gag, Hank waved him off, pointing him away from the crime scene so he would throw up away from any evidence that might still need to be collected.

"This is the demon," Hank said. "Jared DeGregor."

"What? No, he's not," the detective insisted. "Demons revert to their old form when killed."

"Actually, no, they don't," Hank said. "You're thinking of shapeshifters."

"Wait, there are shapeshifters, too?"

"Not that we've encountered," Jack said, around a few dry heaves. He was doubled over near the yellow tape, leaning against the tree that it was wrapped around, and safely away from anything that would need to be documented.

"And even if we had, we wouldn't be able to discuss that with you," Hank said. He focused on the body and the ground around it, trying to commit everything there was to see to memory. He would also take as many pictures as he could, once the crowd had dispersed fully and he had command of the crime scene. Still, he knew those first few hours in a case were crucial, and he would need the research team to start doing their thing as soon as possible. "How long ago was this reported?" he asked.

"What?" the detective asked. "Oh, the hit and run? That was about three hours ago. We got here soon after to secure the scene. The ME did her preliminary report, saying the body had been here another two hours before it was reported. But, now that we know it's a demon, that could be any amount of time, I guess. I would have figured that the ME would have been able to tell the difference."

"That would have made the shapeshifting quite useless if it could be detected so easily by untrained eyes, wouldn't it?" Hank asked. "We have ways of determining a person's demonic status."

"Oh?" the detective asked. "What are those?" Hank just glared at the man, making it clear that he wasn't about to answer that question. It wasn't just that the actual method was classified Need to Know. It was that he didn't like admitting the simplicity of the process, the almost juvenile nature of it. "I just figured it might be good for the rest of us, you know, the civilians, to know these sorts of things so we know how to handle these cases better."

"That was why the HPS was awarded jurisdiction on these cases," Hank said. "So that you civilians won't have to know information that would only come up on those rare cases when a demon is involved."

"Rare cases?" the detective asked. "Dude, that's all we get around here. And it's not just the demon on human crimes, neither. We have plenty of demon on demon stuff. You think this is one of those?"

Hank eyed the man, wondering how he could be so ignorant of the most basic information on demons if he had to deal with them as often as he was claiming. "I won't know anything until I start investigating," Hank said, simply, trying to signal that the Q&A part of the detective's departure was quite over.

"Alright," he said, thankfully taking the hint. "I'm leaving. I'm sure you have your own secret methods on how to deal with these crimes. Pull out your top-secret gizmos that the demons gave you as part of their whole amnesty agreement, and whatever. Don't let me hold you up. I'm sure you'll have this whole thing solved by suppertime."

"Isn't supper an hour from now?" Jack asked. He looked at his watch as he made his way back towards the body. When he got halfway there, though, he made another gagging sound, contorting on the spot, before turning around and heading back to his supportive tree.

"I really hate when you lose your cool around the locals," Hank said, once he made sure that the area was clear. The last few cars were starting to pull out, carefully making their way around the crown vic, expertly avoiding scratching its stellar paint job. "It's unprofessional."

"Yea, well I hate when you pretend to know stuff that you don't," Jack said, once he managed to get his stomach settled once more. This time, however, he stayed where he was, on the fringes of the scene, away from the sight of the body. Although the smell would have permeated the entire area already. "You even do it with me, and I'm your partner."

"No, you're the idiot that I got stuck with for the past twelve years," Hank said. "Maybe once you grow up, we'll discuss you becoming an actual partner."

"Yea, I'll do that," Jack said, sarcastically. "In the meantime, why don't you pull out our 'top-secret gizmos'?" He snickered at the thought that the demons would be able to provide us with any technology at all. "Civilians," he scoffed.

Hank rolled his eyes at his erstwhile partner, as he pulled out his smartphone. Though it was state of the art, for three years ago, it wasn't the least bit tricked out or had anything to do with demons. That is, at least, other than the several thousand contact information entries that were listed inside of it. All the registered demons in the area, their charges. He pulled up the contacts, scrolling down to one of the seven non-demon entries in the list and hitting send.

Before the phone had a chance to ring, Danielle had already picked it up in the home office. "Homeland Protection Services, how may I direct your call?" she said.

"They still have you manning the phone?" Hank said, as way of greeting. "Tell Herb to get off his lazy ass and hire an actual receptionist already."

"Hank," she said. Her voice took on the usual sunny disposition that they all knew her for. "He's hired three since you've been in the field. All of them were just here to get a sight of the demons we have locked up here. I kept telling them that there's no way for us to hold a demon for long, the usual company line. You have no idea how much I miss Lynette."

"Yea, that poor, poor girl," Hank said.

"Oh, don't give me that," she huffed. "She's just on maternity leave. Now, what's up? I know you didn't call in just to catch up."

"No, you're right. I called in to see if you have anything for me on my case."

"What would you boys do without me?" Danielle asked.

"Starve," Hank said. "Die hopelessly alone and destitute."

"Maybe one day you'll realize that and actually let me out in the field," she said.

"But then who will keep Herb company?" Hank joked, trying to change the subject. Danielle often complained about being stuck behind a desk for the past two decades. Even before the New York incident, back when the group was part of a larger, more clandestine organization. When almost all of the old organization was unceremoniously terminated, in a very gory manner, those that were left behind fell into their own little niches. There was little support to let any of them branch out and develop their careers.

"Alright, let me pull this up. Oh, no. Not Jared. He was nice. You know, for a demon."

"Well, now, that's just specist," Hank said. "I've known plenty of demons that were... well, not as nice as you, but certainly nicer than me."

"Yea, and that's saying something," Jack said. Hank just waved him off as he focused on the call.

"You just only get to meet the bad demons because you're stuck in the office all the time and those are the only ones that we bring in. Maybe if you got out more..."

"Maybe if Herb would hire the fifty people we need around here, I'll be able to get out more."

"Yea, with what budget?" Herb's voice could be heard in the background.

"Alright, anyway," Danielle said. "We do have some sat vid of the incident. I'm sending that to your phone now, but it's not going to do you any good. I couldn't get an angle on the plates. The traffic cam system is still light in that area, so we don't have any feed on that. I even tracked the vehicle back to the parking garage it was parked at, but it had been there since dawn. I could try to get the system to work on a longer window, but that can take some time and long jobs like that need to be stuck in the queue, which is like three months behind already. You're better off trying to find it where it ended up."

"And that would be?" Hank asked.

"Another parking garage. It's a mile down the road. I've already sent the address to your phone."

"Great," Hank said. "So, you've already solved the murder for us?"

"Not quite. You did at least get the notes from the officers on scene, didn't you?"

Hank went quiet, his face going pale, as he started to look around him. Everyone had already cleared out, leaving no signs behind that they had ever been there, besides the yellow tape that still framed the scene, three evidence markers, and a cigarette bud that may or may not have been there before the crew had come. The evidence markers, small, yellow plastic signs, marked three seemingly random places around the body. They showed where evidence had been taken away, though he had no idea what evidence it was or where it had gone to. There weren't even any uniformed officers watching the scene, keeping the civilians out of their way.

"Uh, no," he said.

"I'm already halfway through the form to request the files," she said.

"See? You're far too important right where you are," Hank said. "We can't spare you from the desk to have you out in the field."

"Oh, please," Danielle huffed. "If I were a man--"

"Hey, this has nothing to do with gender," Hank said, blocking off the usual argument. "You know my wife is in the field more often than I am. This has to do with the fact that you're not trained to be a field agent. You're an analyst, an amazing analyst. Don't sell yourself short. Not even Lynette can do what you do."

"Yea, right," Danielle mumbled. "I'll send over the report once we get it. In the meantime, the local coroner will be by shortly to pick up the body. Did the ME at least do the initial assessment?"

"Uh... Wait, I know that one," Hank said. "Yes, the detective said something about an ME being by."

"Well, why don't you have Jack babysit the body while you head over to check out the parking garage where the car is at?" Danielle suggested.

"Because I'm afraid to come back to find him having burned the body," he whispered into the phone, holding his hand over his mouth to prevent Jack from hearing him.

"Oh, please. He hasn't burned anything in five years. Well, at least nothing that he's not supposed to burn."

"That we know about," Hank said. He eyed his supposed partner over his shoulder. Jack was just standing over by the tree, leaning against it, as he eyed the body. Hank still didn't trust the guy, not even after all those years. He always felt like Jack was little more than an adult child, needing to have his hand held the entire time he was outside. Leaving him unsupervised was completely out of the question. "Besides," Hank said, in a normal volume. "It's not like the car is going anywhere. If they were going to torch it, they would have done so already."

"Huh?" Jack asked, as if the word torch had pulled him out of some internal discussion.

"It was parked there minutes after the accident," Danielle agreed. "Which was a good eight hours ago, by the way. Just get as much documentation of the scene as you can before heading out. If you're not going to leave Jack behind, you're going to have to release the crime scene once you leave. Herb isn't going to approve any payments for crime scene guards this time."

"Pfft, for a murdered demon? Hell, no," Herb said, in the background. Danielle and Hank tried not to laugh at the unintentional pun that he had made. Herb hated being laughed at when he wasn't in on it.

Chapter Three
Quick Work of the Search

Hank hated having to close down the crime scene before he was certain that all evidence was collected. It just went against the grain for him. Usually, the HPS came in after the fact, after the locals had done all the legwork. It allowed them to come in and sweep up. They'd usually put in the finishing touches in order to finish the case where the locals couldn't. Provide some evidence or knowledge of the demons that the local police didn't have. Supply the equipment that they had access to. It didn't exactly make them popular, as they were still taking credit for other people's work. But it was what needed to be done. Besides, it allowed the group to over deliver, despite being under budgeted.

    He missed the days, just ten months earlier, when they weren't so bogged down. Their mandate was to investigate the unexplained, the unexplainable, the cases where words like magic and wormholes would end up in the final report. Heck, their first official case had a time traveler in it. Though it had been happening a lot more often as of late, it wasn't until the demons showed up that their ten person organization was suddenly not enough for it. When not having enough field personnel actually made the difference. Herb kept insisting that their budget would increase at some point. But Hank was beginning to think that would never happen.

    So, it was with a heavy heart that, once the local coroner had come to pick up the body, Hank got back into their crown vic and drove right through the yellow tape that marked off the intersection. The people from the neighborhood had started to congregate around the scene, especially after rumors that the deceased was actually a demon. He knew that the tape wouldn't keep them out for long. He was just thankful that they had been able to get the body out of there before the neighbors had started to rush the scene.

Jack watched the intersection fade into the distance in the rear-view mirror as Hank concentrated on the road in front of them. The address to the parking garage was already entered into the GPS, though he needn't have bothered. The place was just two blocks up the street, on the same street that had flowed through the crime scene. As he turned into the garage, he could just see the faintest fluttering of the yellow tape up the street from them.

"Not exactly the best hiding spot in the world," Jack said. "Think the driver is still in the car?"

"I'd be a little surprised if they were. The question that's been running through my head is why they only ran this far. Why didn't they just keep on driving?"

"They ran over a demon," Jack said. "Don't you think the car would be damaged by that? At the very least, the tire would need to be changed, because it drove through Jared's blood. The acid would have gotten on the rubber and eaten through it in the first few minutes. They probably had to ditch the car here because they couldn't drive it any further on flat tires. I was just wondering why they didn't drive down a side street and hide it in an alley somewhere."

Even after all these years, it always surprised Hank when Jack showed how smart he was, proved his worth to the team. When he was first under investigation by the secret organization, the predecessor to the HPS, he had already burned down twenty buildings. The local police departments, stretching over several towns, were completely clueless about the perpetrator, who seemed to have more ways of burning down buildings than they had buildings to destroy. Still, he found it rather refreshing that Jack's intelligence could be turned to something more productive. It kept him on the straight and narrow and, more importantly, the right side of the law for the past twelve years. Then again, Jack might not feel the same way about it.

"Right," Hank said. He reached over to press the button on the machine barring his entry into the garage. It spit out a ticket, letting out a buzzing sound as it waited for him to take it. Once the machine detected the removal of the thick piece of paper, the barricade dropped down into the ground in front of him, revealing the interior of the garage. "We're looking for a light SUV, probably showing damage--"

"And flat tires," Jack added. "And I imagine it's that one right there." He pointed off to the side, barely three spots from the entrance on the first row of parking spots. The lane continued onward for the entire stretch of the block, with cars clogging up both sides of the aisle. The spots closest to them, the ones near the entrance, were mostly empty, as those that had gotten into the structure early enough to claim those most sought after spots had already started to head home for the day. The SUV in question was alone, surrounded by several empty spots, which practically placed a bright spotlight on it, the spotlight of the sun streaming in through the entrance. "Do I get a prize?" he asked.

"This isn't a game," Hank said. "This is homicide."

"My money is on vehicular manslaughter," Jack said. "I like giving strangers the benefit of the doubt."

"Why? Because no one gave you it?"

"No, no, no. I so didn't deserve it. But, well, you know me. I always like to look on the bright side of things."

"Yea, and if you can't find one, you'll light it on fire to give it a bright side," Hank said, regretting it immediately.

Hank pulled into one of the spots on the other side of the lane from the SUV, giving it plenty of space so as not to contaminate any evidence that might have survived the intervening hours since it had parked there. With little more than a passing glance at the windows as they passed, he knew that no one was inside. Still, as protocol dictated, he took out his gun as he got out of the car, slipping it free from his shoulder holster in one swift motion. Seconds after Jack slammed his own door, Hank could hear the man notching his gun, despite the fact that doing so had no effect on his ability to fire the weapon. Together, the two of them cautiously moved forward, heading for the abandoned vehicle.

Hank crossed paths with Jack as he went for the driver's side, their usual pattern when approaching a suspect vehicle. He trained his gun on the Nissan logo on the back. The silver of the logo blended well with the light gray of the vehicle itself, the overhead lights reflecting off the unmarred paint job. He pulled out his cell phone, double checking the aerial view photo of the SUV as it hit Jared. Hank wanted to make absolutely sure that this was the car they were looking for. The rear tires were both flat. The rubber was peeling away, almost melting, joining in with the noticeable pool of oil and other fluids that had been accumulating beneath it. After taking a deep sniff of the air, trying to detect the more explosive chemicals one usually finds in a car, he made a quick glance over at his partner, who would be the first to recognize the dangers of anything blowing up. With no signal coming from Jack, Hank took two shuffling steps to his left before heading along the side of the car.

The windows showed no signs of added tints. The interior was easily visible through the glass. The back seat was spotless, as if the car had never been used, had just been driven off the dealership's lot. Although the child seat in the back was certainly not standard for that model. As he came up to the front seat, he wasn't surprised to find it similarly pristine. The leather seats and steering wheel glistened as if recently polished. Once he got there, though, he noticed the damage that had been hidden from his view of the rear. The hood was busted open, with a huge hump in the middle that would make seeing while driving difficult, if not downright impossible. The front bumper was simply missing, though he didn't remember seeing it at the scene, or along the drive to the garage. The hubcap on the driver's side was no longer attached to the wheel; instead, it was somehow embedded into the fender, the metal bent back around the place of its insertion. The engine still gave off a low hum, though he could already see that the keys were no longer in the ignition.

Hank glanced over at Jack, who seemed to be in pain as he stared at the injured car. He had never taken the man as much of a car guy, except for how well they burned, but it was clear that he sympathized with the vehicle. Jack had holstered his weapon at some point, probably, hopefully, after it was clear that there was no one inside the car. After another glance around the area, Hank followed suit. He let his jacket flop back down over the holster, hiding the weapon from sight, though still readily available if needed.

"It looks wiped down," Jack said. "I'd be surprised if we get a single print from it."

"Yes, but we'll still need to run the scene," Hank said. "Why don't you call it in while I search for clues."

"Oh, wow, are you really trusting me to make a case related phone call?" he asked, sarcastically. "I wonder if Huey and Dewey are even available right now."

"Don't call them that," Hank snapped. He hated Jack's animosity towards the in-house CSI team, something that he never quite understood. While Dr. Howard and Dr. Davidson were very much on the nerdy side of things, they were perfectly decent people for what they did. The pair of them had been added to the team soon after the New York incident, along with Hank's wife, Blanche, and her partner. They had all been a part of a different clandestine organization that had been defunded at the same time as the incident, and the HPS inherited them. Perhaps he always had a soft spot in his heart for the pair of them more due to their proximity to Blanche than their own merit. "Just make sure you have Danielle run those plates. Now that we can actually see them, perhaps they'll lead us to the culprit."

Jack rolled his eyes at Hank, perhaps at the condescension that was plain in his voice, before heading off to the garage entrance to get a signal. Hank jogged back to the crown vic to get gloves, from the glove compartment, of course, before trying to examine the SUV. Once the gloves were in place, Hank headed over to the passenger side door first, wanting to leave the driver's side untouched for the CSI team. Even if there had been a passenger in the car when they had run over poor Jared, it would be the driver that they were looking to arrest.

Carefully, Hank tried the passenger side door, though he wasn't surprised in the least that it was locked. He peeked in through the window, looking around for evidence, or for any sign of the keys inside. The inside looked as clean from that angle as it had from the driver's side. Reluctantly, he made his way back over to the driver's side door, trying that one as well. He was surprised to find that door unlocked. It swung open freely and easily, despite the damage. Still, he avoided touching the inside of the car, merely reaching in to hit the unlock button on the door, unlocking the passenger's side. Before he closed the driver's side door, however, he noticed something in the well by the pedals. The one item marring the otherwise pristine interior of the car was a pile, a pool, a puddle of dark dirt spread across the floor. There was a dark footprint of the stuff on the accelerator, but only a single print on the brake. That print, perfectly preserved in its singularity, its solitary, showed the perfect cross print of the driver's boot. And it was a boot, that much was clear from the print, the width too great to be anything less substantial. The tread marks themselves were almost familiar, a song playing in his mind that he couldn't quite remember the tune to.

By the time he made it back over to the passenger door, Jack had returned from his call. Still, he ignored his partner for a moment as he reached into the car. He did a quick search of the glove compartment, trying to find something on the driver other than the boot print. As he opened the compartment, a random assortment of papers fell out, spilling across the floor and seat. Those that fell on top were mostly menus for takeout and old receipts. He started poking around in them, trying to pull information where none was available.

"Any luck?" Jack asked.

"Shouldn't I be asking you that?" Hank asked.

"I got the address of the owner of the car, and the CSI team was already on its way here. They were just three states over, so it will take them some time to get here. I gave her the location of the car, so, I'm hoping we're not going to waste time babysitting this place as well."

"I doubt we'll be getting much from the car," Hank admitted. "I don't know. Something just isn't sitting well with me."

"Oh, not that again," Jack said, with a huff. "You are not psychic. You can't tell the future, no matter what you think of yourself."

"I'm not talking about that," he said. "Though you have to admit that I do get feelings sometimes. Impressions of something that's about to happen. I'm not talking about actually knowing the future, knowing what's to come, just that something was about to."

"Yes, Hank, something is always about to happen. That's how time works. Without things happening, nothing ever will."

"Alright, alright, no need to get snarky with me," Hank said.

"Get?" Jack asked. "When am I not snarky with you?"

"That's actually a good question. Why is that, do you think?"

"I don't know, maybe it has something to do with how you recruited me into your organization twelve years ago."

"No, I don't think that's it. You wouldn't be holding a grudge all this time. Besides, it's not like we didn't give you an alternative."

"Yea, yea, yea, I kept your secrets and you kept me out of prison," Jack said. "Let's just get on with it."

"Prison?" Hank asked. "Did you really think that after the New York incident, prison was still on the table? Anyway, is the car's owner far from here?"

"That, I don't know," Jack said. "But her address isn't far from the garage that the car came from. We'll be there in about twenty minutes, if we can leave here at all."

"Fine, fine," Hank said. "We're not getting anything here."

He tossed the random assortments of papers back into the glove compartment, snapping it shut afterwards. Three pieces of paper, three receipts, flitted down in the air displaced by the slamming shut of the compartment. They danced down in the air, playing with the light as they found their way through the open doorway. Once they landed on the floor, Hank scooped them up, one at a time, depositing them in an evidence bag that he always carried around in his pocket.

"Did you set up the spy cam?" Hank asked. As part of their investigations, they always set up spy cameras in key locations. Hank had set up the one by the crime scene, embedding it into the tree that had held the yellow police tape, trained on where the body had been. Over the years, they had developed quite a network of the cams, not having bothered to go back to retrieve those that were no longer useful to them. The network had solved four cases that year alone, without having to put in any more field work. Herb liked the camera network mostly because it was cheaper than hiring new personnel.

"Of course," Jack said. He pointed towards the wall near the car, where the small camera was just barely visible from their position. If he hadn't known where to look, he would have missed it completely.

Hank nodded his approval at his choice of positions. He made one final glance around the inside of the car, making sure he hadn't missed the one piece of evidence, plain to the eye, that might solve the case. When none presented itself to him, he slammed the door shut, leaving it and the rest of them unlocked for the CSI team that would be along shortly. As they walked back to the crown vic, he pulled the gloves free of his hands, snapping them twice in the process, and slid them into his pocket along with the evidence bag.

Chapter Four
The Owner Did It

They parked the crown vic in the parking garage that the car had driven out of, barely nine hours earlier. The parking spots were all labeled with numbers, though one section was filled with spots simply labeled "guest". All of these spots were filled, all the way up to the fourth floor of the garage. This was the top floor, open to the sunlight above. It was getting late, the sun already setting in the distance. Hank knew that Jack would be complaining about missing dinner soon, and they would be stuck taking a break before heading back to the office. He just hoped that this next stop would have the answers that had eluded him at the other parking garage.

As they made their way down through the building, they stopped off at the second floor, where Hank had noticed the number 2852 emblazoned on an empty spot. This was the address that was on the registration for the SUV. He wasn't sure what to expect from the place, the vacant space that must have housed the car so recently. There were cars on either side of the spot, blocking the lights from above and bathing the empty slot in darkness and shadow. Hank pulled out his cellphone, using the display to light up the area. The only thing that he saw in the low light from his phone was a single boot print, an echo of the one he had found on the brake pedal in the SUV. The rest of the area was too disturbed to find anything of use. He took a quick photo of the boot print, hoping that it would help narrow the suspect list down.

"If that belongs to the driver, I'd hate to run into him in a dark alleyway," Jack said, pointing at the print. "That dude must be huge."

"I'm no expert on boot size; I'm hoping the CSI team will be able to get something off of it. In the meantime, we have the car's owner to interview."

"I doubt that Cassidy Masters would be the owner of the boot. She's probably a bubbly twenty-something that has a tendency to date older, bigger, scarier men that love to borrow her car to commit vehicular manslaughter with."

"God, you have a weird mind," Hank said, and not for the first time. "And, yet, you remain hopeful that this wasn't a murder, despite the fact that the victim was a demon. I just don't think a coincidence like that is possible right now. Not with the invasion still fresh in everyone's mind."

"That's like saying a gay person being run over is a coincidence," Jack said. "There's no way for most people to tell the difference between a human and a demon, certainly not while driving a car at the time. At least not one that we know of. All we know for certain right now is that he was run over by that SUV and the owner lives here."

"And, yet, I've seen it enough times to know that it's never that simple," Hank said. "Trust me, this will come back around to someone who had a grudge against Jared for some supposed wrong. Perhaps even something that had nothing to do with Jared himself. Maybe it was the invasion as a whole, or he wasn't even their intended victim. Believe me, this had murder written all over it."

"I'll remain cautiously optimistic, if that's alright with you."

"Whatever," Hanks said, rolling his eyes at the naivety of his partner. "Let's go. We're not going to find anything here."

By the time they made it back to the ground floor of the parking garage and out into the open, the sun had set and the street lights drained out the last few rays that the buildings didn't block. Jack led the way around to the north most of the three buildings that bordered the garage that serviced them. There were several signs posted on the building displaying the number two all over it. They indicated that it was building two, and, thusly, the one that belonged to their current person of interest, Ms. Cassidy Masters, the owner of the SUV.

Cloistered within the four buildings, the three apartment buildings and the parking garage itself, was a small sitting area and garden. The trees hung over the path that led through them, giving shade where none was needed, except perhaps at high noon when the sun could beam down between the buildings. Still, the place would have provided a decent amount of nature in the otherwise developed city. As they passed through it, Hank watched as Jack eyed the trees around them. He wondered if he was simply enjoying the little bit of nature or if he was thinking of burning them down to the ground. It always irked him that Herb had offered him a position in their organization. He would like nothing more than to report on him to the boss man and get him fired. Or, better yet, locked in prison for the rest of his life like he should have been. Just as they left that little piece of nature, Jack looked back towards Hank. There was a bright smile on his face as if he knew exactly what the man was thinking.

The path led directly to the front door of the building, as it was facing the inner courtyard. The outer door was locked, as was typical for most apartment buildings in the city, with an intercom system built into the wall by the door. Instead of a listing of the tenants, each with their own button, the intercom had the standard 12 button dial for any regular phone.

"What do you think?" Jack asked, nodding towards the intercom.

"I don't like it," he said. "I don't like needing to announce ourselves to a possible suspect like that. She could make a run for it."

"Out of where?" Jack asked. "Isn't this the only door?"

"Why don't you take a loop of the building and see?" Hank said. His question was more of an order than a suggestion. Jack, knowing full well that he wouldn't get away with not following the order, started heading off around to the left. Hank waited until his partner had gone out of sight before picking up the phone handset that hung from the intercom and entered the 2852 of the apartment number, hoping that he wasn't about to have to chase after the woman.

"Yes?" came a voice from the handset. The woman had answered almost immediately after he had dialed, as if the woman had been waiting by the phone. Perhaps she had been waiting for someone to come, perhaps to ask about her missing SUV.

"This is Agent Gorning of the Homeland Protection Services. I have a few questions to ask of a Ms. Cassidy Masters."

"Oh, yes, that's me," the voice said, sounding much older than Hank had been expecting. "Why don't you come up." The intercom let out a click before going silent.

A few seconds later, the front door buzzed. Hank quickly grabbed hold of the door handle, pulling it open. He paused there, looking between the inside of the building and the path that Jack had followed to take a circuit of the building. He knew he should wait for his partner, knew that he shouldn't go in alone. But he didn't want to risk the suspect bolting, running out some back door that he didn't know about. As a compromise, Hank grabbed a rock that was just inside the door, placing it inside the doorway to hold the door open before heading into the building.

The entry area was small, with little more than two elevators standing side by side. There were doors on the two side walls, extending into the building in either direction, leading to the ground floor apartments. Hank paid little mind to those doors, taking the three steps that it took to cross the small room and come to the elevators. He clicked the button to call them before he came to a stop. The elevator on his left quickly let off a ding as the circular light above it blinked three times. The doors opened, revealing the usual metal walls and dirty floor. After stepping inside, Hank gave one last glance at the front door, wondering if Jack would catch up with him, before pressing the button for the eighth floor.

The door labeled 2852 wasn't far from the elevator, with 2801 on the right and the numbers heading up as it made the circle around to 2860 on the left. Hank made sure that his gun was loose in his holster before knocking on the door. He hoped he wouldn't need it. As with the intercom, he got a response almost instantly, with the door flying open quickly and cleanly, revealing the last person he would have expected to see there.

Cassidy Masters stood barely five feet tall, if she were standing straight. However, as she stood there, her hand clasped firmly on the door handle, she was stooped over quite a bit. In her other hand was a walking cane that was showing much abuse, with dings and scrapes all up and down its length. She was wearing what appeared to be a nightgown, bathrobe and slippers, and glasses thicker than Hank had ever seen outside of a movie. The old woman's face was covered with deep wrinkles, distorting her features to the point of making her all but unrecognizable to anyone that had known her in her youth. She stared up at him, barely being able to raise her head to look straight at him. "Agent Gorning?" she asked.

"That's right," Hank said, visibly relaxing. He wondered why Jack hadn't mentioned the woman's age. He could imagine him sitting outside under the trees, after only pretending to look for another escape route that the woman might have taken, laughing his full head off at his expense.

"How can I help the HPS today?" she asked, almost as if seeing an HPS agent was a regular thing for her.

"I'm here about your SUV," Hank said. "Do you know where it is right now?"

"It's in my spot, isn't it?" she asked. "I don't know. I don't get much use out of it. The dumb thing costs more than it's worth. I don't drive, myself, you see." She gestured up to her glasses, seeming to indicate that she couldn't see well enough to drive. "It mostly just collects dust in that spot of mine as it drains my limited income."

"Ah, well, okay," Hank said. "Why don't you just get rid of it then?"

"Well, I keep it around for... sentimental reasons, Agent Gorning. I could no sooner get rid of it than use it."

"Uh huh," he said, pensively. "When was the last time you saw the vehicle, exactly?"

"Oh, it must have been, I don't know, maybe a couple of weeks. I don't get out much these days, and, as I said, I don't--"

"Don't use it. Right. So, would it surprise you to find out that the vehicle wasn't in your spot right now?"

"Why, yes, it would," she said. "It isn't there?"

"No, ma'am. It's a couple of miles away, in another parking garage completely. You didn't drive it there?"

"Why, no, of course not. As I said--"

"Yes, you don't drive it much."

"Is the vehicle alright?" she asked. "I'm not getting a parking ticket, am I? I wouldn't think that kind of thing within your wheelhouse, being in the HPS and all. It really is a dreadful cost, that thing. But..."

"Does anyone else use the vehicle on a regular basis?" he asked. "Does anyone else have a set of keys?"

"Oh, heaven's no," she said. "No, it's just little ol' me these days. I have the only set of keys right here." She reached into the apartment, over to her left. Hank heard the keys jangling in her shaking, wrinkled hands, before she managed to show them to him around the edge of the door. "It's the only set of keys left right now."

"So, then, it would surprise you to know that the SUV was used in a hit and run a few hours ago?" Hank asked, exasperated, confused, and thoroughly annoyed as their only lead turned out to be a complete dead end.

"Yes," she said, sounding completely surprised by this revelation. "Was anyone hurt?"

"I'm afraid they were killed, ma'am."

"Oh, that poor dear. I hope their family is alright. I know how hard it is to lose someone suddenly like that."

"He actually didn't have any family," Hank said.

"Ah, well, thank God for that. At least no one else should suffer such a loss as that. Now, is there anything else you need from me?"

"No, ma'am," Hank said, shaking his head. "That should be all. Sorry for the bother."

"Oh, no bother at all. Really. Come by anytime. I don't get many visitors these days. Uh, any chance I could get the SUV back at some point? It really is such a waste to not use the thing, but I just couldn't bear parting with it for long."

Hank nodded to her. "We'll see about getting it back to you as soon as we're done with it, though it took some damage during the accident."

"Oh, well, that's fine. As I said--"

"You don't use it much, right," Hank said. He nodded to her again, feeling like he should be tapping his hat or something, before turning away from the overly unhelpful woman. He retraced his steps back to the elevator, heading back down to the ground floor, completely empty handed for all his efforts.

As the elevator doors opened up again, revealing the small entry room, Jack was standing there, his gun free, aimed directly at him. For a split second, he glared at the man, thinking "This is it. This is the moment that he turns on me, that he kills me. He'll probably frame it on the same person that killed Jared." But, then, just as suddenly, Jack lowered his gun. Relief spread across his face, quickly followed by a smile.

"There you are," he said, his voice full of concern. "What happened to you? Why didn't you wait for me? Did you find her? Why didn't you arrest her? Is she dead? Should I call the coroner over here?"

Hank just stood there, in complete annoyance and incredulity, for almost a complete minute before saying, "Why the hell didn't you tell me the woman was almost ninety?"

Chapter Five
The Home Office

"Hank, I swear, I didn't know. Would you look at this report? It said she was twenty-eight."

"Will you stop trying to show me the damn report?" Hank snapped. Granted, it was the first time that Jack had offered him the report when he wasn't driving. Jack had brought it up on his phone on the way over and kept throwing it at him when Hank was trying to focus on the road. He continued to present it to him out in the open, as they tried to make their way to the home office. With the team as small as it was, they had to share the floor with another company, which made security a delicate thing.

Before the invasion, the HPS was still a covert organization, working behind the scenes and usually under the mantle of some other group. Whichever would open the most doors on the case they were working on. Hank still had his badges for the FBI, the DEA, the NSA, and ICE, though he had lost some of the badges for the lesser organizations, like the fish and wildlife service. He even had a badge made for the Medical Information Bureau, just to be funny. Back then, they shared the floor with Almanarc Insurance. And, since they dealt with personal information and contracts, they agreed to have badges be required to access the floor. Life was a whole lot simpler back then.

However, after the invasion, when the president had come on to address the issue, he heralded the HPS as being the go to organization to solve all the problems that the new arrivals would bring with them, pulling them out of the shadows and into the light, so to speak. The group had suddenly become overt overnight, their mandate, both old and new, made public. A few weeks later, Almanarc was moving out, under the excuse that they were looking for a bigger space. Everyone at the HPS knew they just didn't want to associate themselves with the demons.

Since then, their new neighbor has been Angel Corp, some diversified construction corporation that seemed to have come out of nowhere. They made it clear from day one that they had an open-door policy, which led to the HPS's drop in security. It left the floor open to anyone that walked in off the street. Even with the doors to the office themselves being locked, people still managed to find their way in. Most of them were there to complain about their new demonic neighbors, whether or not they really were from hell.

As the two of them came off the elevator, Hank swatted at the phone, trying to get Jack to put it away. He wasn't the least bit surprised to find five people standing outside of the office, trying to get a peek inside through the fogged glass. Their office location had never once been advertised anywhere, not even on their hastily made website that showed a picture of the outside of the building for all of five minutes before Herb had them take it down. Still, it didn't keep the gawkers away in the least.

"Angel Corp is on the other side, people," Hank shouted out, as he and Jack pushed their way through the crowd towards the door. He flipped his badge at the reader that was bolted to the doorframe, which gave a satisfying beep before unlocking the door itself. The crowd reluctantly parted as he pulled back on the door, opening it just enough to let Jack in, before scooting in himself. Two members of the crowd tried to slip in after them, but they blocked each other in the process, giving Hank just enough time to close the door in front of them.

"Oh, it's you two," Danielle said, as way of greeting. She was sitting behind the receptionist's desk, taking on Lynette's role in addition to her own. The desk took up much of the main room of the office, blocking off the entire width of the small space, with only one small section that lifted up to allow passage to the other side of it. Behind the desk were four doors, two of which were currently closed, that lead to the individual offices. Jack and Hank were stuck sharing a space, as were the two CSI techs and the other two field agents. A hallway directly behind Danielle, seeming like a dark halo around her otherwise heavenly figure, led to the CSI lab, where most of their actual work was done.

"Were you expecting someone else?" Hank asked.

"Will you please tell him that--" Jack started to say.

"Oh, enough already," Hank said, exasperated. "I don't care what the stupid report said. The woman is ninety. There is no way that she was driving the car."

"Why?" Danielle asked. "What do you have against ninety year olds? My grandma is ninety and she still drives just fine."

"Yea, well, she's one of those youthful ninety year olds, then," Hank said. "Not this woman. She could barely see as it is."

"Which would give her the perfect excuse for accidentally running over poor Jared," Jack said.

"First off, no, there's no excuse for running someone over, accidentally or otherwise. Certainly not when there was a stop sign right there. Second, she didn't even know that the car was gone, and I somehow doubt that she would have been able to get back to her apartment on her own between the accident and when I got there."

"That was hours apart," Danielle said. "She could have had a friend drive her, no problem."

Hank just rolled his eyes, wanting nothing more than to have the matter drop instantly. In his mind, Cassidy Masters was not a suspect. She didn't even seem like the type to have run off like that. Even if she had been driving. Even if she had accidentally hit someone, demon or otherwise. He was still insisting that this was an intentional murder, and there wasn't anything he had seen so far that would change his mind.

"Have we heard from the CSI team, yet?" Hank asked.

"They promised to have their report on the car first thing in the morning, though I don't know how they'd be able to work that quickly without working overnight," Danielle said. "Please don't throw a fit in the morning when they come back with nothing."

"As long as they know what that black dirt on the driver's side is, I'd be satisfied with whatever they give me," Hank said, surprising both her and Jack. "What? You saw the car, Jack. That thing was spotless. I'd be surprised if they get anything off of it at all."

"Well, there's a little more in the report from the local PD," Danielle said, helpfully. "It's in your office right now. Cliff Notes' version is that there was no sign of the car stopping, or even trying to stop. Unless the breaks weren't working at all--"

"Which we'll hopefully find out about from the CSI team," Hank added.

"This was definitely a murder," Danielle finished.

"I told you," Hank gloated at Jack. "Aren't you glad you didn't want to put a wager on it?"

"Whatever," Jack huffed. "I'm still hoping there's an explanation for this other than a hate crime against demons."

"Well, I never thought that the driver was just running over any old person on the street," Hank said. "God, that would make this case downright impossible."

"It's not impossible enough for you already?" Danielle asked. "You have no leads, no evidence, and no prints. What exactly do you have to work on?"

"First thing tomorrow, if the black dirt doesn't come back as anything important, I'll be interviewing the people who knew Jared. The guy was a demon. Nice or not, he probably had some enemies. I'm not going to call this case impossible until after that comes back empty."

"Don't we have some records on that already?" Jack asked. "Aren't you guys tracking them while we're out cleaning up after them?"

"We track their movements, sure, to a degree," Danielle admitted. "But most of that is automated and done via satellite, making sure they don't flee the area or anything. They do enough damage when we limit them to the pacific northwest without them moving all over the world. Plus, people would freak out more than they already do. I mean, we still get calls from France about their new president supposedly being a demon, despite the fact that the man was on live TV when the invasion happened and no one popped out of a portal behind him. He's no Sami."

"But you can give us a record of his movements over the past few days," Jack said. "Jared, not the president. That should help us."

"I don't see how, but I can print it up. Is it just me or does this case seem sort of... backwards?"

"What? You mean about trying to solve a case about a murdered demon instead of a murdering demon? No, of course not. I don't see how that is anyway backwards at all," Hank deadpanned. "When I told the local PD that Jared was a demon, they couldn't get out of there fast enough. Nobody wants to touch this case in the slightest, which makes it all the more difficult. We need to put a policy in place where we don't interfere with a case that's already been picked up, unless the demon is actively threatening someone. We don't have the resources to track down every single case like this."

"And we're bound to have a lot more of these now that people are starting to get over the original fear of these demons," Jack said.

"No one is getting over anything, just yet," Herb said, coming up behind Dannielle from his office. Hank was startled by Herb's sudden appearance. He looked over to one of the previously closed doors, surprised to see it open. "The humans are just getting more brazen, to the point of striking back. Jared is just the first. I expect many more to come. And, no, we're not going to offload our work onto the local police departments. That's not our mandate."

"Neither is investigating the murders of demons," Hank said. "We're supposed to be keeping a lid on them, not getting justice for their deaths."

"Are you saying that Jared doesn't deserve justice because he was a demon?" Herb asked, glaring over at him.

"No, sir," Hank said. "I'm saying that we have enough on our plate already without having to add this to it."

"Well, it was made rather clear to you earlier that no one else is about to do it, wasn't it?" he asked. "What does that say to you?"

"That we're stuck doing it, sir."

"Exactly," Herb agreed. "I expect this sort of attitude from that one, not from one of my best agents."

Hank would have found the sideways compliment flattering, except for the fact that there were so few agents there. He knew that the agent that Herb would consider his best would be Blanche, of course. Hank was often torn between pride and jealousy over his wife's success, but that rarely got in the way of their relationship. He looked over to the other closed office door, the one to her office, wondering if she was back from Montana, or wherever it was that she had gone off to on her latest case. The two of them had a very important day coming up, and he hoped that he would be able to take some time off for it. But, if he didn't close this case in time, he'd be stuck working through the planned vacation.

"Now, I expect you both to make some progress on this case tomorrow," Herb said. "And I don't want to hear any more grievances about being overworked. I'm just as stretched as the rest of you, and you don't hear me complaining, do you?" Herb looked to all three of them, in turn, before spinning around and heading back to his office, closing the door lightly behind him.

"Seriously, I think he has the outer office bugged or something," Jack whispered, conspiratorially.

"Either that or he just has really good hearing," Hank said.

"Oh, please, he has a video feed of the office," Danielle said. "He saw you come back and opened the door to eavesdrop. The guy is still paranoid as all hell after what happened in New York. At least you guys get to spend time outside this office."

"Ah, so that's the reason why you want to be a field agent," Hank said. "You just want to get away from the boss."

"Sure," she said, sarcastically. "It has nothing to do with the fact that field agents tend to get promoted faster and have better pay. I swear, even Huey and Dewey get paid better than me."

"Oh, not you too," Hank said, exasperated. "They have names, you know."

"And doctorates," Jack added. "That's probably why they get the better pay. Maybe if you got an advanced degree--"

"With what time?" Danielle asked. "I have no spare time to do anything like that. If I'm not here, answering the phones, supplying you four with intel, coordinating with the CSI techs, or ducking Herb, I'm sleeping. I barely have time to eat these days. When is Lynnette going to get back from her leave?"

"We'll hopefully have a better temp by then," Hank said. "She still hasn't even had the kid yet, has she? She's due any day now, though."

"Is Blanche up on all the baby gossip?" Jack asked.

Hank glared at him, knowing full well the look he would have gotten from Blanche for the suggestion. "Why? Just because she's a woman, you figure that she'd be into all of that stuff?"

"What? No, pfft, of course not," Jack said, quickly. "You're not... you're not going to tell her that I said that, are you?"

"I make no promises," Hank said. "I might just need to get her on my side against you at some point, or off my back, as the case may be. You never know how good ammunition will come into play." Hank looked over at Danielle, knowing she'd be on his side for once. She just rolled her eyes at the both of them as she went back to her work. "Anyway, enough wasting time. We have some paperwork to do before we can go home. Plus, there's the report from the local PD to go through. Tomorrow is going to be another long day."

"Do we have any other type of days these days?" Jack asked. "It's kind of feeling like one long day that never ends."

"Well, you could always revisit the alternative," Hank suggested, knowing that the threat of jail, or worse, usually was enough to motivate Jack to do his work.

"It's getting to the point where the threat of a dark hole is starting to sound pretty good," Jack said. "At least then I'd get a decent night's sleep once in a while."

"Who said they'd let you sleep there?" Danielle added, without looking up from her screen. "I hear they're really up on the sleep deprivation."

"Well, with how they work their agents, I wouldn't be surprised."

Chapter Six
The Office at Home

It took Hank another two hours before he finished up enough work to call it a night. With how busy they had been lately, ever since the invasion, the paperwork would just keep piling up unless he got it down to a controllable level every night. There were some days when he didn't manage to get home at all, sleeping on the couch in their break room. He'd complain, but the only person to complain to would be Herb. He already knew just how overworked they all were, and kept offering promises to expand the team once the financing came in. There was never any word on when that would be.

Still, even with staying at the office past ten, Hank hadn't managed to crack open the report from the local PD. Instead, he grabbed a copy on his way out the door, with thoughts that he would read it a little before bed, knowing full well that he wouldn't last long once he managed to get home. As he stumbled through the door, tripping over the growing pile of mail just inside the apartment, he noticed that the lights were still off and the old-fashioned answering machine was blinking that it had a message. He tried to think of anyone that still called him on the landline, though he figured it was probably just a wrong number or a telemarketer. Still, his sleep deprived brain managed to bring him over to the machine, hitting the right button in the dark to play the message.

"Hey, honey," Blanche's voice came to him out of the machine. There was distortion on the line, as well as loud background sounds that made it difficult to hear her properly. "This mission is going to keep me out for a while." Gunfire could be heard in the background of the message, despite Blanche's calm voice. "I seem to have misplaced my phone in all of this, so I'll be calling into the machine to check messages until I can get it replaced. You know me and my memory, who would have thought that the landline would be the number that I remembered." She laughed it off as more gunfire, louder this time, played out. The machine let out a screeching sound when the noise got too loud for it to record properly. "Anyway, don't worry. We're both fine. We'll be back in a couple of days, though, hopefully before the big day. If not... well, send my love along with yours." The message ended abruptly with another set of crackling sounds.

"Ah, typical Blanche," Hank said, laughing it off. He was too tired to be concerned for his wayward wife. If he wasn't, he would also be able to remember that she had been in far worse scrapes and come out just fine in the end. As he tossed down his keys in the bowl next to the answering machine, he glanced over at the computer in the corner. The monitor was always on, running one of those old screensavers left over from the days when screens still needed them not to have images burned into the glass. It showed a pattern of pipes forming all over the screen before disappearing. At the center of the menagerie of metal was a small box, with three circles in the middle. All three circles were green, showing that his whole family, himself included, was alive and well. If Blanche had been injured by anything more than a papercut, the center circle, representing the center of his world and family, would start moving towards yellow. He wouldn't start worrying until it was a bright, fiery orange.

Once the slight wisps of worry were abated, he took the three steps from the table by the door to the couch that dominated the living room. He flopped over the armrest, not bothering to walk around it, letting his legs dangle over, flapping in the air. After about a minute of him lying there, his mind a silent buzzing, he reached up over the other side of the couch, past the other armrest, to the end table near it. He scooped up the picture that always sat there. It was the only thing on the table besides the lamp that was rarely used. He pulled it over to him so he could look at it in the low glow that filled the apartment.

The picture had been taken over a year ago, back in the summer of 2012, back before all of this had happened. It was back when the HPS had only been dealing with the unexplained. Blanche was standing on a giant boulder overlooking Lake Chelan. Her arms were wrapped around their daughter, Marissa, holding her tightly to keep her from the precipice of the boulder. Hank was off to the side, sitting on the ledge, his feet dangling over air, much like they were on the couch. A passing hiker had taken the picture of the three of them, capturing one of the last moments they had together as a family.

Soon after the picture had been taken, barely two weeks later, they had sent Marissa away to a new boarding school, up in Ontario. The school had been set up for the children of high profile individuals, mostly politicians and royalty from all around the world. The offspring of field agents for the more clandestine and high risk agencies were also being taken. It was still months before the invasion, but, as soon as the brochure had been passed around at work, Hank had a feeling that they would need to send Marissa away. Blanche didn't like the idea at first. But, once the invasion happened, once they were fully consumed by the new workload, they were both glad they had made the decision. And, with the HPS in the public eye, it had become all the more important to protect her. In fact, barely a month after the invasion, Herb had said, in no uncertain terms, that, if she hadn't already been at that school, he would have insisted that they send her there, or they couldn't both still be in the field.

Hank missed his little girl, though they video conferenced almost every weekend. The school had an archaic view on technology during the week. But, on the weekends, when they had time, they always talked with her. It made it easier, at first. At least during the school year. But, as the summer vacation rolled around, they had both been so busy dealing with crisis after crisis that they were forced to keep her at school. She wasn't the only student there over the holidays, and the school administration promised that there would be special activities for her during the summer break. It still hurt to go so long without seeing her. He just wished that she could be with them and safe and well cared for all at the same time. But he knew that it wouldn't be the case.

With a sigh of longing, Hank placed the picture back in its spot on the end table. The footprint of the frame showed in the dust that collected on the surface, as it did with all the surfaces around the place. Whenever he saw the dust and dirt that soiled his home, Hank always thought to himself that he would get around to cleaning up around there eventually, knowing full well that he would never have the time. Instead, he just shook his head, picking up the folder with the report from the local PD, and made his way over to the computer.

The computer was placed in a corner of the living room, set aside from the rest of the room by an invisible line that Marissa had quickly learned never to cross. The area was designated the home office, and the two of them usually switch off using it, on those rare instances when they were both home. He flipped on the desk lamp that was clamped awkwardly on the ledge of the window behind the monitors. The piles of paperwork on the desk were starting to rival those in the office. Most of it had been completed already, just waiting for a return trip and a good filing. Hank pushed the piles aside, clearing some of the desk away for him to start a new one, one dedicated to his current mission. In the process, he tapped the mouse, dismissing the screen saver.

Family Minder was up on the main screen. It was the application that everyone had been buying lately, ever since the demons invaded. His heart rate was showing on the top of the window, with the trend over the past few hours spreading out on a graph that continued to scroll on its own. The biometrics came from his fitness band that he was always wearing, as were Blanche and Marissa. They were fed into the application through their cell phones and sent to the main server for the service. As it was Monday night, Marissa's feed wasn't showing anything. Her band would cache the readings until the weekend when she could sync it with her cell phone. However, Blanche's readings, showing in the middle, were live, as were his. They showed a spike in heart rate a few hours back, around the time that she had placed the call to the machine. But there was no disruption, no signs that she had been hurt at all. Though the green dots that had shown up in the middle of the screen saver had said as much, he still liked to look at the readouts whenever he had the time, just for that extra level of assurance.

Not only did the software track a person's biometrics, it also compared it against the database. If the person wearing the fitness band wasn't the registered user, the application would be able to tell immediately. The system was one of the many good things that Angel Corp had released over the past few months, and had led to their meteoric rise. After all, in a world where demons could disguise themselves as your family members, what everyone really wanted was peace of mind. And Angel Corp sold it to them at $10 per person per month.

Hank clicked the application off, sending it to the tray in the corner, before getting down to business. He flipped open the report, which was a lot thinner than he had been expecting, scanning each page in turn before doing a proper readthrough. Danielle had been right about the tire marks. Written on one of the first pages, in a barely legible scrawl, were the words "No tracks. Murder?". The note was typed out in the report, in the same phrases, though easier to read. Other than that, and a few pictures taken of evidence collected on the scene, there wasn't much to the file. He could have gotten through the entire thing in five minutes back at the office and left without anything to take home. But he hadn't realized how little there was in it.

It was the pictures of the evidence that took up the brunt of his time with the folder. He kept looking at each picture over and over again, as if trying to pull some information out of the seemingly mundane items. A cigarette bud, burned down to the filter, was seen just inches away from Jared's hand, which showed up in the corner of the picture. This didn't tell him anything as he knew that the demon was a smoker. You didn't really have to worry about getting cancer when you were already dead. A broken off piece of a headlight, with a mini placard showing a 2, was in another of the pictures. As they had already found the car that had hit him, that wouldn't give them anything they didn't already have. On and on, the pictures went, 22 in all, each more insignificant than the last.

He had been hoping that there was something in the report. Something that he had missed from arriving on the scene so late. Something that the cops would have caught if he hadn't arrived on the scene so early. There had to be something that he was missing. Because, if there wasn't, then this case was really starting to look hopeless, and he knew that he wasn't going to be able to get out of it before Wednesday. Unless he somehow managed to solve the case within the next 36 hours, he was going to miss out on the trip they had been planning for weeks.

Wednesday would be the 26th of September. It had been a very important day to Hank for almost seven years now. It was the day that Marissa was born. He had missed out on celebrating it with her the year before, due to wanting her to focus on settling into her new school, her new home, with her new friends, under the thought that they would still see her again at Christmas and over the summer. When neither happened, he promised himself that he wouldn't miss this day. That he wouldn't miss out on celebrating this most special day with his special little girl. And, yet, it was starting to look like that wasn't going to happen.

"Not unless I somehow manage to solve the unsolvable case," he said to himself, as he, dejectedly, tossed the folder down onto the desk, into the recently cleared space. "Maybe Herb will just let me head up for a few hours at least, if the case was stale enough by then. No sense in missing out on her birthday when there's no progress to be made on the case, is there?"

He stared daggers at the infernal case file, the oppressive monster that was promising to keep him from her. To keep him from fulfilling the promise he had made to himself. Thoughts of quitting flitted through his head. Of leaving the agency that he had been a part of, in one form or another, ever since he graduated from college almost twenty years beforehand. It was a hollow threat, he knew, but one he had been contemplating a lot recently. There was nothing like being overworked and underpaid to make a person rethink their priorities.

With a final sigh, Hank pushed himself up out of the chair. He reached over, snapping off the desk lamp. He left the computer open and on, knowing that the screensaver would kick in again in a few minutes. Right before heading off to bed, he scooped up the folder once more, hoping that, once he had gotten a few hours of sleep, he'd be able to make something more out of the mishmash of documents that represented the entirety of the case. At least, that is, until the CSI team came back to him in the morning.

It was going to be a long night, and he already knew that he wasn't going to be getting much sleep.

Chapter Seven
But He Was So Quiet

The folder continued to tease him as it sat there on the dashboard. The three hours of sleep he had managed to get, according to his fitness band, had done little to aid in his attempts to find leads that didn't exist. He had a huge coffee in his hand as he tried to find a spot for it amongst the trash that had taken over the cup holders in the crown vic. Jack was sitting in the passenger seat, looking well rested and practically jumping out of his seat to be working the case. Hank always wished he could let the kid loose on the case and see what happened, but he couldn't afford to lose the time he was bound to waste.

"We still haven't heard back from Huey and Dewey. They might have something for us," Jack said. "Don't lose hope just yet."

"You are way too bubbly for the morning," Hank said.

"Well, you know me. I'm a morning person."

"Are you sure you're not a demon?" he joked, though he had made the joke often enough over the past few months. In fact, prior to the invasion, he had been using several other remarks to explain the man's unusual perkiness in the morning. But, since the invasion, it was always that the man was a demon, because it made perfect sense. Thankfully, his excess energy tended to lapse over the course of the day. Although he often made morning investigations almost torturous, he was much more manageable closer to lunchtime.

"Last I checked," he said. He made a show of pulling on his ear. "What do you think?"

Hank just rolled his eyes as he pulled the car through the intersection, through the crime scene, that was showing little signs of the flurry of officers that had been there the day before. There was some yellow tape still stuck to the mailbox, though the rest of it had been collected, or blown away in the wind. Still, the few people that were walking past were eyeing the intersection, as if the asphalt itself would provide some answer to their prying, questioning eyes. Hank only wished it would, so that he would be able to close the case in time.

"So, where are we starting?" Jack asked. He was looking around the neighborhood where Jared had been killed. Clearly, he was looking for something, but Hank had no idea what that could be. Knowing Jack, it was likely that he was looking for something to set fire to.

"I say we start at his house," Hank suggested. "It's just up here on the right."

"It's scary that you know where all the demons live off the top of your head."

Hank smiled at that thought, at the illusion he had let his partner believe. Of course, he didn't remember the address off hand. It was in his phone, along with the contact information and addresses of every demon in the area. He had looked up the address before picking up Jack that morning, making a show of entering it into the GPS from memory, though he had been repeating it to himself the entire time. To maintain the illusion, Hank did his best to hide the surprise that he felt that Jared actually lived right up the block from where he was killed. It made perfect sense, though, given the fact that he had been on foot at the time.

"What can I say?" he said, feigning modesty. "It's a gift."

"One of these days that gift is going to get you in trouble," Jack said.

"Here it is." Hank pointed at the yellow house as they pulled up in front of it. The mailbox at the curb said

Housanstien, though he was pretty sure that Jared's last name had been DeGregor. He just wrote it off as laziness on Jared's part, figuring that the house must have belonged to some other family before he had bought it and he hadn't gotten around to changing the mailbox.

"Think he's home?" Jack asked.

"No, I don't think Jared is home," Hank said, well aware of the joke. "But we don't have any records on whether or not he lived alone. He might have a live-in girlfriend or a roommate that would know more about him than we do. If not, then we can let ourselves in and snoop around a little."

"Oh, we're going to do some breaking and entering?" he asked, as if that surprised him. "Why didn't you just say so?" He smiled a gleeful, self-indulging smile that consumed his entire face, before jumping out of the car.

"Why did I have to be stuck with the criminal?" Hank grumbled to himself, as he slowly moved to follow.

Jack was halfway up the sidewalk before Hank made it around the car to the curb. The lawn was expertly tended to, with three trees, each still small, each with their own perfectly symmetrical circle of dirt around it. The houses on either side of Jared's had the same setup, same appearance as his. However, their yards weren't as well maintained and the paint was all faded. Jared's house looked freshly painted. As Hank approached the front door, he was thinking Jared's laziness was less likely to be the reason for the old mailbox, though he couldn't think of another reason for it.

"Hey, you guys HPS?" came a question from his left, seemingly out of nowhere. Hank looked over in the direction of the voice, spotting someone's eyes over the edge of the perfectly trimmed hedge that lined the lot. After a quick glance over to his partner, who was waiting impatiently for him near the door to the house, he made his way across the perfectly manicured lawn towards the neighbor.

"Yup," he said, once he got close enough to not need to shout.

"Can you believe that guy was a demon?" he asked. His head peaked the rest of the way out from behind the obstruction.

"Well, yes," Hank said. "We knew he was a demon since the invasion."

"Wait, really?" he said. "Why didn't anyone tell us?"

"Well, there wasn't a reason to," Hank said. "Just because they're demons doesn't mean they're overly likely to commit crimes."

"Pfft, yea, right. That's why you guys never have anything to do," he laughed. "I watch the news; every day there's some demon or whatever killing or stealing or generally screwing over us normal, regular human beings."

"Those are the exceptions, of course," Hank said. Although, he had to admit, those exceptions did keep him pretty busy. Still, given the fact that there were only ten of them, with only four field agents, and thousands of demons, that wouldn't be that hard of a thing to do.

"Yea, well, I have to admit, it took me a bit by surprise to find out the guy was a demon," he admitted. "I mean, he was such a quiet guy, you know? And look at this yard; puts mine to shame. I never had any problems with the guy."

"See?" Hank asked, giving a half smile. "There are plenty of nice demons. You just have to give them a chance."

"Uh huh," the guy mumbled. "So, who killed him? Was it some other demon? Hell on hell action, so to speak?"

"I'm afraid I can't comment on an ongoing investigation," Hank said. Besides, he hadn't the faintest idea.

"Aw," the man said, disappointed, before disappearing back behind the hedge. Hank just shook his head in amazement before making his way back over to his partner.

"Are we ready?" Jack asked him. Hank grunted his ascent, and Jack took that as his cue, ringing the doorbell. He hopped up and down on the balls of his feet, trying to peer into the house through the windows that framed the top of the front door, looking for someone coming. No doubt he was hoping that no one would come so that he would have an excuse to practice his lock picking skills. He was quickly disappointed, though.

The man who answered the door was short and petite, looking more like a teen than an adult, though the full stubble across his face said otherwise. He wore wire-rimmed glasses, which were askew, improperly framing his red, tear filled eyes as he looked up at the two agents. Though it was almost nine in the morning on a Tuesday, the man was still wearing pajamas. He had a robe around him that was clearly far too big for him, with the sleeves swallowing his hands and the bottom of it dragging behind him on the floor.

"What do you want?" he snapped at them, glaring as if they ruined a perfectly good cryfest.

"Is this the house of Jared DeGregor?" Hank asked, knowing full well that it was.

"It was," the man said, falling into what appeared to be another round of hysterical crying. "He-He's d-dead," he managed to get out around a wracking line of sobs.

"Are you his roommate?" Hank asked.

"I'm his boyfriend," the man clarified. "Or, at least, I was. He was k-killed yesterday, barely a block away from here. I have to drive past the place where it happens on the way to work."

"We know," Jack said. "We're HPS. We're investigating his m... his death."

"HPS?" he asked.

"Yes," Hank said. "Homeland Protection Services. Did you know Jared was a demon?"

"Well, of course I knew he was a demon," the man snapped at him. "I was his boyfriend. You don't keep that sort of thing from your boyfriend."

Hank let the comment go, though he knew of several cases where the demons hadn't told their significant others of their demonic status. There were even cases where they went as far as marrying them before it was reported. However, once the marriage certificate is on file, the HPS would get a copy of it, and it was their responsibility to verify that the human spouse was aware. In most cases, the notifications don't go well. In fact, in one case down in California, the recently married wife had become pregnant before they were able to notify her. That complicated things considerably. However, on the bright side, the growing discussion on abortions didn't seem to have any bearing on these demonic offspring. No one, not even the most outspoken against the practice, had any problem with aborting a demonic human hybrid. After all, can they even be considered alive when their father isn't?

"Do you know of any reason why someone would want to hurt Jared?" Jack asked.

"Oh, you mean, besides the fact that he was a demon?" the boyfriend asked.

"Yes, besides that," Hank said.

"No, of course not. Jared was a sweetheart, the most kind, generous man I've ever known. He was perfect and everyone who knew him loved him. No one would ever want to hurt him."

"Who knew he was a demon, then?" Hank asked.

"You mean other than you guys? No one. Jared kept that a secret, not wanting it to color people's opinion of him. He was a bit vain that way, I guess. Of course, he was a pride demon, after all, so it makes sense that he would keep up the practice. I don't even think they knew down at the bar."

"The bar?" Hank prompted.

"Yea, the bar where he worked. Didn't you guys know he worked at a bar? I thought you guys spied on everyone these days."

"No, just the demons," Jack said, trying to make a joke of it, but failing miserably.

"We'll be heading over there next," Hank said. "Though, if they weren't aware of his demonic status, I'd be surprised. Most businesses ask that on the application these days."

"He got the job soon after the invasion," the boyfriend said. "Before people were asking. He was having trouble finding better work because of it. It was the only thing that we ever fought about, really."

"How did you and Jared meet, if you don't mind me asking?" Hank asked.

"At the bar," the boyfriend said. "They don't really encourage bartenders to date customers, but he said he couldn't help himself. As soon as he saw me..." He trailed off before breaking into another round of sobs. "I'm sorry," he said. "Can we finish this later?"

"Actually, we don't really have any more questions for you at this time," Hank said, looking over to Jack for confirmation. He just gave a slight nod and a shrug. "We'll keep you apprised of any developments in the case."

"Thank you," the boyfriend said, nodding his appreciation, before retreating into the house. He closed the door softly, his sobbing audible for several seconds after as he headed away from the door.

"So, what do you think about that?" Hank asked.

"A gay demon?" Jack asked.

"Why not?" Hank asked. "If he was gay before he died, it would make sense that he would be gay afterwards. That wasn't exactly what I was talking about, though."

"Well, the guy was too distraught to have killed him," Jack said. "I know the whole 'the significant other did it' angle is there, but I don't exactly think him capable. Not unless Jared was cheating on him or something."

"Jared didn't seem the type," Hank said, shaking his head. As they headed back down the sidewalk, towards the crown vic, he tried to think back to the last time he had met with the guy. Jared had made an impression on him, mostly because he didn't seem all that demonic. The pride demons tended to be some of the nicer ones of the bunch, though that wasn't saying much. However, he had noticed a tendency for each type of demon to favor their given sin, even after returning to Earth.

"Well, yea," Jack agreed. "He was a pride demon, not a lust demon. Just think, if he had been an incubus, no one in this neighborhood would have been safe."

"Well, I imagine the straight ones wouldn't fall victim of his seductions," Hank said. "Though I guess anything is possible when demons are involved. Shall we knock on a few more doors around here before heading over to the bar?"

"Do we even know which bar he worked at?" Jack asked.

Hank pulled out his phone, pulling up Jared's entry, which was still open in the recent apps. While the name and address of the bar wasn't listed, there was a business phone number under his profile. A quick internet search on the number brought him to a site for a bar named simply Hell's Bar. He was pretty confident that this was exactly the place that Jared would have worked at. The website was covered in fake demonic symbols, most of which weren't anything new, used throughout the decades when people could worship demons openly. However, the seven most potent of true demonic symbols had a prominent position near the top of the page. These were the ones depicting the seven deadly sins, those that symbolized the different factions of demons.

"Yea, I think I got the address for the place," Hank said. "It looks like the boyfriend might have been wrong about them not knowing he was a demon, though."

"Well, then, let's just head over there," Jack said. "I'm thinking that the boyfriend was right. If anyone knew that he was a demon around here, no one would have been able to keep the secret. It's a suburban neighborhood, after all, filled with gossips and busybodies. God, I miss the city."

"What? Seattle isn't city enough for you?" Hank asked.

"No, it's not, and it never will be. That's why they call New York THE city."

"You know, I just noticed something," Hank said, his hand hovering over the handle for the driver's side door. "We never got the boyfriend's name, did we?"

Chapter Eight
Hell's Bar

It took them a good hour to drive out there, further away from the city center. The bar didn't look like much from the outside. The building was low, squat, spanning across a large area in the middle of nowhere. However, the entire lot, which was made up of mostly just the one building and the parking lot around it, was in the middle of an area that seemed like the ground itself had been scorched clean of the forest that was visible in the distance. The trees seemed to quiver, perhaps in the wind, or, more likely, out of fear that the fires that raged so close to them would consume them next. The smell of burnt wood was still fresh in the air as they stepped out of the car.

"Yea, this seems like the perfect place to put a demon bar," Jack said, gazing around at the place. Smoke rose into the air all around the edges of the parking lot, as if the fires still raged, just out of sight in a fiery pit that was invisible to the naked eye. "How could anyone work here and not be a demon?"

"Actually, the place has been here for over a decade," Hank said. He had noted the date on the website as he plugged in the address, a date that was remarkably close to that of the events in New York. The coincidence made him a little uncomfortable, but he tried to put it out of his mind. After all, the place was on the other side of the country from the city. "Someone must have worked here before the invasion."

"That doesn't mean they weren't demons as well," Jack said. "We never were able to determine if there had been demons on Earth before last December. It would kind of make sense for certain demons to come through ahead of time, making room and laying the groundwork for the others to come."

"Not that conspiracy theory again," Hank said. "They would have been a lot better acquainted with the world if that had been the case, at least enough to avoid hitting the studio while they were broadcasting live across the area. We owe our very knowledge of their presence to their lack of preparation."

"Oh, we would have found out about it soon enough," Jack said. "We're the HPS. Nothing paranormal escapes our attention."

"I'm sure there were plenty of things that happened over the past few months that we were too busy to find out about. But, yes, we would have found out about the demons, eventually. I'm just worried about the kind of damage they could have done in the meantime."

"Like the damage they did on invasion day? Did we ever get the final number on how many people they killed?"

"No, and we never will. Seeing as how almost all of them had been able to find an identity when they arrived, I imagine that number is about one per demon on Earth. But good luck getting any of them to admit to killing the original owner of their identity. Besides, some of them might have been missing before they arrived, and they just took their form from the information they had at hand. I know that one of the succubi had taken the identity of some guy's dead wife. They're happily married now."

"Yea, how are Grace and Mark?" Jack asked. "Still in blissful happiness?"

"Sickeningly so," Hank said. "And, last I heard, she was expecting."

"Seriously? I thought it was only human females that can carry the offspring. Now we have to worry about the demon ones as well?"

"Yup, looks like."

"Let's hope that doesn't get out anytime soon."

"Yea," Hank agreed. "The last thing we need to deal with right now is a rise in anti-demon hate crimes that revelation is sure to cause."

"That's what this was, wasn't it," Jack said, more than asked. "An anti-demon hate crime?"

"Only if the person knew that Jared was a demon," Hank said. "But, yea, it's looking like that. If he really was as beloved as the boyfriend seemed to think."

"No one is ever that liked," Jack said. His words sounded almost jealous of the demon.

"Well, I guess we're about to find out. Shall we head in?" Hank asked.

"It's not even ten in the morning yet. Do you really think anyone is going to be in there?"

"The website says the place opens at eleven, so, yea, I imagine someone is here, getting things set up. We can't exactly afford to sit on our laurels while we wait for people to be ready to answer our questions."

"Well, you can't, at least," Jack said. "I don't have a daughter's birthday to go to tomorrow."

"Yea, and whose fault is that?" Hank asked.

He left it at that, with no answer forthcoming from Jack, as the two of them made their way towards the front door of the bar. The smell of burnt wood quickly gave way to the fumes of alcohol and other, less desirable smells that tended to arise from such establishments. The parking lot was mostly empty, with just the crown vic and three other cars parked there. It was impossible to tell if those other cars belonged to the staff or were left there overnight by those patrons too wasted to drive home safely.

When they got to the front door, they found it locked tight. The thick wooden door had no windows in it. Neither did the wall it was in. So, Hank wasn't able to peek inside. Not being deterred by this, he made his way around to the back of the building, looking for another entrance that might be unlocked. Around behind the building were two more cars, parked in a small section next to the dumpster, and a metal door that was locked just as tightly as the front one.

"Can I pick the lock?" Jack asked, a malicious smirk spreading across his face.

Hank was about to answer him, about to give him permission to break into the place, when the door suddenly opened. A short woman, only slightly taller than Jared's boyfriend had been, stepped outside carrying a huge garbage bag. The woman had tattoos running up and down her arms, with piercings all over her face and ornamental horn implants parting her hair. The trend in the horn implants was relatively new. It was meant to be a show of solidarity with the demons that had arrived, though none of them had shown horns in their human forms. She had earrings completely covering her ears and, when she looked up at the two agents, they noticed that she was wearing demon colored contact lenses. They made it appear that she was a demon herself, though it was clear to both of them that she was quite human. When she saw them standing there, she gave a small jump of startlement. She tried to recover quickly, putting on a false air of indifference.

"The bar doesn't open for another hour," she said, as way of greeting. She pushed her way past the two of them, tossing the large trash bag into the dumpster, before turning back to them. "And neither of you are going to be fitting in here. What? Are you guys supposed to be disguised as the men in black or something?"

"Something like that," Jack joked.

"We were actually looking for a manager or someone we could talk to," Hank said. He pulled out his HPS badge, flashing it at the girl. "We're here to talk to them about--"

"Jared, yea," the girl interrupted. "That asshole went and got himself killed yesterday. I had to find a replacement for him last minute. It totally screwed up the schedule. I try to keep at least one demon on shift every night. But with only three of them on rotation, well, two now, it can make things a little difficult. Any news on the guy that did it? Was it a demon?"

"We can't comment on an ongoing investigation," Hank said. "We did have a few questions for the manager, though."

"I'm the owner," she said. "There ain't no manager. What is it you want to know?"

"Well, clearly you were aware that Jared was a demon," Hank said.

"Duh," she said, simply.

"That was common knowledge around here?"

"Duh," she said, again.

"Were there any problems with demon haters coming around?" Jack asked.

"It's a demon bar, always has been. Only people that come 'round here are demons and people that want to hang out with demons. If a demon hater came here, looking for trouble, they'd find it. But it would be them that went home bloody, not the demon. Demons can take care of themselves just fine. That's why I'm so annoyed at Jared for screwing up like that. I hear it was a stupid car that did him in. A car. Can you believe that?"

"Well, technically, it was an SUV," Jack said, as if the size of the car would have mattered.

"Same dif'," she said.

"What about the clientele," Hank asked, trying to get the conversation back onto the right track. "Did any of them have any problems with Jared?"

"None that I knew of," she said. "A couple guys didn't think he was demon enough to be in a demon bar. But they just stopped coming in on Jared's usual nights. They'll probably be here at eleven, if you want to hang around to bother them. Scare some sense into them about what is or isn't a proper demon."

"I would have thought you would have agreed with them," Hank said. "With how Jared was killed, and all."

"Hey, I ain't specist one way or the other, but getting hit by a car is just plain stupid. And that dude was from Earth before he went and got himself killed the first time. Grew up in the early 1900s, if I recall correctly. He should have known not to tangle with a car like that."

"But, other than this one group, he had no problems here?"

"Nothing out of the ordinary," she said. "We just have some rabble rousers every once in a while, same as every bar. But he always outsourced that to the bouncers. The very human bouncers." She rolled her eyes at the thought of a demon doing such a thing. "Naw, everyone really liked him. It was sickening how well he was liked. I don't really see that as a reason to kill someone, though, do you?"

"Not usually, no," Jack said. "I guess his boyfriend was right on that front."

"Boyfriend?" she asked. "Really? Well, no wonder why the guy was so worried about his manicure. I mean, seriously, that actually makes some sense, for once. The dude was a complete pompous puff. I bet he didn't even get anything out of his deal with the dark lord."

"Deal?" Hank asked. He was confused for a moment, before he remembered the typical misconception most demon worshipers had, even now that the demons were there on Earth. "Do you even know what a demon is?"

"Of course. It's someone who sold their soul to the Devil."

"That's quite ridiculous," Hank snapped. "Your soul is the very essence of what you are. You can't sell it and it would be of no use to the Devil or anyone else. No, a demon is someone who died in sin and was forced to pay for it in hell. It's as simple as that."

"Wait, seriously?" she asked, seeming almost offended by the simplicity of it. "No selling souls? No corrupting innocents? What a rip off. They should have at least gotten something out of it."

"Well, there are the muscles and cool powers they had in hell," Jack said. "But, nope, on Earth, they're pretty harmless."

"But I've heard plenty of my guys boasting about dragging others into their work," she said.

"Well, yea, there were some of them that did that," Hank admitted. "Most of the demons just tried to repent in their forced labors. But some of them had preferred to spread their misery in the hopes that it would lessen. Those are the ones that tempt others to sin, further spreading their ranks. Those are the ones you should be looking out for, even on Earth."

"I think I'll take my chances," she said. "Pfft, no selling your soul, eh? No wonder why Satan never answered my prayers."

It was pretty common knowledge what a demon was and wasn't, despite the misconception that still survived alongside the truth. From the very beginning, from the first interviews that the HPS had done with the first group of demons they were able to track, the demons wanted to make it very clear that becoming a demon had never been a conscious effort on their part. Yet, for some reason, that part of the news had been downplayed, had been largely forgotten, much to the annoyance of the HPS. It seemed weird to Hank that the demons working there hadn't corrected that misconception repeatedly.

"Would you mind if we talk to some of your staff?" Hank asked. "We'll try to stay out of the way of the prep work."

"Pfft, suit yourself," she said. She held the door open for the two agents.

They entered the small kitchen that was at the back of the bar, just inside of the back door. The short woman disappeared as she headed off to finish opening the place for the public. She didn't seem overly concerned about their continued presence in her establishment. Hank managed to find the way through the tight area to the door leading out into the bar proper. The place looked like any old bar. The actual bar lined the wall to their right, with stools lined up in front of it. Five small tables were clumped together around the central area. Tall wooden pillars holding up the roof. A pool table was in the corner. The only thing that told that the place was anything other than a normal, everyday bar was the color scheme, which was red on black. The walls were black with red trim, making the space seem bigger and darker than it actually was. The tables and bar were all a dark gray, just a few shades off the walls to offset them from the backdrop. All the chairs and stools had black wood with red cushions. Even the pool table was a black frame with red felt, the pool balls all different shades of red rather than the standard colors.

Plus, there was a demon standing behind the bar, carefully drying off some wet mugs before sticking them out of sight. Hank was a bit surprised to find one of the octuplets there, not having known that any of them had been working at a bar. He made a mental note to try to make some time for them to cross reference all the demons' workplaces, trying to figure out just who worked with whom. What was the point in having the database they had without getting all the information that was available to them?

Hank made his way up to the bar. He tried to remember which one this was, though they were almost impossible to tell apart. Seven demons, one of each sin group, had all come through into the same spot, the same apartment of a guy that had lived just outside of the city. Instead of killing him, like most of the demons had, all seven of them had taken on his form. Now, all eight of them, including the human, lived in a house together, closer than any set of brothers Hank had ever heard of.

"Hank," the demon said, surprised, when he spotted the agents. "W-What are you doing here?"

"Hey, um... Jason?" Hank asked, taking a stab at which one it was.

"Justin, actually," Justin admitted. Justin was the human of the group, which took Hank by surprise even more. Justin had a very successful line of ties that he had designed, running the company that made and distributed them. It seemed odd to Hank that the man would be working in a bar, in any bar, let alone acting as a demon. "The brothers help out at the office, and I get to work here, every once in a while. It helps keep me grounded, and get better ideas for ties," he explained, unbidden.

"How?" Jack asked. "I wouldn't think anyone wore ties in a place like this."

"What do you mean a place like this?" he asked. He seemed overly offended, though the pretense didn't last long. "Naw, I've been going with the whole demonic theme since the brothers arrived."

"And no one has a problem with a human working here?" Hank asked, in a whisper.

"It's not like many people would be able to tell," he said. He pointed to his eyes, which had the familiar yellow shade to it, the tell-tale shade of demons, though they shouldn't be flaring like that. "It annoys the brothers to no end that they have to wear these things too," he said. "It's standard attire for the bar, the uniform, if you will."

"Ah, okay," Hank said. "Anyway, we're here about--"

"I didn't do it," Justin said, quickly.

"What?" Hank asked.

"It was Mike," he said, just as quickly, naming the incubus brother. "He only told me this morning. I would have said something, but I had to get over here."

"Justin, Justin, Justin," Jake said, disappointment flooding his voice. "You know better than putting on that excuse. You should have called us, even if you were late for work."

"Mike?" Hank asked. "Really?"

"Well, I guess this means you'll be able to get to that vacation after all, eh, partner?"

"But why would Mike do that?" Hank asked. "Mike always seemed the nicest of the group."

"Well, I don't think he meant any harm by it," Justin said, defending his brother.

"Any harm?" Jack asked. "A guy is dead, Justin."

"I know, but... wait, what?" Justin asked. "What are you talking about."

Disappointment hit Hank like a wave before he had even realized that he had begun to hope that the case was going to solve itself. "We're talking about Jared, Justin," Hank said. "You know, the guy that your brother killed?"

"What?" Justin asked, shocked. "What? No. No, no, no. That's not... Can we start over?"

"What did your brother do, Justin," Hank asked, in that menacing tone that he had once reserved for his daughter, before the invasion completely changed his life around. Now, it seemed like he was using it on fully grown men and women that just didn't seem to understand the rules of society anymore. "What did Mike get himself into?"

"Well, he... and then... I mean, it's just wolf's bane."

Hank stared at the man in stunned silence for the longest time, before bursting into a fit of hysterical laughter. Jack started laughing soon after as well, with Justin joining in near the end. "He's smuggling wolf's bane?" Hank asked, as the laughter eased. "Again? Well, we'll have to handle that, but later. No, we're here about Jared."

"Wait a sec, what about Jared?" Justin asked. "Which Jared? The Jared here? None of my brothers killed a Jared."

"Pfft, a likely story," Jack scoffed.

"Jack, it's alright," Hank said, placing a restraining hand on his partner's shoulder. "We believe Justin, don't we? I mean, he wouldn't lie to us, would he? Would you, Justin?"

"No, o-of course not," he insisted.

"Uh huh," Jack said. "Just what do you know about Jared's death then?"

"Nothing, I swear," Justin said. "Wait, when did this happen?"

"Why do you ask?" Hank asked. He tried to not let his suspicion taint his tone of voice, but he wasn't sure how successful he was.

"Well, David was called in here last night, all last minute. That's why I'm covering now."

"Just how many of your brothers work here?" Hank asked.

"Officially? Just David. It's always been David, Jared, and this succubus Claire. Claire gets all the tips, of course. Unofficially, me and some of the brothers switch in and out from time to time, though it is mostly David here. Just... Just don't tell the boss, okay? Sam is scary, even to the brothers. I mean, some humans just take it way too far, and she's definitely one of them."

"That little thing?" Jack asked, pointing towards the back room where she had disappeared. "She seemed harmless enough."

"Yea, tell that to the guy whose arm she broke a couple of weeks ago. If I didn't know better, I'd say she's the demon here, definitely on the wrath path, if you know what I mean."

"And what does BB think of that opinion?" Hank asked, referring to Bone-Breath. He was the wrath brother, the only one of the group that had never been human. The rumor was that he used to be an orc or something similar, largely due to his bad vocabulary. But none of the brothers would confirm that.

"BB actually wants to date her... well, not exactly date, but--"

"Yea, we get the picture," Jack said, shuddering at the thought of the guy with her. Even though the eight of them looked exactly alike, even down to the freckle on the tip of their nose, there was just something about BB, his stance or the way he walked, that just made everyone's skin crawl. BB was the easiest to pick out of a lineup of the group.

"So, you're telling us you know nothing about Jared's murder?" Hank asked. "Other than David being called in to cover for him."

"Nothing," he said. "Sorry. Was he really murdered?"

"It's looking like it," Jack said.

"Do you know of anyone, here or otherwise, that would have a reason to kill him?" Hank asked.

"What? Kill Jared? No. No one. Well... I mean, Sam had to have been here last night, though, right? To call in David like that."

"Why do you ask?" Hank asked.

"Well, I'm just saying, and I'm not saying that she would ever..."

"Oh, just spit it out," Jack snapped.

"Well, she wanted him gone. Not like that, though, not with no notice. She just didn't like the guy. Not sure why not, I mean, the guy got along with everyone. He was the nicest guy I ever met, demon or human. He just didn't live up to her standards for what a demon should be."

"Yea, that was the impression we got from her," Jack said.

"But I don't think she would have killed him for that, not really. Maybe fired him, sure, if she could figure out how to do that with cause and all. But Jared was awesome at his job, super overqualified. Hell, he could have done Sam's job. I would have hired him at the company, but, well, with the brothers, I'm already overstaffed as it is. I don't even have much to do on most days, when I'm not designing the new line. Thus me being here. Jason has those books wound tighter than BB's abs."

"Would David be able to confirm that she was here yesterday?" Jack asked.

"I guess so," Justin said. "I could ask."

"But when was he called in," Hank asked.

"Around six or so, I think."

"Oh, yea, that wouldn't help, would it," Jack said.

"Well, earlier than that, you'd be able to ask the regulars when they get in. She's almost always here from around nine-thirty to six, later if someone doesn't show up for their shift, like she would have last night. You should wait around to talk with one of them. They'd be the ones to ask about someone out to get Jared."

"Speaking of which, Sam mentioned a group that wasn't too fond of Jared," Hank said. "Something about him not being demon enough for them either?"

"Oh, right, them. Yea, they'll be around shortly, I'll bet. Why don't you pull up a stool and stay for a while? They'll be beating down the door soon enough."

Hank looked at the clock displaying on his fitness band, wondering just how long "soon enough" would be. And would "soon enough" be soon enough to close this case. Or, would this lead come to nothing, just as all the others had. Just how long could they pull at this single string, coming up with nothing, before it ran out as well.

"Fine," he said. He rolled his eyes, as he, reluctantly, sat down on one of the stools.

"Works for me," Jack said, as he joined him. "I'll have a beer." When Hank just glared at him for that, he quickly retracted the order. "Better not. We're on duty, right?"

Chapter Nine
The Hellish Bikers

It was getting towards noon and the group of regulars still hadn't shown up, despite Justin's continued insistence that they would be there soon. Hank was starting to think that they should move on to the next lead. But he wasn't sure what that would be. He knew that the forensics off of the SUV would be back shortly, if they weren't already. But he wasn't sure if he was quite ready to head back to the office just yet. If the forensics didn't provide anything, he would be stuck coming right back to the bar, with no other leads to follow.

Hank looked at his watch again, for the fifth time since it turned 11:53. He downed the last of his third Diet Sprite, letting the glass hit the bar with a loud bang, a mix of frustration and annoyance.

"They'll be here," Justin said again, as if the sound had begged an answer.

Immediately after he said this, the front door swung open again. The late September breeze, already telling of a cold winter yet to come, pushed its way through the room. Hank barely managed a sideways glance at this latest group of patrons. They had been coming in, off and on, since the place had opened. Whenever Hank would look to Justin, to ask if these were the ones they were looking for, he would shake his head, insisting they would be there soon.

This time, it was different. Hank had barely noticed the group of six men standing inside the door before Justin called out to them.

"I told you they'd be here," he insisted. Justin waved the group over, smiling at them like they were his favorite people in the world.

"David," one of the men said, nodding in his direction. He obviously was confusing Justin for his brother, the one that was supposed to be working there. The six of them were tall and stocky, each with a full beard of varying lengths and levels of grayness. They each wore a leather jacket with the same emblem on the back, an inverted pentagram, with the point on the bottom, pointing down to hell. Embossed in the center of the pentagram were the demonic symbols of sin, one symbol per person. Hank checked each symbol in turn, noticing that lust was the one missing, though the other six had a representative standing there. He wondered briefly if these men intended to be champions of their selective sin. If they predicted that their death would be from that sin. Or if they had just chosen them at random, liking the symbols in general and for their closeness to the demons they were fans of.

"Mark, these guys have some questions for you," Justin said, quickly.

"I don't have any answers for them," Mark said. He was the one that greeted Justin. He had barely glanced over at the two agents as the group moved past them, heading for the pool table in the back. Jack reached out his hand, grabbing Mark by the arm before he could move out of their reach. "And this one had better get his hands off my leathers," the man said, menacingly.

"Just a couple of questions," Hank said. He stood up from the stool he had been sitting on the entire time. Hank was as tall as the group, though he wasn't nearly as broad as they were. He knew that, if it came to brute force, he would be no match for the six of them. Fortunately, with him, it rarely did. "We're with HPS," Hank said, flashing his badge.

"Good for you," Mark scoffed, pulling his arm out of Jack's grip. The leather let out a little squeal of displeasure as

Jack's nails made their way across their surface. Mark looked down at the offended sleeve. He brushed his hand against it, before glaring down at Jack, who barely came up to the man's chin. "I've killed men for less than that," he threatened.

"Well, you'll be hard pressed to kill us," Hank said. He flashed the butt of his gun, in the shoulder holster beneath his jacket.

"Now, now," Justin said. "There's no need for that. They just have some questions about Jared's death."

"Jared's dead?" Mark asked, with a laugh. "Well, good riddance. What did he do, drown in the bathtub?" The entire group broke out into uproarious laughter.

"He was murdered," Hank shouted over the din. The group's mirth slowly died, though the look on Mark's face alone could kill.

"By who?" he asked. "By a demon? That dingus didn't deserve the pleasure."

"We don't know who killed him," Jack admitted. "But there were no demon signs at the scene." Both agents knew that the absence of demon signs at the scene of the accident didn't tell them anything. Hank figured Jack was banking on the men not knowing that.

"Killed by a human, then," Mark said. "That's appropriate. Killed by the very people he wanted to be one of. I only wish that I had had the pleasure myself. I'm assuming that was your question; no, I didn't kill him."

"Where were you yesterday, around this time?" Hank asked. The surveillance footage of the SUV leaving the garage had been at nine o'clock, with the accident shortly after that. However, he wanted to keep the exact time of the incident secret, to prevent false confessions. Besides, if the group was far enough from the scene, they still wouldn't have been able to perpetrate the accident.

"Well, we weren't here," Mark said. "We don't set foot in this place when that pretender was working."

"Though, now, we can come here all we like, can't we?" one of the others said. This gained another round of laughter from the group, though it didn't last as long as the news of Jared's death.

"We were down in Woodland," Mark said, "at the bar that doesn't hire people like that. They hire real demons, the ones that will scare the skin off anyone that even looks at them. He wouldn't even dare step foot in that place. If he had, they would have rid the world of the little pissant. Though, I'm sure you know all about that place, with your fancy spy stuff. Hell, I bet you already knew we were down there. You just didn't know to be looking for us."

"Damn spooks," another one of the group said. The man looked towards the others, as if expecting a round of laughter to follow his statement, but got nothing in return.

"We're pretty big in those circles," Mark gloated, barely noticing the interruption. "I'm surprised you didn't already hear about us."

"Contrary to what some might believe, we don't actually spy on all the demons that are out there right now," Jack said. "There are thousands of them and only so many of us."

"Yea, but what about all those cameras out there?" Mark asked. "The traffic cameras and the ones you keep planting all over the place. I bet you even have five more of them on you right now, just waiting to be stuck in someone's face."

"Uh, Mark, wouldn't that mean there are cameras in here, too?" the first guy asked. He slapped his friend on the back as he looked all over the room, looking for cameras that weren't there. Although they would often plant cameras in public places, overlooking crime scenes and locations of importance, it was against policy to post them in private establishments. This was more because the owners would just find and destroy them than anything else.

"Good point," Mark agreed, similarly eyeing the place. "Maybe we should hang out at Woodland for a while longer, just until Sam finds all the cameras and throws them out. I hope they're expensive as hell, so you run out of your spy camera funds quicker."

"Uh huh," Hank said, letting their growing paranoia sweep past him. "Anyway, if you didn't kill him, do you know of anyone else that would want him dead?"

"What?" Mark asked, barely paying attention.

"Hey," Justin shouted, slamming his fist into the bar. The six of them all jumped in unison, their eyes going to the faux demon. "The nice agents asked you a question. You are going to answer them. If you don't... well... Let's just say, they tend to outsource their more troublesome interviews. Actually, now that I think of it, I hope you don't answer their questions. I could use a little fun." He let out a low, guttural, maniacal laugh that almost made Hank doubt the man's humanity. It was clear, though, that Justin was spending far too much time with his demonic brothers.

"I'm sorry, agents," Mark said. His voice squeaked a little, his eyes never leaving Justin. The faint smell of urine that had been part of the general potpourri of the place seemed to flare up, to dominate over the other smells, both foul, pleasant, and otherwise. "W-what was the question again?"

"Other than the six of you, who would want to see Jared killed?"

"W-we never would have wanted the guy dead," Mark said. "No, no-no, we just wanted him gone-I-I mean from the bar, from the bar. No, we wouldn't have killed him. That was all just talk. No, n-no one would have wanted him killed. He was a nice guy, that's all. Certainly not what-what we were expecting from a demon."

"N-no, that's what we expect from a demon," said the second man, the one that had called them spooks. He sounded almost adoring, grinning stupidly at the very human bartender.

"Oh... kay... When was the last time you saw Jared, then?" Hank asked.

"Uh...," Mark said, his eyes still locked on Justin.

"Easily a month ago," said one of the other men, one of the ones that hadn't spoken yet. He was hiding in the back of the group, though, when he spoke, the rest of them backed out of the way, allowing for a direct line of view to the man. He was easily the shortest of the bunch, shorter than Jack by the same amount that Mark was taller than him, with the longest, blackest beard. When Hank saw him, the word dwarf came to mind. Not the normal, human dwarves that have inhabited Earth for centuries. Rather he looked more like the kind that had found their way into fairy tales and fantasy, the ones that some of the demons, mostly those that hadn't come from Earth, had spoken of in their interviews. "When Sam made it clear that she wasn't putting up with us... well, putting him down, we made ourselves scarce on his nights. We haven't seen him, here or otherwise, since then. If he had problems with anyone, other than us, it would have happened during that month."

"Uh, yea," Mark agreed, pointing towards his friend. "What Heath said."

"Alright, then," Justin said. He finally relaxed as he stepped away from the group, going back to busying himself behind the bar.

"David," Sam snapped. She had seemingly come out of nowhere as she came up behind the group of six. She pushed them out of the way easily as she made her way to the bar. "What have I told you about pounding on my bar?" She pointed at the dent that he had seemed to have made in the wood where he pounded on it moments before. Hank stared at the place, surprised to see the damage. "You're paying to repair that."

"What's one more divot in this thing?" Justin said, barely looking over at his brother's boss. "It gives it character, and makes it look like demons really do work here."

"Well... alright, you got me there," she admitted. "Now if you idiots will excuse me." Without another word, she pushed her way past the agents, whisking around the bar and disappearing from sight once more.

"Wait, where did she go?" Hank asked.

"How did she do that?" Jack asked.

"That girl is a demon waiting to happen," Mark said. "She sold her soul to the devil, much like David over here had, for magical powers."

Justin rolled his eyes at the comment, but he didn't correct the man, letting it slide. Instead, all he said was, "There's no such thing as magic; not on Earth, anyway."

"Says the demon," Mark said. "Anyway, is there anything else you need to ask me?" He was directing the question to the two agents, though his eyes still hadn't left the bartender.

"No, I think that's it," Hank said. "For now, at least." Mark nodded to Justin before leading his group back the rest of the way to the pool table, all thoughts of abandoning the supposedly camera riddled bar gone. "Well, that wasn't all that productive," Hank said, once the group had left earshot. "Anyone else you think we should talk to in this... place?"

"I'm sorry, Hank," Justin said, shying away from his ire. However, when he noticed the group looking his way, he reversed his position, coming back over to stand by the two agents so his voice wouldn't have to carry. "I just think you were barking up the wrong tree on that one."

"More like grasping at straws," Jack muttered under his breath.

"Everyone loved Jared here, and I can't think of one person that would want him dead."

"I'm so tired of hearing that," Hank said. "There has to be at least one that did."

He eyed the other bar patrons, trying to see one of them that looked suspicious. One of them that was staring at them or purposefully averting their gaze. The bar wasn't all that populated to begin with, barely ten customers other than the group of six, and none of them seemed interested in the two agents in the slightest. They weren't even the only ones in there in suits, with a group of executive types taking a corner table as they drank their lunches and cheered their latest success.

"So, we hit one more dead end," Jack said. "So, what? We've been getting a lot of them on this case. We still haven't looked at the forensics yet. Let's go back to the office and see what Huey and Dewey have found out about the SUV."

"SUV?" Justin asked. "You already have the car that hit him? Shouldn't that be enough to find out who did it?"

"It should have been," Jack said. He glanced over at his partner, as if afraid he was saying too much.

"There wasn't much there," Hank admitted. "And I don't hold out much hope that the forensics will be much help. It's like this case is conspiring against me or something."

"Well, how about another drink for the road?" Justin suggested. "Something stronger, perhaps? Something to get your mind off your troubles?"

"It wouldn't help," Jack joked.

Hank just grunted, not hinting at whether or not he agreed with the sentiment, before heading for the front door to the bar. Jack downed the last of his drink before hurrying to catch up. Hank stopped just outside of the bar, stepping aside from the door to let another group of two men in suits enter, while he let his eyes adjust to the bright sunlight that filled the outside world. Once he could see properly, once the parking lot had come into focus, he noticed the group of six bikes standing in a row. From the paint job it was clear that they belonged to the six leather clad men inside. They were covered in blacks and red, with depictions of demons in battle against angels.

"That just figures," Hank muttered to himself, as he led the way over to the crown vic. "Of course, the leather clad demon worshipers are bikers."

Chapter Ten
Huey and Dewey

"Don't you always say 'the case isn't over until the forensics are in'?" Jack was saying as they got off the elevator.

The crowd of people outside of the office door was as big as the previous evening, despite it being the middle of the day on a Tuesday. The group gawked at the two of them as they approached the office, as if expecting for one of them to be a demon. Of course, they would have had no way of knowing if they were. But that was why most of them swarmed around anyone that came into the hallway and didn't immediately head over to the Angel Corp doors.

There were rumors that some demons would flip over to their full, demonic form at the slightest provocation. However, such a thing was quite impossible, even for those who were actually demons. Well, except for the Hellians, those demons that were always in that form. Those were the demons that had never taken human form. The whole lot of them had lost their shapeshifting capabilities minutes after their arrival on Earth. Or, at least, that was the party line, and the whole lot of them were sticking to it.

"We should have come back here first thing in the morning," Jack said, ignoring the usual gawkers as the two agents pushed their way through.

Hank refused to say anything on the case, or anything at all, until after they managed to push themselves back through the throng that filled the hall. He could have sworn that two of the men standing in the corner had been there since the day before, since they had returned from Cassidy Masters's apartment. Admittedly, he didn't remember seeing them on his way out later that night. For once, the crowd parted to let them through to the door, though their constant barrage of questions and requests for entry never faded until the door closed behind them.

"It was nothing but a pile of dirt," Hank said, responding to Jack's earlier comment. "Unless it was special dirt from only one place in the world, it's not going to lead us anywhere."

"It was special," Dr. Howard said, as way of greeting. She and Dr. Davidson were standing off to the side, behind the main desk. Danielle was sitting in her usual chair, not having bothered to so much as look up at the two of them as they came in the door. The two scientists were leaning against the door to Hank and Jack's office, wearing matching lab coats. The coats were blue, though Hank had seen the two wear similar coats of several other colors. They were always the same shade, always matching. The two would almost always be wearing the same outfit, though it was never clear to Hank if they coordinated beforehand or if they just knew each other well enough to know what to wear each day. They even wore matching glasses, despite the fact that Dr. Davidson didn't need them.

Other than their attire, the two women couldn't be any less alike. Dr. Howard was a short, latina woman with a small frame but an ample bosom that would put a Barbie doll to shame. Dr. Davidson was tall and stocky, of Irish descent, with a skin shade made paler due to her tendency towards the indoors, solidly built and easily the strongest of the two. It often made Hank think that their coordinated outfits were harder to accomplish than strictly necessary, for the two geek chic women.

"The only problem is that it isn't dirt," Dr. Davidson finished for her, her low, booming voice easily filling the space. "It's ash."

"Ash?" Hank asked.

"But... special ash?" Jack asked.

"Very special ash," Dr. Howard said. "It's demonic ash."

"Demonic ash?" Jack asked. "Like as in coming off of a demon? Which type of demon gives off ash?"

"None that I know of," Hank said.

"No, not coming off of one," Dr. Davidson said.

"Well, not really," Dr. Howard said. "It comes from hell, left over from some of the furnaces that power the place."

"Think of it as volcanic ash, only from hell," Dr. Davidson said.

"So... but, wait, wouldn't that have come off of them long before now? Like back in December?" Jack asked.

"Exactly," Dr. Howard said. "So, why would there be so much of it all in one place like that?"

"I'm hoping you have some answer to that question," Hank said. The two scientists just looked at him with blank faces, neither showing interest, curiosity, or any hint that they knew, or even cared, about the why of it. "Any thoughts at all?"

"The why's are your department," Dr. Howard said.

"Ours is the what and when," Dr. Davidson said.

"Okay, then when did the ash get to Earth?" Hank asked, trying to trick them into giving a straight answer that might actually give him some hint as to the source of the ash.

"There's no way of knowing that," Dr. Davidson said. "Carbon dating doesn't work on demonic artifacts."

"We still have that sword in the lab that one of the wrath demons brought with them," Dr. Howard said. "When we tried to carbon date it, the machine told us it was older than the universe."

"Did you at least try it with the ash?" Hank asked. "Maybe it's not really from hell."

"Oh, it's from hell alright," Dr. Howard said.

"And, yes, we tried it," Dr. Davidson said.

"It's older than the sword," Dr. Howard said.

"Well," Jack said, pensively. "Maybe someone just collected the ash in a plastic bag."

"No," Hank said, simply.

"What?" Jack asked. "Why not?"

"Well, for starters, I don't remember the stuff falling off any of them in any large enough of an amount to collect it in anything. They would have had to dust it off of every demon that came through in order to get that much. And why would anyone do that? Just on the off chance that they would need it to suggest that it was a demon?"

"Plus, it would mean that the ash was completely useless as a clue," Danielle said. She had been sitting there, quietly, at her desk, focusing on her work, listening in on their conversation the whole time. "It would mean that he would be back to square one, with less than twenty-four hours before his trip to the school, with nothing to show for it."

"Yes," Hank said. "That too."

"Well, while I agree with the fact that it is unlikely that someone had collected it in a bag, it wouldn't have taken that many demons to get that much ash together," Dr. Howard said. "It's just that none of the demons we know about had been covered with that much ash when they came through the portal."

"And, given what we know about the mass migration--" Dr. Davidson started to say.

"You mean the invasion," Jack interrupted.

"The mass migration is what the demons call it," Dr. Howard explained.

"And most terrorists call themselves freedom fighters," Jack said. "It doesn't make their suicide bombings honorable."

"It is in their minds," Dr. Davidson said. "And the demons never meant to invade. They couldn't stay in hell, so they migrated to somewhere they could stay. Thus, it was a mass migration. And, given what we know about it, about the fact that the whole lot of them had been together in one of their training fields before entering the portal, it would make sense that none of them would have been covered in ash. The ash covered plains are in a completely different part of hell."

"Sounds to me like you've been talking to the prisoner again," Hank said.

"She is a veritable font of information that isn't tapped nearly as much as it should be," Dr. Howard said.

"I'd like to tap--" Jack started to say.

"Jack," Hank interrupted, expecting the comment as soon as Dr. Howard had said it.

"What?" Jack asked, feigning ignorance. "She's hot. Or, at least, she was hot last time I saw her. Is she still hot?"

"Yes, she's still hot," Dr. Howard said, rolling her eyes at the man. "She still looks like Sami, so of course she's still hot."

"And, now that we have the video conferencing set up in her cell, we can talk to her anytime we want to," Dr. Davidson said.

"Dibs," Jack said, raising his hand as if someone was taking volunteers.

"Except that would only help so much," Hank said, ignoring his partner. "It's not like she would be in a place to help us out with this case. She's been in prison since the invasion, or mass migration, or whatever you want to call it. All we know from her is that the ash could have come from anywhere, which is obvious enough already. And, now, she knows something that she shouldn't. Something about a case that is almost actively trying to not be solvable."

"I never said it wasn't solvable," Dr. Howard said.

"You didn't have to," Hank said, exasperated. "You already told me that there's a lot to know about this special ash, but there's nothing that can be known about it that would help in any way to this case. What you haven't told me, what you can't tell me, is that there is a way to pinpoint the origin of the ash, or that it would help in any way to find the person, or demon, that it came from."

"But it wasn't just the ash that was found at the SUV," Dr. Davison said.

"What else was there?" Hank asked. "The boot print?"

"Exactly," Dr. Howard said. "The boot print."

"Which was also in demonic ash," Dr. Davidson said.

"And the tread was very distinctive," Dr. Howard said.

"Very distinctive indeed," Dr. Davidson agreed.

"Will you two stop that?" Hank yelled.

"Hey," came a call from Herb's open door. "Do I need to come out there?"

"No, sir," Jack called after him. "All under control."

"The boot tread was of the demonic symbol for wrath," Dr. Davidson said, finally. "Which means that the boot was straight from the wrath training camps in hell."

"Another bit of information that we wouldn't have had without Semi's help."

"Semi?" Hank asked. "The faux Sami's name is Semi?"

"We don't know if that was her name before taking on Sami's visage, but it is the name she goes by now, yes," Dr. Howard said.

"So, what? It was a wrath demon that killed Jared?" Jack asked. "Are we going to pull in every wrath demon out there and ask them where they were yesterday?"

"It doesn't even have to be a wrath demon," Hank said. "Or a demon at all. They just had to have access to the boots. It's not like there was anything special about the boots that make it so only wrath demons could wear them. Not all the demons were able to find work right away, and they came here with just the clothes on their back."

"And the boots on their feet," Jack added.

"One of them could have sold their boots in order to buy food," Hank said. "It's just another dead end."

"On the contrary," Dr. Howard said. "I said the boots are from the training camp, not from one of the demons that came through."

"I... I don't follow," Hank said.

"None of the demons that came through, at least none of the ones we interviewed, were recruits," Dr. Davidson said.

"Those boots are only worn by recruits," Dr. Howard said.

"According to Semi, after they become full-fledged demons, they get new clothes, because their old ones were destroyed during the process," Dr. Davidson said.

"New clothes means new boots."

"And new boots means new treads."

"So, what? One of the demons brought through some old boots they weren't wearing?" Jack asked. "Did they bring them along as a memento?"

"Not if their old boots were destroyed during their... graduation ceremony, or whatever it is that elevates them to full demonhood," Hank said. "But, if someone did bring an old pair of boots through, that might explain the ash. They weren't wearing them on the way through the portal, but they, or someone else, was wearing them when they drove the SUV. The problem is that anyone could have had those boots. They'll help to prove our case against whoever it was, but it's not going to help us find them now."

"Well, yes, okay, I can see that being a problem," Dr. Howard said.

"But, still, you have to admit, it is rather interesting," Dr. Davidson said.

"Yes," Hank allowed. "Interesting, but worthless."

"Well, that's rather rude, Hank," Blanche said, as she came in the front door to the office. "Jack is standing right there."

Chapter Eleven
The Wife

"Oh, ha ha," Jack said. "It's about time you two got back. Are you done saving the world already?"

"That depends, are you done trying to destroy it?" she asked.

"Oh, come on, that was one time," Jack said. "It's not like I knew that was what that stone was going to do. If you were there, you probably would have done the same exact thing as me."

"Trust me, there was no way that I would have done... that, with anything, let alone a stone with glowing glyphs on it."

"In either case," Hank said, getting between the two of them. "It was a long time ago, and I'm very glad you're home." He kissed Blanche lightly on the cheek, a chaste show of affection, though more than she usually liked in the workplace. "After the message you left yesterday, I was starting to worry about you."

"Why would you go and do a thing like that?" she asked. "I told you not to worry, didn't I? I thought I specifically said don't worry."

"If I told you not to worry when there's the sound of gunfire in the background, would you worry?"

"Of course, not. If you told me not to worry, it would mean you had it under control, just as I had. You really need to trust my judgement, as I do yours."

"You shouldn't," Jack said. "His judgement is pretty bad sometimes."

"Never as bad as yours," she said, through her teeth, glaring at the man. Jack always had a way to anger her, even in the best of conditions. He was also the only person Hank had ever seen get under her skin in that way. Usually, she was a calm, cool, collected person who thought showing emotion was a weakness, one that must be guarded against lest your enemies use it against you. It had turned Hank off at first. But once he managed to find the soul of the woman underneath, he knew the reason, knew why she was always so guarded, and loved her all the more for it.

"But your case is over?" Hank asked. He wasn't even sure what her case was, just that it was a few states over and involved gunfire. Hers were always the more secretive of missions, working within the more hidden worlds of the demons, trying to keep them from uniting against the humans. It was better that he didn't know what she was doing, as he usually had to deal with the demons as actual people, rather than a group that was to be feared.

"Completely over," Blanche said. "Just in time for our trip."

"Yea, about that," Hank said, hesitantly.

"You walked in on us talking about how impossible our case is," Jack finished. He seemed to take enjoyment in breaking the news that Hank would most likely not be joining her on their trip to see their daughter.

"You're stuck here?" she asked. Hank was just barely able to detect the edge of disappointment in her voice, something that had taken him years to manage.

"For now," Hank admitted. "But I'm still hoping that I'll be able to find a break in the case. Maybe I'll take a redeye later tonight and meet you over there."

"Come on, Hank, you know my rule," she scolded him.

"Don't make promises you can't keep," he intoned.

"Yes, I know. And I'm promising that I'll try."

"Promising to try is no promise at all," she said. "Of course, you'll try. I wouldn't have married you if I thought you weren't someone that would try. The problem is trying won't be enough, and you can't promise me that you'll solve it in time."

"No, you're right."

"In either case, I'll head out tonight, as planned. There's no sense in her being completely alone on her birthday. Not again. Not when I'm available to be there with her. If you can make it, great. If not... well, we'll miss you."

"I'll get there if I can," Hank said. "But you do know, there might be a time when neither of us are going to be able to be there for her. And I'm not just talking about when we're both busy. She's going to have to get used to the idea of us not being able to be there for her; you know, not making promises that we can't keep and all of that."

"Hank, she's turning seven, not seventeen. Let's keep our little girl as little as possible," Blanche said. "Besides, she does have her school and her friends, people she can rely on when she can't rely on us. She's strong; she's our daughter. She can handle anything."

"Great," Jack said. "Now that that's settled, can we get back to the case? I have my own plans that I don't want to be putting off myself."

"What plans are those?" Hank asked. He was a little afraid of what they might be.

"Oh, wouldn't you like to know," he teased.

"Well, I have a little extra time before my flight. What do we know so far?"

Hank went over the case, first as an overview, then in greater detail. With as little as they had known so far, it went by rather quickly. The review only made him feel more depressed, more like the case really was hopeless. He knew that Herb would have none of that. He wouldn't let any case, no matter how small, no matter how little evidence they had, slip by them, without a bigger case to take its place. It always made him wonder about all the smaller cases that they were missing out on, that were slipping by them. However, he knew that most of those were still handled, just on the local level, by departments that weren't as strapped as theirs.

"You do know where you went wrong on this case, right?" she asked.

"Getting there too soon," Hank said. "If we had let the locals handle it longer--"

"They'd be even worse off than you are now," she said. "You at least knew who Jared was, that he was a demon, had the resources to track the car and who it belonged to. The locals wouldn't be anywhere at this point."

"We're not anywhere at this point," Hank said.

"Well, that's debatable. Anyway, no, the place where you went wrong was that you're not seeing the bigger picture here. That's why you and that one are on cases like this, and why Jenkins over there and I take on the bigger ones." She nodded over to her partner just as he ducked into their office. The man had managed to slip into the office without anyone noticing he was there. The short man was easy to miss. It was his job to sneak into uncertain situations to get the lay of the land, so to speak. He was a scout and spy, keeping Blanche safe in the most dangerous of situations. Hank was immensely thankful to the man, though he didn't know much about him. "The ones that run on multiple levels. You should have left this one to me."

"Are you offering to take it over?" Jack asked.

"Oh, hell, no," she scoffed. "I'm going to see my little girl, and nothing is going to get in the way of that. No, I'm saying you need to think bigger."

"Bigger than one demon being run over by an SUV by someone who is, as of yet, unidentified, for reasons we don't know, going on nothing but a boot print and some ash, neither of which we know the origin of? What's bigger than murder?"

"I don't know that, yet," she said. "Neither do you. That's the problem. However, there is someone that might know what we don't. Someone that we already have access to. You just don't want to talk to her, because you're scared that she has an ulterior motive that you wouldn't be able to detect before it came to fruition."

"Oh, not you, too," Hank said. "Please tell me you haven't been talking to this Semi character."

"She's an asset, one that is totally under our control. She knows more than she's letting on, more than most of the demons that had come through in the invasion."

"And you think that's a reason to trust her?"

"No, of course not," Blanche said. "Never trust her. But, if we start using her more, if we get her to let her guard down. Or, better yet, make her think that we've started to trust her, to rely on her. Then maybe her real agenda would come out. Then we stop that, break her, stop the real reason why the demons came here, and, maybe, just maybe, they'll leave and we can go back to our normal, boring workload."

"Is that why Herb refuses to put in a request for more funds?" Hank asked. "He thinks they're just going to, what? Go away? All of them? What about the ones that have made a life here? They're not just going to give that up, not to go back to hell."

"We won't give them that choice," she said. Her voice went low, conspiratorial, almost menacing. It was the facade that she had put up when he first met her all over again, renewed on a level that always scared him.

"And what about those demons that haven't done anything? That didn't help out in whatever plan Semi tries to play out? What about the ones like Jared, or the brothers, that have adapted to life here better than some humans do? Are you going to banish them as well?"

"Hank, they don't belong here. They never had, never will. The sooner they're gone, the better it is for everyone, including the demons."

"I don't believe that, Blanche. I never will. They're just a different form of immigrants, providing a new take on life. Once they integrate with society--"

"They're demons, Hank. They don't have a new take on life, they have a take on death. They're not going to integrate with society, they'll destroy it."

"Some already have integrated," Hank said. "Like I was saying, the brothers, Jared. Plenty have made a life here. You're too busy watching the forest to see the trees."

"And you're too busy watching the trees to see the forest," she said.

"Well, how about this tree? How about Semi? What can she possibly know about this one accident, this one hit and run, when she was locked up the entire time? No one outside of this organization even knows where she is. She'll be even more clueless about the whole thing than we are."

"You'd be surprised," she said, with a slight smile. "Some of these demons have powers you couldn't begin to explain."

"You know just as well as I do that the magic in the prison doesn't reach beyond those walls. If Semi had any powers, they're blocked by the glyphs. Magic has its limits, even when it comes to demons. And there's nothing I've seen, not even since the event, that would make me think otherwise."

Despite the company line, there really was magic out there. It was just in too small quantities to impact the world. Most of the known areas of it, like the prison, were under the control of the HPS. Those that weren't were closely monitored. Nothing happened in those known pockets that the group didn't know about.

"You don't really believe that, do you? Considering all that we've seen? Planes disappearing out of thin air doesn't make you think that there are other forms of magic we haven't found yet?" Jack asked. "Or are you on team 'the aliens did it'?"

"Hey, I believe that aliens did it," Danielle said. "It's the only explanation that made sense at the time. It's still the only explanation that makes sense, given that the demons were still all in hell."

"But were they?" Jack asked.

"There are other explanations," Hank said, though he didn't put word to his suspicions. When a plane disappears only a few hours before a leather clad maniac took a self-admitted time traveler and just disappeared, the coincidence was more than enough for Hank to hang it all on the girl's shoulders. It wasn't a popular theory in the group, though. "Even the demons have said there is no magic here. Semi will be no different."

"But it's not like it would hurt to ask her," Blanche suggested. "Besides, do you have any other leads to try right now?"

Hank hung his head, knowing that she was right. Knowing that, despite the fact that he doubted the woman would know anything, he had no one else to turn to anyway. And, if he was going to be stuck on the case from hell, he might as well make the most of his time.

Chapter Twelve
HPS Penitentiary

Samantha Sanderson had an amazing career before all of this started. Hank had been a fan of hers from early on, though he never let on to Blanche. He knew that he would never have heard the end of it from her, even though he had never met the woman, never would have met her. They didn't exactly run in the same circles, not even close. And Hank feared and loved his wife far too much to ever go there.

Still, it wasn't her beauty that attracted him to her. She was beautiful, of course; she had her own show, she had to be beautiful in the world that they lived in. Blanche was just as beautiful, more so to him. No, what attracted him to her was the fact that she got to where she was, despite having been where she started out barely eleven years before then. It was a little-known fact, one held closest in the hearts of her biggest fans, that she had spent some time in a psychiatric facility in upstate New York. The place was only a few hours away from the complex that Hank had been working out of at the time of the incident. In another world, perhaps one where the planes had hit and there were no such things as time travelers, the two of them might have even met.

So, it was with great difficulty that he tried to put all thoughts of the woman out of his mind as he made his way into the complex. It wasn't Sami they were coming to visit anyway. She was dead, killed on live television. It was her murderer they were visiting, and the fan in him wanted nothing more than to kill Semi for what she did.

The place had been an old prison, long since condemned, with tales of ghosts keeping most of the locals away, and high, electrified fences keeping the rest of them out. There weren't any guards, at least not on the outside, as they would have only attracted attention. The complex worked best in secret, hidden away in the wilderness of Washington, of which the state had more than its fair share.

"We could have just talked to her on the video conference equipment they have set up," Jack said, as he followed behind Hank. The crown vic was parked in the parking lot that was cleverly disguised as a field that desperately needed to be mowed. The two of them were heading towards the main gate, the same one that had fed into the place since the original facility had been opened, over a hundred years earlier. The place had been retrofitted for their needs, increasing the strength of the bars that framed the prison cells and putting certain safeguards in place. Otherwise, it largely remained the same way it had been for decades.

"You can only see her face on that thing," Hank said. "The face can only tell you so much when trying to interpret a person's body language."

"Oh, so you wanted to see her squirm under your interrogation," Jack said. "I can understand that. The girl was hot."

"And, what? It wouldn't have been a tragedy if an ugly woman had been killed on live television?"

"No, it would have been," he admitted. "I just wouldn't have cared as much. And neither would you, whatever you tell yourself."

Hank just grunted, not wanting to show just how much he really had cared about the woman's death. When he got to the gate, he pulled out his badge, the same badge that got him into the HPS offices. He flicked it in front of the sensor that was nearby, disguised as an extra fence post. The gate gave a resounding click, followed by a low buzzing sound. The low hum that came off of the fence shut off, a split second before the gate started to roll open on its own, opening the pathway to let the two agents into the complex.

They made their way along the main lane, down through the old exercise yard. Hank eyed the abandoned yard, expecting trouble to jump out at him, even through the protective barrier of the fence. The place had always given him an eerie feeling, even before they started using it to house their demonic prisoners. Before the HPS had taken possession of it, the prison had been used by an old devil worshiping cult as their secret base of operations. They had gotten hold of a charged artifact, one of the few sources of real magic in the world. The cult had been completely wiped out in the raid, which meant the existence of the place was still secret. That was essential for their use, but it still made him feel like the place was haunted.

Although the HPS had been outed to the public, they still kept some parts of their job a secret. No one knew, no one was allowed to know, that the prison existed. That they kept those demons that needed to be locked up imprisoned there. They couldn't very well tell people that they had demons under lock and key, without revealing just what kind of locks they were using. However, due to certain financial restraints, they were forced to outsource the place to the DOD, allowing them to use it for some of their own harder than normal to detain prisoners.

At the far end of the main walk was the second checkpoint. This, too, was unmanned, as it was just outside of the front doors, still in plain view from outside the fences. The only thing that can be seen to indicate that the place might be in use were a set of lockers placed against the wall next to the door. From far away, the lockers looked worn out and rusted. However, they were only a few months old, put in place when the prison's latest guests had been locked up. Each locker, barely larger than a mailbox, had a key sticking out of the lock. All but the six along the bottom, which were used by the six guards inside.

Hank and Jack were well versed in the use of, and the need for, the lockers. They went straight to them after coming in the inner gate. After using the key to open the top left locker, Hank put in his cell phone, his fitness band, his keys, the badge he used to open the gates, everything that had the slightest bit of electronics in it. While he was at it, he also added his gun and wallet, just in case. Once it was all inside, he locked the locker, taking the key with him. The key was a simple thing, solid metal with a plastic circle on the far tip with the number to the locker painted on it. It was too simple for it to be affected by what was inside.

He barely glanced at his partner as he made his way over to the panel next to the door. He placed his hand on the panel, on the scanner, letting the green lights play across its surface as it scanned his handprint, verifying that it matched what was on record. At the same time, another panel, this one in the door itself, opened up, scanning his face in similar colored lights. No matter how perfect of a copy the demons were able to make, they were never able to copy the person's fingerprints. At least not in the few minutes they had to make their transformations in. The two panels chimed their approval of him at the same time and, seconds later, the door clicked unlocked. Instantly, a protective shield slammed over both panels, coming out of the door and the wall, before the door slid open.

Hank jumped back a step, clutching his hand to his chest as he eyed the shield coverings. He knew they would slam into place. He knew the whys and the hows. It always startled him whenever it happened, and he was always grateful that he would automatically drop his hand away from the panel when the chimes played out. He had heard of a guard, soon after the security system had been put into place, that hadn't moved his hand quickly enough. They bought him the best prosthesis that money could buy, on the DOD's dime, of course.

The door swung inward with an audible squeak that resonated up and down Hank's spine. The DOD sigil was carved into the stonework of the entrance area, lit by torches flaring out along the walls of the room. The sigil had been placed right where the devil worshipers had laid their pentagram, erasing it as the replacement was carved into the stone. As the wind from outside made its way through the entrance, the torches all flickered, two of them going out from the force of the wind. There were no electric lights anywhere in the complex. Even the old lamps and sockets had been removed, just in case. It gave the two agents the feel of stepping into another world, almost as if doing the reverse transition from the ones that the demons had experienced.

It only bothered Hank the slightest bit that the inside of the prison felt no different to him from the outside. He didn't have the strange ability to use the magic that lay within. This capability seemed quite independent of the world that the person was from. He couldn't feel the mana as it flowed past him, like air flowing towards a vacuum. It flowed passed him through the open door, out into the world, only to dissipate in the air. There was enough magic within the prison to bring down empires if they could only just use it out in the world of science. Most of the mana was sealed deeper in the prison, behind doors that were closed while the two of them were coming inside.

Just before Hank made it to the sigil on the floor, he heard a series of popping and fizzling sounds coming from behind him. He spun around, staring over at the source of the sounds. His hand went to his gun that was no longer there. Jack had just stepped across the threshold of the door and was dancing around in place. He made hissing noises as he tried to pull something from his back pocket. Hank just managed to get a quick peek at the white badge as Jack pulled it out. As Jack tossed the thing in the air, Hank could see the plastic and metal flared up in front of him. Before the melted mess hit the floor, it was completely unrecognizable.

"Damn it, that's the fifth one of those I've fried here," Jack said. "I keep forgetting about that stupid thing because you always badge us in wherever we go. I hate it that magic completely fries anything electrical. It makes me think that science is somehow inferior to it."

"After all that I've heard from these demons about their use of it, I'd have to agree with that," Hank said. "More powerful, and easier to wield, at least for those that have the gift for it."

"Gift," Jack spat. "You make it sound like being a mage makes you chosen by god or something."

"Or a goddess maybe," Hank joked. "It's a much bigger multiverse than what we were led to believe in Sunday school, isn't it?"

"I never went to Sunday school. It was CCD for me, and it was on Saturdays."

"Ouch."

Jack gave one last sidelong glance at the melted pile by his feet before heading over to Hank. Three chimes rung out above them, marking the time they had had to get inside. Once they were done, the front door slammed shut, much like it had opened. The two agents were dropped into the darkness of the low torchlight. Seconds later, the door leading further into the facility slammed open. Those few torches that had been blown out by the wind burst forth to life once more as the magic from the facility filled the chamber.

The two of them continued onward, deeper into the prison. They rounded the corner through the main hallway, around to within view of the front desk. There was a guard behind the desk, tucked away in a small room behind it. He was the first person they had seen since entering the place. A glass wall separated the room that the guard was in from the rest of the waiting area, which was little more than two cells next to each other without the wall in between them. Both agents knew that the area back there, behind the glass wall, was shielded from the rest of the facility. It was one of many strategically placed cavities that allowed the modern world to exist within the confines of the place. Hank could just make out the screen of the computer against the far wall around the bulk of the man behind the desk.

They had called ahead, telling the guards that they were coming. So, the man behind the desk simply waved them through. He pressed a button next to him that unlocked the door to the corridor leading further into the place. The corridor ran in a spiral around the center of the prison, passing by each of the gen pop cell blocks in turn, starting with A and heading all the way up to E at its center. Next to the entrance to each cell block was another guard station, each one a small island of the outside world within the ocean of magic that surrounded them. The guards each gave the agents a single nod, acknowledging their presence, their right to be there, as they continued onward.

It wasn't until they had gotten to D block that they first heard anything from the prisoners. The DOD's prisoners were stored there, in D block, second furthest from the main door. These were the worst of the worst among the full-blooded humans. The terrorists that were too dangerous and too valuable to the enemy to keep in Guantanamo, or any of the hundreds of black sites they had access to. The facility was its own black site, though one filled with black magic, rather than cloaked in the darkness of secrets. The two agents flitted by the entrance to D block, barely glancing in through the bars. Even so, the prisoners gave them hoots and hollers, even a few wolf whistles, as they passed.

The two of them stopped at the last guard station, the one across from the entrance to E block. This guard, unlike the rest of them, they knew. He was, technically, a member of HPS, another drafted man like Jack. He was the missing tenth man of their team. Donald Grayson had been in New York for the incident, had been there as Jack's lawyer. He had originally signed on with the team as their legal department. After the incident with the devil worshiping cult, he threatened to go public about the entire organization. Instead, he ended up getting stuck at the far end of the prison, as far away from the rest of the world as they could get him. As much a prisoner of the place as the actual prisoners he had to see every day.

"Grayson," Hank said, in way of greeting. He leaned against the glass walls of Grayson's guard station, his cell, tapping on the walls as if he were a kid at the zoo. Grayson presented his middle finger to the agent, his typical response to the greeting. "Care to let us in to the visitor's room?" Hank asked, ignoring the gesture.

"The prisoner isn't taking guests today," Grayson said. His voice was muffled as it came through the glass. They weren't able to put the usual air holes in the glass, not without compromising the little pocket of science friendly space within. Instead, there was an intercom. It was something of a hybrid between the scientific and the supernatural that one of the demons had whipped up for them. They only seemed to work about half the time.

"What do you mean 'the prisoner isn't taking guests today'?" Hank asked. "We came all the way down here."

"Come off it, Donny," Jack said. "We know this is just another one of your power trips, like when you threatened to go public. We both know you're going to give in to our request eventually. So why don't you just save us both the hassle, eh? The guy is missing his daughter's birthday for this case."

"Oh, well, in that case," Grayson said, before blowing a raspberry at the two of them. His spittle spread across the glass on his side, obscuring his face momentarily before he wiped it down. "She's been playing with the wards again, trying to escape from her cell. I had to get George to strengthen them twice last week and another time this morning, after that stupid call with Huey and Dewey. She's too familiar with the wards and keeps breaking through them too quickly. We stuck her in the SHU until we can get one of the pride demons down to change them. I'm not taking her out of the SHU for anything, least of all you two idiots."

"Fine," Hank said. "Then let us into the SHU. We can talk to her there just as easily as the visitors' room."

"Fine," Grayson said, in a huff. "Suit yourself. Don't come crawling to me when she pulls your eyes out of their sockets and beat you to death with them."

As Grayson continued to stare daggers at the two agents, his face seemed to light up with some idea playing out in his head. His smile started to show through his facade, just as he reached over to the panel next to him. The panel was hidden from view by the walls that bordered the glass barrier. When he pressed the button, the mechanism that it triggered hit with a loud bang, accented by Grayson's laugh. A split second later, Hank's world went dark.

Chapter Thirteen
Visiting the Prisoner

"I hate magic," Jack muttered.

Hank rather agreed with the sentiment. Wherever he was, it was dark. He had fallen at an odd angle. His head was pressed under his body, forced into the stone floor beneath him. He was completely disoriented by the sudden darkness, the reorientation of his body, and, of course, the magic that was the cause of it. It was several seconds before he managed to feel the direction of gravity beneath him. Once he was certain of which way was down, he flopped himself over onto his side, then his back, so he could stare up through the darkness at a ceiling that he couldn't see.

"Where are we?" Hank asked.

"I'm guessing we're underneath the prison," Jack said. "Maybe a basement or something."

"Oh, good," Hank said. "I was a little afraid that Grayson had banished us to some other world or something."

"Well, I wouldn't put it past him. He is a lawyer after all, surrounded by terrorists and demons that might actually be capable of doing just that. If the glyphs didn't keep their magic at bay, that is."

"That's assuming the glyphs do what they're supposed to. The demons that provided them could have just given us crap, in the off chance that we have to arrest them as well."

"No," Jack insisted. "Remember, we tested them out that one weekend? What was it, like two weeks after the invasion?"

"Jack, I was in DC all of January, briefing the president and all of congress on what we had learned so far. I must have missed the sleepover."

"It was more of a shut in, really. It was fun. Grayson nearly messed himself when we wouldn't let him out of the cell."

"Maybe that was when he decided to try to go public about the cult," Hank suggested. "That happened around that time, right?"

"Actually, I think he had decided that earlier. He had been all grumpy all that weekend, moaning about ghosts that haunted this place. That was why we decided to lock him into the cell. Granted, yes, it might have been the last straw, but he totally deserved it."

"Great, now you got me feeling sorry for the guy," Hank said.

"If you two are finished..." came a voice from the darkness around them.

Hank eyed the area, trying to will his eyes to see the room, despite the absolute lack of light to see by. Suddenly, a flash went off in the distance, a spark of light that started to glow. The light gradually approached them, slowly revealed the area around them. They were in another corridor, this one lacking in the sporadic torches that had led their way through the one above. To Hank's left was an old elevator shaft. The doors were opened, showing nothing but the empty shaft. He could easily see below them as the light source came closer. Instead of the shock absorbers, the shaft simply ended in a flat, solid stone floor. After seeing that, he looked up, trying to see the rest of the shaft above the floor they were on. There were no torches inside, leaving much of the shaft too dark to see in.

"I'm here to lead you to your prisoner," said the voice that had spoken before.

Hank looked towards the source of the voice. The owner was the one holding the light, the ball of fire, in his hands. Hank's eyes bugged out so far that they might have fallen out. He wasn't sure what to expect down there, in what he had been taking for the basement of the prison. A fully formed demon was certainly not on his list of things to see. Instead of looking like a normal human being, as most of the demons that currently resided on Earth did, this one looked like something out of a horror movie. His skin was a blood red, though it looked almost fiery in the dancing flame. The ball of fire floated above his skin as if repelled by it. The ball was only slightly larger than Hank's own hand, though dwarfed in the hand of the demon. The demon stood tall, having to stoop down to not scrape his head against the normal height ceiling above them. Every inch of his torso and arms were covered with muscle, stretching out the red skin to an almost bulbous, hideous sight. He wore a pair of tight leather pants that seemed to have been melded with the rest of his body and nothing else. No shoes, no shirt, but no one seeing his face would dare deny him service. Though Hank could see something human in that face, that only made the rest of it that much more horrifying. The major parts of his facial features that were almost beyond description. And, to top it all off, his horns grew out from his forehead, looping up over his head to scrape against the ceiling, carving deep grooves into the cement above.

Yet, despite all the fierce, demonic vision before them, the demon himself had a broad smile as he looked down at the two agents. "Oh," he said, in that deep, booming, echoing voice that seemed to fill the entire corridor. "I remember you two guys. It's Ralph."

"Oh, right, Ralph," Hank said, feigning familiarity, though he couldn't for the life of him remember any demon named Ralph. If he had his phone with him, and it wasn't a steaming pile of goo from the magic flowing around everywhere, he could at least look at his notes. He had a specific subsection of his contacts list dedicated to the hellians like Ralph. "How you doing?"

"Eh, it's a living," Ralph said. "I never was that good at transformations, and it beats being screamed at everywhere I go. Anyway, you're going to see the boss lady?"

"The... Semi? Yea, we're here to see Semi," Hank said.

"Alright, follow me."

He turned around and started heading down the way he had come. As he turned around, his horns sparked against something in the ceiling. He lifted his hand high enough so that the light from the ball of fire could be seen over his right shoulder, illuminating the floor in front of the two agents. They tried to keep up with the demon, though his long stride made that difficult.

On either side of the hallway were doors, each facing one another, the typical isolation cell doors that were used on all the prison movies and shows. They each had two slots in it, one at waste height for the meal trays and one a couple of feet higher for the guards to look through. However, unlike in those movies, the only sounds they were hearing were their own footsteps and the flickering of the ball of fire in Ralph's hand. No one was shouting, crying out for mercy that wasn't going to come, or trying to scare the people heading past their cell. As Hank stared at each door in turn, he half expected one or both of the pair of doors to be open, with hungry demons waiting to pounce on them. He had no doubt that, if anyone was inside, they knew that they were there and were just biding their time until they could attack.

"There's one thing I don't quite understand," Jack said. Hank jumped a little at his partner's sudden words. "Not all humans can use magic, right?"

"Yes, only those gifted with the talent."

"But can all demons?"

"Well... yes, and no," Ralph said. "I don't quite understand it myself, but demons can use magic to do certain things. It was limited in Hell and Heaven, because, well, afterlife and all of that. But out in the world, just the smallest amount went a long way. We were taught to use the excess energies from the portal itself to transform once we got here. My spell just fizzled when I tried it.

"If the demon had the talent for magic when they were alive, they can still use their magic. But the ones that weren't mages can still do a few things; balls of fire like these, shapeshifting, if you're good enough at it to make it stick, minor illusions, teleporting--"

"Woah, wait, teleporting?" Hank asked. "You mean these demons, the ones imprisoned upstairs, could just teleport out of here?"

"Oh, no, of course not," Ralph said, much to Hank's relief. "That's what the glyphs are for; well, some of them anyway. Some of them work against the strength of the demon themselves, and that is rather substantial. It would have been enough to tear apart any prison bars, no matter how much you reinforced them. At least that's the case for some of the factions. Wrath, like me and the boss lady, for certain. Lust usually, too. Sloth, greed and gluttony, not so much."

"What about envy and pride?" Hank asked.

Ralph just shrugged in response, before turning around the corner. As the agents turned to follow, Hank saw that they had come to the end of the corridor. There was a small section leading off from the main. It was barely large enough for Ralph to stand in with the agents beside him, though there was enough room for two more doors. In the far wall was another door, this one with light glowing through the two slots. When Hank saw this, he looked behind them, down the now dark corridor, noticing that none of the doors they had passed were glowing in that manner. He figured this meant that none of the other units were occupied and felt a bit relieved. He didn't want to have dangerous demons at his back. But he couldn't help but wonder why they had felt the need to put Semi in this one, all the way at the end of the corridor, away from the entrance.

"Uh, you don't need me to go in there with you, do you?" Ralph said. He spoke in a whisper, though his voice still resonated in the pit of Hank's stomach. "She scares me."

Hank stood there for a moment, wondering at that thought. The thought that this huge, strapping wrath demon would be scared of anything. Of course, the fact that this Semi was a wrath demon as well hadn't escaped him. She might very well be older than Ralph. More powerful, even, perhaps. One of the ones that had tortured him during his transformation. But, still, he was left with wondering if this whole trip wasn't just one large mistake.

"No, Ralph," Jack said. He placed his hand comfortingly on the demon's elbow, which he had to stretch up to reach. "You can stay out here. We just need to get let in."

"Shouldn't we be worried about having her restrained?" Hank asked.

"That happens naturally," Jack said. "The glyphs will spark up once we're inside."

"Let me guess, you tested those out on Grayson as well." Jack gave a malicious smile at that comment, seeming all the more insidious from the low firelight beaming down on him from above his head.

Ralph reached down, clasping firmly on the door handle, which was dwarfed in his hand. It slid through his grasp a few times before he pulled his hand away. He ended up using his thumb and forefinger to pinch it instead. His face was scrunched up in a strained expression as he seemed to be restraining his own strength, to put only the slightest amount of force behind turning the handle. The handle rattled in its socket, threatening to break even under the light touch. It eventually turned, revealing the cell within.

Samantha Sanderson was curled up in a ball in the far corner. Seconds after the door had opened, far too long for Hank's liking, thick cell bars of fire were flung up from the floor, filling the space between them. The woman flinched at their activation, curling in tighter as she let out a little whimper. A single torch was mounted in the ceiling, letting light flow down around the prisoner, illuminating the small cell. There was a proper bed, though she wasn't sitting on it, a toilet in the other corner, and even a desk, though that was empty.

"Please," Samantha said, her voice coming out as little more than a squeak. "There's been a mistake. You don't understand. I'm not supposed to be in here."

Hank, confused, looked between the prisoner and Ralph. Or, at least, where Ralph had been moments before. It appeared that Ralph had fled soon after he had opened the door, as he was nowhere in sight. Hank laughed a little to himself at the thought of anyone, least of all a big strapping demon, could ever be scared of this little slip of a woman.

"Come off it, Semi," Jack snapped. "You're not going to fool us."

Hank looked towards Jack for a moment, further confused. Sure, the woman was in the cell where they were supposed to find Semi, the wrath demon that was impersonating the woman that she had killed on live television. But this seemed like the same woman, that same news anchor that he had watched almost religiously before her death. If he hadn't known any better, he would have thought that the whole thing was just one big mistake, that the woman before him was the real Sami, and that there really was just a huge mistake being made.

So, it was only out of the corner of Hank's eye that he spotted the desk being thrown in his direction. He jumped backwards, ducking in on himself as the wooden furniture flew through the six feet of space between the two of them. It smashed into the fiery bars. Instead of passing through them, or breaking apart on impact as it should have done against metal bars, it bounced off of them. It came back at Semi in the same time that it had taken for it to fly across the room. Semi caught the thing in a single hand, holding it over her head with little effort. She had stood up while the desk flew through the air, an evil grin on her face as she stared down the two agents.

Hank hadn't had any interactions with the woman since she had come onto the world stage on live TV. In those few times that he had come to the prison, he had almost purposefully avoided the woman. So, he wasn't sure what to expect from her. She wasn't wearing a typical prison uniform, or even the clothes that she would have come in with, the copy of Sami's suit that she had worn on the last day of her life. The demon was wearing a torn-up tank top that looked more like a bra and an overly frayed and damaged blue skirt that revealed more of her legs than hid them. An orange armband, presumably all that was left of the prison outfit that she had been issued, was wrapped around her upper arm, doing little for the look. Now that her facade had been dropped, she was flexing her paltry, human muscles as she tried to look intimidating. It was hard for her to do, stuck in the petite form of the demure news anchor.

"What do you two want from me?" she asked, anger filling her voice. "You're interrupting my day."

"I'm sorry, were you busy doing something?" Jack asked. He hadn't moved from where he was standing while the demon was still cowering in the ball, showing no outward sign that he was affected by the flying furniture. Hank tried to straighten himself, to put back on his airs of professionalism that had slipped under the duress. "Were you trying to talk to your lord and master?"

"Satan never responded to me before. Why would he begin now?" she asked.

"Jack, can we not bait the murderous demon?" Hank asked. He tried to pull the conversation to the matter at hand, rather than letting the two of them continue in what appeared to be well practiced banter.

"It's not like she can get to us, stuck like that behind these wards," Jack said. Still, Hank had to look at the fiery bars, and the gaping holes that stood out among their structure. He wondered why the demon didn't just reach through them, past the restraining bars, and snuff out their lives where they stood. Unlike the other demons that he had dealt with, Semi was a known murderer, someone known to have killed the person whose identity they assumed. This made her seem that much more dangerous. He took a hesitant step away from the bars, closer to the door.

Semi's eyes darted towards him, following his movement. Her smile widened. Her tongue came out to lick her lips. Though the tongue looked to be quite human as it darted across, it didn't make the maneuver any less spine tingling. "No, come closer," she teased. "Let me bathe in your blood."

"Can it, Semi," Jack said. "We just came for some information."

"Ah, information," Semi said. "The only thing I have left to bargain with. What makes you think that I would provide such a thing to the likes of you?"

"Because we're going to get you out of here," Jack said. Her eyes lit up for the slightest second, as her posturing slipped the slightest bit. Hank looked over to his partner, unsure what exactly he was offering there. He knew that they would not be letting Semi out anytime soon, not for all the information in the world.

Semi seemed to read that out of Hank's mind. "You don't have the power to do that," she accused. "I'll be stuck here, in this prison, for the rest of my eternal life."

"You don't know that," Jack said. "Your life might not last any longer than mine. Your immortality might be tied to your connection with hell."

"A connection that will never fail me," she said. Her eyes literally glowed as her ire rose. They flickered with demon sign, something that Hank hadn't thought them capable of without the proper trigger. Then again, he hadn't seen a demon get as angry as she seemed to be getting.

"Jack, stop baiting the demon," Hank ordered. "Semi, put the desk on the floor and sit down."

Semi looked up at the desk, still looming in her hand, as if she had forgotten it was there, despite its weight. She placed it down on the floor, in the same place it had been in when Hank had come into the cell. At first, it didn't seem the least bit affected by being thrown against the bars. However, after a few seconds, the leg that she had been holding it by popped out from its place. It fell to the floor seconds before the rest of the desk did. The desk fell apart on impact, confusing Hank all the more by its timely destruction. Once the debris settled in a pile, Semi sat on the tallest part of it, where the desk top had been, taking Hank's orders to heart.

"Now, then, what can I do for you?" Semi asked, seeming to have calmed down completely.

"Like we said, we have some questions," Hank said.

"Well, I'm always happy to answer questions... for a price," she said, her smile still locked in place.

"What do you want?" Hank asked.

"As your fine friend offered, I want out."

"I don't--" Hank began to say.

"Done," Jack said, interrupting him.

"Excellent," she said, barely blinking. "Now, what are your questions?"

"Do you know a demon named Jared?" Hank asked, figuring it best to jump right into the questions before she thought they were breaking a promise with her.

"Oh, yes, of course," she said, nodding her head. "I know all of the thousands of demons that came through personally. I remember when Jared first came to hell like it was yesterday. I even pulled him from the masses myself, escorting him straight to the torture chamber where he would get his red skin."

"Jared wasn't a wrath demon," Jack said, confused.

"That was sarcasm, Jack," Hank supplied. "She doesn't know who we're talking about."

"No answers, no deal," Jack said.

"I knew this was going to be a monumental waste of time."

"Ah, you're as impatient to get out of here as I am," Semi said, staring at him. "How delicious."

"It's not even like she would care about demon on demon violence, let alone a demon killing one of their own," Hank said.

"Oh, that," she said. "That's never really been an issue. There has been infighting for centuries. Millennia, even. If you really want to see some demon on demon violence, I'd check out one of the fight clubs."

"What fight clubs?" Hank asked. In all the months that the demons had been there, he hadn't heard anything about a fight club starting up. It unnerved him a little to hear of one being spoken of so casually from someone that wouldn't have had contact with anyone from the outside, as if one was bound to show up eventually.

"We've never heard of any fight clubs," Jack said.

"Well, no, of course you wouldn't. They would be keeping it under the radar, to prevent you guys breaking them up. I'm sure you've put a load of laws in place that would make such a thing illegal."

"Yea, like limiting the gathering of demons in one place," Jack said. "And, oh, yea, assault and murder laws that were already in place, demon or not. I'll bet there's even illegal betting there."

"Exactly. So, why would they advertise their location to the likes of you?"

"Advertise," Hank said, pensively. "They would need to advertise in order to get new people in, wouldn't they?"

"Oh, it would all be word of mouth, I assure you," she said. "Demons only, maybe some humans, if they can be trusted, if such a thing were possible." She practically spat the word humans as if she couldn't get it out of her mouth fast enough.

"Huh," Hank said, as an idea came to him, a lead that he hadn't thought of pursuing, as it seemed unlikely to go anywhere. Yet, suddenly, it was the only way he could see forward. "Thank you so much for your help. Seeing you wasn't a complete waste of time, after all. Go figure. Alright, Jack, let's go."

"Wait, I helped you?" Semi said, completely surprised. "Does that mean..."

"Wait, what's going on?" Jack asked. "I hate when you don't tell me things."

"Hey, that means I go free, right?" Semi asked. "I'm getting out of here? Seeing the sun again?"

"Oh, shut up, you," Jack snapped. "Of course, you're not getting out of prison."

"But you said... you promised... You can't break a promise to a demon."

"Of course, we can," Jack said. "Why can't we?"

"Because of the magic that binds us," Semi said, gleefully. "And there's magic here. Structured, restricted, so much so that I can't change from this detestable form. But enough that a broken promise earns me your soul."

"That's ridiculous," Hank snapped. "If anything like that were true, the other demons would have told us that. Any of the demons would have told us that. They've all been very cooperative."

"Fine," she spat. "But it's never a good idea to break a promise to a demon."

"Fine," Jack said. "I promised to get you out of here, and that's exactly what I'll do." She laughed, hysterically, maniacally, as she jumped up from her place on the pile of wood. She ran towards the bars, reaching towards them. Her hands were repelled before she could touch them, even as she aimed for the gap between them. "I'll speak to Grayson about getting you out of here... and back into your old cell. I'm sure the glyphs have been recharged by now."

"But... no," she said, her glee gone instantly. "No, you promised to get me out of here."

"Exactly," Jack said. "I'm getting you out of the SHU. Neither one of us gave a specific clarification on where here was."

Jack turned on his heel, heading out, past Hank, into the hall. Hank was left standing there, shocked by that interaction as Semi started screaming her head off, slamming herself against the bars. She bounced back off of them, much like the desk had, coming back to her feet in the perfect position to make another jump. This continued as Hank left the cell, following Jack down the hall. Right before Hank turned the corner in the hallway, the door to the cell slammed closed behind him. The next few bangs were of Semi slamming herself into the magically reinforced door.

"Seriously?" Hank asked, when he caught up with his partner. "Was that always your plan? Sometimes you really scare me."

"Not really," he admitted. "It just kind of came to me when she was giving me gripe about breaking a promise."

"Oh, no, that's real," Ralph said, coming out of a nearby cell. His ball of fire was still lit, still in his hand, lighting the way down the hall. Behind him, the cell that he had been hiding in was completely empty. "The effect of breaking such a promise is completely random, and not controllable by the demon themselves, but there's always a price. It just relies on magic, so no one thought to say anything about it. Um... is she gone now?" He looked towards the corner in the hallway, but didn't seem brave enough to head that way.

"Yup, the door is closed. She's locked in there once more," Hank said. "We'll, apparently, be talking about moving her back upstairs, so you won't have to worry about her much longer."

"Oh, good," he said, sounding relieved. He led the way back to the entrance, barely sparing another glance behind him as he did so.

"Sometimes I scare you?" Jack asked. "What about you? What was it that you thought up back there? Do you know about one of these fight clubs?"

"We both do," Hank said. "It was something about what one of those bikers was talking about."

"Bikers?" Jack asked. "Those idiots back at the bar? What about them?"

Chapter Fourteen
The Fight Club

Hank pulled the crown vic into the parking lot for the club a few hours after dark. The sign stuck up in the air over the building named it The Demons' Pit, which made it sound like they had the right place. They had called into the home office as soon as they managed to get free of the magic within the prison. It didn't take Danielle long to track the place down, once she knew what she was looking for. The bar that the bikers had mentioned was listed online as little more than a bar. The trip down to Woodland took too long, though, and they lost the rest of the day to it. While it helped that they had a direction to go, a place to look into, it was looking less likely that Hank was going to make it up to the school at all.

The two agents pulled into a spot near the entrance, one of the few that were still available. Despite the late hour on a Tuesday night, the place was packed. Once they pulled into the spot, they waited there for a few minutes, trying to gage what they were getting themselves into. There was an almost non-stop flow of people heading inside. And, yet, in the ten minutes they sat there, not a single person came out.

"There could be any number of people in there," Jack said.

"People, demons, other, absolutely," Hank said, staring at the front door. Just like at the bar, The Demons' Pit had no windows, hiding its interior from the outside world as if those fighting within were vampires, rather than demons. "It's a good thing we're not here to cause any trouble."

"Why are we here? This lead is pretty thin. We're just as likely to find the killer in some abandoned building that you randomly pick to search."

"It's probably the thinnest I've ever worked with, but it's all I got. I should be on an airplane right now, heading up to see my daughter. Instead, I'm chasing down any angle that might lead me where I need to go. You can stay here, if you want."

"No, I'm coming with you," Jack said, sounding almost disappointed. "I'm your partner. I always have your back. Even when you do weird, stupid things like walk straight into... where exactly are we?"

"My guess is that this is one of the fight clubs that Semi was talking about," Hank said. "In either case, this is the bar that the bikers had gone to on Monday. We can see if anyone inside might have known Jared and wanted to kill him. If it is a fight club, we should have known about this place already. If we weren't so tied down in bigger cases like murder, we would have. I think it falls under our jurisdiction. We should probably have it shut down."

"Oh, you're no fun," Jack said. "Let the demons blow off their steam if they want to. It's no skin off my nose. Should we really expect them to play by our rules?"

"Oh, you mean like those rules about assault, murder, stealing, and all that?"

"No, I mean about beating the crap out of each other, willingly, for money."

"If this were a legally established fight club, then we'd let them be. But how much do you want to bet that they haven't filed their paperwork. I doubt demons would be up on the details like that."

"Wouldn't it be faster to check that out before heading in there?" Jack asked.

"No need," Hank said. "If there was a demon that had a fight club registered, it would have been flagged in our system already. It hasn't, so they haven't. It's as simple as that."

Hank waited as the latest group of patrons headed inside before exiting the crown vic. He didn't want to be immediately associated with the sigil on the hood when he made his move towards the door. Jack's footfalls followed him towards the front door, echoing his own, though without the purpose he placed in his. Another car pulled in behind them, but they were far enough away from the crown vic that Hank didn't worry about anyone seeing them. By then, they were just another couple of patrons looking to see the fight, or whatever it was that was going on inside.

The lights that filled the room surprised him as he made his way inside. Once his eyes adjusted to it, he could see a crowded room, which looked to take up the entire interior of the building. Pillars could be seen everywhere, over the heads of the packed crowd, holding up a balcony section. Although the pillar closest to the door was made of steel reinforced cement, the rest of them were made of simple wood, as was the floor above them. The crowd was cheering something on, but he couldn't make out anything beyond their raised fists and jumping forms.

Hank pushed his way through the crowd, trying to make it towards the center of the room. The crowd cheered on what it was seeing, though Hank couldn't make anything out but the backs of the heads in front of him. Even those next to him, the ones that were shorter than his substantial height, seemed to not have any trouble seeing the events in front of them. He had quickly lost track of Jack in the crowd, though he knew that the man would be able to take care of himself. It was only his lack of ability to keep himself out of trouble that worried Hank.

Just inside the door was a group of five men shouting their heads off. Once Hank got past them, he started hearing something besides the yelling of the crowd. The unmistakable sound of a fist impacting with a face was immediately followed by a cheer from the audience. After getting past another two, the packed people seemed to open up in front of him. There was a slight downward slope that allowed those close enough to the center to see everything in front of them. He made it into the open just in time to see a man leaping off of a metal fence. The fence had been erected in the center, forming a cage where the fight was happening. And a fight was exactly what was happening. In the center of the ring was a woman who seemed stunned. Hank watched as the man practically flew through the air at her, his fist leading the way.

A split second before the man came close enough to hit her, she unfurled her wings, extending them over her head to block the incoming blow. She flipped out her wings in the same motion, blasting the man away from her and back into the fence. He bounced off of it, coming into a crumpled ball on the floor. The woman stood up in the center of the ring, staring down at her latest opponent, her wings stretched out to her side. The wings identified her as a demon more than anything else about her.

She was clearly a succubus, one of the lust demons. Unlike their cousins, the lust demons didn't have a need to change form. In fact, most of them had opted to remain in their original form. In their full demonic form, they looked like beautiful men and women. The only thing that showed them as being demons was their demon sign, the wings, and their feet. The wings were capable of retracting so tightly against her back that no one would be able to see them, even without clothing over them. If this woman's wings were fully retracted, she would look no different from anyone else in the crowd. As for their feet, there was a very popular line of pumps out that simulated them.

As Hank made his way closer to the ring where the fight was happening, he was able to get a better look at the woman. She was wearing a pink tank dress, which he felt was an odd choice for a fight. The gaps on the back had been enlarged to accommodate her wings. As he watched her, the man managed to get a punch through her defenses. She took a glancing blow from the man's attack, reeling backwards and into the cage closer to Hank. When she hit the fence, he noticed that her ears were pointed. They reached upwards into her blond hair, which was pulled up in a ponytail. Hank figured that the woman had been something akin to an elf in her previous life.

During the lust demon training, the process of turning them into a demon had the effect of making them more beautiful, more striking and alluring. They tended to look something similar to what they looked like when they were alive. The process also made them stronger and faster, though less so than some of the other demon types. Her strength was made clear as she bounced back from the blow. She swung an uppercut at the man and forced him upwards. The punch was so strong that he flew free from the ring and up into the balcony section.

Hank looked up and over, trying to get a better angle at the man where he landed. Despite her obvious demonicness, it wasn't clear what the man's status was. Though no human would stand a chance on equal footing with a demon in hand to hand, it wasn't clear if that was why he had lost to the woman. A wrath demon, unfamiliar with the reduced strength of a human form, could just as easily be dispatched by a lust demon in all their glory. The balcony extended so far out that Hank had to make it all the way to the side of the ring before he managed to see the man. He was crumpled on his side near the edge of the balcony. His arm dangled down from above and his eyes were closed. Someone was standing over him, taking his pulse to make sure that he was still alive.

A hush fell over the crowd as they waited for the results of the fight. Hank wasn't sure of the rules, if a death was looked on more or less favorably than an actual knockout. But, when the person standing over the prone man came up from his examination, nodding his head with a smile, the crowd erupted in a final round of cheers. Behind Hank, the cage was opened up and the ref came over to the woman's side to herald her the victor. The ref was obviously a pride demon, a hellian, and had been all but invisible next to the gate during the fight.

"Such a wonderful fight," came a booming voice above Hank's head. He looked in the direction of the source, surprised and disgusted by what he saw up there. The demon was sitting on the balcony, just above the cement support. There was no question that he was a gluttony demon.

Gluttony demons were perhaps the most distinguishable of all the types of demons. Their bulbous forms, distortions of what they had been before, stood as testament to just how fat people can become. Even the lightest of the lot were morbidly obese, without having to worry about the morbid part. This one, in particular, was more on the other side of the spectrum. His fat extended over several seats on both sides of his own, overly large chair. He wore no clothes, at least not that his pockets of fat hadn't swallowed whole. Even with as fat as he was, there was a large buffet in front of him and a roast chicken leg in his hand as he congratulated the winner. As he spoke, he waved around the chicken leg as if it were a wand or scepter.

"I do so love to watch a succubus at her best. Ah, if only I were a lighter fellow, perhaps we could see her at work in another manner." He managed to get a decent amount of chuckling from the crowd.

The crowd let off a small round of applause for the fight before heading off to the sides of the overcrowded room. With the crowd falling away from him, Hank was left standing there, in the center of the room, mostly alone. He spotted Jack eyeing him from the edge of the crowd, but he was just walking away from him with the rest of them. Hank looked back towards the ring and the succubus that was still there. She was leaning against the cage, her wings retracted once more. As she struggled to regain her breathing, her eyes were locked on her defeated opponent. Sweat flowed freely down her face, which she unconsciously dabbed at with her towel.

When she realized that she was still being watched, her eyes fell onto Hank standing in front of her.

Recognition instantly played across her face, and the woman ran for the still open door in the cage. Once she was out, her wings came out again. They whipped at the air as she jumped up the incline, heading for the back of the room. The crowd that still lingered on that side were all hunkered down near the sides of the room where vendors were hocking their wares. They quickly made way for the woman as she ran from the agent like a literal bat out of hell.

"HPS," she managed to scream out, right before she burst out of the back door. Her wings hit the EXIT sign above it and knocked it loose.

The entire crowd looked towards her departing form before, collectively, turning towards Hank. He was still standing, dumbstruck, in the center of the room. He had lost sight of Jack again, though he was certain that his partner was somewhere in that crowd. However, he wasn't as confident about the man coming to his rescue if needed. Hank could feel the beady eyes of the gluttony demon staring down at him from above, knowing full well that he wouldn't be able to flee if needed. Gluttony demons were used mostly as fodder in the wars between heaven and hell, blocking the enemy forces and literally rolling over them. They weren't all that mobile.

Hank looked up at the demon, standing his ground against the obvious leader of the club. The demon's eyes went wide as he stared right back at Hank. The audience that had been sitting around him during the fight were slowly slinking away. They were perhaps trying to avoid detection from the otherwise distracted demon. Unfortunately, the demon's fatty hand, the one not still clutching the chicken wing, was just as firmly clasped on the woman sitting beside him. The woman's face made it clear that she didn't want to be there any more than the rest of the fleeing spectators. Hank pointed towards the demon, then to the woman in distress, and was about to yell for him to release her when he was interrupted with the strangest reaction that he had ever gotten from one of their ilk.

The demon laughed, a deep, belly laugh that went on for a while. And, with a gluttony demon, a belly laugh really means something. His stomach jiggled noticeably, even as far away as Hank was. The pillar beneath the demon groaned under the added effort of holding his weight, showing the need for the added support. In his overzealous guffaws, he lost his grip on the scared woman. She quickly fled from his side, passing some of her fellow audience members that had left earlier. When she made her reappearance, she was clutching at her wrist as she fled through the front door.

"Finally," the demon's booming voice came, once he was able to control his laughter. "An HPS agent has come to my humble establishment. Don't mind these fools that flee at the very sight of you. I do not fear anything that you could bring upon me. Come, enjoy the sights. Participate if you see fit. I would love to see what one of your ranks could do against some of my more powerful fighters."

"Aren't you worried I'm here to arrest you?" Hank asked, assuming that was why so many had fled.

"Why would I be?" he asked. "This place is completely legal, even by your rules."

"An unregistered sporting and gambling establishment?" Hank asked.

"Oh, it's registered, alright," the demon said. "Just not under my name. My silent business partners handle all the legalities that have changed over the years since I had run my old gladiator pits. They assure me that everything is on the up and up. As for the gambling, well, do you see any going on here? Everything is paid for by the overpriced alcohol that is served at the bars on the edges. And, I assure you, we also have our liquor license as well."

The remaining members of the audience laughed at that comment, raising their glasses to toast their host. The ambience of fear that had filled the room quickly dissipated, just as suddenly as it had risen. That might have to do with the sudden lack of demons in the room, other than the gluttony demon and those that had fully taken human form during the invasion.

"What about... the fire code?" Hank said. He was trying to find some reason to break up the fight club, some reason to take the demon down to the HPS offices for questioning. He wasn't sure what this lead was going to provide to him, or if it was going to help at all with the case. He just wanted something to come of that trip. And, if the demon was telling the truth, there might very well not be anything illegal going on there. Hank had no way of knowing if the place had been fully licensed under a human's name, or perhaps an LLC that was protecting the demon's identity.

The audience laughed at Hank's comment, at the futility in his argument that even he could hear. "What the hell is a fire code?" the demon asked, over his own round of laughter, which only spurred on his audience more.

"Relax, fat man," said Jack, who was suddenly on the balcony next to him. He patted the demon on the shoulder as he plopped down in the seat next to him. It was the seat that had only just recently been vacated by the scared woman. "We're not even here for you. We just came for some information about a dead pride demon."

"A dead pride demon," the demon said. He shrugged. "Not that much of a loss. Though our dear lord was the first to fall to that sin, those that followed were nothing more than a hollow echo of him. However, I assure you, I had nothing to do with their demise. While there is no love lost between me and the demons of the pride core, we have a healthy trust of one another. Not like those foul wrath demons." He spat onto the floor beneath him, dangerously close to where Hank was standing. When the spittle hit the wood floors, a hissing started up, smoke billowing up from where it had hit. Hank waved the stench away from his nose, trying to preserve his sense of smell, which the smoke had been known to compromise in humans. "What can I do to help right this wrong?"

Jack waved Hank up to the balcony, obviously not wanting the rest of the room to hear the discussion. Hank rolled his eyes at his impetuous partner, but followed his lead nonetheless. He headed for the stairwell that he had seen the fleeing woman leave just moments earlier. The wooden stairs groaned under his weight as he ascended. They were obviously damaged by the comings and goings of the beast above, though they seemed only barely broad enough to allow for his passage. The stairs let out just behind the demon's chair. The floor was empty of all obstacles between them and the demon in front of him, except for the deeply stained red carpeting that led the way.

Though the balcony hadn't seemed more than a floor higher than the main level, the view from the above made the area down below seem that much smaller. The crowd was still congregating around the bars that almost completely lined the outer wall as they waited for another fight to start. None of them seemed the least bit concerned about the two agents that were now looking down on them from above. All of the people that remained looked human enough, but Hank knew that wasn't enough to go on. He found himself scanning the faces that he could see, trying to find any that he recognized from one of his interviews with the masses. They all seemed to just blend in with the crowd, none standing out in any way.

"Will you get over here?" Jack snapped at Hank, jarring him out of his perusal of the crowd. "Now, what questions did you want to ask the fine gentleman?"

"What? You mean you don't know?" the demon asked, looking between the two partners. "You mean you just barged into my fully licensed establishment to cause a scene? Thanks so much. Maybe I could interest you in spending some time in the ring. You know, make it up to me and all that."

"I don't think so," Hank said. He came over to stand on the other side of the demon from his partner. Before he could sit down in the seat there, he had to move a few empty popcorn buckets, and less identifiable debris, that had accumulated in the seat. "And I have questions in mind."

"Like where were you yesterday afternoon?" Jack asked. It was the obvious first question to ask. Hank didn't think it would lead anywhere, though. He wasn't disappointed.

"I was right here," the demon said, gesturing to the chair he was in. Hank took a closer look at the chair, which seemed to be some kind of reclining lounge chair. It must have been specially made for him, as it was extra wide, wider than Hank had thought a chair could be before becoming a loveseat... or a sofa. And, yet, even as wide as it was, it seemed that the demon's girth had swallowed it up hole. His excess fat fell over the sides and was almost welded into the cushions. If Hank had to guess, the demon probably couldn't have left that chair for days, weeks maybe.

"God, I thought you were a gluttony demon, not a sloth demon," Jack said.

The demon flinched at the reference to the all mighty. "Both sins are near and dear to my heart," he admitted. "However, it was gluttony that did me in. It was a close call, I'll tell you, but I'm glad it worked out the way it did. Have you seen the sloth demons in their full demonic form?" He shuddered at the thought of it.

"Do you know of a demon by the name of Jared DeGregor?" Hank asked, the next question on the list he made on the way over.

"Is that the pride demon that was killed yesterday?" the demon asked.

"So, you do know something," Jack snapped, pointing an accusatory finger at the man.

"No, idiot," Hank said. "We already said there was a dead pride demon. And, since we asked him where he was yesterday, it was rather obvious that that was when it happened."

"Oh," Jack said.

"Well, unlike you two, I don't have the name of every demon in my rolodex," the demon said.

"You mean every demon that came through the portal," Hank amended.

"Yes," the demon said, simply. "I did not know of this Jared person directly, though I could ask around. That doesn't mean he hasn't fought in my ring, though, mind you. I don't know the names of all the fighters that come here. I just know of the ones that win, and win often enough to earn my favor. I don't associate myself with the losers."

"Which means it's unlikely that you would have developed a grudge against him," Hank said, answering several of his remaining questions himself.

"Yes, if someone had it out for him, I would have bet on the man once or twice in his time here."

"I thought you said no gambling happened here," Jack said.

"Oh... well... I... uh... well, no official gambling goes on here. I can't be responsible for every little personal bet that happens under my roof, can I?"

"Maybe the ones you participate in," Hank sniped, but he wasn't about to make any case over a little light betting. Not when he still had no leads for the murder he was trying to solve.

"I assure you, that's all it is. And I declare all my winnings on my personal taxes."

"You shouldn't have filed taxes yet," Hank said. "Unless you won bets in that ten day span between the inv... the mass migration and the end of 2012."

"Yes, all the bets I made during that time," the demon said. "I didn't have this place up and running just yet, and I needed the capital to make it happen. Money doesn't exactly grow on trees, at least not on this world."

"What about the bikers?" Hank asked.

"Which bikers?" the demon asked.

"The uh... the ones that... well..."

"The ones that practically worship demons and have them painted on their bikes," Jack supplied.

"That doesn't really narrow it down any," the demon said.

"They have the sin glyphs on their jackets," Hank said.

"Oh, those idiots," the demon said, smiling his familiarity. "Yes, they drain their bank accounts here on a regular basis. That short one had even gone into the ring a few times. He didn't take on any of my heavy fighters, I keep those specifically for fights against other demons. He managed to take on some of my pride demons. Those guys are always interesting fighters. This one time--"

"Let's not reminisce right now, shall we?" Hank broke him off.

"Oh," Jack whined.

"Of course," the demon said. He turned towards Jack, seeming to signal something to the man. Jack's face seemed to light up with something, perhaps excitement. "Anything else you'd like to ask me?"

"Yes," Hank said. "What's the name of your silent business partners?"

"Who?" the demon asked. "Oh, them... Why?"

"So that we can look up your license and make sure--"

Hank was interrupted in mid-sentence by the shattering of glass beneath him, followed by a sudden whooshing sound. He couldn't see the source, but he felt the result almost instantly. The floor beneath his feet suddenly went from room temperature to an inferno.

Chapter Fifteen
The Fire

The floor glowed red where it wasn't covered by the carpet, matching the color perfectly. Hank knew that wasn't a good thing. Screams started up below them as the crowd ran for the exits. The two agents had more important problems to attend to, though.

"Help me get him out of the chair," Jack said. He started trying to pull the gluttony demon to his feet. Hank wasn't even sure if he still had any. But a more important thought was dominating his mind.

"The fire is right below us," he said. "That means it's blocking the stairs."

"Who cares? We can jump."

"Oh, no, I'm not jumping," the demon said. His eyes were focused on the floor down below. He was showing no signs of trying to help Jack extricate him from his chair, and Jack's concerted efforts were barely budging him. It was starting to look like they would need a forklift to get him out in time.

"This building is completely made of wood," Hank said. "It's going to go up like a match. We need to get everyone out of here before that happens."

"It would help if you'd help me get him on his feet," Jack said, groaning with the effort.

Hank tore his eyes from the stairs, trying to ignore the fact that the red carpeting was starting to smoke. He wasn't sure just how fire retardant the thing was, but he somehow doubted that a demon would care about such a thing. "Aren't demons resistant to fire?" Hank asked, as he took up trying to pull the demon up from the side opposite Jack.

"No, of course not," the demon said. "Why on earth would you think a thing like that?"

"Well, you're from hell," Hank said. "Isn't that entire place one big fire pit?"

"No, just the fire pits. Most of it is actually rather nice... well, you know, for hell. I don't know what your people are thinking on that subject; a snowball would last as long in, say, a training castle as it would in this room right here."

"You mean the room that's on fire right now?" Hank asked.

"Less arguing, more pulling," Jack said.

"Actually, I have a better idea," Hank said. He let go of the demon, knowing that the two of them weren't going to be strong enough to get him out of the chair anyway. Instead, he turned to the table that still stood in front of the demon's chair. There was a red table cloth spread out across the surface, slim protection between the food that was sprawled across it and the wood of the table. From the look of the table cloth, it hadn't been changed in days, weeks perhaps. The red color did little to hide the stains, both old and new, wet and dry. Hank pulled up the corners of the table cloth, one by one, turning it into a sack, with the food that had been left over pulled within it. Without a second thought, he pulled up the newly formed sack and tossed it off the balcony to the floor beneath.

"My food," the demon shouted, when he realized what Hank was doing. This was barely a second after he had thrown it. The demon surged forward an inch, chasing after the lost food. But his chair was not having that. He was pulled back as quickly as he had moved, the chair rocking slightly under the weight.

"Was that your idea?" Jack asked.

"No," Hank said. "But if it had worked, I would have said it was." The sound of wood splintering came from off to the side as the fire from below started to lick the floor. It snapped him out of his momentary humor, bringing him back to the task at hand.

Now that the table cloth was removed, he turned to the table itself, his true target. He was only slightly surprised that the table was only a long, plastic folding table. He had been expecting something sturdier, something made of wood or, perhaps, even stone. Something that could hold the weight of all the food that the demon must eat in a day. Hank only took the briefest of moments to note the plastic nature before scooping the table up. He was no longer sure if it would be strong enough for his plan, but he didn't have another one in mind at the moment.

It took him a painfully long time to slam the legs down into the compact position, given the proximity of the fire. The demon was a demon, of course, but that didn't mean he wasn't worth saving. He knew he would regret it if he didn't at least try. With the table now resembling nothing but a long, wide board, he circled around behind the demon. The edge of the table fit nicely underneath the chair, exactly where he needed it to be. But then his plan fell completely apart.

"Uh, that's not going to work," Jack said, once he realized what his partner was trying to do. "You're going to need some kind of fulcrum if you're going to pop him up and over the edge of the balcony."

"What is he doing?" the demon asked. He tried to look over his shoulder, but his neck fat was getting in the way.

"I was hoping that I'd be able to take the top off the table and use the legs for a fulcrum," Hank said. "I wasn't expecting a cheap table up here."

"I'd go through the expensive mahogany ones too quickly," the demon admitted. His voice took on an edge of desperation as the situation slowly dawned on him.

"Grab that chair," Hank suggested, gesturing to the one Jack was sitting in. "We can use that."

"What about the counterbalance?" Jack asked. He scooped up the chair, which was easier to lift than the occupant of its neighbor.

"That would be us," Hank said.

The two agents positioned the chair underneath the table. It was an awkward placement; the back was too high for use as a fulcrum, the seat was too low, and the back would have been in the way, so they had to use one of the armrests. It meant that the two of them had to stand in the seat itself in order to put their weight against the table. There wasn't enough room on the chair, so Jack ended up standing on the other arm. His hand was pressed against the table top to steady himself.

"Ready?" Hank asked, once the two of them were in position. Jack just looked behind them, towards the stairwell that was alight with fiery flickers as the flames started making their way up it. He nodded, not having strength to fill his voice. "Alright. Let's jump on it together, on three. One... Two... Three."

They both jumped onto the table together. Hank missed the top, his feet hooking underneath it. He toppled forward, falling on the table on his knees instead of his feet. The table bent for a moment, leaving them hanging there on top of it, before breaking right down the middle, along the seam where the table was designed to fold. They both went tumbling to the hardwood floor, their half of the table coming down with them.

Hank hissed in pain when his hand hit one of the nails in the floor. It was red hot with the heat of the fire below. The floor couldn't last much longer. He was surprised it wasn't on fire already. By the time they managed to get the demon out of there, there wouldn't be anything left of the ground floor to run through. Yet, despite their efforts, he was right where they had first found him, stuck in his chair that wasn't going anywhere soon.

"Got any other bright ideas?" Jack said. He was kneeling not far away from Hank, trying to get his foot out of a hole that had opened up in the floor beneath him. His pant leg had been torn in the endeavor and blood was flowing down from a cut near the newly formed hem.

"I might," Hank said, pointing towards the hole in the floor.

"He's a demon, not a vampire," Jack snapped. "I know the difference. Blood isn't going to motivate him out of the chair any more than the food had."

"No, not the... Oh, never mind," Hank huffed.

Ignoring his partner as Jack continued to try to extricate himself from the floor, Hank picked up the chair that they had just used as a fulcrum in their last failed attempt. When he lifted it, he overbalanced, almost toppling onto his back. He used the momentum, though, redirecting it to bring the chair over to the edge. When he regained his balance, he thrust the chair downward as hard as he could, bashing the pointed feet directly into the floor in front of the demon. The demon made to move his feet out of the way, but he was too slow, and quite incapable of doing so. It didn't matter, though, as the floor had been Hank's target, and it was hit straight on.

It took several strikes against the hardwood floor, even as weakened as it was by the fire below, before a fissure finally opened in it. While the cement supports were directly under the demon, the rest of the balcony wasn't reinforced. Two more hits had the gap widen enough that it compromised the seating of the demon's chair. The chair was finally dislodged from its previous position. It, along with the demon, toppled forward. Hank barely made it out of the way before the chair hit the floor on the other side of the gap. It bridged the gap almost perfectly, with the demon's legs down in the hole and his torso on the floor next to Hank. Once the demon's weight was no longer supported by the cement pillar, once it was fully on the no longer supported section of flooring, the wood quickly buckled. Both the demon and the human dropped to the inferno below.

Hank only just barely managed to avoid getting crushed by the demon, as they both fell to the ground floor. He rolled and slid down the incline, hitting the cage of the fighting ring with his back. His eyes went wide as he looked back up the incline, back up to the rotund demon rolling his way, a boulder down the mountain side. Suddenly, their role in the wars made perfect sense, as he hurried to get out of the path of destruction. The demon continued to roll, straight through the metal fence, straight across the newly open ring, only to come to rest against the fence on the far side.

"Now, that was what I was talking about," Hank called out, towards the other side of the room, where he knew his partner must still be.

From the better vantage point of the ground floor, Hank could better make out where the fire was. It was starting to make its slow way across the room, lighting up the floor as it went. The only reason why the entire building wasn't alight already was the fact that the fire started right next to the cement pillar. Being the only thing in the building that wouldn't easily burn, it blocked much of the fire's progress towards the center. Instead, it redirected it towards the stairs, focusing it beneath where the demon was. Once the fire managed to spread around the barrier, it quickly made its way around the edge of the room.

What confused Hank the most was the placement of the crowd. Though it had been a couple of minutes since the fire started, they were still clustered around the far door, clambering to get out. With the front door blocked by the flames, it was the only exit still available to the fleeing people. But it didn't seem to be enough for them to escape through in time. He looked towards the demon, wanting to point to the crowd and tell him that such a scene was exactly the reason for the fire code that he was so ignorant about earlier. His voice caught in his throat as he stared at the standing behemoth that was the gluttony demon. The demon was clinging to the fence for balance, though the fence was bending around his hand, whining against his weight.

"Clear out of the way," the demon shouted, his voice barely registering in Hank's ears over the shouting of the crowd and the roaring of the flames heading his way. The demon flapped his free hand through the air, the one not maintaining his tentative balance. However, no one was in the direction that he was waving at. All that was in his way was another wall of the fence. The rest of the room was clear all the way to the outer wall of the room. Still, he stood there, flapping his hand for a few more seconds, before he started lumbering his way across the floor. He didn't stop at the fence, didn't change directions. His momentum was already enough to knock the thing down without slowing him in the least. The sloping floor barely slowed him as his one demon stampede flowed towards the wall. He led the way with his enormous gut. As the excess fat hit the wood of the outer wall, Hank could see his entire body vibrating with the impact, even as far away as he was.

The wall quickly buckled under the impact, breaking outward and opening a huge hole in the side of the building. The night air flowed in around his humongous form. He stood there in the open gap, the dark night sky seeming the perfect background to his supposed glory. No one else could have knocked down the wall as easily, opening another exit for the screaming crowd. The demon turned around to stare at his work, his hands firmly planted on his sides, taking on the visage of the conquering hero. However, no one in the crowd seemed to have noticed the effect he had on the building or the new exit. They all remained near the one door, trying to force their way outside before the flames reached them.

With the new source of oxygen flowing into the room, the fire found a second wind and started eating up more of the room. It drew Hank's attention away from the antics of the demon, reminding him of his still absent partner. He stared towards the door, then the balcony area above, back to where he had last seen Jack. Hank scrambled to his feet, moving back towards the stairs. He didn't get far. The heat from the flames was too much for him. It forced him back to where he had fallen, back to the fighting ring. He knew he couldn't stay there much longer. Knew that he would need to get himself out before it was too late for either of them. Still, he took a moment to stare up at the balcony, trying to make out some brief glimpse of his partner amongst the flames. No matter how much he hated the guy, that was a far worse fate than he would have wished on anyone.

Seeing no sign of his partner, Hank turned towards the people that he could still save. "Everyone, this way," he shouted, gesturing to the crowd. However, no one turned towards him. No one seemed to have even noticed his call. Frustrated, he grabbed up one of the fence poles that had been knocked over by the demon's passing. It had been severed down the middle, making it into an only somewhat unwieldy metal staff. It was awkward for him to handle as he swung the pole against one of its brethren, the ones that were still standing as part of the fence structure. The din rang out throughout the room, over the cries of the crowd. He had to do it several times before he managed to get their attention, or at least the attention of those few that were on the outskirts. "Run for the hole in the wall," he shouted, once he was certain they would listen to him.

After one last glance towards the balcony, Hank followed his own suggestion, running for the gap in the wall. By the time he made it to the top of the incline, the demon was no longer standing in the gap. He was out in the middle of the parking lot, a proper distance away from the burning building. When Hank cleared the building, he started to hear the distinct sounds of sirens from the fire trucks heading their way. People were still shouting all around him, cries of pain, of anger, of fear, sweeping out from the crowd that had managed to flee the inferno within. Some were still coming out of the one door, as more fled through the gaping wound in the structure. What he didn't hear, however, was a single word from his partner. He knew that he shouldn't go back inside. That he was as likely to find Jack outside as he was to be able to survive the flames long enough to get back to the balcony. The fire had already reached the roof and was starting to burn away at the tiles above.

"Can I get a little help over here?" someone shouted. The voice was familiar to Hank, but, as it was filled with fear and pain, he couldn't immediately place it. He headed off towards the source and, once he spotted him, gave out a heavy sigh of relief.

"Jack," Hank shouted. Hank had never been so happy to see his partner in his life. He ran towards Jack, who was leaning against one of the cars, favoring the leg that had been stuck in the floor the last time he saw him. "How the hell did you get out of there?"

"Oh, ha ha," Jack said. "No hell in there. Just fire. I managed to get my leg out of the floor, no thanks to you. But the flames had started eating at the outer wall before I could follow you off the balcony. Once I saw the sky, I made a jump for it. I twisted my ankle in the process." He winced as he placed more weight on his offended leg, as if to demonstrate the injury. "Think I'll survive?"

"You'd better," Hank joked. "Herb isn't likely to get me a new partner anytime soon."

"What do you think happened here?" Jack asked, looking over at the inferno they both barely escaped. "Do you think this has something to do with Jared's death?"

"Maybe," Hank said. "I don't like coincidences." For a moment, he considered the possibility that Jack had a hand in the fire. It was the sort of thing he'd do. But he was sitting right next to him at the time, and didn't have any fire-starting items on him. At least, not that Hank knew of.

"Think they knew we were in there?" he asked.

"Well, it's not like we hid the crown vic."

"And, yet, whatever their intent, it wasn't like we were about to get any answers from the people inside. Maybe we should interview the crowd?"

"I think they're too panicked about the fire to give us much information," Hank said. "Besides, I don't even know what to ask anymore. I was about to call this another dead end, but..."

"In trying to direct us away from our answers, could the murderer have led us right to it?" Jack asked.

"Damn it," the demon shouted out. His voice easily carried over the cacophony of the crowd. "My club."

"Well, on the bright side, I guess we don't have to check up on that license after all," Jack said.

Chapter Sixteen
Interviewing the Survivors

The firefighters did their work well and the blaze was out less than an hour after it started. However, in that time, the building was converted into a smoky skeleton of its former self. The fighting ring remained mostly intact, but the rest of the place was barely recognizable. The bars that had once framed the outer ring of the building had sacrificed their undrunk liquor to the fire gods and showed no signs of ever being there. Much of the crowd had dispersed, driving off as soon as their cars had a clear path to the highway that flowed past the lot.

By the time the fire was out, there was just a small handful of survivors still standing around. This was in addition to the two agents and the demon, who didn't seem to have anywhere else to go. The firefighters promised the arrival of an arson investigator the next day before they, too, left the scene of the inferno. Jack went about setting up a few cameras, extending their surveillance network to include the fiery pit that was once a fight club. Hank wasn't so sure it was worth the effort.

"Any thoughts on who would want to burn down your club?" Hank asked the demon, once they were alone. The demon had found a new seat to settle into, the back bed of someone's truck. Hank hadn't noticed any of the few people that were still milling around looking his way. He wasn't sure if the owner had abandoned it or was no longer around to own it. There were no signs of any bodies left inside the burning husk of a building, but that didn't mean there weren't casualties there that night... or some other night.

"Isn't that your job?" the demon asked. "I'm sure there are loads of anti-demon organizations that would have loved to burn the place down. Humans Now comes to mind."

Hank knew he was right, of course. There were several anti-demon groups out there, though none had turned violent just yet. At least, none that he knew about. If the HPS hadn't been strapped so much by keeping the demons in line, they might have had time to do proper investigations into the groups. As it were, they were barely keeping up with documenting their online activity. He made a mental note to reach out to Danielle, ask if there were any groups that were active in the area. Perhaps one of them had claimed credit for the fire.

"They wouldn't have attacked here unless they knew it was a demon fight club," Hank said. "Just how well known had this place become in the area?"

"Well, you know the first two rules of fight club, right?" he said, laughing at his little joke. "It's mostly been word of mouth, between people that can be trusted. We've had problems from time to time with anti-demon sentiments. But it's been a pretty decent, stable crowd mostly."

"For a fight club," Hank said.

"Well, yes. Most fights were in the ring, though, and not among the crowd. I'd have to say this is by far the biggest reaction I've seen from anyone about my club."

"But there have been incidents before this?" Hank asked. "Which groups did the perpetrators belong to? And what, may I ask, did you do with those individuals."

The demon gawked openly at Hank for a moment, seeming offended by the suggestion, however light, that he might have done something more nefarious to those that would enter his establishment with violence on their mind. Violence other than the kind that could be channeled in the ring. "I'd have some of my fighters redirect them outside, where they couldn't harm anyone. They'd preoccupy them until the local police can handle them. You can reach out to the cops, if you'd like. The latest incident was last week, when some idiot came in with fliers spouting anti-demonic rhetoric. Some members of the crowd didn't take too lightly to that. When he was ordered to leave, the guy kind of flipped out. He broke the arm of one of my best fighters in the process, before the rest of the group could get him outside. If you want to start somewhere, I'd try with that guy. He must have been on something, some kind of drug, to have that kind of strength. But he was perfectly calm by the time the police showed up."

"Sure, we'll look into that," Hank said, nodding. "Do you happen to have one of the fliers he was passing out?"

"No," the demon said, definitively. "And if he had stuck any somewhere, it would have been destroyed in the fire. When I heard the disturbance, I had sent one of my girls to check on it. They brought one of the fliers up for me to see, so we could have a good laugh about it. Speaking of which, have you seen them? I haven't seen either of them since the fire."

"I'm sure they made it out. I haven't heard any reports of bodies in the... in the building. Are their cars still here?" Hank looked around at the almost abandoned parking lot. The crowd was dropping like flies, barely numbering six that he could see, with a similar number of vehicles still left behind in the parking lot. He couldn't know for sure without asking everyone that was still there. But it seemed like the truck was the only one that didn't have an owner still in the area.

"Their place is around the corner from here," the demon said. "They usually just walk to work, leaving their cars there. They wouldn't have left me behind like that, though."

"We can look into that once we're done here," Hank said. "Do you have a place to go?"

"I don't exactly have a spare club to go to, if that's what you mean. Like I said before, I lived in that chair upstairs. I loved that chair."

"How about these women of yours? Can you stay with them until you get back on your feet... so to speak?" Hank looked down at the demon's feet, which were bloated and seemed under used. The bottoms, covered in soot from the fire, showed no signs of calluses. At the same time, they were clearly not pedicured. The nails were long, gnarled, and starting to curl under. If Hank hadn't just seen him move, he would have thought him incapable of doing so.

"That does sound like a rather lovely idea," he said, smiling broadly. He seemed oblivious to Hank's comment as he lost himself in thoughts that would probably make a lust demon blush. "But I'm afraid you'd have to drive me over there. I should still have the keys to this old rust bucket." He slapped the top of the cab to the truck lightly, though it still shook the whole thing. The suspension whined under the strain and sounded like it was about to give out. Before the truck stopped rocking, he started poking around near his waist. As his hands slipped into what appeared to be pockets, it suddenly became clear to Hank that the demon was, in fact, wearing a pair of very small shorts. Small, of course, being a relative term. They were probably custom made to fit over his enormous form. Even so, they strained against his excess fat to the point that they might have been cutting off his circulation, if demons still had that sort of thing. Either way, the shorts were straining to contain his girth and left him little room for his hands to reach inside the pockets. Hank was just about to offer his own hands, much to his own revulsion, when Jack came back over to them. He was tucking one of the cameras back into his jacket pocket, having run out of places to put them.

"Still no sign of casualties," Jack said, as if the news would have changed in the ten minutes since the firefighters had left. "I've spoken to a few of the people that had been hanging around, though many of them slipped away before I could talk with them. No one seems to know anything more than we do, at this point."

"Has anyone said why they're still hanging around here?" the demon asked. "I would have thought they'd all have abandoned me by now."

"They were still a bit stunned when I spoke with them. They'll probably clear out in the next hour or so, like the rest of them."

"Rats from a sinking ship," the demon muttered.

"Well, it's not like there's going to be another fight here tonight, right?" Jack asked. "Are we waiting around for the arson investigator to get here? I think it's going to be a while."

"I was just planning on having Danielle follow up with him tomorrow," Hank said. "We're going to drive the demon over to his employees' house."

"You do know I have a name, right?" the demon said. He seemed offended by Hank's use of the term.

"And what is that?" Jack asked.

"Phil," the demon said, simply.

"After that, I'm thinking we're going to call it a night," Hank said, mostly ignoring Phil.

"Giving up so soon? I would have thought you'd stay here all night if that meant it got you one step closer to closing this case."

"If there was anything to help with the case here, I think it went up in smoke with the rest of the place. Right now, we're going to be stuck waiting around for more information. So, we might as well go home and get some sleep. We'll start at it again fresh first thing in the morning."

"Fine by me," Jack said, shrugging. "How far away are these employees?"

"They're just around the block," Phil said.

"I'll drive him over in the truck, if he ever finds his keys," Hank said. "Mind following behind us in the crown vic?"

"Seriously?" Jack asked, feigning surprise. "You're going to let me drive the car?"

"Well, kid, I think you're old enough to handle it," Hank said, knowing that Jack was only a few years younger than he was. "Just don't go driving into any telephone poles."

"Oh," Jack said, in feigned disappointment. "Can I at least run over some stray demons?"

Hank stared at him in shock, trying not to glance behind himself at the demon over his shoulder. However, Phil let out a few random chuckles at the continued banter between the two agents, so he figured that no harm was done. With a shake of his head, and a deep sigh, Hank reluctantly passed Jack the keys to the crown vic. He hoped that his baby would remain in one piece for the short while that it was in the hands of his partner. Jack half ran, half skipped over to the car, seeming far too eager to be behind the wheel.

"Any progress on the keys?" Hank asked. Phil just looked at him as he continued to fumble around in his pockets. Hank would have thought that any keys that were in those pockets would have been digging into his flesh from the strain of the fabric. However, Phil seemed unsure just where they would have been. "How about I just hot wire the truck instead?" Hank asked, figuring they'd be there a while if they waited for Phil to find the keys.

Chapter Seventeen
The Twins

Hank drove slowly down the highway. He didn't feel comfortable with Phil's position in the bed behind him. The demon's bulbous form blocked much of his rear view, and Hank was forced to rely on the side mirrors to make sure that the crown vic was still behind them. Their slow progress also made it easier for Hank to hear Phil's directions through the open window, not having to hear it over the roaring winds. Even with the slow speeds, however, the truck didn't appreciate having to lug the excess weight of the demon. The old engine sputtered and popped as often as it purred, and every pothole brought about another agonizing squeak from the suspension.

Still, it was faster than having the demon walk the half mile to the employees' house.

The house was a squat, low roofed ranch that showed signs of rot in the wood that it had for shingles. An old AC unit was laying out on the grass beneath one of the open windows. The window frame had split along the bottom, a gaping wound in the side of the building. The paint was still white in certain places, but most of the walls had yellowed with age. As the truck pulled up in front of the house, it quit running several feet shy of its mark. The pair of them seemed to match.

Hank was overjoyed to see the crown vic pull up next to the dilapidated truck, a taste of home among the cemetery of a society long dead. He practically jumped out of the truck, hugging his car in the same movement, before landing on his feet next to it.

"Do you two want to be alone?" Jack teased, as he stepped out of the car.

"That truck is a rust bucket," Hank said. "I was afraid the thing would blow up with me in it."

"Well, excuse me," Phil said. "I bought it old when I got to this gods forsaken country of yours and haven't used it since I opened the club months ago. I'm sorry if it doesn't live up to your standards, but it's more truck than I really need."

"I beg to differ," Hank said. "The thing probably would have worked fine without--"

"Hank," Jack snapped. "Just leave it. We're just dropping him off here anyway, right?"

Hank looked towards the decrepit house. There didn't seem to be any lights on, and no one had looked out at the noise of the truck's approach. He wasn't sure that anyone was even home. While Phil wasn't technically his responsibility, at least not in that respect, he felt bad about just abandoning the guy outside a house that might fall on him if he sneezed wrong.

"Let's just make sure his employees are home and are alright with him staying here," Hank said. "A couple more minutes aren't going to make that much of a difference."

"Aw, thanks, Hank," Phil said. "I didn't know you cared." He was still sitting in the back of the truck, having made no move to get out of it. Hank wasn't sure if the demon would need help to get out of there, but he wasn't about to offer any. There were limits to what that job was going to require of him, and that was far beyond them.

Hank headed over to the front door of the house. The low porch that stood in front of the door groaned when he stepped on it. His second step broke a gaping hole in the old wood, large enough that his foot wasn't caught in the process. The third step brought him to the door, the only place that the wood didn't look like ants were holding their hands together to keep it in one piece. The only new thing on the entire outside of the house was the doorbell, which was hanging at an angle outward from the doorframe by a single screw. Hank had to straighten it before he was able to ring the bell, though the toll rang out clearly and loudly through the open windows on either side of him.

After a few seconds, a woman came to the door. It was the same one that he had seen earlier at the club, when everyone had been staring at him. She was rubbing her eyes and yawning as if he had woken her, though Hank knew she couldn't have made it back home that long before they had. He remembered seeing her right before the fire started. That couldn't have been more than a couple of hours earlier. Still, she glared over at the agent as if she had been in a deep sleep before he had awoken her.

"What?" she asked, as way of greeting.

"Hello, miss," Hank said, trying to keep as pleasant as he could be. "I believe I saw you at the club a little while ago."

"I don't think so," she said, around a deep yawn. "I haven't been there all day."

"But... well... um..." Hank said, flustered by the unexpected response.

"Oh, spit it out so I can go back to bed," she said.

"So, you didn't hear that there was a fire?" Hank asked, still confused.

"A fire?" she asked. Suddenly, she was wide awake. "Is my sister alright?"

"Sister?" Hank asked. He tried to take a better look at the woman, though she was only illuminated by the headlights of the truck behind him. She still looked exactly like the woman he had seen at the club. Considering how the world worked these days, it started to make a little sense to him. She and the woman he had seen at the club must have been doubles, with one or both of them being demons. Though the James brothers had been the record on duplicates, there were several doubles, and even triples, that had been found over the weeks of tracking all the demons down. It would have been easy enough for him to have forgotten the two of them. "I'm not sure. Isn't she here?" Hank said, once he recovered from the shock. "I had seen her before the fire, but not after. Phil suggested that she probably went home." Hank gestured over his shoulder, back to the demon, still sitting comfortably in the truck bed.

"Did he?" she said, almost ominously.

"There were no casualties reported," Hank assured her. "And the firefighters didn't find any bodies. If she's not here, we may have just passed her on the road."

"One second," the woman said, sticking up a finger before ducking back into the house. "Sara? Are you home?"

They waited for a response from the missing sister, but none were immediately forthcoming. After a few moments, the woman turned back to Hank, worry plain on her face. Hank looked back towards the truck, the demon, and his partner, before turning towards the road behind them, in the direction they had come. He didn't remember seeing anyone on the road, though he wasn't paying too close attention on his way over. He could have just as easily missed her. If that had been the case, though, he would have figured that Sara would have flagged them down. The demon poking out from the truck bed wouldn't have been hard to miss, unlike the lone woman on the side of the road. She probably would have asked for a ride.

With no sign of Sara coming down the driveway, Hank turned back to the sister. "I'm sure she'll come home," he assured her. "I can check the road between the club and your house on our way out of here. However, about Phil..."

"Right, the stupid ass boss man," the woman muttered.

"I heard that," came a call from the demon.

"Good," she muttered. "I don't exactly think our couch is going to support him. Plus, if the club burned down, it's not exactly like we still have jobs."

"Oh, can it," Phil called out. "I have inpurmance, or whatever it's called. My business partners assure me that I'm covered if anything like this happened. That probably includes your salary. However, if you don't think you're still employed by me, I can find some better accommodations somewhere else. There's probably an inn around here somewhere."

Hank wasn't about to tell the demon that the hotels in the area weren't likely to be able to support his weight any more than the woman's couch would. That was even considering they didn't reject his business outright. Despite some efforts in congress to establish demons as a protected status, covered by the same laws that govern discrimination based on race, sexual orientation, and gender identity, those demon advocates were still in the minority. Several of the businesses in the area tended to exercise their right to deny service to all openly demonic individuals. That is, of course, other than those businesses that specifically tailor to them. Hank didn't know of any demon hotels.

"Is that a promise or a threat," she muttered. The woman glared over at the demon, her eyes staring daggers into his heart. It was clear that there was no love lost there. Her steely-eyed gaze offered him no welcome into her house. Hank was starting to think that he might just be stuck bringing the demon home with him. It wasn't the first time he brought his work home, and certainly wouldn't be the last.

"Look, if you're not going to allow him to stay here with you--" Hank began.

Suddenly, the woman's expression turned completely around. Instead of the open annoyance she had been showing for the demon, she was actually starting to smile. Hank looked behind himself, trying to see if Sara had come down the road or if there was some sign of the missing sister. However, the road was just as empty as it had been before. Hank wasn't sure what the source of the woman's joy was, but he wasn't sure if he trusted it just yet. There were some demons who had unusual mood swings, and they were never to be trusted.

"Oh, I think we can find somewhere to put him," the woman said.

Hank didn't like the way that she said it. It seemed like she had some hidden meaning in her words. Like she had meant the words as a threat. He went back over the course of his conversation with the woman, trying to remember if he had identified himself as being an agent of the HPS. From the look on her face, though, he wasn't sure if that would have mattered. Slowly, he reached for the inside pocket of his coat, reaching for the badge that was there.

When he moved his arm, the coat dropped open. His gun in the shoulder holster was suddenly in plain view. The woman looked directly at it, and her smile quickly faded. Suddenly, she took a huge jump backwards, covering several feet. Hank looked behind her, trying to see a flare of wings that would have identified her as a succubus. Instead of wings, though, he saw an echo of her. A twin. Double vision.

And they were both holding very large shotguns.

Hank cursed loudly as he jumped to the side, out of the entrance to the house. The first blast of buckshot shredded clear through the wall above him, showering him with splinters. He tried to continue the movement, to dive headlong for the corner of the house. But the force of the shot, barely reduced by the wall, forced him out into the yard. He rolled to a stop at the side of the truck, bumping against the mud-covered tires.

Hank stayed on the ground for a moment, searching his body for some sign that he had been shot. Before he could get a decent look at himself, though, another two blasts came from the house. He started scrambling behind the truck, trying to get out of the way of the gunfire. But he was met with the worried eyes of his partner. Jack was crouched in front of the truck, his gun at the ready, as he stared at the front door and the twin attackers.

"Are you alright?" Jack whispered. The words were blocked out by another blast from the twins' cannons. Hank just nodded, before taking another rolling dive to the side. He was trying to get behind Jack and the added protection of the truck so he would be able to pull free his own piece.

The truck suddenly rocked, jarring Jack from his covered position and right into Hank. Both of them were knocked to the ground. Jack's gun went sliding across the dirt, coming to rest in open ground between the truck and the house. It was too far away for either of the agents to reach. Hank looked over to the truck, trying to figure out just what caused its betrayal. The demon was standing again, his hand against the side of the vehicle to steady him.

Phil jumped down from the bed of the truck. A huge cloud of dust and dirt billowed up from his impact with the ground. His eyes shone out through the cover, giving an ominous sight that didn't properly represent who the demon was, as a person or as a demonic visage. The earth shook beneath Hank as the enormous demon made his approach to the house. He should have looked like so much fat moving across the ground. But the image that he intoned for Hank was of the stay puffed marshmallow man, making his rampage through the city. Hank wanted to reach out to him, to stop him, to warn him of the danger that loomed before him. But his words were stuck in his throat.

When Phil was halfway to the house, two more gunshots went off, renting the still night air. The sounds echoed around them, making those two shots seem like a thousand. Phil took one of the shots straight in his gut. The excess fat there seemed to absorb the buckshot rather than being affected by it. He took the second blast in his face, though. That laid him out on the ground so easily, so simply, that it looked like the demon was dead before he hit the ground.

Hank wasn't entirely sure that he wasn't.

Cheers struck up from the twins inside the house, a celebration for the demise of the demon. Hank looked over to them, the twin forms he could make out through the many gaps in the walls of the house. They were so preoccupied by their latest success that neither seemed to have noticed the two agents out in the open in front of the truck.

Hank finally managed to get his gun out, coming up off the ground into a crouch. He was still too far away from the truck for proper cover, but he didn't seem to need it. The twins continued to ignore him as they celebrated. He took his time to sight in the two girls, aiming for the one on the right. He wanted to aim for her shoulder, a shot that he could make when he took the time. But with his unarmed partner out in the open next to him, he had to go with policy. He had to go for the kill.

Two bullets hunted the buckshot to its source. Two bullets hit the women, one a piece, straight into their chests while they still celebrated the destruction of the beast. Two guns hit the floor, one of them at just the right angle to fire off another shot. Two bodies joined that of their victim on the floor.

Hank kept his gun drawn as he came up from his knees, rushing forward to the house. When he got to Jack's gun, he kicked it backwards. He was aiming for Jack's still prone form, but missed entirely. He cursed his miss, not taking the time to head over to where the gun lay. He hoped that his partner would get up off the ground and cover him properly, but he wasn't banking on it. His eyes stayed glued to the two women, his gun swinging between them, daring either to move. For either to show their true colors, their demonic nature. If they were the right kinds of demons, if they were wrath or lust, it was possible for either to survive a direct shot from a gun if they took it just right. Even into the center of their chest.

The sound of his footsteps on wood startled him. As focused on the woman as he was, he hadn't realized it when he made the porch. He half expected for the woman to be similarly startled. For them to jump up and attack him. For demon signs to fly freely. For their wings to sprout as they jumped to tear his throat out. Instead, the two bodies remained where they were.

Blood pooled around their still forms. The lights from the truck, blocked by his body as he came into the house, didn't offer enough light to tell the color. He couldn't tell if it was the red of a human or the black of a demon. Their eyes were turned away from him, hiding any flair of light that might still be flickering in them. Neither of their backs were exposed, their clothes covering any signs that they had wings ready to fly free.

Hank couldn't tell which of the sisters he reached first. He had long since lost track of the two, back before the first shot had gone off. If he had to guess, he would have said that Sara was the other one, the one further from the door, the one who was pointed away from him. He reached down to the closer one, the other sister whose name he never got. He shook her lightly at first, then more steadily. Her skin was soft, smooth, supple, and already cooling to his touch. He rolled her over onto her back, her dead eyes staring up at him accusatorially. There was no life within them, no life within her, and no demon signs to speak of.

He continued further into the room, his gun automatically going to the remaining sister. If the first was human, the chances were pretty good that the second one wasn't. She would have been the one to arrive in the invasion. She would have been the one to have seen this human and take her visage, in an attempt to hide that she was otherworldly, that she didn't belong on Earth. She would be the one to worry about. To shoot again if she so much as moved an inch. There was nothing more dangerous than a cornered wrath demon.

Instead of reaching down to this one, instead of lowering his guard so that he could handle her gently, Hank simply nudged the second body with his foot. The second woman rolled over onto her back. Her eyes flashed over to him, showing more pain than he would have ever wanted to see in another individual. Emotions played out over them in rapid succession, confusion, accusation, hatred, fear, pain, concern for her sister. Her hand was against her chest, as if trying to hold the wound closed. But there wasn't much strength behind it. When she wasn't staring at Hank, she was looking around her. Trying to find her sister perhaps, or the shotgun. Both of them were right next to her, easily within reach.

Hank kicked the gun away from the girl before kneeling down next to her. His hands went to her wound, adding his own strength to hers, desperately trying to stop the blood. As dark as it was in the house, the blood looked just as red as his. He needed her to be alright, needed her to have answers to the burning questions that were plaguing him. Did she have a hand in the attack on the club? Was she involved with Jared's murder? Just why had she attacked the three of them without any warning, without any provocation?

"Why did you attack us," he asked. He figured that would be the easiest for her to answer, the one that she would have an answer to, though certainly not the most important of them all. He leaned down closer, trying to hear her words that barely made it past her own lips.

"Remember Sami," she whispered harshly, before she joined her sister.

Hank leaned back in confusion, staring down at the dead woman. That was the only thing that saved him from being bombarded by a large cloud of blood as it spluttered out of her dead mouth. He backpedaled, swatting at the cloud as he desperately tried to escape it.

"What the hell was that?" he asked, once he was far enough away from it to breathe freely.

Chapter Eighteen
Remember Sami

"Remember Sami?" Jack asked.

"That's what she said," Hank said. He was back by the truck, trying to wipe the blood off his hands. Even looking at it close to the headlights, the blood still looked red. Though that couldn't be. One of the girls had to be a demon, didn't they? "How's Phil?" he asked.

"I don't know," Jack admitted. He was kneeling next to the demon. His hands were on his neck trying to find a pulse. "I can't feel anything, but his demon signs are still flashing." To demonstrate, Jack pulled open Phil's left eyelid with one hand while squeezing his ear with the other. The telltale flash of yellow spread out across the iris of the exposed eye. It was the one demon sign that all demons had, no matter which faction they belonged to. One that only worked while the demon was still alive.

"Try by his wrist," Hank suggested. "His neck might just be too fat for you to feel it there."

"Oh, I've never been able to find it on the wrist, not even my own."

"His chest then?" Hank asked more than said.

"He's got boobs there," Jack said. "It's weird."

"Hey," came a weak groan from the demon. "I heard that."

"Well, you do," Jack said. "I mean, seriously, you need to go on a diet or exercise routine or something."

"Do you not get the whole concept of a gluttony demon?" Hank asked. "He's fat because that's where his power is. Losing the weight would be like taking away his identity."

"Plus, it's impossible," Phil said. "I tried it once, back in hell. I've heard of a few that tried it here on Earth. It doesn't happen. We just get hungrier until we can't control ourselves. Better to embrace who we are than struggle for no return."

"The real question is how are you still alive?" Hank asked. "You took a blast of buckshot to the head."

"What's buckshot?" Phil asked.

"A spread fire round of metal that comes out of a shotgun," Jack explained. "That's what took out the wall over there, and what hit you in the face."

"I was hit in the face?" Phil asked. "Do I still look pretty?"

"You... uh... you look about the same as you did before," Jack said. "You basically took a bunch of tiny knives to the face in rapid, hard jabs."

"Oh, we gluttony demons are made of stronger stuff than that. In the last great war, a few of us were shot out of cannons straight into the enemy lines and survived."

"Yet those two in there were taken down by bullets to the chest," Hank said.

"And Jared was run over by a truck," Jack added.

"Jared was a pride demon in human form, as vulnerable as any human. Even in hellian form, they're not that great in an attack. They're sneaky backstabbers, quite literally, relying on stealth and complete lack of scruples to get the job done."

"And your employees in there?" Hank asked, pointing over towards the house.

Phil struggled to sit up, but the ground around him held him in place where it had become indented with the force of his fall. It took both agents to pull him free, even with Phil's help. Once free, he glared over to the twins, mere silhouettes on the floor of the house. Yet, somehow, it seemed like the demon could see them just fine. "Oh, right, those two," he said. "They weren't demons."

"They... they weren't?" Hank asked. "Neither of them?"

"Nope, just human twins. I'm an equal opportunity employer, or so my business partner tells me. Even some of my fighters are human... were human. Anyway, as long as you can do the job, you're good in my book."

"That's a bit odd coming from a demon," Jack muttered.

"Not all demons are evil," Phil said, having no trouble hearing him.

"Why would they want to kill you, though?" Hank asked.

"I don't know," Phil said, shrugging. The simple shrug knocked both of the agents off of him, but he managed to stay upright on his own. "Maybe they didn't get the message that not all demons were evil?"

"Do you know what Remember Sami means?" Hank asked.

"Well, I think you'd be in a better place to answer that than me," he said. "I imagine Sami refers to that poor woman that died the night of the mass migration. Maybe she wanted you to remember her, and what that one demon did to her? I don't know. Maybe the attack on me was in retaliation to that because she couldn't get to the other one, the one that actually did it. Or, maybe they blame all demons for that one murder."

"But why attack now?" Hank asked. "How long did she work for you that there was no incident?"

"Well, they both have been working for me for months, maybe since I opened the club. They probably didn't attack me sooner because I was never alone with them before. Maybe they just saw their chances now and took it."

"But what does that have to do with the fire?" Jack asked. "Or Jared's death?"

Phil shrugged again. His hands hit the ground afterwards, sending a small microtremor over at the agents. "Maybe everything, maybe nothing."

"This has to be the most infuriating case I've ever been on," Hank muttered.

"This isn't a case, it's a rabbit hole," Jack said. "The more we uncover, the less we know. I'll secure this scene, put up the surveillance, and wait for the coroner. Why don't you take Phil to see a doctor? He may say he's fine, but he took a hit to the head. That's got to have an effect, even on a demon."

"Except I doubt that there's a qualified infernologist out here," Hank said. "The closest one I know of is back in Seattle, and she's closed by now. We can't just take him to any old ER. They won't know how to treat him. Heck, they might just turn him out on principle."

"I'm fine," Phil insisted. He actually stood up, taking a few wobbling footsteps until he could reach the truck. Once there, he climbed back up onto his seat in the truck bed, showing no less stability and capability than he had before. He looked like just any old massively obese demon, rather than one that was just shot in the head.

Hank didn't like the look of it one bit, at how quickly Phil recovered from his injuries. More than anything else, he was worried about what would happen if the inmates at the prison ever escaped. When they were first arrested, the demons weren't familiar with Earth, with the customs and law enforcement personnel. They had been disoriented by coming through the portals. If they hadn't been, they never would have been brought in, not without an army at their backs. There were several other demons, whose crimes could actually be proven, that were still at large. Still running free out in the world. In fact, 9 out of the FBI's top 10 most wanted were demons. The sixth was a domestic terrorist rumored to have made an attempt on the president's life soon after the announcement of HPS being tasked to handle the demons.

"Let's just see if there's something here that can lead us in the right direction," Hank said. He turned from the demon, and from his concerns about the prisoners, and heading back towards the house.

"Hank, uh, wait up," Jack said.

Hank didn't slow down, but Jack's footsteps quickly caught up with him before he made the porch. He was more careful this time, trying his best to step on the areas that weren't obviously rotten. As focused as he was on his feet, he moved to knock on the door before remembering that it wasn't there anymore. It had been blown free on one of the barrages from the shotguns, leaving the front of the house a gaping maw.

Once Hank got past the doorway, he took a step to the side to allow the headlights to flow into the house. Jack still blocked the beams, so Hank had to pull him aside once he got over the threshold. With the area as bathed in light as possible, Hank started looking around for a light switch. The place looked like it was about ready to fall down, and that was before the wall had been unceremonioudly destroyed. And yet, there were still lights in the ceiling and a fan running in the room on his left. If there had been a switch for the lights, it would appear that it had been destroyed in the gunfire.

"Check the kitchen," Hank said. He pointed towards the room on his right. As Jack started heading that way, he pivoted in place and went into the living room. He did his best to ignore the bodies in the hallway, but the blood had spread to cover the entire area. The pool was stretching into the living room as well. The smell already permeated the house. Hank knew that other, less pleasant smells would soon follow.

Hank headed into the living room with his weapon drawn. He knew the two girls were dead, and were probably the only ones in the house, but he wasn't taking any chances. His hand explored the wall upon entering the door, first on the left, then the right, before he found the switch. He flinched away from the glaring light while his eyes tried to adjust to it, his gun up in front of them to help shield them.

Once his eyes adjusted, he started to kick himself over the stupidity of it. Fortunately, no one was in the room, so the mistake didn't cost him anything.

The living room didn't seem to have much living done in it. There was a single couch against the inner wall in the corner and the fan standing in the middle of the room. Both windows were open, letting the breeze enter the house. The fan was turned to blow out the heat of the day. It had been an unusually warm day for late September. With the AC unit in the front yard, the fan would have been the only source of relief for the house. There was nothing else in the room. No places to hide, for people or clues. Nothing there helped explain why the two women were so interested in killing Phil.

"Ah hah," Jack called out from the other room. This gave Hank hope that the trip wasn't a complete loss. He spun around, retracing his steps back to the hall and across to the kitchen.

Hank slipped on the blood as he passed the bodies, and he slid more than walked into the kitchen. He was able to grab hold of the back of one of the chairs at the table to steady himself before he fell. Jack was turned away from him, staring at the front of the fridge, so no one had seen his stumble. He walked over towards his partner, doing his best not to attract attention to his previous blunder.

"What did you find?" Hank asked.

Jack pulled a piece of paper from the collection of magnets that cluttered the fridge. There were postings of job positions and takeout menus that took up much of the space that wasn't covered already. But the flier that Jack had found wasn't like the rest. He presented it to Hank like it was the holy grail.

"I give you 'Remember Sami'," he said.

The flier read "Remember Sami" across the top, in bold, overly calligraphied lettering. Below the title was a picture of Sami, an old stock photo that was often used in memory of her. Hank didn't remember where it originated from, though he knew it was the one used on her IMDB page. Below her photo was an address, the date of September 25th, and a time of midnight. There was no other information on the flier, on either side, though Hank flipped it back and forth several times just to check. "Now that's what I call a clue," Hank said.

"Not much of one," Jack said. "I mean, yes, we're obviously going there tonight, which means our early night off is... well, off. Do we even know where this place is?"

"No, but Danielle will be able to get us directions if I can't find it in the GPS. We'll have aerial surveillance before we get there. Don't worry, we're not going into this one blind."

"Yea, 'cause that's stopped us before. What are we doing about Phil? We can't bring him with us. Whatever this thing is, I doubt they'll be that welcoming to a demon in their midst."

"Phil can stay here," Hank said. "It's not like the twins will be using the house anytime soon. Once their estate is settled, he might need to move again. But it'll do for tonight. Why don't you start putting up the cameras while I get him settled? He can look over the bodies until the coroner gets here. Nobody is going to mess with a guard demon on duty."

"Are we really going to trust a demon to watch over a crime scene?" Jack asked.

"Well, that's what the cameras are for, aren't they? Besides, as long as he has enough food..." Hank turned back to the fridge, pulling the door open. The fridge was filled with takeout leftovers and the makings of salads and sandwiches. They might not be that appetizing to the demon, but it would keep him from starving. "That should last him a few hours at least," Hank said. "He's not likely to eat the bodies anytime soon."

"Sometimes, you are way too trusting, Hank."

"Yea, but if you trust no one, you're only relying on yourself."

"Well, I'm not likely to let myself down. Other people can only disappoint you."

"Other people can only disappoint you if you put more faith in them than they deserve." He tried not to think of the fact that he was forced to trust Jack a lot more than he would have wanted.

Chapter Nineteen
The Rally

They left as soon as they could get Phil settled in the dilapidated house. He seemed content enough, and they needed to get out of there if they were going to make it to the rally on time. As they left, Phil spotted the flier and commented that it was the same one that had been passed around at his club. Hank hoped that was a good sign. That they were on the right track to find whoever it was that had killed Jared.

The GPS led them to an old warehouse in the city. Hank felt relieved to be back in more familiar territory, though it took them so long to get back that they were strapped for time. Danielle had grumbled about being held late at the office the entire time she was on the phone. She told them that there were a lot of cars already there, cluttering the parking lot, but that there was little else to be seen from the skies.

"Can I go home now?" she grumbled, on the handsfree. "It's almost midnight and I'd like to get at least a little sleep before I have to go back to the office tomorrow."

"Why don't you just use the couch in Herb's office?" Jack suggested. "It's comfortable enough."

"Says you," Danielle grumbled. "I've tried sleeping on that thing before. There's no support. I fall right into that thing."

"Yea, that's what I said," Jack said. "It's like sleeping on a cloud."

"More like sleeping in a lake. It makes me afraid that I'll drown before I wake up."

"Nonsense. If you ever have trouble breathing, you'll wake up before you drown. It's feathers, not water."

"Can it, you two," Hank said. "Danielle, go home, get some sleep. Hopefully we won't need you as support on this. It should just be an easy stealth mission."

"Assuming we don't drive the crown vic right into the warehouse," Jack said.

"With those numbers, there should be a substantial crowd inside. We should blend in easily. Don't feel like you have to stay in case we get in any trouble."

Silence filled the other line of the call, stretching out so long that Hank had thought Danielle had just left the line open. He was about to hang up the call when Danielle came back on. "Fine," she grumbled. "I'll hang around until you get inside the warehouse. I'll give you two minutes after you enter the building to call me back. If no one screams or tries to kill you, I'm going home."

"Thanks, love," Jack said. The phone went dead right after he said that, so neither knew if she had heard him say it.

"We should be fine," Hank said. Immediately afterwards, he was pulling into the parking lot.

Danielle had been right; the place was packed. The parking lot was bigger than Hank was expecting. There were three warehouses there, standing on every side of the parking lot other than the one facing the street. The lot was big enough to accommodate a decent sized supermarket, and yet all the spots were filled. After making a pass through the lot, Hank settled on parking on the street. They had to drive a block away to find a spot. Hank wasn't sure what to expect from all of this. But whatever it was, it wasn't going to be good. He had an ominous feeling the entire time he was walking from where they parked the car back to the warehouse, all the while thinking it was an awfully long way to be chased by an angry crowd. He eyed the other people that were making the long walk from the street parking. Waiting for them to turn on him. Watching for them to draw torches and pitchforks.

The clock on Hank's fitness band read 12:05 by the time they got inside. The crowd glared over at them as they made their way into the building. No one seemed to recognize them. No one drew weapons or fangs. After a few seconds, they all went back to staring towards the other side of the room. The place wasn't as packed as Hank was expecting, allowing for easy walking through the crowd and a decent view across the inside of the building. Hank liked his place right where he was, though. Standing just to the side of the door was close enough to the exit to make a swift departure, but not in anyone's way. It made the perfect place to disappear into the crowd. Jack was much better at doing that, disappearing even from Hank the moment they were inside the door.

At the far end of the main room was a stage, under some catwalks that ran the entire perimeter of the place. Judging by the height of the people nearest to it, it was easily five feet high. This was what everyone was looking at, other than those few people in the crowd that had turned to look at the agents as they entered. There were three people standing up on the stage, two women and a man. They were all staring out at the crowd around them. The man was pacing back and forth across the length of the stage like a tiger in its cage, stalking the prey that were just out of reach. None of them were saying anything, and it seemed like they were waiting on something, or someone.

One of the two women was blond, with a short bob. She was standing in the center of the stage, right by a microphone. Her gaze went out across the crowd, looking at each person in turn. When she saw someone she recognized, or perhaps just at irregular intervals, she would nod her head in welcome to that person. There seemed to be more people that she recognized than those that she didn't, though. As her eyes slowly scanned from left to right, it was like she was some kind of bobblehead toy, always shaking her head.

The other woman was a redhead. She was standing in the back, near the far exit. Instead of paying attention to the crowd like the other two, she was watching the man. Whenever he came near her in his pacing, she would reach out to him, as if she wanted to keep him by her side, to keep him calm and stationary while they waited for whatever it was that they weren't finding in the crowd. Whenever he came close to her, though, he would be out of her reach before her arms went up. The only exception, the one time she managed to get a steadying hand on him, he simply shook her hand off and continued in his pacing.

After a couple of minutes of watching this, the door behind Hank opened up again, letting in more people. First to come in was a cluster of three, which quickly stepped off to the side, blending into the crowd. They were quickly followed by another, fourth individual who came in far enough away from the other three to noticeably be alone. When he came in, all three of the people on stage stopped; stopped moving, stopped scanning the crowd, simply stopped. They may have even stopped breathing, though Hank was too far away to tell.

Even though there was already a substantial path through the crowd, leading from the front door to the stage, the crowd quickly parted, giving him more space than he would ever need to make his way across the room. A few members of the crowd even bowed to the man, as if he were some kind of royalty, though Hank didn't recognize him. He looked almost indistinguishable from any other person there, yet he commanded a level of fealty in them that was almost tangible. It was obvious that there was something going on there, but Hank hadn't the slightest idea what that was. He was left to wonder if Jared had found out about this group, if their secrets were what got him killed.

The man jumped up onto the stage in a single bound, easily clearing the five-foot height and then some. Hank thought the man was a demon, though there were no signs of wings or any flaring of demon signs that he could see from so far away. And, from the first words that flowed from his mouth, it was clear that he wasn't. Without any further ceremony, he headed straight to the mic, taking it and the stand away from the blond with barely a glance her way.

"Death to the demons," he called out, his deep, low voice resonating throughout the room.

"Death to the demons," the crowd cried, an obviously over practiced response to his call. The crowd went immediately silent after the battle cry, as they all focused on the man, waiting with baited breath for every word he would utter.

"We all know why we are here," the man said. "This is our world, and those wretched demons have no right to be here." A few members of the crowd called out some utterances of agreement to those words. The rest of the crowd glared at them until it was clear that their talking part was over. "I see we have a few newcomers here tonight. Our numbers grow strong, while theirs only dwindle. Even tonight, I've heard that a blow had been struck against them, straight at their heart, so to speak. Not that any of them have a heart. One of their gathering places, a sick, wretched hive just a couple of hours outside of this city, our city, was burnt to the ground. That is one less place for these creatures to hide from our righteous fury."

The man raised his hands and the crowd cheered on, jumping at the obvious signal to cheer out their approvals. Hank used the fervor of the crowd to hide his actions as he drew out his cell phone. He was kicking himself that he hadn't already been recording. That he hadn't gotten what could very well have been an admission of guilt on tape. He palmed the phone as he flipped it into record, holding his hand against his shoulder to hide it. The camera was just barely visible through the cracks between his fingers. As the crowd's cheers died down, perfectly matching the man's arms dropping back to his sides, the phone was in place, recording everything that followed.

"Now while I, while we all, applaud the actions that had been taken in the memory of our great Sami--"

Without needing any visible cues, the crowd, as one, called out "Remember Sami".

"Yes, remember Sami. It was ten months and three days ago tonight that we lost our beloved Sami. We continue the fight, in her name, against these invaders that took her life. So carelessly. So ambivalently. But we must not lose sight of what we wish to accomplish. It isn't enough to kill every last one of them. It isn't enough to make sure that they have no place to hide. No sanctuary. No friends. We must make sure that they never wish to return to this place. We must make it clear to them and all that follow them, that Earth is just as bad for their ilk as the hell that they come from."

Another cheer struck out at that comment, at first subdued before reaching a crescendo when the man raised his hands again. Hank was at a loss for words, unsure what exactly he should do there. Of course, the group had every right to be there, to gather in a non-violent assembly. Provided they weren't planning out another attack. Provided they weren't directly involved in the attack they were already celebrating. And, as far as he could tell, that was all they were doing. They were celebrating the destruction of the fight club. No one was claiming responsibility just yet, and he almost hoped that they never did. He didn't like the idea of having to arrest anyone in that crowd. The rest of them would likely tear him to pieces if he ever tried.

Hank scanned the crowd, trying to spot someone that he might have seen at the club. Someone that might have been responsible for the fire. The man on stage continued in his diatribe, calling out for more actions to be done against the "foul scourge", as he called them. However, even with all his bluster, he never once went into any detail, never made any plans. Hank would have to defer to Herb on this one, but he was pretty sure that the demagogue did his best to skirt the legality of it all. Encouraging action without actually calling for it. Spurring anger at the demons without actually directing it.

He kept his phone recording, pointed at the stage, as he slowly made his way through the crowd. It was remarkably easy, far easier than it was at the club, as most of the crowd was perfectly still as they stared up at the stage. Everyone there seemed captivated by the man as he touted his anti-demon agenda. Calling out how evil they were, despite the fact that most of them weren't really evil. Sinful, sure, that's what they were, but not evil. He wasn't exactly sure how it worked for evil people, but there had never been anything that he had seen or heard since the mass migration that would have led him to believe that any of the demons were straight out evil. Even Semi, with her rage filled nature, didn't seem evil. Just angry, lost, perhaps even scared. And, surrounded by those people, the group that was so hell bent on killing any demon that they could, he could easily see why.

Hank made it halfway to the far left wall before spotting someone he recognized. It wasn't someone that he saw at the club. Not a possible suspect in the fire. Instead, it was someone related to Jared's murder. Someone he had thought he had already eliminated as a suspect. When he spotted her, Hank ducked behind one of the pillars that were spread throughout the room, trying to hide from the one person there that could identify him as being an HPS agent. As riled up as the crowd was, he doubted they would care that he was supposed to be on their side. That he was supposed to be policing the unpoliceable demons.

But that fact probably wouldn't have mattered to Cassidy Masters. The old woman was looking considerably less old and feeble than she had when he had gone to interview her about the SUV. She was cheering right along with the rest of the crowd, her voice carrying over the throng to him. Louder than it should have. Louder than she should have been capable of. The woman had made it seem like she never left her apartment. That she wouldn't have had use of the SUV, and wouldn't have noticed if it was stolen. Yet, there she was, chanting along with the crowd. The two girls on either side of her seemed to know her rather well. Together, the three of them cheered on the man on stage, leaning on each other and screaming at the top of their lungs. Hank wasn't sure just what her involvement in this group was, or even what this group was, but it was clear that she wasn't one of the newer ones.

"Yes, my friends," the man was calling out. "We are a force to be reckoned with. We will not go quietly into the night. We will not vanish without a fight. No matter what the so-called Homeland Protection Services--" The crowd let out a collective jeer at the name of Hank's organization. "No matter what the HPS says about these hell spawns, we know the truth. We know that there has been an increase in disappearances these past few months. We know that those demons need identities, ones that weren't compromised by taking them on in view of others, or on national TV. That same demon that had killed our beloved Sami is still out there, still killing. It is just doing a better job of hiding its tracks."

"Yea," the crowd cried.

"I saw one of them kidnap my little cousin," came a call from the other side of the room.

"The one that lives down the road from me seduced my wife," came another.

This seemed to open the floodgates, with a round of accusations, both believable and unbelievable, coming from everyone there. They all seemed to have perfectly reasonable reasons for being at the rally and for hating the demons. Hank knew that it was mostly just hate speech. The same hate speech that had been around for as long as there have been other groups to ostracize. Hank had known far more than his fair share of the demons, and they didn't seem any more deserving of the hatred they were getting than any other group out there. Like any race, or in this case species, there were good ones and bad ones. Far too often the entire group was painted by the sins of the worst of them.

Hank laughed at that thought, the sins of the worst of them, given the fact that they had all died from a mortal sin. It was obvious that, even among demons, some sins were worse than others. Yet, none of the protesters there seemed to make that distinction. None of them seemed to even know that there were different kinds of demons. He heard about the cloven hooved man, obviously a greed demon, who had supposedly seduced one man's fiancé. A humpbacked one that had killed an entire church choir over an apparent snub, though the pride demon would have been more likely to try to sell them a used car.

It amazed Hank a little that so many of the reports were of demons that hadn't transformed during the mass migration. He knew that hellians were in the minority, though it was obvious to him why they had been singled out. The demons that had taken human form were less likely to be identified as being a demon, which was the whole point of the facade. Their actions would be more likely to be attributed to a human, and not even worth a mention from this crowd. Everyone was used to the misbehaving of humans, long before people could blame it on demons.

"Yes," the man on stage called out, over the raging voices of the crowd. "We all know that there are plenty of reasons to want these demons gone from our world." This comment elicited another round of cheers from the crowd, but the man quickly raised his hands to abate them. "We must also remember, though, that there are laws protecting these creatures from our righteous justice."

"But they don't follow any laws. Why should we?" was shouted by several members. Their cry was all but drowned out, as the crowd went wild with the man's remarks. The jeering lasted almost a whole minute before the man was able to regain control of the crowd.

"There are laws, and we must work within those laws to remove these demons from our planet. I've heard, from a very reliable source, that the HPS is now investigating the deaths of these demons themselves. Protecting their charges from us, not the other way around."

"But they're already dead," came the familiar cry. Hank looked over to the source, over to Cassidy and her friends, who were shouting out their incredulity. "How can you kill something that's already dead? Good riddance to the lot of them. It was worth the loss of the car."

"If the HPS comes to your door," the man continued, "remember to be cordial while you tell them to go shove it."

The crowd let out another round of cheers, louder than before by far. Hank felt a hand tugging at his shirt behind him and he jumped. His hand went to his gun in its holster. He spun around, spotting Jack there just before the piece went free. Jack's finger was at his mouth as he motioned for Hank to follow him.

Hank kept his eyes on the crowd, half expecting them to gang up on him and his partner, as the two agents made their way through it. The cheers continued the entire time they walked to the door. The man on stage appeared to be absorbing the sounds as if he were the demon, draining the very essence of the people there. It was nothing like anything that he knew the demons were capable of, though. Hank was pretty sure that the man was quite human. However, just before they ducked through the door, Hank imagined what it would have been like had the crowd thought that the man was a demon, seeing them rush to the stage wanting nothing but to tear him apart.

The quiet of the night was startling once they got free of the noise from inside. The stragglers they had seen coming in were nowhere in view anymore, all having already gone inside to join in the hate speech. Jack continued to make his way through the parking lot, past the cars that shouldn't be blamed for their owners. They went far enough from the building for their voices not to be overheard before Jack turned back to Hank.

"I really don't think we should have been in there," Jack said, his voice sounding more panic stricken than Hank had thought possible. "If those people knew--"

"If they knew we were agents, we wouldn't have made it past the door," Hank agreed. "And at least one of them had, but I don't think Cassidy saw me."

"Who?" Jack asked. "Oh, the SUV owner? Was she in there?"

"Yes," Hank said. He started leading the way back to the crown vic, not wanting to be at that rally any more than Jack did. "And she's going to have to answer a lot of questions first thing in the morning."

Chapter Twenty
Research

It was after 1AM before Hank made it home, and all he wanted to do was go to bed. However, as had become his normal lately, he had brought work home with him again. There wasn't much point in staying at the office once they got back there. Danielle had eventually crashed on Herb's couch, despite her earlier protests. Jack went straight to his car, with just the quietest mutterings about subways. With no one else to work with, and nowhere else to crash at the office, Hank just went home. Still, he knew he would be up for another couple of hours researching this hate group that he had stumbled upon.

However, when he got home, it wasn't the computer that he had gone straight to. Hank was barely in the door when the light on the answering machine claimed his attention. He let out a deep sigh before heading over to hit the button, knowing full well that it would be a message from Blanche. Something in the night's activities must have registered in the family tracking system and given her quite the scare. The display on the monitor showed three solid green lights as it bounced across the screen. Whatever it was that caused her the distress, she must know that he was alright, that he had gotten through it alright, without any lasting damage.

Hank was about to hit the play button on the machine when he was interrupted by the phone ringing. He gave an involuntary chuckle, smiling at the phone as he picked it up. "Hello, my love," he said.

"You have a lot of nerve," Blanche yelled into his ear. "Not one phone call. Not one call."

"How was your flight?" Hank asked. He brought the phone over to the computer with him, knowing that the call would last a while anyway. "It's gotta be about 4AM where you are, isn't it?"

"Don't change the subject," she said, though her voice was quieter with the reminder of the late hour.

"Are you at the hotel already?" He tucked the phone into the crook of his neck as he brought up a web browser and started to google Remember Sami. The query brought up a slew of pages, most of them in memoriam sites with the same picture of Sami that he had seen earlier. It wasn't until he added the term Rally that he managed to get anything close to what he was looking for. The link, which was thirtieth on the results list, only led to a scan of the same flier that he had seen at the twins' house.

The entire time that he did his very basic searches, Blanche was droning on about how concerned she had been for his safety. About what would have happened to her if he had died in the line of duty. He didn't want to mention the fact that she made more than he did, being the more senior agent, and that his income would continue even after his death if he had been killed that night. As strapped for cash as the HPS was, they made sure the agents' families would be well cared for if they passed. Otherwise, the agents would be too concerned about their families to do their jobs properly.

Hank had quickly lost track of Blanche's swirling diatribe as he tried to focus on his work. He knew the contents of it, almost well enough to recite it with her at times. In fact, he didn't think much of it when he interrupted her in mid-sentence to ask her the question that he had been trying to answer himself. "What do you know about these Remember Sami rallies?" he asked.

"And what if the plane had gone down, too?" Blanche continued. "You would have made Marissa an orphan, and... wait, what? Have you not been listening to me this whole time?"

"What? Of course, I've been listening to you," Hank lied. "Riveting stuff. Anyway, Remember Sami rallies?"

"Has... does that have something to do with what happened tonight? Why, I have about twenty notifications about you being in distress? I mean, one or two, sure, I can get past as long as your light is still on, but twenty?"

"Oh, I hardly think that it was twenty," Hank said, waving off her concern. "It was just a fire."

"A fire?" Blanche asked. "You were in a fire? Were you burned?"

"Not hurt in the slightest. Even if I were so much as singed, the app would have told you, wouldn't it? It was probably just registering my elevated heart rate as I tried to get the demon out of there."

"You were rescuing a demon from a fire?" she asked. "Did they start the fire?"

"No. Why would you think that?"

"Experience," she said. "That might have explained the three I had when I got off the plane, but then there were another five when I got to the hotel."

"Oh, you're at the hotel?" he asked. "Is it nice? I tried to find a good one, but the school is out in the middle of nowhere, so I didn't have much of a selection."

"What happened after the fire?" she asked, her words stretched out as she tried to control her temper.

"It was just a little gunfight. I'm fine. It wasn't like I was even hit. The demon was, but--"

"I don't care about the demon," she screamed. "Who was shooting at you?"

"A couple of the demon's employees. They're dead."

"Good. What does all of this have to do with Remember Sami?"

"There was a flier on their fridge about a rally tonight."

"Tell me you didn't," she said.

"Didn't what? Go to it? I thought it could have something to do with the fire, or with my case."

"Damn it, Henry. Do you have any idea who Remember Sami is?"

"Some kind of hate group?" he asked.

Silence filled her side of the call for a moment before her words started coming out in a torrent. "That's it," she said. "I'm coming home immediately. You have no idea what you're dealing with. Remember Sami is bad news, tantamount to a terrorist organization. You basically went to a Klan meeting and you don't even know about--"

"Hey, it was pretty clear that we weren't going to be welcome there early on, so we skedaddled before anyone knew we were agents. There's nothing to worry about. Now, you have a birthday party to be at in a few hours and we both need our sleep. Give Marissa a kiss for me."

"Oh, we are not done with this conversation," she yelled.

"Oh, right, yes, you still haven't told me anything about the group," Hank said. "Is there a briefing on them in the system? I hadn't thought to check there."

"Seriously?" she shrieked. "You're still trying to do work right now? Do you have any idea about how worried I've been for the past few hours?"

"Yes, Blanche," Hank said. "I know how worried you've been. I worry about you when you go out in the field all the time, but I trust your abilities to keep you safe."

"That's not the same thing," she insisted. "I'm..."

"You're a capable field agent," Hank finished for her. "As am I. I didn't take any unnecessary risks and I made it out alive and unhurt. You would have done the same as I did in my position."

"Well, that's debatable," she said, in a huff.

"Yes, you knew about Remember Sami before me, so you wouldn't have gone to the rally. Well, I'm glad I did, because I have another lead to follow up on tomorrow because of it. Bottom line, you wouldn't have even known that anything was wrong if we hadn't gotten that tracking system."

"And you think that's a good thing? Me not knowing that my husband and the father of my child was going into dangerous situations? That he might have died at least twice tonight?"

"Just twice," Hank insisted. "That rally was mild by comparison to the fire and the shootout. I honestly don't know what the system was so worried about there."

"Well... okay, maybe I exaggerated on how many times the app went off tonight. But, still, without it--"

"Without it, you would have gotten sleep tonight. And you would have been fine tomorrow when you met up with Marissa. And I would have called you up, just like I'm going to be doing tomorrow. I might have even told you about what happened tonight."

"Might have?" she asked.

"But the point is, with or without it, I'd still be alive right now. The app didn't save me, it just made you worry unnecessarily. Besides, why didn't you call me on my cell if you were so worried? Why did you only call the landline?"

"Um... my... my phone died again. I brought a charger this time, but... I forgot the cord that connects it to the phone."

"Your phone died?" Hank asked.

"After I got the notifications from the app. I think the app going off drained it or something. Anyway, I think I need a new phone."

"So, I should call you on Marissa's phone tomorrow? It'll be at about two in the afternoon here, assuming you're not dead on your feet. Why don't you tell me about this group and then get some sleep?"

"There's not much to tell about them," Blanche said, finally calming down from her rant. "They haven't claimed responsibility for any of the anti-demon activities that have been popping up over the past few months, but I've been able to tie some of their members back to a couple of them. There were rumors of the group existing before the demons even arrived, but I haven't been able to corroborate that. Besides, seeing as how they are almost exclusively a demon hate group, I don't see how they could have existed before there were demons to hate on. It wasn't like demons came to earth in any real numbers before December. Yes, from the folklore about them that had spun up over the years, it's clear that there was a trickling of demons coming to Earth. That would never have been enough to spawn that kind of hate."

"Especially since the demons were mostly confused for the people they were impersonating," Hank agreed. "The whole 'possessed by demons' thing was just a demon being found out."

"So, whatever ties they might have to some previous group, that other group had to have some other purpose besides hating on demons. Maybe they had a different target for their hate, or maybe they knit sweaters."

"But you don't know," Hank said. "Maybe I can find out as part of my invest--"

"Or maybe you can stay the hell away from these people," Blanche interrupted. "Seriously, Hank, these people are dangerous. The Portland bombing last month? That was them."

"All the more reason for us to find out all we can about the group," Hank said.

"Hank," Blanche whined.

"Relax, Blanche. I promise you, if something comes up, if something happens with them, I'll err on the side of caution and call you immediately."

"Well, maybe take Jenkins with you. He can keep you safe."

"Isn't he on vacation? What with you out of the country and all. Let him have his time off. We don't get nearly enough of it. I have Jack."

"Pfft, yea, like he's going to keep you safe," Blanche said.

"I'd rather have Jenkins well rested and keeping you safe. Your missions have always been way more dangerous than mine, even with me dealing with this hate group. And that's all they are, as far as either of us can tell. A hate group, with terrorist ties. At worst, there's a terrorist faction within it. Now, what else can you tell me about them?"

"Nothing, really," she admitted. "Just a few of the suspected members, and the three arrests we've made in their attacks. We haven't been able to tie the group as a whole to any of it, yet. Anyway, the list should be in the file, as are all my notes and Jenkins'. Check under Sami Terrorists, or something like that. Make sure you go over all of it before approaching any of their members. Better yet, don't approach any of their members. Just stay safe and call them over the phone."

"But then I wouldn't be able to tell if they're lying," Hank said. "I can promise that I won't go anywhere with any of them alone, though. How about that?"

Blanche let out a deep sigh, huffing out her exhaustion and frustration all in one blast. "Fine," she agreed, reluctantly.

"Now get some sleep," Hank insisted. "And kiss our daughter hello from me. Tell her that I'd be there if I could."

"She knows that," Blanche said. "She may be turning seven, but she's a smart seven. Besides, you can tell her that yourself when you call her at two."

"Absolutely," Hank agreed. "Bed, now."

"You're not the boss of me," Blanche joked. "Good night. I love you. Be safe."

"I will, I promise. I love you, too."

Chapter Twenty-One
Cassidy Masters Is in Trouble

Hank stayed up for another hour, reviewing all the notes that were in the file. There wasn't much, and Cassidy Masters wasn't on the list of suspected terrorists. He also put in a request for the four cases that were referenced in the notes. The cases were two arsons, a shooting, and the bombing that Blanche had mentioned. All four cases involved known members of the group either taking an active participation or straight out leading the actions.

The bombing had quickly been heralded a terrorist attack, with over thirty killed and fifty more injured. The attack was the biggest one to hit the continental United States since the failed attack back in 2001. However, despite the loss of life, he felt a little more comfortable about dealing with the group when he read the report. The tie to Remember Sami wasn't with Jerold Cooper, the well-known head bomber, or with Henrietta Lowenstein, the bomb maker. It was with the third man, a low-level guy that no one even remembered the name of. It was Cooper and Lowenstein that had gone down in a blaze of glory barely a block away from the demon bar they had hit. The Remember Sami member, someone by the name of Eric Smith, had surrendered soon after. He traded his information about the three other planned attacks for leniency. If their target had been anywhere else, it would have been a high-profile case, getting all sorts of media coverage. After the first day of reporting on the incident, most had simply forgotten about it, chalking the loss of life up to their proximity to demons. After all, twelve of the dead were demons themselves.

Hank had looked at the mug shots of the dead demons when he was reading the file, but he couldn't remember any of them. Even with as great of a memory as his, they hadn't made enough of an impression on him, among the thousands that he had interviewed in those first few months. He even flipped through his contacts to look each of them up. He hadn't put down any notes and his information was months out of date. He hadn't even known that three of them had moved to Portland, still having old Seattle addresses on record. As always, whenever he noticed such discrepancies, he promised that he would make more of an effort to keep track of his charges. He was beginning to trust his own word less and less.

With the late night, he was exhausted when he swung by the office to pick up Jack. He had told Jack that they would be swinging by Cassidy's apartment first thing the next morning. So, he wasn't surprised to find Jack just sitting on the curb outside, waiting for him with a single, tall cup of coffee. Jack didn't say anything as he climbed into the passenger seat. Instead, he took a long, pointed draught of his coffee, practically licking the cup's cover in the process, claiming the drink as his own, before placing it in the cup holder between them. Hank stared down at the cup for a moment before pulling away from the office. He wished that he had poured himself another cup for the road before heading out of the apartment.

"A little homework for you," Hank said, sliding the printouts of the file onto Jack's lap.

Jack stared at the folder for a moment, before sliding it up onto the dashboard. "I'll read it when we get there," he said. "I can't read in the car while driving."

"Except I'm the one driving, not you," Hank said. "And, yes, I agree. It's very dangerous to read while driving."

"You know what I mean. I don't think you want bile stinking up your shiny car."

"You know my rule about bodily fluids and my baby." Hank practically petted the steering wheel of his much beloved vehicle.

"Then it can wait till we get there. It's not like it's going to tell me the old bat has an Uzi hiding under her bathrobe."

"Nope. Nothing on Cassidy. It's just on her friends and the people she seems to be hanging around. We should be careful, and tread lightly with this bunch. They tend to get a little explodie."

"Well, who doesn't before they get enough caffeine in them," Jack said, before taking another sip of his coffee.

They came to a stoplight, giving Hank the opportunity to flip open the folder, thumbing through to one of the pictures of the aftermath of the explosion. He left it there as his attention went back to the road, letting Jack properly absorb the importance of the situation. The very real danger involved with dealing with Remember Sami. Jack was silent for the rest of the drive, while he stared at the file. His eyes flickered between the road ahead and the pages of death and destruction. When they got to the apartment complex, his mirth had been properly abated.

Hank managed to get the same parking spot in the garage as he had the evening of the hit and run. It had only been 36 hours but it had felt like so much longer. He glanced at the clock on the dashboard before turning the engine off, making sure that he still had time to make his call with his family. It was just after nine in the morning, giving him three hours, plenty of time to ask a few more questions of the old woman, arrest her if possible, and get back to the office for some privacy.

As the two agents passed by the still vacant spot that the SUV had been parked in, Jack waved over at the camera that they had stuck there when they were leaving that first night. Hank looked in the direction of the camera, but it was so small that he couldn't see it. He knew it was still there, that it would be there for years to come, without anyone the wiser. They more often had to replace the cameras due to insect intervention than human.

Neither agent spent much time admiring the foliage in the courtyard this time. Both headed straight for the call box by the door. Anger seeped into Hank's mind as he dialed Cassidy's apartment. The fact that he had to come back there angered him greatly. He missed out on his trip to see his girl, simply because this one woman hadn't been straight with him. While she had seemed so frail and helpless, it was clear that it was just a facade. He did his best to get his anger under control. He had to remind himself that, if he was guilty, the last thing he would have done was come clean about it to the police. Unfortunately, he wasn't able to tamp it down by the time the old woman's voice came through to them. "It's Agent Gorning again," Hank said. Even he could tell that his voice was tainted by the uncontrolled emotion. "I have some follow-up questions for you."

"Oh, of course," she said. Her voice sounded overly crotchety, cracking at what appeared to be strategic moments. "Come on up."

The front door buzzed, allowing for their entry. The elevator doors opened quickly to the first of many jabs that Hank had made to the button. As they ascended the few floors, he fidgeted in place, wanting this second interview to be over with already. He always hated having to do follow-up questions, always wanting to get everything out of the way on the first interview. It seemed like every case had at least one of them. There was no getting around an improperly worded question, or a missed lie, that would hold up an investigation. He just hoped that, after this interview, after he got the answers that he should have gotten that first day, that the case wouldn't seem so impossible to solve.

Mrs. Masters was waiting for them at her door when they arrived. She was, again, holding her cane, leaning heavily on it as she had the first time that he had seen her. Hank didn't remember her needing one at the rally. In fact, he didn't remember her wearing the coke bottle glasses either. No matter how old she was trying to look, he had to remind himself that she was no innocent grandma in all of this.

"What can I do for you two agents?" she asked. Hank noticed her skip a beat when she looked between him and his partner. Unfortunately, he wasn't able to detect anything further. Her surprise to see two of them there could just as easily have been confusion, based on the assumption that he was working alone.

"We have some follow-up questions," Hank said, again. "Like where were you last night at around midnight?"

"Oh, I was fast asleep, in bed. I'm afraid to say that I was quite alone, so no one can confirm that." She laughed at her little joke, which seemed a lot less funny now that he knew the truth. "Why? Was someone else killed? I'm afraid I don't know anything about anyone else dying. I hope they didn't use my SUV this time."

"Can it, grandma," Jack said.

"Oh, I'm afraid I'm not your grandma, though I must admit you do look a little familiar. Are we related in some way?"

"Do you have any other family?" Hank asked, using a little more tact than his partner. "Say, perhaps, an identical twin?"

"Oh, I did have a sister at one time," she admitted. "But she wasn't my twin. She passed a few years back, though. Why do you ask?"

"Because I saw a woman that bore a striking resemblance to you, last night, in a warehouse downtown."

"Now, how would I have gotten downtown?" she asked. "I don't have a car anymore, now that my SUV was--"

"Oh, come on," Jack interrupted. "We know it was you. Drop the whole old person act."

"I'm old, sonny. It's no act."

"Funny," Hank said, with a tone that made it clear that he didn't find anything about what was happening there amusing. "You looked awfully spry from where I was standing." He stared her straight in the eye, daring her to deny that she was there, daring her to say that--

"I don't know what you're talking about," she said.

"You and your two friends were cheering along with the crowd very animatedly at the rally. I believe you even said something about using that SUV of yours for something. Now, what was that again?"

"Oh, that is quite enough of this nonsense," she huffed. "I don't have to stand here and take this. In fact, it's not good for me to stand here. Unless you have some serious questions, I'm afraid I must insist that you leave."

"You can answer our questions here or down at our office," Jack threatened. "I assure you that you would very much prefer the first one."

"But these questions are just completely absurd," she insisted. "What would two HPS agents even be doing at a Remember Sami rally?"

Hank smiled as the truth finally broke free from her lips. "I never said that it was a Remember Sami rally," Hank said. "Just that it was a rally."

"Well... what other kind of rally would an HPS agent be interested in?" she asked.

"And, yet, just a moment ago, you were wondering why we'd be there?" Jack asked.

"Oh, alright, fine, I was there," she said. "So, what? Is it a crime to go to a peaceful rally?"

"No, but it is a crime to run over a man in the middle of the street," Jack said.

"That wasn't a man," she yelled. As her anger flared, her face turned red, and she stood straight up to full height of barely 5'2. Her cane, long forgotten, went slack at her side. She stared up at the two of them, not bothered in the least by the difference in height. "That was a demon. He had no right being in this world to begin with."

"So that gives you an excuse to run him down?" Hank asked.

"Yes, it would have," she said. "Had I done it, that is. They're a scourge, a plague on this world that must be eradicated. I wouldn't feel the least bit guilty if I had killed him."

"You wouldn't feel guilty about killing an innocent person?" Hank asked.

"Person?" she asked. "Person. Hah. Demons ain't people. They're monsters. Plain and simple. Never heard of an innocent monster in my whole life. He had to have killed someone, unless he wasn't in human form or something."

"That is not true in the slightest," Hank said. His anger was getting the better of him as he practically screamed at the old woman. "There are plenty of demons that copied old photographs, rather than having to take a person's identity. Even those that never took human form are quite capable of leading a normal, law abiding life. What's your excuse?"

"They killed my granddaughter," she yelled back. Her voice filled the whole hallway. Three doors opened up behind Hank, and two more further down. Several of Cassidy's neighbors popped their heads out to see the source of the disturbance. Hank simply flashed them his badge, pointing for each one of them to return to their homes. "That car, the SUV, that belonged to my granddaughter, Jennifer. She had been all I had left of my own daughter, my little Heather. Now all I have of either of them is that blasted car, all because of those damned demons."

"Was she killed in the mass migration?" Jack asked. His voice took on a much calmer tone than Hank's and Cassidy's.

"No," she spat the word. "They killed her after the invasion. She was out with her daughter, my great granddaughter, Ginny. Two of those goat-footed freaks barged into the bank with guns. Guns if you would believe it.

They insisted on getting everyone's money, not just the banks. A bank robbery, of all things. Have you heard of anything so atrocious as a demon robbing a bank?"

"Was this here in Seattle?" Hank asked, confused. He didn't remember hearing about anything like that.

"Pfft, no. It was down in Portland. But they got their due. Those goats were hanging out at that bar. They went up with the rest of them. Let God sort 'em out." She crossed herself at the mention of God, as if she actually cared about his opinion of her, despite the hatred in her heart. "And I bet you were the ones that arrested my friend for it. So, yea, go ahead. Arrest me for going to that rally, if you want. I wish I had killed that demon, but I didn't. I'll probably never see the SUV again, anyway."

Jack pulled Hank away from the door. He held up his finger to the woman to indicate that they would be back. Hank glared at her the entire way down the hall, not wanting to let her out of his sight. They stopped by the elevator, just far enough away from the door that their voices wouldn't be overheard by her, or any of the neighbors who were still peeking out from behind their half open doors.

"We're not really going to arrest her, are we?" Jack asked. "I mean, I kind of understand where she was coming from on all that. Heck, if I lost a daughter, I might have gone to one of those rallies myself. Maybe not more than one. I mean, I actually know these people. But still."

"Unfortunately, she didn't do anything wrong," Hank said, annoyed. "Well, nothing illegal anyway. It was a peaceful assembly and all that. Maybe if they were trespassing, but I didn't think to check that last night."

"Yea, we can come back later if that's the case," Jack said. "She's not going anywhere. If we're going to build a case against her, it's going to need to be more than just circumstantial stuff. You guys had more on me back in the day and I still walked."

"I wouldn't exactly call this walking," Hank said. "You're stuck with us, just not in a cell."

"And, yet, my lawyer is, sort of," Jack joked. "So, what now?"

"Now we go back there and scare her straight."

"What does her sexual orientation have to do with anything?" Jack asked. "And I don't think you can--"

"No, it's... Seriously, you've never heard that expression before? I would have thought a lot of people would have tried it with you growing up."

"If they had, they never told me about it."

"Well, alright, just follow my lead, will you?"

Hank led the way back up the hallway. He pulled all of his anger and frustration about the case into his stride. His eyes burned hotter than the fires of hell as he stared down his latest adversary, this woman that seemed hell bent on ending up a wrath demon herself. Cassidy stood her ground, leaning against the doorframe, as if stealing herself for what was to come, preparing for the oncoming storm that was Henry Gorning. Jack followed close behind him, his eyes on his partner, waiting for the cues that he would be expected to follow.

Hank was about to throw down the hammer and made it perfectly clear how unacceptable it was, or at least that it should be, to hate on a group that had no real control over what they became. But, then, the strangest thing happened. A flash of recognition played itself out across Cassidy's face, as she pointed her finger, almost accusatorially, at Jack.

"I knew you looked familiar," Cassidy said. "You're Jack, right? Judy's son? I thought you died in the fire that claimed her life. Wow, such a small world."

"Um... what?" Jack asked, completely stunned.

"What? You don't recognize your own aunt? I mean, sure, you were like yay high when I last saw you, but... Wow, you look great. I can't say I approve of the company you keep, though."

"Aunt?" Hank asked, staring daggers at his partner. All the anger he had been stoking suddenly found a different target.

Chapter Twenty-Two
The Birthday Girl and the Gift for Her Father

Hank slammed the bars on the small cell closed with a high level of amusement and glee. The small holding cell was just across the hall from the break room, and often doubled as a storage closet. At least he knew that the new occupant wasn't about to starve, as most of the snacks were still in there with him.

"This is going a little overboard, isn't it?" Jack asked. His hands were clasped firmly on the bars as he stared out through them. "I don't even remember ever meeting my aunt the first time. How was I supposed to recognize her now that she was all old and wrinkly? I don't even think I've seen a photo of her when she was older than like twenty. Besides, you didn't arrest her. Why arrest me?"

"Because I can," Hank said. "You know the agreement we made with you. I think not telling us you have an aunt in the area breaks about two or three of the items on the list of rules. So, you can sit in there and stew while I start processing the ending of your agreement."

"You're just thrilled that you can finally get rid of me as a partner," Jack said. "I hope your next partner is worse than me."

"I don't really think that's possible," Hank said, though he didn't deny the accusation. He didn't even deny it to himself. He knew very well that he had jumped at the possible chance to get rid of Jack. Herb would need to sign off on the paperwork, and that was about as likely as them getting a replacement for Jack. But, in the meantime, Hank enjoyed the thought that it might actually happen. "On the bright side, maybe I can get you a cell next to Semi. You can enjoy her doing impersonations of Sami for the rest of your life."

"They're not going to send me there," Jack said. There wasn't much confidence behind his voice.

"Sure," Hank said, before turning away from his former partner and heading back to his office. He wanted to enjoy having the office to himself for as long as he had it. Plus, after he was done filling out the paperwork, it would be about the right time to call his family for some facetime.

"You do know that Herb isn't going to sign off on that, right?" Dr. Howard said. She and Dr. Davidson were hanging out in the main office again, removed from their usual hiding hole in the lab. Hank hadn't seen them when he came in with Jack, so they startled him when he walked past. "Jack has been way too useful of an asset to just throw away over a long-lost relative."

"Emphasis on the word asset," Dr. Davidson said. "Jack had never been a proper employee of this organization, and he never will be. Besides, don't rain on his parade. He's been wanting to throw Jack in a cell for over twelve years now. Let him enjoy it a bit longer before Herb makes him let him out."

"Well, you two are no help," Hank said. "Anything new on the car, or anything else we've managed to get in this case?"

"What else did we have in this case?" Dr. Davidson asked. "Was there other evidence that you didn't bring in to us?"

"There's nothing new with the car because we already found everything there was to find the first time around," Dr. Howard said. "No sense in beating that particular dead horse."

"I got in touch with the local PD and the arson investigators about the club and the dead bodies," Danielle said, calling their attention to her. She was back in her usual chair at the front desk. She must have gone home for a fresh change of clothes, or had some stored somewhere in the office, because she was wearing a different outfit from the one that she was wearing the day before. This one was black while the other was most noticeably blue, otherwise Hank would have missed the fact completely. "They're thinking that the girls were responsible for the fire. They found some shards of glass near the point of origin. There were fingerprints on it and they matched one of the girls. They're not sure if it was planned or a spur of the moment kind of thing, but they're closing the investigation. As for the bodies, well, the police don't like the fact that you left the scene without calling it in to them. But they understand that our jurisdiction supersedes their own, and they're not going to be pressing charges. Besides, the evidence they have from the scene is matching up with your report, so they're declaring that case closed as well."

"Thank you, Danielle," Hank said. "At least one of us is doing work around here."

"Hey, if you want us to do work," Dr. Davidson said.

"Give us work to do," Dr. Howard finished.

"We can't exactly examine evidence if we have no evidence to examine."

"I know," Hank said. He pressed the heels of his hands into his temples, trying to squeeze the stress of this case out of his head. Now that Cassidy's return to the suspect list was revoked, he was back to square one with nothing to show for it. Whoever had done it, whoever ran over poor Jared, had covered their tracks too well for him to ever find them. And, yet, that was his task, his complete job, until he managed to solve it. "What about the recording of the rally?"

"There's nothing we can use on it," Danielle said. "If they did say anything incriminating about taking out the club or killing Jared, it was before the recording started. Besides, with the arson investigation closed, we'd need to have pretty damning evidence of their involvement. And a recording of someone saying they were involved wouldn't be enough. We can't even get them for trespassing."

"Why not?" Hank asked.

"The man on stage, the one you had the camera on the whole time? His name is Rudolph Judd. He owns the warehouse they were meeting in. Obviously, they were all there with his permission."

"What do we know about this Rudolph Judd, then?"

"Nothing there, either. He owns several similar warehouses around town. The meetings probably shift between them, as I wasn't able to find evidence of similar meetings at that location in the satellite records. I was looking through the recordings on some of the other locations, but he has dozens of them. It'll take days to look through them all. And with both field teams out of commission right now, I'm still coordinating with the local police departments to pick up the slack on the demon related cases. Blanche is still back tomorrow, right?"

"As far as I know," Hank said. "Though, considering this case is suddenly related to Remember Sami, I wouldn't be surprised if she's on an earlier flight."

"I don't really think the cases were related," Danielle said. "I mean, you only went to the fight club because of Semi's advice, right? What would she know about a demon being hit by a car a couple of days ago? The only contact she has with the outside world is through us."

"And, what? It was a coincidence that they lit the club on fire while we were there looking for evidence?" Hank asked.

"Maybe," Danielle said. "Maybe they weren't worried about you finding evidence on them so much as wanting to kill a couple of HPS agents along with all the demons that were there at the time."

"Most of the demons scattered when we were recognized. Phil was probably the only demon still in there when the fire started."

"They probably didn't know that at the time. If they did, it might not have mattered. You said the fire started right below Phil, right? He might have been their main target to begin with. If I had to... service a fat gluttony demon day in, day out, I might feel the need to light him on fire myself."

"We're right there with you on that one," both Dr. Davidson and Dr. Howard said in unsettling synchronicity.

"I don't think I'm quite ready to treat these as two separate incidents just yet," Hank said. "If someone at Remember Sami was behind Jared's death, it would make sense for some of their members to try to silence us. If they weren't involved, then I have nothing to go on. No leads. No clues. And no theories. I'm going to look into this Rudolph guy. If I can tie him back to either of the crimes, then I'll have some leverage to squeeze him about the other."

"Except he was clear across the state at the time of the fire," Danielle said. "I hate to say it, but your partner was more likely to be involved in that fire than Rudolph Judd was."

"Ex-partner," Hank corrected.

"For now."

"In either case, I have a mountain of paperwork to catch up on. Can you please try to find something on this guy? Something that I can take to him to leverage a confession, or at least a misstep? And find out where I might be able to run into the guy. I want to interview him later today, if possible."

"I can try to schedule something with his assistant," Danielle said.

"No. I'd rather try to ambush him somewhere. Does he have a public calendar?"

"A guy like that isn't going to be easily ambushed. He probably already knows you're going to want to talk with him, and has his lawyers standing by him the entire time. A scheduled appointment would at least put him in a more cooperative mood."

"Fine, I guess," Hank said. "I miss coming in after everything goes south and just cleaning things up. It was so much easier. People actually wanted us there."

"And a whole lot of people got hurt before we could help anyone," Danielle said. "At least now we have a chance of getting there before we're needed."

"Tell that to Jared," Hank said. He instantly regretted it. He regretted not being able to save Jared, though no more so than the kids that died at a school a couple of months after the demons showed up. There was no evidence connecting the dragon to the demons, especially since that incident had taken place down in Louisiana and no demon had shown up further south than Medford. However, the timing couldn't be ignored.

With his words still in the air, Hank headed into his office without looking to any of the ladies. He made a great show of tossing Jack's chair out into the main office, letting it roll right over to Danielle's station. But, when he turned back to the office, back to Jack's desk, he chose to stop there. He didn't like the thought of trying to lift the furniture. Besides, Herb would have made him replace the computer out of pocket if he broke that. Instead, he simply closed the door, leaving him in a peaceful silence that was rarely known in that office. This gave him an opportunity to settle into his own desk and get through most of the paperwork that was still waiting for him.

The paperwork, of course, included writing up the reports on the fire and the shooting. HPS's policy on shootings while on duty was quite lax, compared to some of the other agencies and police departments. But it still involved writing up a report on the incident, and a few mandatory therapy sessions that he would put off till later, after the case was closed. He had already dictated his immediate after-incident report to Danielle the night before, during the drive over to the warehouse. This put him ahead of the curve. But he would still need to write the whole incident up again, as well as his impressions of the shooting in hindsight and what, if anything, he could have done differently. It helped that the civilian authorities had already completed their own investigation, that he could attach their casefile to his report before sending the whole thing off to the oversight committee. Oversight on shootings was another of the many of their functions that they had been forced to outsource to another agency, this time the FBI. He had dealt with the process before and had no doubt that the whole thing would fly through their review quickly enough. In the meantime, he wasn't even required to give up his firearm, which still hung in his holster.

By the time he had finished the paperwork on the open case, including his own personal notes on the events that had been happening, it was almost ten minutes before he was scheduled to call his daughter. Still, knowing his wife as he did, she would no doubt be at the school already, chomping at the bit to celebrate Marissa's seventh birthday with her. He took a quick peek out the door to make sure no one was looking for him, then checked his email one last time, before pulling out his cell phone.

The line rang four times before a small voice answered it. "Hello?" Marissa said.

His heart ached at the simple sound of his daughter's voice, a sound he hadn't heard nearly enough over that past year. What pained him more, though, was that it sounded so uncertain. As if she hadn't been expecting his call, hadn't been expecting to hear from her father on her birthday. "Hello, my little one," he said, before breaking into a verse of Happy Birthday.

"Who is this?" Marissa asked, once he was done singing.

Hank's face fell. Certainly, it hadn't been that long since they had last spoken. "It's... It's your father."

"Oh, Daddy, hi," she said. Her voice finally took on the sense of glee that he had been expecting.

"Should I put on the video?" he asked. "Is your mother there?"

"Mommy? No. No one's here but the teachers. The headmistress pulled me out of eighth period, but she didn't say why, other than it was a surprise. Class was fun though. We were talking about how the witch in The Lion, the Witch, and the Wardrobe relied too heavily on fear and her spy network of animals, and not enough on winning the loyalty of the people."

"That's... nice, honey. I would have expected your mom to be there by now, though. She was at the hotel last night, but I haven't heard from her."

"Did you try her cell?" Marissa asked. She sounded way too grown up for his liking.

"It was drained the last time I heard from her, and she didn't have her charger, so... hold on a moment. I want to check the family tracker."

"Oh, that stupid thing," Marissa said. "I hate wearing this stupid watch everywhere I go. It keeps cutting into my wrist."

"I know, honey," Hank said, adjusting his own band. "But it lets Mommy and Daddy know that you're alright."

"I know," she said. "That's what the headmistress said. She said you both have very important jobs and that worrying about me was like another job and that the band helps you not worry so much."

"Worrying about you isn't a job," Hank said, trying not to laugh at her. "It's our life. It's part of what being a daddy is all about." As he was talking with her, he shifted his phone onto his shoulder so he could use both hands. His work computer didn't have the family tracker application installed on it. Instead, he pulled up the website and logged into their account that way. He could have pulled up the app on his phone, but he didn't want to hang up on Marissa in the process. "And we worry about each other, too, you know," he said, when he realized he was doing just that. "Fortunately, your mother's band last synced three hours ago, and she was fine then, and in Toronto. She was probably still at the hotel, where they have a hub. She might just be on her... Wait, she's syncing up now, maybe on your cell?"

He watched as the progress bar that had popped up on Blanche's status started to fill up, waiting for the location stats to populate so he would know if she was at the school, or just on her way there. There were family tracker hubs all over the place, in public areas, restaurants, train stations, and at every Angel Corp location, including the one across the hall. They were supposed to be coming out with bands that didn't even need a hub or a cell phone to sync with the network, that had built in cell transmitters that would constantly broadcast the information. As Hank watched the progress bar, he swore to himself that he would get three of them as soon as they were released, one for each of them.

"Is she coming?" Marissa asked, impatiently.

"Uh, no," Hank said, almost as disappointed as Marissa must have been. "She's here, actually."

The Last Known Location field for Blanche's information listed Angel Corp, Seattle Office.

Chapter Twenty-Three
How to Disappoint Your Daughter on Her Birthday

Hank switched on the video for the call, wanting Marissa's disappointed face to be the first thing that Blanche saw when she got in the office. He headed out into the main room, coming around to the front of the desk. There was a brochure holder off to the side, filled with their brochures about how to handle demons for those that didn't interact with them on a regular basis. No one at the office ever used the brochures, so they were just collecting dust. However, the holder was the perfect place to stick the phone so that it was propped up. Hank made sure that Marissa had her arms crossed, with her patented pouty face on in full, before Blanche could get through the door. When the two rapid beeps and the solid click signaled her arrival, they were in a united front about how they felt about her choices.

Blanche came in through the door with her eyes to the floor. At first, Hank thought that she was already properly mollified. But then she pulled through her suitcase, complete with someone's foot. The crowd outside hadn't died down in the least. Blanche had to fight off those that were ambitious enough to try to get in around her. As she held the door closed behind her, she had to stomp on the foot in the door several times until its owner retracted it. When the door was finally clear, she slammed it home, bracing herself against its steady frame as she regained her composure.

Hank didn't move a muscle from his stance the entire time she was doing this, though he did have the urge to check on Marissa. He doubted that she would be able to stay mad at her mother long enough. Although as Blanche's face fell, he figured the point was properly made. "Why aren't you at the school with our daughter?" Hank asked.

"Yea, Mommy. Why aren't you here?" Marissa asked.

"Hello, to you, two, too," Blanche said. She left her suitcase by the door, where it quickly toppled forward onto its front, while she took the three steps between the door and Hank. She leaned over the desk to Hank, kissing him lightly on the cheek, before doing the same to the phone. "I'm so sorry we're both missing your birthday this year, little one," Blanche said. "It couldn't be helped, I'm afraid. We'll try again next year, yea?"

"Okay, Mommy," Marissa said. "I'd better go anyway. They're going to have cake for dinner."

"You mean cake with dinner, right?" Hank asked.

"Gotta go," Marissa said, quickly. She disconnected the call before anyone could say anything further. Hank saw the screen go blank out of the corner of his eye before it went back to his lock screen, which was a copy of the photo of them at the lake. It stayed on that shot, almost teasing him about the missed opportunity, before going to black.

"How could you do that to her, Blanche?" Hank asked. "I told you to go to the school."

"You guys do know I'm here, right?" Danielle asked, from her place right behind Hank. "Maybe you want to take this to your now private office?"

"What?" Blanche asked, her face going pale. "Did you get your partner killed? Did you go after Remember Sami without backup?"

"Don't change the subject," Hank said. He started to lead her around behind the desk, though she quickly took the lead, heading for his office so they could be alone while they yelled at each other. "Jack's fine. He's just... well, Jack. He's in the cell for now. That's not the issue, though. Why didn't you go to the school?"

"I told you why last night," Blanche said.

"And we agreed that you should go, that I could take care of myself."

"No, you agreed. I just allowed you to agree with yourself."

Hank hid his involuntary eye roll by turning around to close the door. Danielle was the only one in the outside office, and she was showing no signs of interest in their conversation. He knew the place enough to know that their voices would likely carry down the hall. The two scientists were still hanging out in the lab, and his former partner would like nothing more than to get his hands on some ammunition against him. He also tried to use the added time to come up with a decent retort to her answer, but he didn't think of much.

"You could have just told me that you were coming home," he said. "I was getting a little worried when you didn't show up for our daughter's birthday."

"Well, you saw her on the vid call. She's fine. She's off with her friends eating cake."

"There are hundreds of students at that school. Do you really think they have cake for every one of their birthdays?"

"Sure, if they have cake every day," she said, smiling. "Don't get me wrong, I would love nothing more than to be with her right now. For both of us to be with her for every day of her life. But there are some things more important than us being with our daughter. Like both of us being alive."

"I'm not going to get myself killed over a murder investigation," Hank said. "I don't even have anything else planned today besides more paperwork, perhaps going home early. Danielle managed to get me an appointment with this Randolph fellow tomorrow. You could have gone to the school, gotten your regular flight back home later tonight, and still been home before I was in any danger, even by your standards."

"Randolph?" she asked. "As in the head of Remember Sami? Are you really going to go into the lion's den?"

"Wanna come with?" he asked. He watched as excitement and worry played an intense battle across her face. He wasn't sure just which one won out, though.

"How about I take the meeting for you?" she said. "I've been wanting an excuse to meet with him over some of the things his members have been doing. But I've never managed to get any evidence even close to pointing to him, and he's refused all my requests so far. How did you get him to agree to meet with you?"

Hank just shrugged, saying simply "Danielle."

"I don't know why that girl wants to go out into the field. She's absolutely perfect right where she is. I think she's even better than Lynnette."

"Oh, there's no question of that," Hank agreed. "If only we could have two of her, instead of having Lynnette back."

"That reminds me, did we ever get a baby shower gift for Lynnette? That's this weekend, right?"

"Blanche, that was two weeks ago," Hank said. "You were there. We got her a car seat. Then you were called away halfway through it to go on another mission."

"I remember the mission, but the rest of that weekend is a total blank," Blanche said. "Maybe I'm working too hard."

"There's no maybe about it," Hank said. "We really needed this vacation. I'd say we should schedule something for Christmas, but things are probably going to get worse for the anniversary, not better. We need to schedule some alone time, just you and me. I feel like we never see each other anymore."

"We don't," she agreed. "We're ships in the night. I spend more time talking to that answering machine than you."

"Well, maybe if you charged your phone more often, that wouldn't be the case. Let's try to schedule at least one hour, just the two of us, every week. If it's not in person, let it be in video chat. Alright?"

"Just one hour every week?" she asked, pulling him close to her. She was already leaning against Jack's empty desk, making the movement that much sexier, that much more sensual. Her mischievous smile made it very clear that her own mind went exactly where Hank's was.

"Well, I thought we'd start with something that was actually achievable and work from there," he said.

A moment later, he was very glad that he had closed the door, as she pulled him into a kiss. He was never that fond of public displays of affection, and Blanche was even less so. There were times when she wouldn't so much as touch him when they were in public. She always presented this image of the warrior princess, with no interest in anything that didn't involve blowing stuff up. Those close, lingering moments between the two of them were few and far between, made so much more so due to their suddenly hectic work lives. There were times when Hank wondered how they conceived Marissa at all. But then there were times when their hungry, fiery passions were ignited, lasting for hours, days sometimes. Then the starving couple would gorge on each other more so than any lust demon ever could. It was beginning to feel like another one of those times would consume them, would take them away from their worries. The open case. The disappointed child. The threat of danger from the mysterious terrorist organization.

Then the sound of shattering glass came to them through the closed door, breaking their concentration, their lust for each other. It was brief, a momentary slip, at first. But then Danielle's voice came to them through the door, with a level of panic that shocked both of them out of their embrace.

"Guys, I need help out here," Danielle yelled. Moments after she yelled it, before they could move to the door, a gunshot went off and a bullet broke through the wall next to the door, lancing through the air over their embracing forms.

Chapter Twenty-Four
The HPS Under Attack

Hank immediately pulled out his gun as the two of them ducked beneath the desk. The door was still closed, blocking their view of the office outside. Two more gunshots went off while they knelt there, before they could collect themselves enough to make it to the door. Danielle screamed again, as laughter came from the front room.

"Give me your gun," Blanche said, holding her hand out to him.

"Where's yours?" he asked, not willing to give up his only weapon that quickly.

"Hank, I just came here, straight from the airport. I wasn't expecting to be shot at in my own office. It's still packed in my suitcase."

"Which is where, exactly?"

"It's out there, out with the people we need to be shooting. So, please, let the better marksman handle the gun while you stay behind me."

"Fine," he said, as he reluctantly handed over his weapon.

"Don't you have a backup gun somewhere? Or, what about Jack's gun?"

"I've never needed a backup gun before. I've barely even needed that gun before the demons arrived. And Jack's gun is with the rest of his stuff in the lab."

"Great, so Huey and Dewey have a gun but you don't," she said.

"Uh, no, I have a gun, you don't. You're just borrowing mine until we can get to your suitcase. Now can we get out of here before they kill Danielle?"

"Come out, come out, wherever you are," came a teasing voice from the front room. Though it was female, and familiar somehow, it was most definitely not Danielle. "We have your secretary, and we're going to kill her if you don't show yourselves. We know that there are five of you in here. We've been watching this door for weeks now. It was so nice of you to not arrest us for trespassing."

"Wait, what?" Hank asked. They slowly made their way to the door, staying close to the floor in order to reduce the likelihood of taking a stray bullet. There hadn't been any further shots fired, but they both knew it was only a matter of time.

Blanche got into place near the crack in the door. Her gun was pointed upwards towards where the voice was coming from. Hank came up behind the door, using the thick wood as a shield. He looked over to her, signaling a question that he couldn't speak. Not without telling the shooter exactly where he was. She nodded her agreement, her preparedness for him to open the door. He reached up, his hand slowly approaching the knob.

Two more gunshots went off, the bullets shooting through the door. He ducked back down onto the floor, his hand falling away from the knob. Blanche jumped on top of him, shielding him from the expected debris and further gunshots, though none came. They lay there for a few more moments, waiting for their hearts to settle down. Hank watched his fitness band, as the indicator that showed both his status and Blanche's started to blink green. This showed that their heart rates were elevated when it wasn't indicated that the user was exercising. With both his cell phone and the hub so close, their statuses would go out through the network, to the only other person on their account, to Marissa's readouts on her own band all the way in Ontario.

Hank hoped that they had turned her phone back off. That she was saved from having to worry about the two parents that barely knew her anymore.

The lights never stopped blinking, but it was time for them to make their move. Blanche came back up into a crouch, Hank quickly following. They jumped back into position, and Hank didn't bother to see if Blanche was ready before pulling open the door. Blanche popped off two shots into the main office, a quick double tap through the barely opened door. Hank threw the door closed again, and both agents put their backs against the thick wood, ducking their heads between their knees. Instantly, another barrage of bullets, this time in rapid succession, tore through the door above their heads. Bullets and splinters flew all over, but all hitting too high to hit them.

The bullets rang for several seconds as they huddled there. While they went off, Blanche signaled what she saw out there. She was using hand signals that they had been trained on, though Hank had never needed to use them in the field. "There are ten targets, maybe more," her fingers signaled, flapping almost quicker than he could understand them. "I shot one of them. Three are on the left of the door, four on the right, and two in the middle." Hank nodded his understanding. He didn't like the odds, especially with just the one gun between them. He hoped that his more experienced wife would know what to do.

Once the bullets stopped hitting the door, Blanche jumped up to her feet. Hank followed quickly after, pulling the door open once more. He watched helplessly as his wife leapt through the gap in the door, his gun leading the charge. Five more shots went off, all from Blanche, before she slid forward on the floor. Hank held his ground, keeping to the more secure cover of the office, as he watched his wife go into the fray. Her five shots took out three of the remaining gunmen, but the other six ducked down behind the main desk. Danielle was off to the side, over by her workstation, with a gun to her head. The gunwoman was holding her to her chest as a human shield.

Hank recognized the face of the woman, who was the only one on the interior side of the main desk. She had been one of the people loitering outside the office door. One of the many almost faceless people trying to get inside the office. Trying to see the random demon pass by or report some random offence they thought a demon was responsible for. They always made it clear that they didn't take petitioners, that they should all move on. Perhaps this was why so few of them did.

"That's enough of that," the woman said. She pulled Danielle tighter to her chest, as her eyes darted between Blanche and me. Her hand shook as it jabbed the barrel of the gun deeper into Danielle's neck. "You know why we're here, so let's just get this over with."

"No," Blanche said. She was crouched down behind Danielle's desk, with the main desk on her right as she stared down the woman. Hank's gun was on the desk, clutched firmly in her hands as she tried to aim at the small section of the woman's face that was visible around Danielle's head. Hank didn't like it, didn't like her lack of a clear line of fire around their colleague.

"What?" the woman asked. She seemed to momentarily forget about Hank as she squared off against Blanche. The woman adjusted Danielle's positioning to make sure she was properly covered. Danielle was a few inches taller than her, which helped the gunwoman stay behind cover. If Danielle had been trained in hand to hand, she would have been on the floor already. Even without the training, Danielle's hand was on the woman's, trying to pull the gun out from her neck.

"No," Blanche repeated. She was adjusting the gun every which way, trying to get the perfect angle to shoot the woman. The six men on the far side of the main desk would occasionally pop up their heads, but the gun was always there to greet them. It was like she was playing whack-a-mole, except with using the threat of being shot rather than actually hitting them with a mallet. Hank only worried that one of them would think to get behind her, to jump over the main desk into the section of space between Danielle's desk and the door to Blanche's office.

"No, what?" the woman asked. "No, you won't give it to us?"

"More like, no, we don't know what you're here for, but you're not getting it anyway," Blanche said.

"We're here for the database," one of the gunmen said, from behind the main desk. "Give it up and no one has to get hurt." Blanche turned the gun towards the main desk, taking a bead on the voice as the man spoke, then fired one shot before turning back to the woman. Two seconds later, Hank heard a body sliding onto the floor.

"Screw this," came another voice from over there. "Give us the database and everyone will still get hurt." Blanche made to point the gun in the direction of this new voice, but she couldn't seem to get a good enough angle around the two desks. The sound of scuffling feet seemed to indicate that the speaker had moved anyway.

"You do know that none of you are getting out of here alive, right?" Hank called out. "At least not with any information. Not without handcuffs. You haven't hurt anyone yet. You could still have a life after prison."

"Speak for yourself," Danielle said. "Shoot the bitch."

"Danielle, honey, you're not helping," Blanche said.

"Yea, and whose fault is that? I told you guys I needed to be trained as a field agent. I'm sick of being behind that stupid desk."

"Danielle, the field has a lot of guns being pointed at you," Hank said. "Do you really want to deal with this on a more regular basis?"

"The three of you shut up and give us the database," the woman yelled.

"What's going on down there?" came the voice of one of the scientists, calling down the hall from the lab. "Are we being attacked or is Blanche shooting at Hank again?"

"That happened one time," Blanche said. "And, yet, I'll never live it down."

"Shut up, all of you," the woman said. "Just give us the database. We have you outgunned and outnumbered."

"You are counting my wife over there as more than just one, right?" Hank asked. "She's more like five, so I'd say we have you outnumbered. Plus, you do know the guys over at Angel Corp have heard your gunshots and have already called the police, right? You might as well just surrender now."

"Your wife, eh?" came another voice from behind the desk. Blanche aimed for it again. But then more gunfire came from the other side of the main desk, shooting through the meager protection much like Blanche had done. Except there were so many more guns on their side. Hank was forced to duck behind the door again, hoping that the stronger wood would protect him from the bullets. At the same time, his wife ducked down onto the floor, trying to get below the bullets flying her way.

Hank watched, helpless, pinned, as a bullet lanced through Blanche's shoulder. Immediately, his fitness band started buzzing, having received the message from Blanche's that she was in trouble. That she was hurt, and badly. He didn't know how badly it was, and he couldn't reach his cell to find out. He could barely look at the band to see if the light was yellow or orange... or red. Worse, as the bullets kept coming, he, too, was forced forward, forced down onto the tile floor, trying to get beneath the onslaught. The gunmen seemed to trade off firing at them as the others reloaded. He wasn't sure just how much ammo they had brought with them. But it would only take one well-placed bullet to take him out.

After a small eternity, the gunfire finally stopped. Hank's ears were ringing something fierce from the loud sounds in the enclosed, confined space. Still, he strained his hearing, trying to hear something, anything, from his wife. The readout on his band showed a blinking, yellow light for her, indicating that she was injured, with an elevated heart rate, but alive. That was little consolation for him.

"Blanche, are you alright?" Hank called out, yelling louder than he needed to. When no sound came from the other room, he started to panic. He edged every which way, trying to see her body around the door without dropping past its protective barrier. There wasn't much left of the door. The lower section had been separated from the rest of it. This had been the section that he had been hiding behind, a section that, thankfully, had a metal kick guard to it. It hung awkwardly from the lower hinge. The rest of the door swung freely, back and forth, on the top one.

One last gunshot sounded out, echoing in his already ringing ears, threatening to take the rest of his hearing away. He couldn't tell who was shooting, or who got shot, but he figured that it wasn't good. Blanche was down, that was all he knew. And she was probably not in a position to be shooting anyone. Everyone else was either hiding, locked up, or one of the bad guys. His place behind the door was too precarious, too tenuous, for him to check. And, with nothing to protect himself with, nothing to help his wife with, he would only get himself killed.

The issue became moot moments later, when a pair of jeaned legs came around his little wall of protection. He looked upwards, his eyes trailing along the seam of the person's pants, before finding the eyes of the woman that had been holding Danielle hostage. She glared down at Hank with utter hatred, right before she thrusted forward with the butt of her handgun.

And darkness claimed Hank's world.

Chapter Twenty-Five
The Return of the Light

Someone was checking Hank's pulse at his wrist. Or, at least, that's what it felt like. It was the only real stimulus he felt as he slowly ascended out of unconsciousness. The ringing in his ear had stopped, though he couldn't hear anything in its place. As this realization hit him, he feared that his hearing was gone. That he would never hear the sound of his daughter's laughter ever again. Slowly, other sensations returned to him. The hard floor that he was lying on. The pain in his head from where the woman had hit it. An absence of something that he couldn't quite put his finger on.

The smell of blood reached his nostrils like a slap in the face. What worried him most of all, though, was that he didn't know the source. He didn't know who it was that was bleeding. Was it Blanche? Was it him? Was he dying as he tried to regain consciousness? The person pressing on his wrist didn't seem worried, as they gently placed his hand back onto the cold, hard, tile floor of his office. He would know if he were dying, though, wouldn't he? There would be more pain. A difficulty in breathing. Something other than the blunt, lingering pain in his head.

Next came his hearing. He silently thanked God when he started hearing a low, electric buzzing over his head. It was intermittent, flickering on and off randomly, and this worried him at first. Then, footsteps came, the soft steps of a rubber sole against the tile. They were steady, solid, growing quieter only because they were becoming more distant. He figured that, whoever it was that had been checking his wrist, they had just left his side, heading over to check on someone else.

Once he was conscious enough to think of it, Hank opened his eyes. It was dark at first, but then the buzzing came again, and a flash of light lit up his office for a moment. The buzzing faded quickly, bringing with it the light. But, another light, this one further away, made its way to him from around the door. He was still in the same place he was during the shootout, still pinned behind the bottom section of the door to his office. The light that was buzzing was the one in his office, a few feet over from the door. This would have placed it right above his head. Instead of it being in place, though, it was dangling down at a weird angle from the ceiling. It swung there, over his head, seeming to be threatening to fall on him. Every few seconds, it would buzz again, sending off a small shower of sparks, when the loose wires connected.

Hank stayed where he was, on the floor, as he tried to hear what was going on in the outside office. He wasn't sure just who it was out there. If they weren't friendly, he would need all the help, and luck, he could get to subdue them. Their shoes squeaked against the tiles as they started to move again, heading back in his direction. They stopped, though, still too far from the door for Hank to get a proper jump on them.

The next sound he heard made his heart soar with joy, at the same time that his stomach clenched with dread. Blanche gave out a muffled grunt of pain. He knew it was her voice. He had heard her grunts often enough over the years to recognize his own wife. The fact that she was still alive was enough to make him fly off the ground. But the thought that whoever it was that was out there might be hurting her, might be snuffing out that life that was only just confirmed, equally filled him with fear.

Fear doesn't cause Hank to lock up. It makes him strike out. To leap into the fray. To run to the defense of other people, especially of those that he loves. So, instead of staying on that cold, hard floor, instead of continuing to play dead, or at least unconscious, he jumped to his feet. His hand went to his holster, before he remembered that Blanche had been using his gun. The swinging top part of the door hit him in the nose before it fell to the ground. When it fell, the wood broke apart, finally succumbing to the damage that it had sustained, both before and after he had been knocked out. With the door gone, the rest of the office dropped into view.

And that did not help his confusion in the least.

Dr. Davidson had jumped to her feet when the door had fallen. A gun was shaking in her hands as it was pointed at Hank. At her feet was Blanche, lying on the ground, unconscious. He focused on her wrist, on the fitness band there. Even as far away as he was, he could make out the display. It showed a solid green light for Marissa, a solid yellow light for Blanche, and an empty space where his own readout should have been. He wasn't sure why his own light was off at first, but he was glad that Blanche's light hadn't grown darker. The solid yellow color indicated that she was still injured, but stable. If she had become worse off while he was unconscious, the light would have changed to orange, or worse, red.

Lying a few feet to her right was Danielle, similarly incapacitated. She had no fitness band, however, nothing to indicate if she was still alive. But, given that Dr. Davidson wasn't scrambling over her, he hoped that meant that she was alright. Or, at least, that she wasn't in any immediate danger. Danielle had always wanted time in the field, and she almost gets killed in the office, barely two feet from her own desk.

In front of the three women was a robot, spinning around on three wheels until it pointed at him. The robot barely came up to Dr. Davidson's waist and looked like something out of a bad sci-fi movie. It had two guns mounted on it, one on either side, similarly pointed in his direction. A red light blinked near the head, right between two cameras that were aimed at him.

"Hi." Dr. Howard's voice came out of a small speaker in the middle of the robot's chest. "Looks like one of you is finally awake."

"What happened?" Hank asked. He put his hand on his head, where it throbbed from his own voice.

"We were attacked," Dr. Davidson said.

"I imagine he remembers that part of it," Dr. Howard said. The robot spun around again, turning 270 degrees, to look over at the other scientist.

"He was hit in the head," Dr. Davidson said. "You never know what that can do. It's not like everything important is up there."

"Not everything. Just the electrical system."

"And without the electrical system, nothing else works. I'd call that important."

"Yes, but not everything important. The heart and the lungs are pretty important, too."

"Guys," Hank said, his hands waving their volume down. "How are they?"

"Alive," Dr. Davidson confirmed. "Which is more than I can say for the rest of these guys." She pointed around her, to the other bodies that littered the office.

Scattered around the rest of the room were several bodies that Hank hadn't noticed at first. As he counted them off, he glanced at what he could see of their faces. None of them looked the least bit familiar. However, when his count came up to five, he figured that he knew exactly who they were. "They're the gunmen that attacked us," he said. "The ones that Blanche didn't take out herself. How did they die?"

"That would be the kill bot one thousand, over here," Dr. Davidson said, gesturing down at the small robot next to her. "You did notice the guns, right?"

"Speaking of which," Hank said. He moved over in front of her, taking the gun out of her shaking hands. She had kept the thing pointed at him the entire time they were talking, even when her focus was on the robot and her colleagues. Only when he took the gun from her did he realize that it was his. He popped the safety and ejected the clip, counting the remaining bullets before re-inserting it. He only had two bullets left, but he was hoping he wouldn't need to use them before he got more. He was about to put his gun back into his holster when he remembered that there had been eleven that broke in. "Where's the other one?" he asked.

"What other one?" both of the scientists said together.

"The woman. There was a woman with these ten."

"Huey?" Dr. Davidson asked.

"There was no woman out here when I got the robot down the hall," Dr. Howard said. "Just the five of them picking through the files. They seemed overly annoyed that none of the files had anything to do with the demons."

"It's a good thing we went paperless last year," Dr. Davidson said. "Nothing to steal unless they broke into the computer systems."

"And those went on lockdown after the first bullet was fired," Dr. Howard agreed.

"I guess she left before then," Hank said. "What about Jack? Did he make it through this whole thing alright?"

"Uh, yea, about that," Dr. Davidson said, hesitantly.

"His cell was empty," Dr. Howard said.

"We heard the bars rattling after the gunfire was over."

"We were busy trying to get the kill bot operational at the time."

"And worried that whoever it was that was attacking us would come further up the hall to us in the lab," Dr. Davidson said.

"You two were playing around with your pet robot instead of trying to help?" Hank asked.

"We were helping," Dr. Howard said. This time her voice came from the hallway, around the corner, instead of out of the speaker on the robot. She was holding a tablet, which seemed to control the robot. He noticed her tap it a few times and the robot raised its guns to point towards the ceiling and away from everyone else. "Us running out here wouldn't have helped anyone, least of all you guys. And the kill bot was almost complete. We had just... repurposed some of the key components for other projects after the trial run."

"Herb wasn't up on the whole automated patrol systems idea," Dr. Davidson said. "Something about blah blah Skynet, blah blah Ultron. I tried to remind him about Robocop, but that was a non-starter."

"Don't worry, we removed the AI components," Dr. Howard said. "It's just a drone... for now."

"No one else is in the hallway?" Hank asked.

"Or the cell, or the breakroom, unless they were hiding in the cupboards. You think Jack ran after the fighting stopped?"

"Either that or the woman has him," Hank said. "I'm still deciding on if that's a good thing or a bad thing."

"Bad, obviously," Dr. Howard said. "We'd have to rescue him, and we have no idea where to start."

"No, the start would be calling an ambulance for Blanche. She was shot in the shoulder."

"Kill bot can do first aid," Dr. Davidson said. "Your wife is fine. The bullet wound was cauterized and wrapped."

"An ambulance is already on its way," Dr. Howard said. "Along with the local PD. They're probably downstairs by now."

"Oh, good. They're going to have a field day about all this. The people in charge of policing the demons get taken down by a group of humans."

"We were outnumbered two to one," Dr. Davidson said.

"I'm sorry, 'we'?" Hank said.

"No need to get snippy," Dr. Davidson said.

"Yea. Who took out half of them, again?"

"Blanche," Hank said. "Now can I at least look at the damage your robot did to my wife?"

Without waiting for an answer, Hank went over to kneel next to Blanche. The robot made way for him, no longer blocking his path to his wife. He swiped at the screen of her fitness band until her heart rate was displayed. At the same time, he checked her pulse himself, not trusting the device. When he checked his own wrist, needing the clock to count the time, he noticed what he had been missing before. His fitness band was gone, leaving his arm noticeably empty. There were tan lines around where it had been, as if to give evidence that it had been there at one point. He wasn't sure what happened to it, or why someone might have taken it, but that seemed to explain why the readout had shown a blank for him.

In the hall, the elevator dinged, drawing his attention away from his injured, but alive, wife. As he stood up to look out into the hall, three uniformed men stepped off the elevator. Two of the men were paramedics, wheeling a stretcher between them. The third was a cop, whose hand was conspicuously near his gun as he eyed the damage that the gunfight had done. Further down the hall, several other people were peeking out from behind the door to the Angel Corp offices, which had also been damaged during the fight. They continued staring on through the gap as if his life had suddenly become an interesting and exciting movie. And, in a way, it had.

"Over here, guys," Dr. Davidson said, calling out to the three uniformed men, waving them over. "We're going to need two stretchers, I think. Blanche is worse off, so she goes first."

"We'll be the judges of that," one of the paramedics said. The two of them fumbled around with the stretcher as they tried to angle it to get through the doorway. The door was jammed most of the way open, though the glass that had made it up was gone, scattered across the floor. They managed to get it part of the way in, but the door didn't want to budge. It didn't want to make way for them.

"One second," Hank said, with a sigh. "I'll bring her over to you."

"I don't think you should move her just yet," the paramedic on his side of the door said. "Let me check on her first." He abandoned the stretcher where it was. He hopped over the top of the main desk rather than moving over to the door. "Why don't you go with the officer over there and answer his questions. He'll bring you to the hospital afterwards."

"I'm not leaving my wife," Hank insisted.

"Hank, you're the senior agent right now," Dr. Davidson said. "We'll watch over her."

"What about Herb?" Hank asked. "Where is he hiding out?"

"Herb went to DC for a meeting, remember?" Dr. Howard said. "He won't be back until Monday. It's just you right now."

"Damn it," Hank swore. "Fine. Just let me try to get some things together."

Hank returned to his office, or what was left of it. He hadn't noticed how much it had been damaged in the gunfight. He hadn't seen much of anything in there besides the door and the light. The light was still flickering on and off, but with the door gone, the light from the main office filtered in, filling the space. Jack's desk took the brunt of the gunfire, collecting the bullets in its wooden panels. His chair, still out in the main office where Hank had tossed it, was in shambles. The stuffing and upholstery was spread out across the floor. The chair spun back and forth in some unseen, unfelt force that still flowed through the area. It was like Jack's ghost was haunting the chair, showing that he would have died had he not been in the cell when it all went down. Hank knew that wasn't true, that he wouldn't have been in the chair when the gunfire started. He would probably have been helping, or at least as much as Hank was. His gun would have been firing right next to Hank's in Blanche's more than capable hands, while the two of them crouched behind the door, trying to stay out of her way.

Unidentified pieces of debris blocked his path around the edge of the desk. In order to get to his desk, he needed to climb over much of it. He fumbled around in the desk drawers, trying to make sure he had all he needed before leaving with the police officer to make his official reports. He needed his badge, which was already in his pockets, his keys, which he found in the top drawer in his desk, right where he always kept them, and his...

"Uh, guys? Do you know where my phone is?" he called out, when he realized that his phone wasn't in its usual place. He usually left it in the cradle on his desk, charging up for when it would be needed. Then he remembered bringing it out into the main office for his call with Marissa, to shame his wife about abandoning her. He didn't remember if he brought it back in. The cradle was right there, though, standing empty in its usual place on the far corner.

There was just no cell phone in it.

Chapter Twenty-Six
The Lost Phone

"Just how important is the phone?" Detective Gregor asked. Gregor had been the detective on the scene at Jared's murder. Hank had made his original report with the uniformed officer that had brought him to the station. After that, Gregor came over to speak with him, to go over the events again. Hank wasn't sure if he was just trying to make sure that every angle of the incident was covered, or if he was really being interrogated for something.

"The most up to date contact information for every demon that we have recorded was in it," Hank said, trying to make it clear with his words and tone just how important it was. "We're talking about phone numbers, emails, work and home addresses. Everything a person would ever need to hunt down and kill every demon in the world."

"Well, not to be overly cynical or anything, but wouldn't that be a good thing?" Gregor asked. "These demons seem like they have been nothing but trouble since they arrived. Half my caseload these days relate to them in some way or another, which means you folk tend to swoop in and take the credit."

"We... that's... We're only trying to help," Hank said. "We're trying to keep the dangerous demons out of the way, out of the public view."

"Which is all well and good, if you're killing them off. You've always made it very clear that containment isn't an option with these things. Heck, half the time we arrest these things ourselves, the demons escape. They end up killing guards and other prisoners in the process. If they can't abide by our laws and they can't be contained if they don't, they should just be killed."

Hank tried not to be pulled into an argument about law enforcement's approach to the demons. From the very beginning, the HPS had made no secret that demons couldn't be contained in normal prisons. However, they couldn't very well make it known that they had a prison that could. The prison was top secret, and for very good reason. If anyone found out about it, about the magic that powered it, there would be no end to the people trying to find it. Trying to break into it. Trying to get at the magic and the dangerous criminals within. Not even the original arresting officers for the demons could know.

"That might be alright," Hank said, reluctantly, "if they were only going after the bad ones. There are far more good demons than bad, I can assure you. You only see the bad ones because those are the only ones you deal with. I've met with them all, good and bad, and neither should be slaughtered outright. I have a feeling that I know who has the phone, though. If I'm right, they're just going to burn the lot of them. They'll kill them and any humans that get in their way or live with them. We're talking about thousands of humans right alongside the demons. Full apartment buildings could be targets as well, not just stand-alone houses. The death toll could be..."

"Who do you think has the phone?" Gregor asked.

"What?" Hank asked.

"You said you think you know who has the phone. Who?"

"They call themselves Remember Sami," Hank said. "Ever heard of them?"

Detective Gregor stared at him for a moment, taken aback. However, when he finally did respond, it wasn't the answer Hank had expected. "I've... heard rumors about them, I guess. I didn't think they were a real group, though."

"Oh, yes, they're real alright, and linked to several hate crimes targeting demons."

"Can they really be called hate crimes when they're against something so hateful, so hate-able, as demons?"

"Demons can't help what they are any more than any human can change the color of their skin. Hating them in general is just as wrong."

"Well, in any case, I'm afraid I won't be able to help in searching out these Remember Sami people of yours. We can, however, provide some added security for your offices, until you are sure it is safe enough to return to them. I heard you are a few men down right now."

"Yes, and, if we're done here, I would very much like to check in on them, especially my wife," Hank said. "Are we done?"

"Oh, yes, yes," Gregor said. "I think that's everything for us. Please, don't hesitate to ask us for any help. We're all in this together, aren't we?"

"Sure," Hank said, halfheartedly. "Actually, now that I think of it, we've come to a bit of a dead end with the murder investigation. This attack would probably derail it even more. I was working under the impression that--"

"Oh, no," Gregor said. "No, no, no. I'm afraid we won't be able to help with that. We are far too busy with our own casework to take on some of yours. Especially when you are just going to take the perpetrator off our hands and claim the win again. I meant helping out with added security for your wife and the other injured."

"Well, if the murderer isn't a demon..."

"And what's the likelihood of that? No, this is clearly demon on demon violence. Tragic, but not exactly in our wheelhouse, now is it? Otherwise you would have let us continue our investigation from the beginning. We've...

reallocated our resources around that case. Now, move along. Some of us have some real crimes to investigate."

Detective Gregor stood up from the desk, his chair sliding backwards loudly on its wheels. He motioned towards the door of the main bullpen, over towards the uniformed officer that Hank had been talking to before. The officer had offered to take him over to the hospital, once the reports were all made properly. It seemed to Hank that that time had finally come. He was eager to see his wife, but he felt like something still needed to be done. He just wasn't entirely sure what that was.

The officer drove him over to the hospital in silence. This gave Hank time to think. He debated whether or not to tell Marissa about the attack. About the fact that her mother was currently in the hospital with a bullet in her shoulder. She had a right to know, but he didn't want to worry her. The attack on the HPS would undoubtedly be news, the people over at Angel Corp weren't likely to keep it silent. However, he wasn't sure just how far that news would travel. Certainly not all the way to Ontario, and not to a collection of school children too young to care about those things. By the time he got to the hospital, he had convinced himself that there was no reason to tell his daughter anything. The whole reason why they had put her in that school was to protect her from their world, from what they needed to do, and what might happen to them in the process. He wanted her to stay a little girl, thinking that everything was right in the world, for as long as possible.

As focused as he was to get to his wife, Hank barely saw much of the hospital. He already knew the room she was in. Dr. Howard had called over to the station once the women had been settled. By the time he made it to the room, Danielle was awake, but Blanche was still asleep. She looked so fragile, so vulnerable in her bed, with the central line coming out of her small hands. That's what really broke Hank, seeing her like that. Whenever she was up and active, she had always been a force to be reckoned with. Yet, when she was down, when she was injured, all he wanted to do was protect her. And it was the one thing he was never able to do.

"I'm so sorry," Danielle said, the moment that Hank came into the room. He barely heard her words as he made his way over to the vacant chair by his wife's side. "I should have stopped them from coming into the office."

"It's not your fault," Dr. Howard insisted. From her tone, it seemed like it wasn't the first time she had to say that. "They smashed the door. We should have gotten extra security to keep them off the floor. It's Herb's fault."

"What we should have done was get more field agents," Hank said, barely getting the words out through the fog that had started to roll in over his mind. "Our workload has us stretched too thin, has us playing defense when we should be on offense. These Remember Sami people should have been tracked down and arrested ages ago."

"They can't be arrested for just speaking their mind," Dr. Howard said. "We don't even know if the people that hit us were Remember Sami."

"It just seems like it's coming from all over these days, doesn't it," Danielle said.

"Well, it shouldn't," Hank yelled. "We should be on this. We have in the past. Sure, we'd be coming by after the fact to mop up the damage most of the time, but we were getting better at tracking these things. Our surveillance network was getting better. We had caught that meteor right when it fell, didn't we? Only one person exposed. And that was while we were still cataloguing these demons. Now, it's like our workload has gone up a thousand-fold, and we're just trying to stay afloat."

"We need to go back to doing what we do best," Dr. Howard said. "That's coming in after the fact and mopping it up, preventing what we can, and leaving these investigations to the experts."

"Except the experts don't want us there," Hank said. "They want their cases to be their cases. If we go that route... we'd need to delegate, we'd need..."

"We'd need to let them in on magic," Dr. Howard finished.

Hank looked towards the door behind him, making sure that no one was listening in. He got up, taking the three steps over to it, to look both ways up the hallway before closing it behind him. "Magic is too dangerous to let it out into the public. We need a way to... I don't know, come up with something that's..."

"Magic light," Danielle offered. "Something that works like magic but isn't. Something that we can offer the civilians that will work to detain these demons without needing to kill them."

"I think this case, this murder, was just that," Hank said. "Them learning that they can kill the demons instead of imprisoning them. We're looking at a lot of dead people on our hands if we can't come up with a solution."

"Let's wait for Herb to come back from DC before we decide on anything," Dr. Howard said. "He's there to beg for more money, insisting that we need more resources. You keep ragging on him for pinching pennies, for not recruiting when he should. But it's not up to him. It never was."

"I know," Hank said. "That doesn't mean I have to like it."

"So, what are we going to do about our offices?" Dr. Howard asked.

"Where's Dr. Davidson?" Hank asked. It was odd for him to see one of the scientists without the other being close by. Even when Dr. Davidson was standing over Blanche, Dr. Howard was operating the robot that was standing next to her. He'd almost think them twins, except that they looked nothing alike. "And Jenkins, for that matter?"

"Dr. Davidson is getting everyone coffee," Dr. Howard said. "Jenkins was out of town on his vacation. We've already reached out to him and he'll be back on Friday. In the meantime, we're just down to the four of us."

"No, we're just down to me," Hank said. "Danielle needs to focus on getting better, and the two of you won't have access to your lab for a while."

"Oh, we don't need to worry about that," Dr. Howard said. "You're not the only one that takes their work home with them at times. Dr. Davidson and I have a spare lab at home. It's not ideal, but we'll have enough to process any evidence that you might be able to collect."

"I don't think there's going to be much evidence to worry about for a while," Hank said. "We need to find Jack. And the gunwoman, for that matter. I think one of them took my phone. Unless... did one of you guys find it at the office?"

"No, I'm afraid not," Dr. Howard said. "Where did you last see it?"

"Before we were attacked. It wasn't where it should have been afterwards, which means that one of them took it. If Jack is working with her--"

"Why would he be working with the gunwoman?" Dr. Howard asked.

"Because he thinks Jack is in Remember Sami," Danielle said.

"It can't be just a coincidence that they attacked right after I put him in the cell. They've been out there for months now, probably just spying on us the whole time. They probably had whatever they used to smash open the door from the beginning. Then, they saw me bring in Jack in handcuffs. The time was just too convenient for them not to have been working together. Jack had never been one of us."

"That was because you never let him be," Blanche said. Her voice was huskier than usual, raw, as if she had screamed herself hoarse. Still, it was a welcomed gift to Hank's ears. He moved to hug her, but stopped in midair, afraid that she might break if he touched her in the wrong place. "Oh, I'm fine," she said, when she noticed his expression. However, when she lifted her arm to return the hug, she winced with pain.

"Are you alright?" Hank asked, knowing that she would just shrug away his concern. "What did the doctors say about it?"

"She should heal up just fine," Dr. Howard said. "Both of them will. They both need rest. They left the bullet in her shoulder because it wasn't near anything critical and taking it out would just do more harm than good."

"We might need it to match ballistics," Blanche said. "Why didn't they take it out while I was under?"

"I just said... We don't even have a gun to match it against anyway."

"And we have the recordings from the internal surveillance cameras," Danielle said. "That'll be up on the cloud already. We won't need anything more than that to prove that the woman was involved in the assault."

"What about the others?" she asked. "There were other men there, weren't there? It was one of them that shot me, right? Did the cameras get a good look at all of them? Can we identify any of them off the recordings?"

"We don't need the recordings for that," Hank said. "They're dead. We have their bodies. It was just the woman who got away. Well, her and Jack, that is."

"Jack wasn't involved. He was still in the cell," Dr. Howard said.

"He could still be an accessory after the fact, or involved in planning the whole thing, making him an accomplice. We won't know until we find him, re-arrest him, and interrogate him."

"What about the recordings of him leaving the office?" Blanche asked. "Was he at gunpoint?"

"We haven't seen the recordings just yet," Danielle said. "I only woke up about ten minutes before you did, and no one thought to bring my laptop."

"You should be resting, anyway," Dr. Howard said. "It's late, and we've had a long, stress filled day. We should all be resting right now."

"Except the gunwoman wouldn't be resting," Hank said. "If she has my phone--"

"It's locked, isn't it?" Dr. Howard said. "She shouldn't be able to get into it."

"Does Jack have your passcode?" Blanche asked.

"No, but they might also have my fitness band," Hank said. His hand unconsciously went to his now naked wrist, where the band had been just hours before. It still felt weird not having it there after wearing it almost constantly for the past nine months. "As long as the two of them are close enough to each other, the phone should stay unlocked. And she would just need it unlocked long enough to transfer all the contacts out of it."

"Okay, now I really need a laptop," Danielle said. "I can track your phone to wherever it is right now. Maybe we can get to it before the damage is done."

"We don't need a laptop for that," Blanche said. "We just need my phone."

"You mean the phone that you forgot to charge last night?" Hank asked. "Where is it? In your luggage?"

"Actually, yea, I think so. Did you guys bring it?"

"Yea, it's in the closet," Dr. Howard said. She went over to the closet, on the other side of Blanche's bed from where Hank was sitting. The suitcase fell out onto the floor on its front with a solid thunk, bumping the bed in the process. She fumbled around with it a little before settling on picking it up and plopping it on the end of the bed, past where Blanche's feet were hiding under the sheet. "Where is it in here?"

"We're going to need a new charger," Hank said. "She lost the cable for it."

"I didn't lose it. I just forgot it at home."

"Well, what kind of cord is it?" Dr. Howard asked. "I have mini USB, micro USB, and Apple on me right now." She fumbled around in the deep pockets of her lab coat, pulling out all manner of odds and ends, including a matchbox car and a golf ball for some reason. When she found the micro USB cord, she presented it as if it were a hard-won prize.

"That'll do just fine," Blanche said. "It's in the front pocket, the one that keeps getting hit when the thing falls over. Really gotta get that fixed one of these days."

Dr. Howard fished around in the pocket in question until she found the phone. With a well-practiced flip, she had the phone plugged into the USB cable, attached to one of her own chargers, and plugged in within a few seconds, handing it over to Blanche with the same motion. "All yours," she said.

They sat there, waiting, for a couple of minutes while the phone charged up enough for Blanche to turn it on, then another couple for it to boot up. Hank moved from his chair over to Blanche's head, so he could watch her work over her shoulder. It took a few moments for the family tracker app to boot up, the indicator popping up into the upper left corner. It was still showing Blanche as a yellow dot, but Hank's circle had turned to blue.

"What's up with that?" Hank asked, pointing at the notification.

"Do you want me to find your phone first or figure out why you're blue?"

"Both, obviously."

Blanche popped up the track my phone app, letting it boot up as she pulled open the notifications window. The full notification didn't show anything more than the minimized one. It just said Family Tracker next to the readout. She tapped the notification, pulling up that app as well, leaving the tracker running in the background. When the full Family Tracker app popped up, it automatically went to the full status window, showing that Blanche was registered at the hospital's hub. There was a link in the corner, where the app connected to the hospital's record system, which would allow for a more in-depth description of her current status. This was used for when family members were checked into the hospital and loved ones weren't able to be there with them.

Next to Hank's now blue circle, however, showed that his fitness band had last logged into the system at a Marriott several miles away from the office. For a status, it showed "Invalid User - Biometrics Mismatch".

"There you have it," Blanche said. "Someone tried to use your fitness band. Someone that isn't you. The system logged it. You'll be able to find them if you track where it's logging in from. It's probably where your phone is, too."

"Well, check the track my phone app, anyway. Maybe they got separated, or whatever. If Jack has the phone and the woman has the band, or something."

Blanche double tapped the last used app button, switching back to the phone tracker. It took a few more seconds for the app to come up, and a few more for it to pull up the GPS coordinates for the three phones on the account. Marissa's was showing spotty connection at the school, which made sense if it was off. Blanche's was, of course, at the hospital. And Hank's was...

"At the office?" Hank asked. "Huh. Maybe they didn't take it after all?"

"Now can you all just settle down and relax?" Dr. Howard asked. "The world isn't coming to an end. Woo hoo." She looked between the two of them for a moment, but the look on Hank's face was clear from the start. She gave out a heavy sigh before saying, "I'll get my keys."

Chapter Twenty-Seven
Touched by an Angel Corp Employee

They hung around at the hospital for a few more minutes, long enough for Dr. Davidson to come back from the coffee run and for Hank to catch up with Blanche's doctor. Other than the bullet to her shoulder, which Hank had been unfortunate enough to see, she also had a concussion and several bone bruises from the attackers. Apparently, they hadn't taken her killing half their team that lightly. None of her injuries were too severe, but they wanted to keep her in the hospital overnight for observation. Danielle, however, only had a mild concussion and would have been able to be checked out, except that it was so late and everyone that could have checked her out were going to already be in the room with Blanche. The hospital room had become something of a new office for them, one that they wouldn't be able to keep for long.

Hank had his own mild concussion, which the paramedics had told him about before he left the scene with the cops. The doctor reiterated what the paramedics had said, that he should be careful and take it easy, watch for any signs that the concussion was more serious. The doctor made it clear that the only reason why he wasn't fitting him for his own hospital bed was because he had come in under his own power, and they couldn't force him to check himself in. Hank had every intention of spending the night in the hospital anyway, by Blanche's side. Just after he had recovered his cell phone and made sure the contacts weren't compromised.

"I hate sitting in the passenger seat," Hank said to Dr. Howard. He was holding Blanche's phone in his hand, as if the cup holder that Dr. Howard had offered wasn't good enough for it. The cup holder was cluttered with coins and trash, but he just wanted the connection, however tenuous, to his wife. He kept flipping between the family tracker and the phone tracker apps, constantly worried that one or both of them would change at a moment's notice. The phone was plugged into the cigarette lighter port to continue charging, but it didn't seem to be making much progress.

"You hate not being in control," Dr. Howard said. She barely took her eyes off the road to glance over at him. "How does that work out with being married to Blanche?"

"No, it's not about control," Hank said. "She prefers that I drive as well. It's because I get motion sickness if I'm not driving."

"Oh... Should I be worried about my car?"

"No, I'll be fine. We're almost there anyway." He flipped back over to the phone tracker, waiting on the screen long enough for the spinning circle in the corner to settle back down. When it did, the dot that marked the phone's location hadn't moved since the last time he had checked. It was still showing up at the office. However, with the limited accuracy of the GPS, and no elevation indicator, it could be anywhere in the building, or any of the buildings around it. The app had a function to make the phone ring, but that would only help if they were close enough to hear it.

"It probably just fell behind the desk," Dr. Howard suggested. "If it took a glancing blow from a bullet, it could have been knocked over without damaging it."

"Jack's desk took a lot of fire," Hank said, going with the suggestion. "It could have bashed into mine and knocked it down."

"Yea," Dr. Howard said.

There were only three other cars in the parking lot when they pulled into it. One of them was the crown vic, and Hank drew a deep sigh of relief when he saw it still there, unaffected by the attack above. He had only caught a brief glimpse of it when he was being hauled off by the cops earlier, as his view of it was blocked by the ambulance. As thankful to Dr. Howard for the ride as he was, he would be driving his own car back to the hospital. Dr. Howard pulled into her usual spot, which was three over from the crown vic, and four over from Jack's car, which was still in its spot as well. The third car, however, didn't belong to any of the HPS staff. But it was familiar enough to Hank for him to not worry about it. There were several other offices in the building, and it could have belonged to any one of the hundreds of employees and staff.

"Why don't you head back to the hospital," Hank said. "It shouldn't take me long to find it." He climbed out of the car, as if the matter was settled, heading for the front door. Dr. Howard quickly moved to follow him, stepping up beside him before he could get far. She clicked the button on her key fob to lock the car doors behind them.

"Shorter still if we both look," Dr. Howard said. "Four ears are better than two. Then we can all get back and rest up for tomorrow, when we get to hunt down the bitch."

"I'm sorry, 'we'?"

"I'll be helping Danielle. No way am I going out in the field after this."

"Well, you seemed to have handled yourself alright with that drone. Maybe we can have you pilot the drone in the field sometime."

"If we ever need the drone out in the field, it might be better to call in a SWAT team. I built that thing mostly on a dare from Dewey. It was all her idea."

"Do you seriously call yourselves Huey and Dewey to each other?" Hank asked. "I hate that everyone else calls you that."

"Eh, it makes sense," Dr. Howard said, shrugging. "I just figured they're kind of pet names for us. Doesn't bother us any. And, why should it?"

"So, if we hire a new scientist at some point, should we target someone with a last name starting with L, for Louie?"

"No, you should target someone who's good enough to keep up with us. We're awesome enough just the two of us. Anyone new would probably just slow us down."

"Well, if we even get any new members to the team, it would probably be in the field agent department," Hank said. "We're completely strapped while you two are wasting your spare time making killer robots."

"Hey, that killer robot saved your ass earlier today. How about a little respect for the kill bot?"

"Yes, total respect for the kill bot. I guess I shouldn't really be talking about expanding the team anyway. This is assuming we even have a team after this. I mean, what kind of--" As absorbed in the conversation as he was, Hank didn't notice the man that had come out of the building until he slammed into him coming out the front door. He staggered backwards with the blow, barely managing to keep his feet. The man was wearing what appeared to be an oversized suit jacket, ill fitted for his form. He just kept on walking, seeming not to have noticed the collision. "Hey," Hank shouted, calling after the man.

That was when he noticed it, the phone on the ground by his feet. Barely thinking about it, he bent down, picking the phone off the sidewalk. The familiar feel of it made him do a double take on his way to offering it back to the guy. The phone looked just like his own, the same make and model. He was about to call after the guy, to accuse him of stealing his phone. But then the display woke up with an alert message. The background on the now broken display showed an Angel Corp logo, looking nothing like the picture of his family. In the dim light of the display, and the far away lamps that encircled the parking lot, he could see that the color was different as well. It was most definitely not his phone.

"Hey," Hank shouted out again. This time he actually chased after the guy when he still didn't respond or turn around. He placed his hand on what he thought was the guy's shoulders. However, as he did so, the jacket seemed to jerk out of his grip, as the man stood perfectly straight. He turned around to look at Hank, exhaustion plain in his eyes. "You dropped this," Hank said, in a more comforting and empathetic voice, before handing the phone over.

"Oh, thanks," the man said, in a thick accent that Hank couldn't place. The man took one look at his phone before swearing in what must have been his native tongue, as Hank didn't understand a word of it. "That's just great."

"I'm sure you can get a new one in the morning," Hank said. "It's the same model as mine, and they had plenty last I checked."

"Right, right," the man said. He waved Hank off before heading over to the car that Hank had noticed before, the one off to the side and away from the crown vic.

Dr. Howard had waited by the door, her eyes covered by a mask of confusion. "What was that about?" she asked.

"I was returning his phone." Hank led the way into the building, pushing the revolving door. He was surprised when Dr. Howard jumped in right behind him, in the same section, but she was small enough that it didn't matter.

"No, I mean him. Why was he here? Do you think he was--"

"He's an Angel Corp employee," Hank said. "The logo was on his phone. It was probably a business phone. I don't know, maybe it's a bigger thing over on that side of the floor. Who even knows what those guys do?"

"Don't they make software? They made the family tracker, right?"

"Yea, but then they're working on that new train network, or whatever. That's not software, it's an outdated mode of transportation. And they're supposedly buying up TV networks as well. It's like they're doing anything and everything. No wonder the guy was so stressed. Our whole shooter situation probably just made things worse over there."

"Are you seriously thinking the Angel Corp employees had a worse day than we did?" she asked.

"Not worse, just also bad. Just because one person gets shot and two others beaten over the head with guns--"

"And ten people killed," Dr. Howard added.

"--doesn't mean that's all the bad luck there is to be had in the world, or even the building. Maybe someone got stuck in one of the elevators as well." The elevator dinged as if in response to its name. Hank didn't remember pressing the button, but the light lingered there long enough for him to see it.

"Let's just find this phone. I'm ready for this day to be over with. Is it still in the building?"

Hank spent most of the ride up pulling the tracking app back up on Blanche's phone. It clicked on, with the indicator for his phone, just as the door opened on their floor. He was startled to find the hallway empty when they got there. It was the first time that had happened since Angel Corp had moved in, even in the dead of the night. Now that he knew that most of the people camped out there were Remember Sami, it gave him a sick, eerie feeling in the pit of his stomach. It was as if he were somehow violated by their presence there. He half wished there had been people there, so he could take out his frustration on them. Even with the loiterers noticeably absent, he knew they would return eventually. He just wondered how long it would take.

"Uh, yea, it's still here," he said.

"Well, ring it. Maybe we'll find it right away."

Hank hit the button on the app while she badged the door. The badge reader beeped twice, but the door didn't click open. Someone had stuck a piece of plywood into the area where the glass had been, making a better door than the glass had. There was yellow police tape pulled across the door in a big X, with a big sticker over the latch saying that the place was sealed. The lights were off inside, and there didn't seem to be anyone there. Dr. Howard pressed her face against the glass of the windows framing the door, using her hands to block out the lights from the hallway.

"No one's home," she said. "Wait here. I know a back way into the offices. I'm going to sneak into the lab and see if I can find it."

"Is that the best idea?" Hank asked. "It's a sealed crime scene. You'll be contaminating it."

"We've been all over it for years. It'll be no more compromised than it already is. I'll try not to touch anything; except for your phone, of course. We gotta know if it's in there, at least."

"I don't hear it ringing," he said, as he clicked the button again.

"Hank, the office is soundproof. You're not supposed to be able to hear anything inside. Besides, the app says it's here."

"No, the app says it's within a certain distance from here, however accurate the GPS is on the phone. It doesn't have to specifically be in this office. It says here within 100 feet. That could mean the parking lot or the building on the other side of the street. It's just more likely for it to be in the office."

"Right. So why don't we eliminate that as a possibility before we go back outside and check the building across the street, alright?" She headed back over to the elevator, hitting the button. The same elevator they just left dinged instantly, the door opening up for her. As she stepped inside, she raised a finger towards Hank. "Just wait here. I'll be right back."

"Uh, alright," Hank said, as the doors closed on her.

Hank was left alone in the hallway for a while. Without much else to do, he started examining the walls and the rest of the hallway, looking for damage from the shootout. Despite the gunfire being just on the other side of the wall from there, there didn't seem to be any damage. There were no bullet holes in the glass wall that opened up into the office, and no sign of any damage across the way at the Angel Corp office. Hank was rather relieved by this, by the idea that their deadly confrontation with Remember Sami hadn't endangered anyone outside of HPS.

But, as he thought about it, the fact that there was no other damage started to make sense. The gunmen had all been aiming into the office, towards their intended targets, towards Hank, Blanche, and Danielle. The only person to have shot towards the hallway was Blanche, and she was good enough of a shot that none of her bullets went wide. None would have missed their intended targets and headed for the hallways beyond. There might have even been more loiterers outside in the hall, ones that had no ties to the terrorist group, that would have been hurt in the crossfire. And, yet, the only deaths had been the gunmen themselves, the only injured being the three of them. It was like someone up there really was watching out for them. Like there really was an angel watching over them, and not just from across the hall.

Hank was startled out of his inner musings by a knock at the door. He turned towards the noise, surprised to find that Dr. Howard had already made her way inside the office. She stood in the light from the hallway, her form visible through the obscured glass as little more than a silhouette. Even though she had told him that she had a way in, he hadn't thought it would be so readily available that she would be inside so soon. She started to flap her hands around in weird movements, but Hank wasn't sure what it was she was trying to say. Instead, he just hit the button to call the phone again, his thumb having stayed on the button the entire time that he paced the floor.

He waited a few seconds after pressing the button, with Dr. Howard continuing her pantomime, before heading over to the door again. He wanted to shout at her, to try to make his voice heard through the soundproof glass. However, he knew the effort would be wasted. Instead, he placed the phone against the door, screen towards the glass, hoping that it would be visible through the white. He pulled it away long enough to press the button again before placing it back there.

The shadowy form of Dr. Howard shook her head, letting it slump in front of her, before disappearing. Hank wasn't sure what happened, though he wondered if she was going to try to set up some way to communicate through the glass. A few seconds later, he thought of actually calling the office line. Of trying to reach Dr. Howard on the phone. It took him a little while, fumbling around with Blanche's phone, to find where she had hidden the phone app, and a few more before he remembered the number for it. The line rang on his end for a while, but he couldn't hear anything through the door. No one picked up, and the shadowy form never returned.

"No luck," Dr. Howard said.

Hank jumped in startlement, dropping Blanche's phone to the floor in the process, before turning around to the scientist. "What?" he asked.

She was standing behind him, right next to the elevator. "No luck," she said, again. "Nothing rang in there when you hit the button. I even tried checking your office. Nothing. Who are you calling?"

"Um... you."

"I'm right here."

"Yea, but... No, I mean... I thought you didn't understand what I was telling you, so I thought to call the office phone."

"I was already in the stairwell coming back to the third floor," she said.

"Wait, that's your big 'secret entrance' to the office? The stairwell?"

"Oh, uh, yea. Oops. Well, the stairwell is supposed to be locked, so people can't get in. It leads right into the back of the lab. The doctor's office on the third floor has theirs unlocked, though, because the doctors all smoke and they want to do it without people knowing. It gave me the idea to hack ours as well, so it's always unlocked."

"Are you seriously telling me that anyone can just walk right into our offices if they come into the stairwell on the third floor?" Hank asked.

"No. No, no, no. Not just anyone. Just Dr. Davidson and I. We're not stupid. We installed a badge reader, so it only unlocks for us. It was a real trick getting it close enough to the other side of the wall to be read without compromising the wall or the door. Now, we just have to slap the badge against the wall in the right spot and it pops open. We've never really had a use for it before now, though, so I almost forgot about it."

"Does Herb know about this?"

"Oh, hell no," Dr. Howard said. "He'd have a fit. I'd appreciate it if you didn't mention it to him."

"I don't know," Hank teased. "It's going to cost you."

"How about I save your wife from six armed madmen?" she said, with a smile. "Oh, wait."

"Yea, yea, yea. Let's go. We still need to figure out where the phone is. It could be anywhere."

"No, it could be anywhere in this building, the grounds around it, or the adjacent buildings. Not just anywhere."

"That's what... Let's just go, alright?"

"Yup," she agreed, almost cheerfully. She reached over to hit the button for the elevator, but the doors still hadn't closed behind her. When she stepped inside, the doors started to close before Hank could join her. She stuck out her hand into the door, triggering the sensors long enough for Hank to get on. Before he could hit the button for the ground floor, though, she hit the buttons for all the floors heading down.

"What? Are you like five?" he asked.

"Ours is the only floor with soundproofing," she said. "We can at least stick our heads out into the hall and see if we can hear anything."

"See if we can hear," Hank muttered. "Sure. Whatever."

He was starting to get a headache, though he wasn't sure if that was from the concussion, the lack of sleep, or the general frustration he had been feeling about the case. Still, he kept his state of mind long enough to join Dr. Howard in sticking their heads out into the hall each time the elevator dinged and the doors opened. There was no sign of any response from him pressing the button on the app, but he couldn't be sure just how far away from the elevator the phone could have been for him to still hear it. Most of the floors were locked up for the night, and they wouldn't be able to get inside any of the offices anyway. Besides, if the gunwoman had taken the phone, she wouldn't have tried to hide out on any of the other floors anyway. When she left the HPS office, no one was after her. She could have just walked out the front door without anyone even noticing.

By the time they got to the ground floor, Hank just wanted to go back to the hospital and check on his wife before curling up into a ball by her side. Even the prospect of the contact information for the demons falling into the wrong hands barely registered in his exhausted brain. He hit the button on the app three times as they crossed the lobby to the front door, but that was more from the habit he developed on the way down than any thought that the phone was there. Staring at the lingering dot on his phone made him think the system was just teasing him. That his phone wasn't really there. That it was long gone and he would never find it again.

"Do you hear that?" Dr. Howard asked, as they exited the building.

"Huh?" Hank asked. He was half asleep on his feet, and he robotically hit the button again. A phone rang into the night, echoing around the empty parking lot.

"I think we found your phone."

Hank just nodded, leaning against one of the light posts by the cars, the words barely registering in his mind. His gaze flitted out into the night, looking for the source of the noise. Looking for his lost phone that he barely remembered losing.

Dr. Howard headed off into the distance, first in one direction, then another, ever searching for the elusive sound that seemed to be getting further away from him as he stood there, before blackness surrounded him.

Chapter Twenty-Eight
Laying Low

Hank woke up to the sight of Blanche's face. She was cradling their joined hands to her cheek as she stared deeply into his opening eyes. Hank smiled. He always liked waking up next to his wife, something that didn't happen much those days. He didn't remember coming back from the office, but he figured he must have passed out in the chair by her bed.

"You gave us a scare," she said, when she realized he was awake.

"What?" Hank asked. He was still groggy, but he was slowly realizing that their positions had been reversed. Instead of him being in the chair, Blanche was the one sitting up, while he was lying in a bed. "What happened?"

"You passed out last night. Dr. Howard had trouble getting you back into her car. You've been admitted to the hospital, so you're going to be here until they say you can go. There's nowhere to go right now, anyway, though."

"What about my phone?" he asked, as the events of the night before slowly returned to his mind. "Did we find it?"

"Huey did. It was out behind the building, in the dumpster. If you had waited a few more hours to look for it, it would have been on its way to the dump. Danielle is working her magic on it right now. She's hoping she can figure out what they did with it."

"They?" Hank asked.

"The gunwoman. It's obvious she took it out of the office. If she was able to get into it, like you were thinking, she could have copied the contact information. Danielle thinks she can figure out what was accessed."

"I don't think I can figure it out. I know I can," Danielle said. She was sitting in the other chair in the room, by the bed that she had been occupying the night before. That bed was now occupied by someone else, someone other than the HPS agents that should have been in there. "They pulled the information on everyone. It was all accessed yesterday, after the gunwoman got away. I'm sending out a mass text message to everyone on the list that their information has been exposed and they should go to ground. I'm betting this isn't exactly going to endear the demons to us anytime soon."

"Well, at least we warned them about it," Blanche said. "We could have just let them all be killed and deal with the aftermath. It would certainly make our jobs easier."

"Except we wouldn't have jobs after that," Danielle said.

"There are other issues under our purview--"

"I mean, we'd all be fired for letting the information out in the first place. Has anyone ever looked into the legality of making such a database?"

"It's not a database, it's a contacts list," Hank said. "If I maintained the list better, and had it available to more people, then, yes, there might be something to worry about. Those demons all gave me their contact information of their own free will. It was there to help me help them better, not to keep tabs on them all."

"Though we probably should have been doing that," Blanche said. "By the way, when this all settles down, I'd like a copy of that list."

"That list, sure," Hank teased. "It'll probably be obsolete by then."

"Doesn't Jack think you have all of that memorized?" Danielle asked.

"Yea, and I let him. I never trusted that guy. Why would I let on that I'm not as smart as he thinks I am?"

"We still don't know what actually happened to him," Blanche said. "He could just as easily be a prisoner of the gunwoman at this point."

"Yea, and aliens abducted the second plane," Hank said, sarcastically. The disappearance of the second plane had always been a mystery, to which many conspiracy theories had been attributed. None were more crazy than that aliens did it. "Why would the gunwoman have broken him out of the cell only to keep him prisoner? No. Either he broke out on his own during the conflict and is avoiding us so we don't put him in the prison, or he's a Remember Sami co-conspirator trojan horse spy type person that we should have locked up ages ago. He never had any right being a field agent, or an agent at all. He should have been in prison these past twelve years."

"Except all the evidence we had on him was destroyed during... the incident," Danielle said. She eyed the supposedly sleeping roommate as she lowered her voice. Even with the HPS being an overt agency, the incident, and everything that was discovered during it, were still classified. Finding out that there are demons and they have invaded caused enough of a panic already without that bombshell getting out. "Speaking of which..."

"I never trusted Jack about a lot of things, but he's not stupid enough to blab about the incident," Hank said. "Not even to get himself away from the gunwoman. He knows that no good can come from that."

"Hank, he's an arsonist. What good comes from that?" Blanche asked. "I mean, yes, I'm not as... overly critical of him as you are. But you seem a little conflicted on what he would and wouldn't do at this point. You locked him in a cell because his long-lost aunt is a member of a hate group that has a terrorist arm, not that she is one of the terrorists."

"And you didn't even arrest the long-lost aunt," Danielle added.

"Alright, alright, alright. Maybe I was a little harsh with him--"

"Maybe?" Blanche asked.

"Yes, maybe, Ms. leaving our daughter alone on her birthday over this group."

"Harsh," Danielle said.

"Sorry."

"No, you're right. They're dangerous. Which is why you should have arrested the aunt, not the idiot. Jack has been by your side almost every waking hour since this whole thing started. Do you really think he's part of this hate group?"

"Emphasis on almost," Hank said. "He could very well be going to midnight meetings when our work doesn't run that late. I know he talks about going out to clubs and parties. Why couldn't a few of those parties be hate group rallies?"

"Has he ever been less than kind to any of the demons that you dealt with?"

"Well, no, not really. But the guy does disappear into the crowd half the time, as to not have to deal with them."

"That's him not wanting to do work, not him avoiding demons," Blanche said.

"Well, the whole issue is moot at this point anyway," Hank said. "Whether or not he was involved with Remember Sami, we're going to have to track him down at some point."

"I've already sent out a BOLO for him," Danielle said. "If he shows up anywhere, we'll hear about it. In the meantime, we--" She broke off when the phone in her hands sent out a ringtone. Hank was pretty sure that the phone was his, but that didn't seem to stop her from looking down at it and checking whatever message it was that came in. He wasn't too concerned about it, though. The only people that would contact him either worked for HPS, worked at the school, or was related to him. However, this time, it was none of them. Danielle let out a little squeal of delight as she jumped up to her feet. The woman in the other bed woke up, glaring at her before rolling onto her side and pulling her pillow over her head.

"What was that about?" Hank asked. He placed his hands over his ears, pretending that her squeal had hurt him as far away as he was.

"You'll never guess who's in the hospital right now," she said, her voice filled with glee.

"Well, given your delight, I'm guessing someone we hate got injured," Hank said. "Who do we all hate?"

"No," she said. "No one got hurt. It's a good thing. Lynnette is having her baby."

"Oh," Hank said. "Did you still want me to guess?"

"And she's here?" Blanche asked.

"Down in the maternity ward. Her husband just texted... well, it looks like he texted the entire team. My phone didn't seem to get it yet, though."

"I turned mine off to save the battery," Blanche said. "Those smartphones run down their batteries way faster than they should. I miss my old flip phone that I had to charge like once a week at most."

"Except the flip phone didn't check your email, track your life signs, and do about a million other things you use on a daily basis," Hank said. "This phone is more powerful, and with great power comes needing to charge it more often."

"Oh, ha ha," Blanche said.

"Will you two stop flirting?" Danielle asked. "Why don't we go down to the maternity ward and see Lynnette. Maybe we can see the baby before anyone else. Wouldn't that be nice? A nice distraction from getting our asses handed to us like we did."

"That would be nice," Blanche said.

"Well, okay," Hank said. "But only because I want to ask Lynnette when she's coming back to work. We're going to need all hands on deck after this."

"You'll do nothing of the sort," Blanche scolded. "She's going to have her full maternity leave without being badgered about coming back to work."

"Can I at least tell her about all the fun she's missing?"

"Well... It might help things to keep her informed about what's going on, for when she does come back."

"If she comes back," Danielle said. "If I were her, and I found out about everything that's been going on lately, I might just stay home with the baby."

"And then you'd be stuck filling in for her for the rest of the year," Hank pointed out.

"Right. Maybe we don't tell her anything," she said.

Chapter Twenty-Nine
Lynnette's Baby

The nurses insisted that Hank take a wheelchair as they all went down to the maternity ward on the second floor. He felt stupid, stuck in the hospital gown as Blanche pushed him through the place. The doctor hadn't been by to check on him yet, and they were waiting on his word before they discharged him. In the meantime, he was still a patient.

None of them had met Bob, Lynnette's husband, before. No one had even known she was seeing someone. The whole thing seemed rather rushed back in March. With the timing of everything, it was obvious that she had been pregnant before the wedding. None of them had been invited, though they were all so busy with getting the demons assimilated into society that they wouldn't have been able to go if they had been. Lynnette had enough trouble getting off work for it, and Herb refused to grant her any time off for the honeymoon. Then, back in the beginning of August, complications with the baby had her stuck on bed rest, and Herb had no choice but to allow for an early maternity leave. Hank had been dreading a very different message from the missing team member, worried that those complications would only get worse. He couldn't even imagine that kind of loss, not while he had his own perfect little angel in Marissa.

Three men were pacing back and forth in the waiting room. Any one of them could have been Bob. As they came in, two of them looked over at the group, expectantly, while the other was just rounding another pass. Dr. Howard and

Dr. Davidson had beaten them into the waiting area and had staked out the corner chairs, with Dr. Howard's back to the wall and Dr. Davidson's towards the nurse's station. Blanche rolled Hank over to the space between them and Danielle sat on the other side of Dr. Howard from him.

"Any news?" Danielle asked.

"Nothing yet," Dr. Howard said. She casually placed her hand on Danielle's leg, supportively, before balling them both together in her lap.

"Which one of them is him?" Hank whispered, as he eyed the three men.

"The one in the middle, I think," Dr. Davidson said, pointing at the taller of the three. The man looked a little familiar to Hank, unsettlingly so, given how secretive Lynnette had been about him. He was certain that he hadn't seen so much as a wedding photo of the two of them together.

"Bob?" Blanche called out, taking a more direct approach than Hank would have. The one in the middle looked over towards her, but didn't halt in his pacing in the slightest. The other two stopped for a moment, just long enough to look between them, before resuming their wearing out of the floor. The delay had synced the three of them up perfectly.

An old man in a white lab coat and a clipboard came into the waiting room. All eyes went to him, and the three men stopped in mid stride. "Drew?" the doctor called out, reading it off the clipboard. The man closest to the group started to look relieved, already celebrating his new arrival as he headed off with the doctor. The other two shook their heads as they resumed their pacing.

"It's like they're robots," Hank said, as he watched the men walk.

"Don't you remember your own daughter's birth?" Dr. Howard asked.

"He wasn't there," Blanche said. "He was in Papua New Guinea, chasing down rumors of an artifact."

"The Marissa Gem," Hank said. "Blanche was kind enough to name our daughter after it so that I would always be reminded of what I missed out on."

"And, yet, you guys never thought to have another one?" Danielle asked.

"We thought about giving Marissa a little brother at one point. But, well, plans change," Blanche said.

Another man came out, similarly dressed as the first doctor, though he was much younger. He wasn't holding a clipboard. His face wasn't as hopeful as the man before. Hank's stomach plummeted when he saw him, as if he knew what was to come. The doctor walked straight over to the man furthest from the group. He talked in a hushed voice, but when the man cried out in pain, they all knew it was bad news. The doctor pulled more than led the man down the hall.

As they left, they passed a woman with a clipboard. Her smile faded only slightly to the sounds of the man's loss. She watched the two of them walk past her, before she continued into the waiting room. She didn't look at the clipboard before heading straight over to Bob.

"Hey, Bob," she said, her voice low, but loud enough for them all to hear. "Your wife did well, and she's sleeping comfortably. There were some complications with the birth, but your son should be fine. We have him in the NICU right now, while we do some tests. I'm afraid there's... well..." She looked over to the group, who were all looking on at the two of them, obviously listening. "Are these friends of yours?" she asked.

"Uh, they're Lynnette's coworkers," Bob said. Obviously, he knew more about them than they did about him. "What's wrong with my son?"

"Nothing's wrong... exactly. These kinds of births are new to us, and we're mostly just being cautious right now. As

I said to the two of you when I recommended bed rest, it is better safe than sorry. There's nothing to worry about." She sounded more like she was trying to talk him down from anger than that she was comforting him. "You can come see him, if you'd like? Would they want to join you? The NICU is a bit small, but they can see him through the window."

"Uh... sure, I guess," Bob said, eyeing the group. "They'll be finding out soon enough, I imagine." He eyed the group again before following the doctor down the hall.

"Shall we tag along?" Dr. Howard asked.

"Let's give them a bit of a lead," Danielle suggested. "Give them time to be alone together."

"What kind of births were they talking about?" Hank asked. He gave Bob and the doctor enough of a lead so that they weren't too close. Then, he started to wheel himself down the hall. The others fell into step next to him.

"Who knows," Blanche said, as she started pushing his wheelchair again. "Maybe some kind of new fertility regiment?"

"No, that's not it," Danielle said. "I think I know what's going on, but..."

"But, what?" Hank asked, but she just shook her head. "Wait, why would it be a new fertility regiment? The timing would be all wrong for that. I mean, getting pregnant, then getting married, all within a span of a month or so, and... No, the timing is all wrong."

"The timing would have been perfect," Danielle corrected. "Just not for a fertility regiment."

The doctor turned into one of the rooms on the left, with Bob following on her heels. There was a window carved into the wall before the door. The group stopped there, looking in on the room within. There were several crying babies, all in lines. Many of them were in plastic boxes, the kinds with holes in the side to allow the parents and doctors to reach into them. A few were in regular plastic baby cribs, the kinds they always showed in movies. Bob was standing next to one of the latter, just a couple of rows back from the front of the room. The baby inside the crib was screaming his head off. His tiny hand reached out to his father, taking Bob's finger in it. The doctor picked up the baby, gently putting him in Bob's arms. She took the time to painstakingly correct the placement of his hands to best cradle the little bundle within them, before heading off to do other doctoring stuff.

Bob came over to the window, nodding at the group. His hands were occupied with the fragile package within them. His smile was wide, encompassing his entire face as he gazed down at his son. The boy in his hands continued to cry, even held as tenderly as he was by the man that was his father. The baby turned his face away from Bob. His eyes opened up as if purposefully looking at the group of agents on the other side of the glass. His eyes flashed yellow before turning to the brown of his mother.

"Holy shit," Blanche said. Her hand automatically went to her side, to where her gun would normally have been.

"What the hell?" Dr. Howard asked.

"Yea, I was afraid of that," Danielle said.

"What... is it?" Hank asked.

"It's a cambion," Dr. Davidson said. "Half human, half demon. I guess it would make sense, at least a little."

"But one of us?" Blanche asked. "One of the HPS having one of... them."

"Oh, am I still on the team?" Lynnette asked. She was in a wheelchair coming up the hall to their right, from further down the maternity hallway. "I'm not fired already for this?"

"No, of course not," Hank said. "I mean, are you even planning to come back?"

"I was... but..."

"No, you're coming back," Danielle insisted. "You're not leaving me with both your work and mine."

"Don't you have temps coming in?" she asked.

"They're all worthless."

"You... married one of them?" Blanche asked. Her voice was a more lethal venom than that of any spider in the world.

"Twice, actually," she said. "Bob was my husband, about twelve years ago, before I joined the HPS. Naturally, when I saw him during the interviews... well, I never did get over his death. And then, it was like some miracle. He had returned to me. I'm sorry I didn't tell you guys sooner. But, well, I hope you can understand why I didn't."

Hank looked between Lynnette and Bob, who was still staring down at his son. She was looking over at them too, torn between wanting to join them and not wanting to disturb the moment they seemed to be having. Hank tried to see the demon in the man, tried to see the evil villain that so many had wanted them to be, insisted that they were. Even his own wife seemed so opposed to these people. Yet, to him, they seemed as human as anyone else. He tried to remember what it was like the first time that he held his daughter, the first time he had seen her, almost a week after she had been born. Had he seemed any more captivated by her than Bob was of his son?

"So, I'm not fired?" Lynnette asked.

"No, of course not," Hank said.

"Not yet," Blanche said.

"We'll have to confer with Herb about it," Danielle said. "I don't think it should be a problem though. It's not like you're a field agent." A bitterness seemed to creep into her voice at the thought.

"Oh, come now," Hank said. "You're not still wanting to be a field agent after yesterday, are you?"

"What happened yesterday?" Lynnette asked. "You're not having fun without me, are you? Wait, why is Hank in a wheelchair? What happened?"

"It's best that you don't know until you're ready to come back to work," Danielle said. "Then you can decide if you even want to come back."

"It's not like I have much of a choice in that," she said. "Bob has been having trouble finding work, as most of the demons have. It helps that he didn't have to take someone's identity, that he still looks like his old self. But, if anyone looks him up, they'll know that he died twelve years ago."

"What did he die of?" Hank asked. Blanche whacked him lightly upon his head, obviously thinking the question rude.

"He was having an affair," Lynnette said, matter-of-factly. "She was married. The husband came back, killed them both. I forgave him long ago, just wanting him back. Who was I to turn my back on a miracle like that?"

"It's not a miracle," Blanche said. "Nothing about them is miraculous."

"Blanche, what is a miracle but something that you can't explain?"

"Isn't that also the definition of magic?" Dr. Howard asked. "Technology that's significantly beyond what you can understand?"

"No, no, no. It's that technology that's significantly beyond what you can understand is indistinguishable from magic," Dr. Davidson said. "Magic is... well... magic." She eyed the hallway to make sure no one was overhearing their conversation, though there was no one in sight besides the babies in the NICU, the doctor, and Bob. The babies weren't likely to tell anyone, and Bob already knew more of the mysteries of magic than the group did. The doctor seemed preoccupied with the other babies in the room, though it was impossible to tell just how much of their discussion that she was hearing. "Maybe not a good idea to discuss it here, though," she said.

"It's not important," Lynnette said. "They're my miracle." She gazed over at her husband and child, and a familiar look flitted across her face. Hank knew that look; he had seen it enough on his own face to know what it meant.

She was in love with her little family, and she'd sooner leave the HPS than betray them.

"It's not an issue," Hank said. "At least not yet. It might be at one point, and we'll deal with it if, and when, it is. In the meantime, enjoy your time with your son. We'll need you at work sooner than you'd like to return."

"Thanks," she said, her eyes not leaving her family as she said it. "Now, if you'll excuse me. Thank you all for coming."

"I don't know what you're thinking, but that is going to be a problem," Blanche said, once Lynnette was off with Bob and their newborn son. "Her loyalties are divided, now."

"No, they're not," Hank said.

"What? You think she'd turn on her son's father, on her son, if it came to that?"

"You mistake me, Blanche. Her loyalties aren't divided because they're with her family, just as mine are with you and Marissa. But, as long as our mission doesn't come in conflict with them, we can still trust her. As long as we remember that not all demons are the same, it won't be an issue."

"Let's give them some space," Danielle said.

"Aw," Dr. Howard said, disappointed.

"But, it's a cambion," Dr. Davidson said. "The first cambion."

"Only the first one you've seen," Danielle said. "The doctor said 'births like these', meaning it's not the first one she's seen. It won't be the last, either. There will be a paper on it at some point and you can read up on it then."

"A paper that will only spawn mass hysteria," Blanche said. She was looking on the bright side of things, as always. "How many people were only begrudging their presence here because they thought it a limited thing? Now they're settling down, putting down roots, having children. This isn't going to end well."

"What does?" Hank asked. "If it ends, it's usually for a reason."

"And, on that uplifting note, perhaps it would be a good idea to get you discharged," Dr. Howard said. She still kept looking backwards, back at the cambion and his parents. It seemed almost like she wanted to dissect the baby or something. But Hank knew that wouldn't be the case. Dr. Howard wasn't likely to kill the baby just to settle her own curiosity.

"Yes, let's," Hank said. "I shouldn't have been checked in to begin with."

"Says the man that passed out last night," Blanche said. "Personally, I'd feel better if you stayed here another night."

"I've wasted enough time lying on my back. We need to get back to the case. Back to looking for Jack and the gunwoman. Back to trying to figure out who killed Jared."

"You nearly got yourself killed over that stupid case several times over already. Do you really think it's such a great idea to go back at it so soon after the latest one?"

"No," Hank said. "But if it were me that was killed, would you want the person investigating my murder to take a day off because he got hit in the head a couple times?"

"Yes," Blanche said. "So that I can track the man down myself and kill him... slowly."

"Well... Okay, but Jared's boyfriend didn't seem the type."

Chapter Thirty
Discharged

The doctor had already done several scans while Hank was out of it. When they met with him again, after seeing Lynnette's new family, he said that the scans all looked fine and that Hank just needed to take it easy for a few days. Hank had his discharge papers together soon after. The whole group was heading towards the front door of the hospital, making their way around the huge atrium.

"Well, that was a nice base of operations while it lasted," Danielle said. "Now where are we going? We can't go back to the office."

"We could just work from home," Dr. Howard suggested. "We have a working lab at our apartment, though not enough space for the rest of you. Hank and Blanche have a decent enough sized home office for their needs. That just leaves you, Danielle."

"And Jenkins," Blanche added. "But, as soon as he's back, we're going back out into the field to track down these Remember Sami lunatics. We'll probably find the gunwoman in the process. It's almost assured that she's one of them."

"That works for tomorrow, but what about the rest of today?" Hank asked. "It's only..." He looked at his wrist again, trying to see the time on his fitness band, before remembering that it had been taken from him.

"Noon," Blanche supplied, reading it off her own band.

"Right. We have half the day still. We should at least try to track these people down while we can. I hate to think that they were getting further away from us this entire time while we've been sitting on our collective asses."

"We haven't just been sitting on our asses. We've been healing, and regrouping," Blanche said. "The last thing we needed to do was go off all half-cocked when we were hit so hard. Now that we're healed up, we can get started."

"Yea, but how?" Danielle asked. "The trails would be cold by now, right?"

"Not necessarily," Blanche said. "We need to get you back on the network, tracking these people."

"You should focus on Jack and the gunwoman," Hank said. "We have enough surveillance on the office and the building to get a decent start from there. I'd at least like proof that they were working together, that they left together. It would be a good place to start."

"I'll drive you all over to the office so you guys can pick up your cars," Dr. Howard said.

"I take the bus," Danielle said. "Mind if you drive me home?"

"Sure, but Hank's car is still at the office."

"Because you drove me back to the hospital," Hank said.

"You were unconscious for eight hours," she said. "Did you want me to just leave you there?"

"Okay, maybe not," he admitted. "Anyway, we go back for the crown vic. Danielle goes home and gets on the network. The two of you head home in case we need more sciencing. The two of us can get a jump on the investigation. It'll be a nice change of pace to work beside my wife for a little bit. Now, how much longer do I have to be in this stupid wheelchair?"

"It's just until we get out the door," Blanche said, patting his shoulder. "We're almost there. Can you wait like, what, twenty seconds?"

She pointed towards the door ahead of them, which was only a few paces away. Hank felt like jumping to his feet and running the rest of the way, worried that something else would keep them there longer than he would have liked. Blanche had been rolling him along slowly the entire time, and the group hung back for the conversation. They, too, seemed overly eager to get back out there.

In his urgency, he almost missed the large collection of people clustered around the atrium. They all looked frightened and worried, but none of them seemed injured. Hank figured that these were the loved ones and friends of injured people entering the other side of the building, since they were approaching the main entrance rather than the ER. He hadn't spent much time in hospitals. The majority of his knowledge of them came from television, back when he had the time for such frivolous things. But he had an odd feeling that there were more people in there than usual. Something in his gut was telling him that it was his fault.

As they passed through the automatic doors, a wrath demon and a greed demon were pushing a sloth demon in a wheelbarrow. All three of them were in full demon form, so it was easy to recognize them for their individual sins. But Hank couldn't remember any of them by sight. The sloth demon was asleep. There was a small trail of black blood flowing down his face, though it seemed to have dried already.

The greed demon ran over to Danielle, scooping her up in a big hug. "Thanks for the warning," he said. He gave off a light baying in his agitation. "We were able to get Igor here out in time, with only minor injuries. I hope you folks are off to track these cretins down. I think it's getting rather bad out there, especially for us hellians."

"I just wish the information hadn't gotten out there at all," Hank said. "I'm so sorry about that."

The wrath demon glared down at him from his domineering 7-foot height. His horns flared up in anger, glowing a low red as if bathed in hellfire. There wasn't enough magic in the area for them to light up properly. His eyes flared their telltale yellow. "You have nothing to apologize for," he practically shouted, making Hank almost jump out of his skin. "It's those damn haters. You having that information saved enough of us already. Just don't let it happen again."

"Right," Hank said, nodding.

The two of them nodded at the group before continuing to head inside. The attendant behind the desk pointed them over to the long hallway that led through the hospital to the ER. Igor slept through the entire exchange, and probably would until long after he was discharged. Sloth demons didn't look like much of anything, a wasted down form of their former selves. It wasn't clear just what role they had had in the wars with Heaven. None of them had stayed awake long enough in the interviews to answer.

The parking lot was packed, with both cars and people. The people were in both human and hellian form. Most of them were hurrying towards the other entrance. Some were sporting injuries while others just looked panicked. Hank's stomach lurched down at the sight. His own minor injuries paled in comparison to the collage in front of him. Most ignored the group as they crossed to Dr. Howard's car, though a few of them darted looks at them that ranged from hatred to gratefulness. It seemed strange that so many of them would have been attacked in such a short amount of time. It wasn't clear just how many of the large congregation that made up Remember Sami were involved in the confrontations. They were easily organized enough to take out the entire list in under a day, if their numbers were large enough.

"We need to do something about all of this," Dr. Davidson said, as they all watched the demons and their humans head into the hospital.

"That's the idea," Blanche said. She rolled the wheelchair over to the car; Hank had forgotten his desire to leave it in light of the march of demons. "We get out there, hunt them down, and stop them."

"Are you so sure you'd want them to stop?" Hank asked. "You seemed to be in the kill them all camp earlier."

"Killing is bad, no matter who's doing the killing or who's doing the dying," she said. "I'm in the lock them all up camp. But, that's why there are two field teams. You handle all the good ones that only want to plant flowers and make the world colorful. I'll handle the rest."

"No, you handle the ones that want to destroy the world, kill the humans, or rob them blind. I'll handle the rest."

"Yea, I guess it's more even that way."

"The workload is, maybe."

"You guys coming?" Dr. Howard called out from the driver's seat. Dr. Davidson was already in the passenger seat, with Danielle slumped in the back behind her.

"What are we supposed to do with the wheelchair?" Hank asked, finally getting out of it. He looked around the parking lot for some place to stick it, half expecting a shopping cart stall like the ones at grocery stores. He couldn't find any. Instead, he stuck it in the yellow marked section next to where Dr. Howard's car was parked. He figured someone would find it or one of the demons could use it to get inside.

"Where are we even going to start in the investigation?" Blanche asked, as Hank climbed in next to her. "Have we got anything to go on?"

"When was that interview with the leader of the group? What was his name again?"

"Rudolph Judd," Danielle said. "He was busy all day today, so I got the appointment for after six tonight. Thankfully we didn't miss it with all the shooting yesterday."

"Yea, that works," Blanche said. "It will give us some time to do research on him and his companies. I don't want to go into this thing cold. We don't know yet just how involved he is in the terrorist arm of their group. With their numbers out in full force, we need to take out their leadership, make a major arrest in order to stop their activities."

"What about in the meantime?" Hank asked. "A lot of people are going to be injured, even killed. What are we doing about it?"

"A lot of demons, you mean," she said. "There's nothing we can do. Not without knowing exactly who it is that's doing it. We'll be running around chasing our tails half the time, even with the surveillance network up in full force. And we only have the one analyst, the one field team. Let the local police handle it for now."

"But are they?" he asked. "Are they handling it? Or are they just sitting on their laurels, expecting us to. The victims are demons; that's our jurisdiction. It should be us, but we just don't have the people to handle it."

"We can coordinate with the local PDs," Danielle said. "If Huey and Dewey aren't busy, I could set them up with access and we could run the surveillance network for the police. That way, we're not the ones sitting on our laurels, either."

"That's fine," Hank said, nodding. "Just make sure they know that we need the help, and that they're going to get all the credit on coming to our rescue on this one. Maybe establish a joint task force, or whatever could actually be set up in time to stop these people. I don't like leaving it to the civilians, but it's not like we have much of a choice."

"And it's humans they're up against, not demons," Dr. Howard said. "It might even help the human demon relations for them to see the human police departments coming to their help."

"Alright, you guys work all that out with them," Hank said. "Blanche and I will focus on researching this Judd guy."

"Well, I could just do that myself," Blanche said. "Maybe you could help the police in the field, be the token agent on the scene, and all that."

"Fine, whatever," Hank said. "You are the senior agent, after all."

"Yes, I am. And don't you forget it. Now, everyone has their assignments. Hank, why don't you start by reaching out to the cop you were talking to yesterday? That'll keep you busy while these three get themselves set up at Huey and Dewey's place."

"He's... probably not the best person to have as a contact with the PD. I think he's still a little peeved with me about taking over Jared's murder investigation. Granted, I don't really have anyone else in mind for the role."

"Exactly. We can't be too choosy right now."

They pulled into the parking lot for the office as she said that. The place was full of cars, from the day staff of all the businesses that were in the building. There didn't seem to be any consideration for the fact that their office had been attacked. No concern in the minds of those other people that worked in the building that they might be next. No one seemed the least bit concerned that demons were being targeted and attacked all over the area. People's lives went on like nothing had changed from a day ago. A week ago. Even a year ago, back before the invasion. Hank envied them; those people untouched, unaffected by this biggest of changes to their world.

Dr. Howard pulled into the same spot she had the night before, right next to the crown vic. Hank was on the wrong side of the car from it, so he had to walk all the way around Dr. Howard's car to get to his. Blanche climbed out right behind him. Dr. Howard stepped out of the driver's seat, leaving the car running, as she went around to the trunk. She popped it open and pulled out Blanche's suitcase, which seemed none the worse for wear from all the excitement. It did, promptly, fall forward onto its front once she let go of it. Hank didn't remember seeing it since he had woken up in the hospital earlier, so he figured they must have snuck it out there while he was unconscious.

"Call us when you get to your apartment," Blanche said, as she pulled the suitcase back up onto its wheels.

"Sure," Dr. Howard said. She slapped the trunk closed, the sound of it booming around the area, seeming much louder than it should have been.

A dog started to howl in the distance, as if in response to the noise. The sound continued much longer than it should have, turning deeper, darker, as the dog gained in confidence. The howl was joined up by several others, all starting up on the same tenor, the same note, echoing their own displeasure to the mix. A chill ran up Hank's spine as he realized that the source of the howls weren't normal dogs.

They weren't even dogs at all.

"Hellhounds," he said. His voice was a harsh whisper, barely audible over the noise as the howls drew nearer.

Chapter Thirty-One
Hellhounds

Hank reached for his gun before remembering that it wasn't in his holster anymore. It had been left behind in the office above, after the shooting. Blanche tossed her bag down on the pavement and started rummaging around inside. She pulled out two guns, but kept both of them for herself.

"How?" she asked, simply.

"Did someone break into the kennel?" Dr. Howard asked.

"Why would anyone do that?" Hank asked. "And how? It's at the prison. If someone broke into the prison, it's likely that they let out more than just a few hellhounds."

"Could we have missed a few?" Blanche asked. "Maybe more had come over since the mass migration?"

"Unless the demons lied about the twenty that they purposefully brought over with them, there weren't any left in the wild after the migration. More could have come over since, I guess, but wouldn't we have heard about another portal opening?"

"Maybe not. They had been opening all over the place for centuries, millennia, ever since there was a hell to open them from. It was just that the mass migration was the only time that anyone had seen it, had documented it. And it was the only time that it happened on such a large scale. Even with so many demons on Earth now, why couldn't more still be back there? Why couldn't there have been another portal opened since? It could be the twenty escaped from the kennel, or it could be fifty, fresh from Hell."

"It was hard enough getting twenty into the kennels, with demon help," Hank said. "I don't want to have to deal with another fifty. Not now. Not today. Frankly, not ever."

"Well, they're coming this way," she said. "We're going to have to deal with them."

"I'm getting the geek squad out of here," Dr. Howard said. She was staring all around the parking lot, as if the hellhounds had already gotten to them. Her eyes were as large as saucers as she ran back to the driver's side door.

"Wait," Hank said. He grabbed onto the door, keeping her from closing it on him. "Any chance you guys have a spare gun in there?"

"Forget the guns, Hank," Blanche said. "Just get in the crown vic and follow them out of here before these things get here."

"I'm not going to leave you to fight off twenty or so hellhounds."

"It might not be all of them. Maybe it's just one or two." Despite her words, the echoing howls of the approaching horde seemed to tell of a larger number than either had ever seen at one time.

"No guns," Dr. Howard said. "Sorry." She kept trying to pull the door from his hand, but Hank wasn't ready to give up the fight just yet.

"What about the kill bot?" he asked.

"What?"

"The kill bot. Can you get it out of the office and down to us before they get here?"

"I don't know how," she said. "It's locked up in the office. It can't get out the front door."

"What about the back door?"

"It runs on wheels. It's as likely to make it down the stairs as it would to survive falling out the window."

"We can try," Dr. Davidson said, leaning forward to see Hank around Dr. Howard. "But we can't try it here. We need to get to the apartment. There's a spare tablet there, and we can access it through the office wifi. Just... let us get out of here before we're nothing but sitting ducks in a can."

"Fine," Hank said. He slammed the door closed. Both he and Blanche backed away from the car, giving them free reign of the parking lot as they sped out of there. "Where do you think they're coming from?" he asked Blanche, once they were alone.

"They hunt in packs like wolves," she said. "Some of them will come at us from straight ahead, while the others swing around and hit us from the sides."

"Let's get inside the building, use the doors for a bottleneck and keep the safety of the building at our backs."

"No, we're not going to do that. If they come at us, let them. If they don't, we're going to need to give chase. No one else is going to die today because of our inability to keep the hellhounds in line."

She didn't say that they weren't going to die. Hank already knew that the possibility was there. He knew that she would be alright with that, as long as no one else, no one besides them, died from their failure. With Marissa safe and sound, over 2000 miles away, they were assured of her safety. She'd be taken care of by people whose job wasn't to go after those too strong and powerful for the normal police to handle, even if they both fell that day.

Loud growls joined in the howling as the first of the group came closer. They were invariably heading in the direction of the office, of the two HPS agents standing out in the open. It was like their preternatural senses were honed in on those that had locked them up. The prison was an hour's drive out of the city, but the hellhounds could have covered that same distance in minutes. Their strong, muscular forms were more powerful than any animal on the planet, even without the assistance of magic.

With it, they were downright deadly, able to destroy a target just by looking at it. Hank mourned for whomever was stupid enough to have set them loose. There was a reason why the pack was kept in a section of the prison removed from the rest of the complex. They were fed through an old laundry shoot so that none would need to enter the room. The walls were reinforced by both steel and magic, forged into a barrier stronger than anything either world could have created alone. And, yet, someone had just let them out.

"They're coming," Hank said, though the sounds would have told her of that already.

"They're here," she corrected, pointing off into the distance.

The first of them were walking down the middle of the street. Those few cars that were driving on the road swerved to avoid running over them, though the three that were in this group leapt and climbed over them as if they were stationary. They had already stopped their mad dash across the countryside, a sprint faster than a cheetah that they could keep up indefinitely. Even as far off as they were, their eyes were locked on the two agents. Their intended targets. Their intended lunch.

The one in the middle, the one leading the charge, was the alpha. It was a three-headed cerberus with a fiery red pelt. When charged with magic, the fire was real, flaring out from its core without it needing to will it so. Hellfire was like that. The other two, flanking him on either side, were smaller than the cerberus, having only one head each. Their fur was red as well, as all hellhounds were, but not as lively. As they approached the parking lot, Hank could make out stretches of charcoal black mixed in with the crimson shades. There were stories told by the demons of hounds that bathed in the blood of their victims in an attempt to hide that blackness, as it was a sign of their advancing age.

Blanche aimed at the central head of the cerberus, but she held her fire, waiting for their approach. Hank searched the rest of the area, looking for the rest of the pack that was undoubtedly approaching them. He even looked above his head, up towards the roof of the building behind them. He half expected the rest of the pack to be standing up there, salivating at the sight of the two trapped agents, their drool dangling down at them the entire way. As he gazed back there, he counted up the five stories to where the office was housed. He held his hand up to the window, trying to will his gun to him. He was unsurprised when nothing happened.

Three bullets fired from Blanche's gun. The sound of the gunshots echoed around the area, but couldn't drown out the sound of the growls. The two hounds flanking the alpha went down. Their momentum carried them forward, forcing their heads into the pavement. The third bullet hit the alpha's center head, killing that one. But the other two heads remained aloft and the alpha himself continued forward. He put on a renewed burst of speed, crossing the distance between the entrance to the parking lot and them in the blink of an eye, a distance easily spanning a couple hundred feet. Hank moved to push Blanche out of the way of its charge, to block harm from her if he could. But the cerberus was already on her, knocking her to the ground. One of its gaping maws clamped down on her hand, the entirety of the gun it was holding stuck within.

Blanche screamed, in pain, in fury, as she forced her finger to pull the trigger again. Hank just stood there, at a loss, incapable of helping her, unwilling to leave her to her fate. As the gun went off again, the head that it was in seemed to explode, spreading blood and brain matter everywhere, covering the two agents. The force of the bullet knocked the cerberus back a step, forcing him off Blanche. But, still, it wasn't enough to kill it. It's one remaining head kept it aloft, kept it alive, or whatever it was that hellhounds were. It stumbled back a step, eyeing the two agents dangerously, as if it had suddenly found a new respect for them. As it walked away, it seemed to stumble on every third step, lopsided by the loss of the other two heads. Both of the dead heads still dangled in front of it, hanging from the neck that connected the three of them together.

"Are you alright?" Hank asked.

He offered his hand to her, trying to help her to her feet. She refused it, batting it away with the gun that had blown apart the second head. Blood covered it and the hand that held it, though Hank wasn't sure how much of that had belonged to the cerberus. Thankfully, unlike their masters, the blood of hellhounds wasn't dangerously acidic. Without getting up from the ground, she aimed her other gun at the wounded creature. Another bullet sounded, causing a ringing to start in Hank's left ear, the one closest to the gun. The cerberus jumped away, avoiding the bullet, before running off again. It headed off back down the road in the same direction that it had come from.

"Come on," Hank said, once again offering to help her up. This time, the gun slid out of her injured hand, falling to the ground with a clatter, as she offered it to him. He pulled her to her feet, gripping tightly on the offered hand so that she didn't slip from him. Her eyes were on the street, waiting for the cerberus's return. Hank, however, tried to gage the damage to her hand, hoping that she would still be able to fire with it. Even with two guns, she was still a better shot than he was. "Can you still shoot?"

"It's fine," she insisted. "I'm fine. It's going to come back."

"I know," he said. "This time it'll come with more than just two of them." Another set of howls confirmed his pessimism. The volume of the howls only seemed to grow as the battle dragged on. "If the prison was breached, why didn't the guards contact us? They should have gotten word to us. We might have been able to help."

"We were in no position to help them," she said. "And a proper attack on the prison would have been over before we could even get there."

"Okay, but at least then we would have been able to intercept the pack while they were still in the woods. Who knows how many people they hurt on their way here?"

"We'll worry about that later. The next wave is coming."

The next wave wasn't a wave. Hank tried to focus on counting the heads as they came into view, except that there were two more cerberuses in the pack. These were smaller than the alpha, each only having two heads instead of three. Though with two of the alpha's heads dead, they now had more than him. Hank wondered briefly if that would mean one of them would challenge him, but he hated the thought of them doing that. Because, if they did, it would probably mean that he had been eaten by the challenger.

"It's the whole pack," he said. His voice was barely a whisper, barely loud enough for himself to hear over the ringing in his ear.

"If you survive this, tell Marissa I loved her."

"If I survive this, you're going to be there with me. No way would I be able to survive that without you by my side." He felt the slightest twinge of gratitude that, if they fell that day, they would do so together.

The pack halted at the entrance to the parking lot. The alpha, front and center once more, glared at them with his good head. Two smaller groups, each spearheaded by one of the cerberuses, flitted off to either side. They were heading off around the edge of the parking lot to flank the two agents and attack them from behind. If the entire pack came at them from the front, they wouldn't need the maneuver. The two of them would be overwhelmed just by sheer numbers.

Blanche picked up the dropped gun. Her aim wavered, unsure where to strike first. Any bullet fired would no doubt signal the entire pack to charge, closing the distance with their preternatural speed. The first few bullets would need to make all the difference in the fight, for they may very well be their last. The pack leader would have been the obvious choice, finishing off the last head. But with it dodging her last bullet, it could just as easily do it again. The bullet would go wide, and probably miss the pack entirely. The pack continued to line up in a single row, showing off their numbers as if they didn't have a care in the world.

"Any thoughts?" Blanche asked, not looking behind her to her husband.

"Drain the clips into them," he said. "No sense in trying to bring the bullets with us."

Hank covered his ears as Blanche started firing. The bullets sailed through the gap between the agents and the pack of hounds. Although Hank knew that Blanche's aim was impeccable, she only managed to hit four of the group, killing each. The rest leapt away, dodging the bullets quite literally, before jumping forward and racing towards them. The bullets that missed went off into the distance, as there were no longer hellhounds behind them to catch those. The alpha seemed to laugh as he dodged two of the bullets meant for him, and a third that was intended for a hound behind him. That hound, the intended target, took the full force of the bullet right in its eye. It was thrown back, knocking into another hellhound and tripping it up. However, the tripped hellhound seemed to avoid taking another bullet just because it had been tripped.

Blanche pulled on empty in both of the guns, and tossed them aside, pulling her hands into fists in front of her. The entire remainder of the pack seemed to start laughing, as if they were more hyena than hound. Hank took his hands from his ears, standing next to his wife in a similar position. He tried to get used to the idea that he might not make it out of there. The pack looked almost hungry as they stalked their intended victims. They instilled a sense of dread in Hank that he hadn't been expecting, even given his impending death.

More gunfire sounded off, filling the area. Hank looked to his wife, who looked right back at him. Both were equally confused about the source, though it sounded like it was coming from above. As the pack started to close the distance between them, triggering their preternatural speed, the two agents looked up at the building behind them. They looked up towards the roof, hoping that there was someone up there trying to help.

Five floors up, a window shattered outward. Glass rained down towards the two agents, though neither seemed inclined to try to dodge it. Not with the hungry hellhounds so close at hand. The glass shards didn't seem to deter the beasts in the least. However, the next thing to fly free of the building surely would. From five floors below, it only looked like a shining ball of gray, flitting through the sunlight streaming down from above. It tumbled downward, a spinning dervish whirling through the air. Bullets fired in short bursts. The muzzle flashes were the only indication that the ball of metal was the source. It wasn't until the kill bot hit the pavement that Hank realized what it was.

Hank half expected the kill bot to stand back up, to pull itself back together from the shattered remnants that were suddenly splattered across the parking lot. One of the cameras had bounced up into the air when the mass impacted, flipping over and over again before it joined its brethren. Hank stood there, stunned, as he tried to take in the wreck that was surrounding him, and the seven bodies of the hellhounds that had fallen barely five feet from the two of them. It was half of the remaining pack, yet still not enough to save them.

The lone hellhound that remained of the main group stood over the body of the slain alpha. He nuzzled the cerberus with his nose, as if to try to wake him. A bullet had taken the alpha in his neck, right near where the three heads had been attached. It would have been fatal even if Blanche hadn't killed the other two heads already. The lone hound didn't seem to understand this, didn't seem to grasp the fact that it was alone, and that the agents still stood.

"Kill it," Blanche said, heartlessly. She scrambled forward, digging around in what remained of the kill bot.

"What are you doing?" Hank asked. He looked towards the lone hound, but couldn't bring himself to go after it, let alone kill it. He had nothing to kill it with besides his bare hands, unless he could find a sizable chunk of the kill bot to hit it with.

"Those splinter groups are circling around. They'll be back soon, if they're not heading back already. I need to find... Here it is." She pulled one of the mounted guns free from the debris.

"Can you even fire that thing?" Hank asked.

Blanche aimed the gun at the lone hound. It seemed weird, awkward, the gun barrel and firing mechanism without the grip. It had been bolted directly to the chassis of the kill bot with the firing mechanism integrated into the inner workings of the drone. Still, after fumbling around with it for a moment, she managed to fire it, and a single bullet hit the hound. It fell in place, its nose still nuzzling the side of the alpha, as if to continue trying to wake him in its own death.

"Keep your eyes peeled for the others. There's still six more of them out there."

Without looking over to him, she immediately placed her looted weapon on the ground and went back to rummaging around in the debris. Perhaps looking for the other gun, though the one seemed heavy enough alone. Perhaps looking for more ammo, though Hank had no idea how to load it. It was hard for Hank to tell how much ammo the thing would hold, or if it would hold any besides the chambered round. If there weren't any bullets left, the remaining six hounds would roll over them like an oncoming storm, like a tidal wave, like their destruction of the rest of the pack had been nothing.

A bush rustled in the distance, over to the left side of the building. It was the first and only sign of the returning splinter groups. Hank shouted a half-formed warning before the first group of three cleared the brush. They ran straight at them, covering the entire distance, seemingly in the blink of an eye. Yet, still, Blanche had been faster. She responded to the initial rustling rather than Hank's half spoken warning.

Her hand slapped down on the gun by her side, the gun responding instantly. The three hounds pounced at him together, but were quickly knocked back by the bullets intercepting them. The gun fired twice before clicking on empty, but the hounds were kind enough to share one of them. The bullets, so much more powerful than those from Blanche's hand guns, both went right through the heads of the first two hounds. They both entered the third at different locations, one hitting it in the neck while the other hit its heart; either would have been fatal. The three of them landed right at Hank's feet.

"We need that second gun," Hank said, not taking the time to feel relieved by the three dead hellhounds joining the collection at their feet.

A howl rent the air, directing their eyes to the other side of the building, to the other splinter group. The one remaining cerberus howled with both heads as the other two flanked him. This howl, however, didn't sound angry or hungry. If anything, it sounded sad. The cerberus just stared at them across the parking lot, his gaze heading towards them along the lines of cars. The hound on its left moved to attack, but the cerberus snapped at him, causing him to jump away and bump into one of the cars.

With one final glare at the two agents, the cerberus led what was left of the pack away, heading off into the city.

Chapter Thirty-Two
Forget About the Hellhounds

"We should go after them," Hank said, once the shock of their departure wore off.

"Forget about the hellhounds," Blanche said. "We have bigger problems right now. Besides, I'm out of bullets. We'll lose them long before we can get more."

"There are more in the office," Hank said, pointing above them towards the broken window. "I know how to get in around the police seal."

"There's no time," she said. She collected her guns, along with the one mounted gun that she had found in the debris, and headed over to the crown vic. "Are you coming?" she asked.

"Where are we going?" Hank asked. He slowly came back to his senses as the stress and adrenaline faded.

"The hellhounds didn't just get out of the prison on their own, and they weren't the only ones in there. We need to figure out just what happened there. What's left of the pack is going to be licking their wounds. They might even be smart enough to lay low for a couple of generations, regain their old numbers before trying to vie for territory again. We'll have time to hunt the last of them down and finish them off."

"What if they hurt someone on their way out of the city?"

"What if they hurt someone on the way into the city?" she asked. "There were a lot more of them then, and they were a lot more ambitious."

"What about the bodies? It's not exactly like we can call animal control."

Blanche came back over to where Hank was standing, the same place he had been standing as the last of the hellhounds were dispatched. She made a show of taking his phone out of the pocket he usually kept it in. Before using it, she took a moment to admire Hank's background, the picture of the three of them together at the lake. She didn't bother using the contacts, which were overflowing and hard to navigate through. Instead, she dialed the phone manually.

"Hey, Danielle. Thanks for... Yea. Already called them? Okay. We're heading over... Yup. Any word from... Alright. We'll keep in touch. You three stay safe." She hung up the phone, handing it back to him. "She already called animal control. They're on their way. Huey says you owe her a new kill bot."

"I owe her?" he asked.

Blanche reached into another of Hank's pockets, pulling out the keys to the crown vic. "Yup. Mind if I drive?"

"But I thought..."

"I don't have time to stroke your ego today, Hank. Are you coming or not?"

"Fine," Hank said, in a huff, as he reluctantly headed around to the passenger seat. "Where are we going, anyway?"

"Don't you already know?" she asked, as she turned on the car and pulled out of the parking spot. "We're going to the prison. Danielle wasn't able to reach anyone over there." She drove out onto the road, heading in the direction that the hellhounds had come from.

"That doesn't necessarily mean anything. With the magic field, they don't have phones in the prison. It's just in those little guard stations that they can use them."

"And, what? Everyone is using the bathroom at the same time?"

"It could happen," Hank said. "More likely, whatever caused the hellhounds to escape simply burst the airlocks on them or something, exposing those little pockets of science to the raw power of magic. Even if it was just for a moment, it would have been enough to fry all the electronics in there."

"Yes, and we can hope that was all it was. It's much more likely that someone attacked the prison."

"Who would have been stupid enough to attack the prison? And know where it is? And have the equipment and manpower to actually succeed?"

"Remember Sami?" Blanche asked.

For a moment, Hank wasn't sure which question she was answering. "Crap," Hank said. "They had my phone, and my GPS history. They could have the coordinates to the prison. But they were so busy with attacking the demons out in the world before."

"Maybe their numbers were bigger than we had thought. In either case, it doesn't matter who attacked. It just matters if and how bad it is. It's not just the worst demons we've encountered that are in there, remember."

"I'm not worried about the humans," Hank said. "They're DoD's problem."

"It'll still be on us if they're loose."

"Except, if it was Remember Sami that attacked the prison, they wouldn't have been interested in the humans, just the demons."

"You really want to gamble on them telling the difference? Or them thinking that actual humans might be in the same prison? If it were only hellians in there, then sure, but..."

"Oh, crap," Hank said. "What about Ralph?"

"Ralph?"

"The guy--demon that works in the prison. He was kind of our tour guide of the lower level when we went there. He's a nice guy, just a hellian."

"I'm more worried about the actual people in there. Like Grayson. We know Grayson."

"I know Ralph, or at least a little. I may not have worked with him for twelve years, but I never liked Grayson anyway."

"You never liked Jack either, but you would have cared if someone tried to kill him."

"No," Hank said. "Probably not. I mean, I wouldn't have let them, if I had a choice in the matter, but, yea. It's not like I would have taken a bullet for him."

"I'll make sure to tell him that when we find and rescue him from Remember Sami."

"Oh, he knows how I feel. I'm more worried about how Herb is going to feel about all of this. Do you think this will help or hurt our chances at getting the funding we actually need to do this?"

"Maybe he'll just not find out," Blanche suggested. "Let's not tell him; at least not until we fix everything."

"What if he gets back before we do?"

"Then we'll move to lake country and be closer to our daughter as we try to find new jobs."

The car turned quiet after that. Hank looked out the window, out at the woods that were already streaming by them. They had long since left the city behind, as Blanche drove the car at a feverish pace towards the prison. Five mile markers passed them by as Hank sat there, thinking over the comment, the half-hearted joke. They both knew that it wouldn't be that simple. That their failure to stop the attack, to stop the slaughter of the demons, wouldn't be enough for them to get fired. They had several other failures over the years, under far less stressful circumstances, that didn't result in anything more than a stern talking to. Yet, as he thought of that possibility, he started to like the idea.

"It wouldn't be too bad of a thing to get the family back together," he said.

After a few more moments of silence, she agreed. "No," she said. "I guess not. It's just..."

"We'd both be incredibly bored as we watched all the things that we could have been helping to fix," Hank said.

"Exactly."

It was a few minutes after that that they first saw it. Hank saw it first, this pillar of smoke on the horizon, streaming up above the trees. The smoke seemed almost normal when he first saw it. Just some campers with a fire, or perhaps a cabin out in the woods. As they continued down the highway, though, the smoke only seemed to get larger. Always staying ahead of them. Always on the horizon. Never passing them by. By the time they were ten minutes away from the prison, it was still there, big enough to indicate a forest fire, one raging through the woods ahead of them. Hank pointed at the smoke, making sure that Blanche had seen it. She simply nodded at his pointing, neither one bothering to say a word.

When they made the turnoff, Hank no longer thought that it was a forest fire. It was a long five minutes up the hidden road. The dirt road was narrow, looking more like a game trail than the drive towards the prison. The road had become overgrown over the years since the prison was decommissioned, with only the HPS and the DoD personnel passing through there anymore. Both made a concerted effort not to disrupt the foliage just for that reason. Blanche wasn't making any effort, barely slowing down. And yet she kept the crown vic perfectly in control on the less stable surface. Hank didn't blame her, as he focused on the column of smoke. It was finally starting to get closer, right when he didn't want it to.

The fence came into view long before the prison, as it usually did. However, when they broke through to the clearing, the prison was still obscured, this time by the smoke instead of the forest. The smoke was everywhere, bubbling up from the ground that surrounded the prison. Hank couldn't tell what it was that was burning, though. The forest seemed untouched by whatever it was that caused the destruction. A waft of breeze swept through the clearing, just as the car approached the front gate. The wind parted the smoke and finally revealed the building.

Blanche slammed on the brakes, spinning the car into a stop. As it skidded across the parking lot, dirt was kicked up all around them, blowing up into the air and joining with the pillar of smoke as it soared up into the sky. She left the car running as she jumped out, barely remembering to unhook her seatbelt before doing so. Hank was quick to follow after his wife as she ran down the corridor in the fence, heading for the front door.

"Hold up," Hank called out to her, as she went straight for the front door. Her hand was already on the scanner, so he had to pull her away from the door before it could scan her face and unlock. She glared at him as she pulled herself out of his grip, flinging his hands back at him. "The lockers," he said, reminding her of the precautions they were supposed to be taking.

"There's no time," she insisted. "In order for that much smoke to be seeping up through the ground, the whole place must be on fire." She coughed a few times as the smoke-filled air filled her lounges.

"All the more reason to hold off a moment," he said, similarly coughing. Once they were within the smoke pillar, it didn't seem as thick, barely thicker than the fog coming off the bay. But it still made breathing a little difficult. "We can't afford to add to the conflagration, anyway. Just... we need to put all our electronics--"

"Do you really think we still need to do that?" she asked. "If the smoke is coming up from below, the mana must have already escaped. There shouldn't be any magic left in there."

"Better to be safe than sorry. Besides, I can't afford to lose this phone. Not again." He made a show of pulling his phone and keycard out of his pockets. When he moved to take off his fitness band, its absence was another punch to the gut, another reminder of just how much had gone wrong lately. Even the absence of his gun, still stuck up in the main office, didn't hurt as much as the loss of that band. He would need to get it replaced, if he never found his old one. But the sky would need to stop falling before he got around to doing that.

He threw all his stuff in a locker, holding it open for Blanche to do the same. She rolled her eyes and let out a huff of annoyance as she followed his lead. She took off her fitness band and placed it, along with her two guns and the keycard, in with his stuff. "Happy now?" she asked.

"What about your phone?"

"Uh... crap, I think it's still in my suitcase."

"Fine. Let's get in there."

Hank placed his hand on the scanner, taking the lead at the door. Nothing happened. The scanner just sat there, cold to his touch, seemingly colder than it should have been. No lights activated, not even a sound. Hank took his hand away, just far enough to look at the scanner. He made sure that nothing was on it already, nothing was blocking the system from detecting his hand. There was nothing there; nothing but the faintest glimmer of a handprint from the last person to use it. Hank used his hand to wipe off the scanner before trying again. But still, nothing came of him placing his hand there. On his third try, he slammed his hand down harder, trying the old "hit the machine to work" trick. The panel let out a couple of sparks before letting off a small wisp of smoke, barely visible in the midst of the smoke coming up from below.

"Great," Blanche said. She pulled him out of position, placing her own hand where his was, but the panel similarly didn't respond to her touch.

Blanche had been more forceful when pulling Hank away than she probably had meant to. Hank stumbled back a step, his hand automatically grasping for something to hold onto. It found the edge of the door. The door pulled forward, swinging open as he stumbled, and wasn't much support for him. As the door pulled open, a burst of smoke came out of the doorway, joining the stream that was coming out from beneath them. Inside, it was dark, the ever-burning torches having gone out at some point.

"That's not good," Hank said, looking in through the open door.

"No," Blanche agreed. "That's not good."

Chapter Thirty-Three
The Great Demonic Escape

Hank went back to the lockers, pulled open the one they had used, and extracted his phone. He didn't like the idea of bringing it with him, not in there. But they had no other source of light to use inside the prison. All of the old lights had been pulled out of there, replaced by the ever-burning torches which worked better, with or without magic. He held the phone up, out as far away from his body as he could get it, and took a few tentative steps inside of the complex. His eyes instantly found the puddle of melted plastic that had been Jack's old keycard, an obvious reminder of the damage that magic did on electronics. Even as he passed the puddle, and the DOD sigil that it had fallen on, the phone continued to work, to give off light into the distance. The door that held in the mana when the front door was open was nowhere in sight. Hank wasn't sure what that meant, but it wasn't good.

"Come on," Hank said, calling back to his wife. He was startled to find Blanche right on his heels, her hands gripping the guns that she must have taken out of the locker while he had made his way inside. Even without bullets, he felt better knowing that she had the guns at hand.

There was no one at the front desk. Hank wasn't sure if that was a good sign or a bad one. He headed over to the glass barricade, the wall that used to separate the magic of the prison from the electronics that helped run it. He expected to find a body, a pool of blood, something to indicate what happened to the guard that had been stationed there when the place was attacked. Instead, he found nothing. No body. No sign of blood. No damage to the barrier. Nothing of note at all. For all he knew, the guard just vanished from his station, or abandoned it completely, long before anyone came knocking on the front door.

"Where is everyone?" Hank asked.

"Do they have any ammo in there?" Blanche asked.

"I don't think so. It's a prison, even if it is a magical prison. They don't want the inmates getting their hands on it. Old habits die hard."

"Damn."

Hank led the way down the hall, keeping the phone away from him as he did. He kept expecting to find the edge of the receding mana field, some point where science would once again fail and magic reign supreme. With the front door open, even the crack it had been open before they had gotten there, the mana should have fled the confines of the prison. It would have headed out into the world where it would be dispersed to a level that would have no effect on the world at large. Even knowing this, Hank was too ignorant about the ways of magic. He didn't trust that it was all gone. For all he knew, the thick, enchanted walls of the prison could have held some of it back, trapping some in pockets throughout the place, keeping part of the prison powered up.

When they came to A block, they got their first sign that the prison hadn't been completely abandoned prior to the arrival of whoever, or whatever, had attacked the place. The light from the cell phone reflected off of a splattering of blood that was on the outside of the glass barrier that surrounded the guard station there. Hank tapped the blood experimentally, finding it still fresh, still wet and warm from whoever it had once belonged to. There wasn't enough on the wall to indicate someone dying, or even being seriously injured. But, still, it didn't bode well for the guards.

"Still fresh," Hank whispered. He felt like his voice could give them away to the enemy that must have left long ago. It had to have been the attack that freed the hellhounds, and they would have left the prison over an hour earlier. There was no reason for the attackers to stay for that long unless they were interrogating the prisoners on site.

"I'm thinking it's a good thing that there are no bodies."

"They could still be alive in here somewhere," Hank said.

Blanche nodded her agreement to that, before pointing her guns towards the cells. "How many prisoners were in there?"

"In A block or the prison itself?" Hank asked. "There might be ten, there might be none. I have no way of knowing without the logs, and they're in the guard stations."

"Then how do we get in?"

"We can't. They were designed to only open up from the inside. People can only go in when someone else is coming out. I don't know why they hadn't just stayed put. The barriers are bulletproof. This whole place was designed to withstand anything either world could throw at it."

"There must have been a reason," Blanche said. "Something that made them think they weren't safe inside the booths."

"They'll need to break them open before we can get the place back up and running again. Even if we had the time to try to get inside there, it would take some heavy equipment."

"We should at least check to see if the prisoners are dead. I hate the thought of having people between me and the exit, at least without me knowing of them."

Hank headed over to the door into the cell block. The keys, like most things they might have wanted, would have been inside the booth. He tested the door, making sure that it was locked, rattling it in its frame loudly. The rattling was echoed by the banging of bars from the inside of the cell block, hands reaching out to wave at the two agents from inside, up and down the row of cells.

"Looks like the attackers weren't interested in the human prisoners," Hank said. "The door is locked tight. They're not going anywhere."

"I still don't like it," she said.

"Think how they feel. They were probably well aware of what was going on out here and thinking that they'd be stuck in there until they starved to death. I'm surprised they're not all whooping for joy right now."

"Yea, that's what I don't like about it. Whoever attacked could still be in here, and we only have the threat of us shooting them to stop them."

"With you on our side, I still like our chances."

Blanche smiled at the compliment, though Hank knew she wouldn't be so easily swayed. With another look down through the gate, they headed off along the main passageway, heading deeper into the prison. They both knew that each step they took could invariably lead them to the attackers. Could lead them to their doom. Each cell block they came to was an echo of the first, an empty guard station, prisoners all too interested in keeping quiet. The prisoners in cell block C didn't even bang on their cells when Hank tried the main door, just waving their hands through the bars to make sure they knew that they were still there.

Hank felt a renewed sense of dread as they approached the guard station for cell block E. Despite what he had said before about Grayson, which was still true, he didn't want the man to die. Not in that way. Not stuck in a box surrounded by people trying to destroy all that they had built over the years. He hoped that Grayson had been the one to escape somehow. That he had managed to get out of the guard station before the attackers had come for his charges.

His hope died quickly as the flashlight on his phone panned across the booth, and a bloody palmprint could be seen on the glass. Blanche ran forward when she saw that, heading for the booth. Hank scanned the rest of the area with the flashlight, making sure that whoever had attacked wasn't hiding somewhere in the shadows. That was when he spotted the door to the cell block wide open, the only one that had been. Instead of heading for the booth, he headed for the cells, headed for the inmates that he and the rest of the HPS had been responsible for. Several of the cell doors were similarly open, though not all of them. As he walked the line, he counted the open cells, looking in each cell as he went, trying to see if any of the prisoners were in there.

Unlike the wings before E, this one was completely empty. Books and cards sat forgotten on beds and desks. The sound of running water came to him from the far side of the cell block, over where the showers would have been. Mist joined with the smoke that, while having died down since they entered the prison, still seeped up at them from beneath their feet. The hot water must have been fed into the prison from outside, out of what used to be the magical field, in order for it to still be hot without the magic in the prison.

"Hank," Blanche called out, making him jump. He whirled around to see her back at the guard station, desperately waving him over towards her. Hank did a quick scan of the remaining cells, the six that he hadn't gotten to before she called to him, and a quick look towards the bathroom door before running back to her. "Don't go wandering off alone," she scolded.

"I thought you were with me," he said. He was so used to Jack staying at his side in dangerous environments that he hadn't thought to look.

"Shine the light inside the booth. I hadn't gotten a decent look inside."

"He's not in there," he said, though he shined the flashlight in anyway. "He's probably with the rest of the guards."

"Yea, wherever they are."

Hank didn't want to look inside the booth. But, when Blanche didn't react, didn't scream, cry out, or just cry, he did look in, only to find it as empty as all the rest. He felt almost disappointed. Not that Grayson wasn't dead. Not that his body wasn't in there or that he wasn't knocked out unconscious defending the booth to his last. He was disappointed that Grayson hadn't seemed to try to leave a note. He should have had a longer warning, far longer of a warning than the rest of the guards. But he didn't so much as mark the number of hostiles in his blood. Other than the hand print on the glass, the booth was almost spotless. Just the normal level of messiness that Grayson had always strived for, even when he had a desk in the main office.

"Do you remember how many demons you arrested and sent in here?" he asked, as he tried the door to the booth. It was as secure as the other doors were, just as it should have been.

"A lot," she said. "Did you really expect me to remember how many?"

"Maybe," he said, with a shrug. "I think I sent seven in here."

"Yea, I sent quite a few more than seven in here. Plus, there was Semi. Why?"

"There were thirty-two open doors in the cell block. Does twenty-four arrests make sense?"

"I'd sooner remember how many I killed than how many I didn't. Neither number comes to mind at this moment."

"Maybe Grayson will remember."

"If we can find him."

"Well, I'm thinking we just follow the blood trail," Hank said. He shined the flashlight along the floor, along the red line that dribbled back and forth, jumping between stretches of the floor. It headed further up the hall, up towards where Hank hadn't gone since they had first hit the place, back when the cult had been running it.

"Well, at least Grayson gave us something to go on."

"You're assuming that was intentional? You give him too much credit."

"You give him too little. He's a lawyer stuck in a glass box for weeks on end. He probably longed for someone to hit the prison."

"You're just saying that because you would have," he accused. She didn't deny it.

"Come on," she said, gesturing towards the blood trail. "Lead the way."

"So that you can cover me with your empty guns?"

"So that I can see where I need to point my empty guns."

He gave her a half smile as he continued down the hallway. With the straight nature of the path, the blood trail didn't help much in their tracking of the assailants. If they weren't behind them, and they were still in the prison, they must be further ahead. Just past cell block E, the corridor turned again, spiraling further inward. As they approached the corner, a red glow started to reach them through the smoke. It had nothing on the flashlight and, with that shining brightly ahead of him, Hank almost missed the glow entirely.

That is, of course, until they made the corner.

"Well, I guess that explains the smoke," Hank said.

Ahead of them was an elevator shaft, the doors wide open, as a blazing fire leapt up at them from the floor below.

Chapter Thirty-Four
The Heart of the Prison

"The entire basement floor must be burning right now," Blanche said, as they both stared at the fire.

"And the blood trail leads right to it," Hank said. "Still think Grayson survived the attack?"

"Well... maybe the attackers brought him out of the prison with them."

"Except there was no blood trail leading back out of here. It leads right up to the shaft, and probably right down into the conflagration. I bet a few of the demons went that way as well."

"It would be nice to think that Semi went out that way, but I somehow doubt they would have broken in here just to kill off the demons. What would be the point? It wasn't like they were in a position to hurt anyone."

"Many of the demons outside of this prison weren't hurting anyone either. That doesn't mean they're not targets. I imagine they would have thought the whole 'burn them in a fiery pit' idea rather poetic."

"But most people think demons are fireproof," Blanche said.

"The twins knew they weren't, else they wouldn't have burned down the club. They must have been part of the terrorist arm of Remember Sami, which means they all know it. And, with them working so closely with demons for months at a time, it was easy for them to figure that little tidbit out."

"So, what now? If the whole basement is up in flames, it's not like we can do much about it. Not without a firetruck and a lot of water, anyway."

"There's not much down there to burn. It was all stone. They must have used some kind of accelerant to start the fire. Once that's burned off, we should be able to get down there. While we wait, why don't we get out of here, get some fresh air. I'm not sure how much more of this smoke my lungs can take."

"Gas," Blanche said.

"What?"

"They must have used gas to start the fire. That's why the smoke is so black, right?"

"I don't know. The twins used a Molotov cocktail, but that wouldn't have started a fire this big down there. How long could a fire like that burn, anyway?"

"I've heard of gasoline fires that went on for days. I'd say we could try to close off the elevator shaft, try to snuff out the fire that way. But with the smoke coming up from the ground, it's obvious that the cement is no longer air tight. Microfractures must have opened all over it. We should head back outside, call Danielle and have her get some firefighters over here with some equipment. We're going to need to get the prisoners out before the smoke gets too bad in here."

Suddenly, the fire flared up, hungrily reaching out for them from the elevator shaft, moving along the corridor floor as if it had a mind of its own. Hank moved back, though he was already a couple of dozen feet away from the shaft. He pushed Blanche back towards the bend in the corridor. The new batch of flames, finding nothing new to burn, still rose high into the air, forming a wall across the hallway. Then, just as suddenly, the entire conflagration expired, leaving both agents momentarily blind as their eyes adjusted to the darkness. Hank raised his flashlight back up, pointing it back towards where the fire had been, only to find the familiar face of a wrath hellian standing right in front of him.

"Boo," Ralph shouted, causing both agents to jump in place. Hank dropped his phone, the beam pointing upward at the ceiling. Ralph started to laugh as he lit his horns with hell fire, which only made the effect that much more intimidating. "You should have seen your faces."

"Ralph," Hank scolded. "What the hell. Were you behind that fire?"

"What? No, of course not," he said, automatically. When both agents continued to stare at him, he repeated it. "No."

"Then how..."

"You were right, of course. Those assholes that came through here had a messload of gas. They poured it all around down there, tossed Grayson and a few of the demons into the elevator shaft, and threw a match down. Several of the demons escaped while they were doing that, though."

"Semi?" Hank asked.

"We never did get around to pulling her out of solitary. She's still down in the hole."

"She survived that?" Blanche asked.

"Yea, of course she did. They all did... well, the ones they sent down there. I should have this place cleaned out in a couple of hours and you can put them back in their cells. Not sure how much good that will do you though. The whole place is aerated. You're going to have to do something about that."

"But... how did anyone survive that kind of fire?" Hank asked. "How did you do that trick with the flames and all of that?"

"Oh, that, yea, that was a bit weird. I'm not quite sure... I don't know, maybe it has to do with my fire affinity."

"Wait, you have an affinity for magic?" Blanche asked. She stared down the demon as if she suddenly trusted him a lot less than she had before.

"Oh, yea. Didn't I mention that? It was part of why I got this job to begin with."

"But... I mean you didn't... you couldn't take a human form when you got here," Hank said.

"Yea, polymorph is a water spell. Water and fire are opposite, so many fire mages have trouble with them. Not all of us, mind you, just many."

"But... there's no magic in here," Blanche said. "Right? I mean, it all blew away."

"Well, not all of it, I don't think. But, yea, the place is aerated, as I said. A sudden dose of my element, in high quantities mind you, must have been enough to restore my mana pools. I can already feel it seeping away from me, though." As he said that, his hellfire halo started to flicker around his horns.

"What about the mana source?" Blanche asked. "Is that still... I guess the word would be functioning."

"I'm not sure," Ralph said, shrugging. "You guys never told me where it was. Or what it was, for that matter. This whole magical versus nonmagical worlds kind of confuse me. Like, why even have a world with no magic? What's the point? How does life even happen without it? How does it happen without magic coming from it? It just... Well, I'll stick with being a guard, and, you know, enchanting bars. Stuff I'm good at."

"What about the kennel?" Hank asked. "The hellhounds got out." Ralph just shrugged.

"Hey, who's up there?" came a familiar voice, calling up through the elevator shaft. "Is the cavalry here already?"

"You're darned right," Blanche called out. "Get your lazy ass out of that hole in the ground, Grayson."

"Would if I could," Grayson said. "Send a rope down and I'll be happy to get out of here."

"A rope?" Hank asked.

"Yea, we're going to need to put something together to get everyone out of the basement," Ralph said. "I used a levitation spell to get out, myself. The ladder got warped in the heat and broke off halfway up. That... machine thing that used to work in there was taken out before they pumped the place full of the mana."

"How long ago did the attackers leave?" Hank asked.

"Who knows. It's hard to tell the time in this place. Could have been ten minutes, could have been ten hours."

"It couldn't have been ten hours," Hank said. "We were attacked by the hellhounds only an hour ago."

"Oh, well, if they got out an hour ago, then the attackers probably left about fifty minutes ago. They weren't here long, just long enough to blow open the front door, storm in, toss some of us in the hole, and leave. They had guns, big guns, probably big enough to take out those booths. And with the mana flowing out through the front door, it was hard to tell if they'd work in here or not. I think everyone was just worried they'd be supercharged by the confluence between the magic and non-magic or something. Can you imagine? I saw some of those things at work when I first got here. They hurt like hell, and that's saying something coming from a demon."

"I'm surprised they didn't blow up in their faces," Blanche said.

"No, guns don't react like electronics," Hank said. "It would be more likely that the mechanism would have jammed up if they tried to use them. But they would have gotten a few shots off. Gunpowder is too natural for it not to work in a magical environment."

"See what I'm talking about?" Ralph said. "Way too confusing. I'll just stick with magic, if that's alright. When can we get back to that?"

"We'll need to get some workers in to reseal the entire place. If the source isn't compromised, we should be able to get the place back to its old state soon after that."

"But how long is that going to take? And are they going to be alright with a hellian in this place?"

"Well, seeing as how it'll be the DoD financing and arranging the whole thing, it will probably take several months," Blanche said. "We'll call them up as soon as we get out of here."

"As for how they'll feel about a hellian, well, we don't really have much control over that at this point," Hank said. "Before we go call this in, though, I'd like to check on the source. Think you have enough magic in you to get me down the hole and back up again?"

"Down, sure," Ralph said, smiling maliciously. His hellfire halo flickered again before going out completely. "Even safely. Back up might be another thing entirely. If I could tap into the source long enough, I could probably teleport you back up here."

"One second," Blanche said, pointing up a finger towards Ralph. She pulled Hank around the bend in the hallway, trying to get out of voice range of the hellian. "I don't think we want to let this one in on where the source is," Blanche whispered to Hank.

"Ralph has been on staff for months now. If he was going to betray us--"

"How do you think they knew about this place? He could have told--"

"Told a demon hate group?"

"That's what he said they were. That doesn't mean--"

"Blanche, he never leaves the basement. Not just the prison, the basement. He's afraid of being out in the world. Given how things have been turning out these past couple of days, can you really blame him? Even if he had someone to betray us to, he wouldn't. I think we can trust him. Besides, the source is locked up tight. Even if he knew where it was--"

"He's a fire mage, Hank. He could just--"

"The walls are protected against magical attacks. He'd have to strip the wards first, and that sets off all sorts of alarms."

"Alarms that he helped put into place."

"So, what? He helped make this place the fortress that it is just so that, at some point down the road, he could get his hands on a source of magic that he helped secure in the first place? If he was going to grab the thing and run, he could have done that from day one. He didn't need to help us secure it."

"Fine," Blanche said, in a huff. "But I'd like it on record that I don't like this."

"Blanche, you're going to be writing up a report on this. I'm not your superior. I only have seniority when it comes to this organization. You have far more field experience than me. Write whatever you want in the report. I'm not going to stop you. I need to visibly inspect the source, otherwise there's no point in us fixing up the place. No magic means no enhanced containment. The demons would be able to break out whenever they want."

"DoD would still want to use it as a black site."

"I doubt that. Can you imagine what people would think if they knew these kinds of prisoners were being held domestically? There was a reason why Guantanamo lasted as long as it did."

"That's why it would be a black site, not a known prison. People don't want to know about it at all."

"Fine, but that would be on DoD, and out of our hands completely. It's of no use for us without magic."

"You'd better go check on the source then," Blanche said. "But make sure you really can trust that guy."

"If I didn't think I could trust him, I'd wait for the rescue team. We don't have that kind of time, though. Herb would want to see the report as soon as he finds out about the attack. Plus, we need to get back to the city for that meeting this evening. It's already almost two. It would take an hour to get anyone out here to get the people out of the hole and put them back in the cells. Longer if we need to wait for someone cleared to know about the place."

"Fine, fine, fine," Blanche said. "If you're going to do it, you might as well do it."

Hank smiled as he finally got her on board. He kissed her on the cheek, taking this one win as a reason to celebrate. It wasn't often that he won an argument with her, and have her not just do whatever she was going to do anyway behind his back. He also didn't often work with her in the field. Even before they started dating, Herb made it clear what the field teams were going to be, and he wasn't inclined to allow switching between without a good reason. After they were married, it was completely out of the question. But, with Jack missing and Jenkins out of town, it wasn't like they had many options.

With a final smile and nod, Hank twirled around, heading back towards Phil. The hellian was standing there, purposefully looking all around as he whistled. His hands were locked behind his back. He was very pointedly not listening in to their conversation, though Hank doubted that he wouldn't have heard every word of it.

"Are we good?" Phil asked, when Hank returned to him.

"Yup," Hank said. "Still got enough mana to do it?"

"Well, yes and no," he said. Before he could clarify, Phil scooped Hank up into a bear hug. He took the three large steps over to the edge of the elevator shaft and jumped.

It wasn't far down, just a little over a story. Still, travel between the floors was difficult without the elevator or any stairs. Hank barely had a chance to scream out in fright before they hit the bottom of the shaft. He caught a brief glance of Grayson's startled face as they passed by the basement floor and kept on going down. Right before they hit the bottom, Hank felt a strong, hot updraft that seemed to come out of the cement floor beneath them. It was enough to cushion their fall so that they didn't break anything on impact, though Phil's arms still crushed into his stomach when they got there. Hank had a feeling he would have a huge bruise across his midsection. He wasn't too concerned, though, as he wasn't inclined to wear anything that would reveal it.

"What was that?" Hank asked, once he managed to get his breath back.

"I got you down safely, didn't I? If you hadn't spent so long arguing with your wife, I could have done it nicer, but I was low on mana. But, hey, any fall you can walk away from, right?"

"You had that saying on your world?" Hank asked.

"Are you kidding? It's all that air mages would say half the time. But, well, they can fly all they like, without needing those... metal thingies."

"Planes."

"Right, those. Now, where to from here? You said the bottom of the shaft, right? I can get you back up to the basement, but that's more strength than magic."

Hank looked up at the mention of the basement. He knew where the source was, but he hadn't been in there before. He was surprised to find the base of the shaft another two stories lower than the basement floor, marked only by Grayson's curious face looking down at him from above. "No," he said, still looking up. "I think... It's supposed to be..."

He started to look around the walls. Though they all looked to be made of solid cement, he knew that one of them had only a thin layer of the stuff. It was thin enough that it could easily be broken through. With the use of a sledgehammer that is. He was hoping that a wrath demon's fist would do in a pinch. The problem was he wasn't sure just which of the walls it was, and he didn't think Phil would be too happy with him if he picked the wrong one. He shined the flashlight on his phone at each wall, in turn. He was hoping to spot something, a glimmer, a glint off of something, to indicate just which wall it was.

"It's that one," came Grayson's voice above him. Hank looked up again to see him pointing straight down.

"Right," Hank said, nodding before he even looked in that direction. "Thanks. Um, Phil? Can you punch open that wall?" He pointed at the center of the wall, right below where the shaft had opened up to the basement, and the ground floor above it. "The wall shouldn't be that--"

Before he could even finish his statement, Phil was already winding up his swing. He punched forward, right into the wall, and through it, to the small cavity back there. It took him several punches to break through the rest of the wall, opening up a gap large enough for Hank to get through, and several more for the rest of the wall to break away from the surrounding structure. The section was higher than Hank had been expecting, coming down to just above his head. They were in the pit below the floor, where the elevator's electronics would have hung. If Phil had been shorter than his domineering almost seven feet, he might have hit below where the cavity was, into the strong, reinforced section of the shaft wall. As Hank watched the demon work, he started to wonder if such a thing would have deterred him at all.

Behind the wall, the sub-basement should have opened up, right where the elevator would have originally led to it. Instead, though, there was a metal door, stretched across the space. It was further in from where the elevator doors would have been. Also, unlike with the elevator doors, this metal door dropped down from above, falling into place rather than sliding across. There was tile on the floor, though it was covered with rock dust and other debris from the destruction of the false wall.

"That's it," Hank said. He sounded more confident than he should have been, given that he had never seen the door. He slid his phone along the floor towards the door before pulling himself up into the cavity. The dust on the floor made his balance tenuous at first, as he came up into a standing position. He came over to the door, picking his phone back up off the floor. The phone was dirty from the debris, but the flashlight still shone strongly.

Hank was surprised to find himself being pushed into the metal door. At first, he thought that Phil had turned on him after all. That he was being forced to open the door. But, then, he realized that Phil had just come up into the small cavity alongside him. There just wasn't room for the both of them to be up there in the enclosed space.

"Sorry," Phil said, when the hellian realized the closeness of the area.

"It's alright," Hank said. His voice came out strained, as his face was still stuck against the door. "Maybe go back down for a moment so I can open the door? I think we'll have enough room once I get in there."

"Oh, right, sorry," Phil said, again, before jumping back down.

Hank had dropped his phone again when Phil had come up, but he decided that it was better on the floor anyway. The light was perfectly aligned to reveal the locking mechanism in the middle of the door. He didn't like having his phone that close to the source of all magic known to the HPS to exist on Earth. But it was his only light source, and it couldn't be helped. Fortunately, all the rest of his electronics were still in the lockers upstairs, far enough away from the door to not be affected by it.

The lock itself was an interesting contraption. The metal door was specifically designed to slam into place the moment that a dip in the mana field was detected. The thought was that any dip strong enough to be detected would have been the result of a breach in the prison, much like the one that had preceded the assault. If the mana field had stabilized after the door closed, the lock was designed to reopen, pulling the door free and feeding the mana field with the source once more. Since there wasn't any mana left in the prison, that part of the locking mechanism wouldn't work anymore. However, there was also a mechanical side to the lock, specifically designed to be usable in both magic and non-magic environments. The mechanical side was something similar to a big combination lock, big enough so that the mechanics weren't messed up when used with mana still flowing through the area. The huge dial, easily a foot in diameter, rested at the base of the door, in the center, just above where the locking handle was.

Hank had to drop down to his knees to use the dial, and it took both his hands to move the mechanism around in place. It was slow going, the dial resisting his efforts to move it. Each time one of the latches locked into place, it did so with a loud, audible boom. It would have made figuring out the combination easy, even if Hank hadn't remembered it. The device had been enspelled to be silent, but without access to mana, the spell had expired.

Once the fourth lever locked into place, Hank got back up onto his feet, positioning himself so that he could still reach the handle. The handle turned easily enough, but, as he tried to lift the door, it resisted his efforts. The door wouldn't even budge. He knelt back down, trying to see if it was caught on something, or if the door was actively trying to keep itself closed. Using his cell phone's light, he swept along the base of the door, trying to see what was holding it in place. Right beneath where the handle was, the bottom of the door came up another millimeter, revealing the gap where the locking bar had been. That section was completely clear, nothing holding it in place anymore. He even tested the handle a couple of times, watching as the locking bar swung down into place, then back up as he continued to turn it.

"Uh, hey, Phil? Would you mind coming back up here?" Hank asked, hoping that brute strength would be the answer. He scooped up his phone and hopped back down into the pit, giving the demon the room that he would need to be in there. Phil looked between Hank and the door a couple of times in confusion. "I think the door is just too heavy for me to lift."

"Oh," Phil said. He hopped back up into the cavity, his arms flapping in the air for a split second as if they were wings. He looked back towards Hank one last time before turning to the door. It didn't even seem like he was putting much effort into it when he pulled the door open, tossing it into the slot that it had fallen out of. He let go when it went up, but the door started sliding right back down into place. "Uh," he said, surprised, as the door slid back onto his shoulder, slamming into it with a blow that would probably have killed Hank.

"Try turning the handle once it's up there again," Hank suggested, hoping the locking mechanism would work in both positions.

Phil tossed the door up again, flipping the lever as he did so. It seemed to click into place this time, as it slid home. Phil looked back down at him with a smile of accomplishment. "Well, that worked. Need a hand up?"

"No, I got--" Hank started to say. But, as he reached up to grab onto the floor again, Phil grabbed his right arm and yanked him all the way up with one hand. "Uh... Thanks, I guess," he said, as he rubbed his offended arm.

"So, now what?" Phil asked, as he looked through the now open doorway.

Hank shined his phone through the gap, showing another door, the inner door, about ten feet further in. Along both walls were more lockers, like the ones up near the entrance. However, these looked pristine, like they had never been used, and had no keys on them. The lockers simply clicked closed, but they would be enough to protect anything within them.

"Head on inside," Hank said. "We need to open the inner door, but not until after this door is closed."

"Oh," Phil said, already halfway across the small room. "Sorry."

Figuring Phil would be too impatient to wait much longer, Hank opened the closest locker, tossing his phone inside, and closed it. The room was plunged into darkness, as the only source of light was blocked by the locker door. Hank reached above his head, feeling around for the latch on the outer door. However, moments later, he heard the door slide down into place.

"Um, Phil, was that you?"

"Don't worry. I can see in the dark. Well, not that well, but obviously better than you. Your hand was like three inches away from it at one point. It was a bit pathetic."

"Gee, thanks," Hank said, sarcastically.

"Sure. Can I open the other door now?"

"By all means, please do."

Hank heard another lever squeaking open. It wasn't in the direction he was expecting, which told him that he had gotten completely turned around in the darkness. Less than a second later, that darkness completely disappeared, as the light from the other room, the room on the far side of the inner door, spilled into the airlock. Hank gave a sigh of relief as he realized what that light meant, that the inside of the source's room was still bathed in magic.

"Ah, that feels so much better," Phil said. He was holding up his hands as if he were taking in the light from the sun.

"Can I see?" Hank asked, when he realized that all he could see was Phil's back, blocking the entire doorway.

"Oh, sorry," Phil said. But, instead of stepping off to the side, he walked forward, into the source's room. Five steps in, he was suddenly walking around the perimeter of the room, rather than continuing inward. He probably didn't think anything of it, but Hank knew that it was the effect of the spells that kept the source out of the wrong hands. Or, perhaps more accurately, out of the hands of anyone that wasn't an HPS employee.

With Phil out of the way, Hank was able to take in the entire room. The room was circular, centered around a raised platform that was fifteen feet in front of the inner door of the airlock. The far wall, where there had once been another corridor, was blocked off by another airlock door, working similarly to the one they had just come through. Through there, he believed, were the kennels, as there weren't many other places in the facility to store them. All along the walls of the room were the ever-burning torches, much like the ones that hung all along the two floors above them.

And, at the center of the room, on the raised platform, was the source of all magic on Earth.

"That's it?" Phil asked, as he stared at the source. "It looks like some kind of rock."

"It is a rock," Hank said. He approached the meteorite, looking all around its surface, trying to find some kind of flaw. He wasn't sure that he would know what a flaw would be, or if it would be enough to stop it from emitting mana. They weren't even sure why, or how, it was emitting mana. Just that it was. "This thing crashed outside of a town in Pennsylvania back in January. We almost missed it, with everything that was happening with the invasion, but there's an Army Reserve base near there. They detected it and, when the thing was destroying their radios, they sealed it off as best they could and called us in. I don't think we would have gotten our hands on it if we weren't in the news the month before. Some civilian kid got mixed up in it, but, otherwise, no harm came from it. I can barely imagine if this thing was strong enough to spread across the whole world."

"But... what is it?"

"It's a meteorite. It's just some rock that fell down from space."

"Space?"

"The place above the atmosphere."

"Oh, you mean the ethereal plane. It's an ethereal fragment. No wonder why it's emitting mana."

"No, it's... wait, what?" Hank asked, confused. "It's space, not the ethereal plane. It's not even another plane of existence, just part of this one. It's just too far away from the Earth's gravity for anything to be in there but debris of other planets and the creation of the universe and... stuff."

"Sounds like the ethereal plane to me," Phil said. Hank figured it was easier to let him think that than explain what space really was to someone who barely understood what science was.

"Anyway, it looks like everything is fine with the source. Mana is still flowing."

"Yes, it is," Phil said. "And it's delicious."

"Alright, alright. Time to go back upstairs. Do you think you'll have enough mana left over for the teleportation after we close the door?"

"Why can't I just teleport you from in here?" he asked.

"Because I can't just leave you in here, and I want to get my phone. I can't bring my phone in here, so you'll have to come out there."

"Aw," Phil said, disappointed.

Phil followed behind as Hank led the way into the airlock. Hank made sure that the demon was all the way in before flipping the lever on the door and letting the weight of it slam it home. For a moment, the room was left to darkness once more, but then Phil ignited his horns again, bathing both of them in the light of hellfire. He smiled down at Hank, his expression looking a lot more ominous and malicious than intended, with the hellfire burning all along his horns.

"Don't waste too much of your magic," Hank said. "We're going to need to open the outer door and leave it open for at least a few seconds before I can grab my phone out of the locker."

"I could just draw in all the mana in the room instead. I think I can store it all, if I just burn off enough of it. Of course, it would be nice if I could always have access to mana, like I did before the place was hit. Ah, if only…" He looked longingly towards the inner door.

"Phil, I can't have you going back into the source room," Hank said. "There's no food or water in there."

"I don't need much of either, and what I do need I can just summon. Summoning water is easy, even for fire mages."

"It's not just you I'm worried about. I... well, my boss might not like the idea that I let you in there to begin with. I might get in trouble."

"Oh," Phil said. His smile faded a little, but he gave a knowing nod before turning towards the outer door. He took a deep breath in, as if he needed the breath to steady himself to open the door. Hank knew that wasn't the case. With the slightest flip of his hand and a pull on the handle, he opened the outer door again. The hellfire on his horns flickered almost immediately, though it didn't go out. They both waited there for a minute, before the horns flickered out completely. "It should be alright now."

Trusting the demon, Hank immediately flipped open the locker, exposing his phone to whatever mana was left in the room. The light from the phone quickly replaced that of Phil's horns, telling them both that the demon had gaged it correctly. Hank scooped the phone back up, closing the locker afterwards. "Can you still get me back upstairs?"

"Sure," Phil said. Without any further warning, Phil reached out a single finger, touching Hank lightly on the shoulder.

The world was suddenly all over the place as Hank's sense of gravity left him. He spun around in the eternal nothingness that was between here and there, then and when, as the teleport brought him from the sub-basement to the ground floor. Hank spilled forward onto the solid cement floor above. His head bashed into the wall, then the floor, then the wall again before finally coming to a rest.

"Are you alright?" Blanche asked, helping Hank back up to his feet.

As he came up, he heard a ripping sound coming from his left. He fumbled around with the phone, which he managed to hold onto during the teleport. The light shined towards the direction of the sound. Several fibers were sticking out of the wall itself, stretching out as if searching for something that was no longer there. Hank's stomach plummeted as he fumbled around with his jacket, finding the huge hole that was now suddenly in it. It was ripped cleanly along the seam, not too far away from where his gun holster was. "Damn it," Hank said. "I liked this jacket."

"What happened?" Blanche asked.

"I think I teleported too close to the wall. Not all of me ended up out of it. An inch closer to the wall and I'd need to be cut out of it."

"Another inch and cutting you out wouldn't have helped," Blanche said. "But at least your phone wasn't killed by the spell."

"It's not the spell that kills electronics. Spells are just directed mana. It's the raw stuff that you have to worry about."

"Where's Phil?" she asked.

"Down here," Phil called out from below, showing just how strong his hearing really was.

"No going back into the source room," Hank called back down to him.

"Aw," Phil said.

Chapter Thirty-Five
Meeting Rudolph Judd

By the time they made it back out of the prison, Danielle had everything scheduled out. The rescue team would bring the guards and prisoners back out of the basement in an hour. The DoD team would come to inspect the facility the next day. The construction team, complete with the proper security clearances, would do the repairs on Monday. There wasn't anything else for them to do at the prison, with still a few hours before their meeting with Rudolph Judd. It was enough time for them to get back home, take a quick shower, put on a fresh set of clothes, and get over to his offices with still an hour to spare.

They didn't waste the hour.

Despite everything that had been going wrong that week, they were both feeling much refreshed and very hopeful that things were going to start looking up after their meeting. Whether or not Rudolph Judd knew what was going on with his group, what the terrorist arm of Remember Sami had been up to, or even if they had anything to do with the death of Jared, the death that had started it all, neither thought they would come out of that meeting empty handed.

Mr. Judd's office was in downtown Seattle, just a few blocks over from their own offices. Or what was left of them. Hank had a feeling that they would need to look for new facilities. Whether that was from the damage done during the attacks or from the building managers not renewing their lease when it came up. Despite their proximity, the two offices couldn't look less alike. Both agents could feel the buzz of the place before they entered the front door.

The building itself was at least ten, if not twenty, stories taller than their own building, which was no slouch itself. Even at almost 6PM, more people were coming into the building than leaving. The insignia for the Judd Group was plastered on the wall when they came in. The insignia looked remarkably familiar to Hank, though he couldn't quite place it. The lobby was huge, three stories tall in and of itself. Escalators were on both sides, leading up to another area that overlooked the lobby. Everything seemed to be made of glass or black marble, or both. It was probably meant to make it look more fancy, more rich. To Hank, though, it just made the area look more sinister and intimidating. Hank had to admit to himself that the impression might have been due to his own expectations for their meeting.

A smiling faced receptionist locked eyes on the two of them the second they came in the door, as if they had been expected. And, given the fact that they had a meeting on the books, they technically were. However, when they approached the woman, she was able to recognize both of them without having to ask their names.

"Ah, we have both Agents Gorning. How lovely. When Ms. Menendez called about this appointment, she hadn't clarified on which would be coming. It is lovely to see both of you well, despite the recent occurrences."

"What recent occurrences?" Hank asked, accusatorially. He eyed her suspiciously, as if the receptionist herself had something to do with everything that had been happening recently.

"Why... the attack on your offices yesterday. It was on the news last night."

"You'll have to excuse my husband," Blanche said, as she placed a staying hand on Hank's shoulder. "We were both injured during the attack and haven't been keeping up on the news."

"Oh, of course," the receptionist said. "I hope you both are alright. You're a little early for the meeting, but I guess you can head up now." She pulled three badges out of a drawer on her left, looking at each before handing two of them over to the agents. "These will get you up to the twenty-third floor. There will be a receptionist there to greet you when you get off the elevator. He will direct you further. You can use the elevator bay over there." She pointed off to her left, towards one of the escalators. "Those are the express elevators for that group of floors. Let us know if you need anything."

"Thank you so much," Blanche said. She smiled at the woman before leading Hank towards the escalator. "There's no need to get suspicious," she whispered, once they were out of earshot of the receptionist. "At least, not yet. This guy is a billionaire. It's not like he's going to have the gunwoman working a receptionist's desk. Besides, don't you think we'd recognize her if we saw her? It's not like they wore masks."

"Yea, I know. I just thought--"

"That they released a companywide memo about their terrorist activities? You don't even know what I'm doing half the time, and we both write reports about everything."

Hank looked at his badge as they got onto the escalator. He was surprised to see that they had printed out an actual badge for him, instead of just a random visitor's badge. It was complete with an old photo that was obviously taken from one of the interviews he had given back in January. Behind him in the photo was a piece of the presidential seal. His name was printed beneath the photo, along with the word visitor in all caps. The badge had been printed on a keycard, rather than just being laminated paper. It was the most well-made badge he had ever seen, at least of those that were designed to only be used once.

As they got off the escalator, Hank grabbed Blanche's badge to look at. Her picture wasn't taken from an interview. Instead, it was a cropped image from their family photo, the one of the three of them at the lake. Seeing that photo used in that way felt like a punch to his gut. He wasn't even sure how they could have gotten a copy of it, unless they took it off his own phone when it was taken from the office.

"They got it from one of those social media sites," Blanche said, answering his unasked question. "I started an account last November. I must have posted it there at some point. Then all hell broke loose, quite literally, and I forgot about the thing until now. Relax. They're not trying to bait us."

She took the badge back, tapping it against the reader next to the turnstile that blocked off one of the elevator bays. Hank looked around them, lost and confused for a moment, before he noticed the sign that said 20-25 over the entrance to the elevator bay. There were two other bays on either side of this one, one for the 15-20 and one for 25-30. He wondered for a moment why they weren't meeting Mr. Judd on the thirtieth floor, where his office would no doubt be. But then he figured they'd be in some small conference room somewhere, lost in the hugeness of the building and away from prying eyes. It was exactly the place that he would have held a meeting that he didn't want people to know about.

There were three other people waiting for the elevators when they got there, and the button was already pushed. They only had to wait a few seconds before the elevator door dinged. Hank jumped a little when it did, having spent too long in the elevator shaft itself back at the prison. His mindset was still stuck in a world where magic ruled and science stood no chance against it. He even looked up at the ceiling, half expecting the elevator to drop right on top of them.

"Relax," Blanche said, though she half smiled at his nervousness.

"I'm fine," Hank insisted, patting her hand where she had placed it on his arm.

Two more people got off the elevator before the five of them went on. Hank watched the two departing workers until the doors closed in front of him, blocking his view. The elevator ride itself was uneventful, with the other three getting off on the twenty-first floor, leaving the two agents to head up the remaining floors alone. Hank watched the numbers light up, one by one, as he impatiently waited for their floor.

"Relax," Blanche said, again. "They're not going to go through all this trouble to attack us in the middle of their own building. People know we're here. They knew that people know that we're here. They're going to be too busy trying to hide their involvement in all of this to do anything stupid like attack us here."

"I know," Hank said. "It doesn't make me feel any better. I've been trying to find these people for days now, and they're just practically rolling out the red carpet."

The elevator came to a stop, dinging one last time at the twenty-fifth floor. Hank braced himself as the doors opened, expecting another attack, expecting something, anything, that would signal their true intent. Instead, all that greeted them when the doors opened was another smiling face. A man in an expensive suit was standing just a few feet away from the doors. His hands were held at ease in front of him, looking well-manicured and sparingly used. It was the last thing that Hank would have expected to have seen greeting them.

"Greetings, Agents Gorning," he said, in a high tenor. "If you will come with me, I'll show you to the meeting room that has been set up for your meeting with Mr. Judd. We've taken the liberty of ordering some food. I'm afraid Mr. Judd doesn't have much time for the meeting, what with his busy schedule, and we've double booked it with his dinner. I hope you don't mind Thai food."

"Thai is fine," Blanche assured him.

They both followed the assistant through the halls, back towards the center of the building. Even with the late hour, people were still busy working all around them, rather than just trying to finish up their work before they left for the day. Several of the workers were even eating food at their desks as they continued to work. Hank laughed a little to himself, wondering if their work ethic had more to do with their boss's extracurricular activities, and his possible involvement with terrorists, than with a desire to work there. He tried to send a mental message to the workers that this would be their opportunity to flag that they're there under duress. As they passed the rows of workers, a few of them glanced up towards the three of them, but none seemed to take more than a cursory interest in the group.

The assistant stopped short in the middle of the hall. He reached his arm up, half blocking their path and half directing them towards the open door on their right. "I hope the accommodations are to your liking," he said, as if he were showing them a hotel room, rather than a meeting room. "Can I get either of you anything to drink? Coffee? Tea? Water?"

"Hard liquor," Hank muttered, jokingly.

"Would you like gin, whiskey, or brandy?" he asked.

"Uh, he was joking," Blanche said. "We're both fine."

"Okay," he said, as if it wouldn't have mattered either way. "It is still early for the meeting, and he might be running a little late. Perhaps you'd like to settle in and get comfortable. Let me know if you need anything, or if you'd like me to show you where the bathroom is."

"We're fine," Blanche said, again, as the two of them headed into the meeting room.

The room had a long window, stretching across the wall opposite from the door. It looked out over the front of the building. The building was taller than its neighbors by quite a lot, giving the window an extraordinary view of the city, including the space needle in the distance. Even with the light streaming in through the windows, the ceiling lights were on, barely adding to the room's illumination. A long, heavily polished table took up much of the space in the center of the room, with several leather chairs placed haphazardly around it.

Hank took one of the seats on the far side of the table, purposefully placing his back to the windows. He found it less likely that someone would attack him from the window than from the front door to the room, given that they were twenty-five stories up. Blanche settled in at the head of the table, with the door on her left, but pivoted her chair towards the exit as well. The assistant continued to smile at the both of them, before nodding to them each in turn and disappearing down the hallway.

As soon as the assistant was gone, Hank jumped back up to his feet. He circled around Blanche to head for the door, taking a long look down both ways of the hallway before closing it. Other than the assistant, heading away from the room, no one seemed the least bit interested in the two agents.

"I don't like it," Hank said, once the door was closed.

"Shh," Blanche said, putting her finger to her lips.

"What? You think they bugged the room?" he whispered. He looked all over the room, expecting to see some kind of indication of the surveillance. There was a black, plastic hemisphere attached to the ceiling in the corner, which was no doubt a camera. But there didn't seem to be anything to pick up sound. He placed his back to the camera as he sat down on the edge of the table next to his wife. "We should go. The last thing we need right now is to be attacked again."

"Why do you think they're going to just attack us out right, here in their offices?"

Hank glanced over his shoulder back at the camera, making sure that it wouldn't be able to get a good shot of his lips. He leaned in close to Blanche as he whispered to her. "Because they're terrorists, or at least involved with them."

"Terrorists against demons," she said, openly and out loud. "They're not going to attack us, now that they already have what they wanted from us. Even if you're right, even if they're behind everything, they went after our offices for the list of demons and the location of the prison, both of which they managed to get from your phone. There isn't anything else they need from us."

"Exactly," Hank said. "Which means we're expendable to them. And we already know too much. About what they're doing. What they're planning. We shouldn't be here at all, not without backup. We should just arrest these people."

"With what evidence? We have nothing on them besides a cursory link between the Remember Sami movement--"

"Which we know he's a part of, if not leading."

"And the terrorists. If we had had anything more than circumstantial evidence against the group, I would have arrested them long before. Remember, I had been on this group for months now, long before you just stumbled onto them like that."

"I still don't like it," Hank said.

"I know. But there's nothing to do about it. If we leave now, it will only look more suspicious. If they are involved with the terrorists, they'd rabbit."

"What makes you think that they're not doing that already?"

"I don't know, Hank. Maybe because they didn't stonewall us at the door. Maybe it's because they have been nothing but nice and accommodating to us the minute we got here. Maybe because I want to think that there are nice people in the world and, until given proof otherwise, I like to think the best about them."

"Yet, you don't feel the same about demons," Hank said.

"Because they're demons."

"That's... Racist? Demonist?"

"Infernalist?" she asked, smiling. "Maybe. I just think they have been nothing but trouble for us since they got here."

"Not for me."

"I know, I know. Maybe we should switch off our assignments when this whole thing is over. Let me handle the normal ones that just need our help assimilating while you take the ones that don't think the war with Heaven will ever be over."

"I would like that, for your sake at least. But you kick ass way better than I do."

"And don't you forget it," she said.

A knock at the door pulled them out of their little argument. They both looked over at the door. Hank stood up off the table and crossed his arms, trying to look intimidating. Blanche kept her seat, her hands crossed on her lap to keep from reaching for her gun. The assistant opened the door slowly, poking his head in just a little bit. The same smile was on his face, though it seemed a little more strained than before.

"I'm sorry to do this to you both, after you've come all the way down here and all, but... Well, I'm afraid Mr. Judd was called away on business, so last minute. Is there any way that we could, maybe, reschedule this little meeting?"

"He's rabbiting," Hank said, not the least bit surprised by this turn of events.

"What? No, no, no. I assure you--"

"You know, we didn't have to do it this way," Blanche said, taking on a more sinister tone to match Hank's. "We could have come up here with a warrant, arrest Mr. Judd in front of all his employees, and pull him out of here in cuffs. But, no, we wanted to be nice about the whole thing. Now, if you'll excuse us, we're going to have to go chase down your boss."

"Welcome to the 'we don't trust Mr. Judd' team," Hank said, under his breath.

"I never trusted him. I was just giving him the benefit of the doubt until proven otherwise. He just--"

"No, no, no. I'm sure that... One moment, please," the assistant said. He pulled the door closed behind him as he headed off again.

"Should we chase after him?" Hank asked.

"No, I think we made our position perfectly clear here. He'll be--"

The door opened again, the assistant pulling it all the way open this time. He stood in the doorway, though, blocking off the exit. "I'm... sorry, but I've been asked to keep you in--"

"You know, you did this whole thing wrong," Hank said. "You should have just left us in here, thinking everything was just fine. Thinking that we were just way early for the meeting, while your boss escaped."

"He didn't escape. He was called away on business."

"No, that's just what you were told to say," Blanche said. "What he's really doing is escaping in his helicopter."

"Um... No?" the assistant said, though his attention was pulled away from the agents by something in the window behind them. Hank looked back there, just in time to see the helicopter flit out of the way. "No," the assistant said, this time with more confidence. "He's running a billion-dollar company. He can't be expected to... Alright, if you must know, he was called away to discuss the prospect of a buyout by Angel Corp. But, please, don't tell anyone. That's insider information."

"Then why are you telling us?" Hank asked.

"Because he knows that if we arrest his boss, the merger will go bust," Blanche said.

"Not a merger, a buyout. Mr. Judd has other business that he needs to attend to, outside of his company, and he wants to make sure that the employees are taken care of. I assure you, there's nothing sinister going on here. Why don't you come back first thing tomorrow morning and we'll get this whole thing squared away... over... breakfast."

"We'll be back alright," Blanche said. "With a warrant."

"I've already discussed that possibility with Mr. Judd and he made it clear that it won't be an issue."

"Well, if it won't be an issue, why doesn't he just turn himself in?" Hank asked. "After he's settled this buyout, of course."

"Once everything is... handled, I'm sure that can be arranged. What exactly is he going to be turning himself in for, exactly?"

"Oh, he knows," Blanche said.

"Yes, of-of course."

The assistant took a step back, away from the door, allowing the two agents to exit again. He followed them as they made their way back to the elevators. Although they hadn't been in the meeting room long, Hank was a bit surprised to see that the scene they walked through hadn't changed in the slightest while they were in there. Everyone there seemed hard at work at whatever it was they were doing. He only gave them the slightest thought to wonder if any of them knew how tenuous their positions really were, before they both stepped back on the elevator that they had only just left.

"I am very sorry about all the issues, and hope you both all the luck on your investigation," the assistant said, waving towards them as the elevator doors closed.

"Yea, I'm sure," Blanche said. Hank laughed a little as the elevator started to descend. "What?"

"I just think it interesting how our positions seemed to have switched."

"You think they are going to cooperate after all of this?"

"Well... no, not really. I'm more thinking how you're the big ball of stress right now and I'm thinking we managed to escape with our heads still attached. That's a win in my book, at this point."

"Yes, it's amazing how low the bar gets after almost being killed... how many times is it now?"

"Oh, I've lost count after the gunfight with the twins," Hank said. "It's been a busy week."

"Exactly. It would have been nice to get some help on at least some of it. If Rudolph Judd hadn't been involved in the terrorist activity in his own group, he might have wanted to help weed out those that were."

"Even if he isn't involved, he might have been on their side. He could be supporting them simply by looking the other way as they recruit his entire group into the cause."

The elevator dinged as 2 displayed on the floor indicator. Hank looked between it and the button that they had pressed when they got on. He was a bit confused to see that was the lowest number that was on the panel, with the little star next to it indicating that that was the ground floor. The doors opened up, revealing the turnstiles they had come through barely minutes before, with people heading both in and out of them in large numbers. With a shrug, he led the way off the elevator.

"Now what?" he asked, turning around to walk backwards so he could watch his wife while they talked. She quickly caught up to walk beside him. As he turned back forward, a familiar face popped out of one of the other elevators. "Blanche," Hank called out, as he drew his weapon, aiming it at the gunwoman.

Chapter Thirty-Six
The Last Gunwoman

The woman was wearing a pantsuit, in a powder blue that perfectly matched her eyes. She was holding some papers that she had been overly intent on as she had left the elevator, the one just further from the turnstile than the elevator that the two agents had left moments before. Still, despite her business appearance, Hank had no doubt that it was her. The woman that had escaped the attack on the office. The one that had held Danielle at gunpoint. That had hit him over the head with her gun. That had knocked out Blanche.

Blanche reacted to his call almost instantly, though she hadn't thought to draw her gun. She turned around, looking in the direction that Hank's gun was pointed, seeing immediately the same thing that he had. "Oh, crap," she said, as she, too, went for her gun.

The gunwoman hadn't noticed their reaction at first, as intent as she was on the papers in her hand. But, as everyone else that was in the area cleared out or dropped to the floor to stay out of the line of bullets, she looked up to see what the commotion was. Her face went suddenly pale, making her entire appearance seem more like ice, as she noticed the two agents standing there. "Um," she said. "Hi."

She was only a couple of feet away from them, close enough to reach out for their extended guns. Hank almost dared her to try. "Put your hands up," Hank said.

It took her another few seconds for her to get over the initial shock of seeing the two agents there. Once she did, she raised her hands, slowly, still holding the papers. When her arms got high enough, Hank reached into his pocket for his cuffs. He didn't get to use them often enough, given the fact that demons could just break out of them. But this woman was no demon.

Once Hank was distracted, the woman threw the papers that were in her hand at the two of them. They fluttered through the air, blocking their view. Hank dropped the cuffs onto the floor, putting his hands back on the gun as he focused forward. The gunwoman was already gone, though, having darted between them in the confusion.

"She's getting away," Blanche called out. Blanche was already through the turnstile, giving chase to the gunwoman.

"Damn it," Hank said. He darted after the two women, slipping a little on the papers in the process.

As he came out of the turnstile, he spotted Blanche heading down the escalator. He didn't see the gunwoman until he was already at the top of the stairs that were next to it. She was already at the bottom, running for the door. Most of the people on the ground floor were either huddling behind pillars or desks or lying out flat on the floor. None of them seemed the least bit interested in helping stop the escaping terrorist.

Both the stairs and the escalator were empty, except for Blanche, who was already near the bottom of the latter. Wanting to catch up to the two women, and figuring no one was actually watching him, Hank hopped up on the railing. He slid down it as best he could. He got about halfway down the stairs before he fell off the railing, his momentum causing him to roll down the rest of them.

"I saw that," Blanche yelled towards him, as she ran past his prone body.

"I meant to do that," Hank mumbled, to himself, as he pushed himself back up to his feet. His left knee suddenly started to complain on the second step he took after them.

"Will you hurry up? She's getting away." Blanche fired off a shot as Hank came out of the doors. She hit the rear window of a car that was already driving off into the distance. "Damn it."

"What? How?"

"She had someone waiting for her in the car. Come on."

They both ran over to the crown vic in the parking lot, Hank favoring his left leg the entire way. When Blanche moved to take the driver's side again, Hank called out to her. "Nuh uh. You're not taking this into a high-speed chase."

"There's not going to be much of a chase if we--"

"Trust me, honey," Hank said. An overjoyed expression quickly spread across his face. "I've been wanting to take this girl into a chase since I got her." Blanche stood there, glaring him down. But Hank just grabbed the keys out of her hand, pushing her out of the way so he could take the wheel. He gave her a quick kiss before sliding into the driver's seat. The engine roared to life as Blanche hurried around to the passenger seat, sliding in reluctantly. "Just remember. There's a reason why they call it shotgun. You do the shooting. Leave the driving to me."

Hank pulled out of the spot at speed, turning the car dexterously around the parking lot and making a bee line for the road. Even as he maneuvered the car around, he was hitting several buttons, on the dashboard and steering wheel. The central panel for the dashboard opened up, revealing the onboard GPS system that he hardly used. As the GPS connected with the satellite system, it automatically called up Danielle on his phone. The police lights, built into the car itself, activated with a switch on the wheel, as well as the siren. By the time they hit the street, the car was in full chase mode, ready to hunt down the fleeing suspect and anyone helping her. Hank was elated. He always felt like the crown vic only came alive when it was in full chase mode, like it actually transformed from its sleeping state, though the only change to its appearance were the flashing lights.

"This is Danielle. What's up?" came her voice on the GPS's integrated hands-free system.

"There was a black sedan outside the Judd building two minutes ago. We need live tracking. Feed it through to the crown vic's GPS system."

"I don't think it--" Blanche started to say.

"Not a problem," Dr. Howard's voice said over the phone. "I was hoping we'd get to test out the new OS we installed on that. The default is just so..."

"Close minded?" Dr. Davidson supplied.

"Yes."

"I got the car," Danielle said. "Nice shot, Blanche. I can't tell if it did any damage to the driver, though. Alright, tracking to live... I got it. They're on--"

"I'm sending the coordinates now," Dr. Howard interrupted. Instantly, the GPS display changed, switching from following the arrow as it traveled along the street to an aerial view of the neighborhood. A second arrow, this one red, popped up several blocks towards their left, and two behind them. After a few more seconds, the red arrow started to travel across the screen, as it raced for the edge of their view.

"Got it," Hank said, watching the GPS out of the corner of his eye. At the next corner, he took a hard left, ignoring the red light stopping traffic in their direction. "Care to give us a little help with the lights? We've got a lot of ground to catch up on."

"Uh..." Danielle said, loudly.

"I've got the car, you do the lights," Dr. Howard said.

"Ah, team HPS, together again, in the action," Dr. Davidson said.

"On the right side of the action, this time," Danielle said.

"Should I try to slow the other car or help you give chase?" Danielle asked.

"Can't you do both?" Blanche suggested.

"Not easily."

"Focus on the other car," Hank said. "I've got this one." As he said that, he was pulling into another intersection, the light against them again. He swerved through the traffic that hadn't heeded the sounds of his siren and the flashing of his lights, easily passing through without so much as a scratch on his precious baby.

"Seriously?" Blanche asked. Hank was too focused on driving to tell if she was surprised or impressed. He guessed both, though, and smiled accordingly.

"I'm throwing up all the red lights on these guys that I can, but it's not stopping them," Danielle said. "They have as much respect for red lights as you guys do."

"I have immense respect for red lights," Hank said. "I just don't think they apply to me."

"Oh, god," Blanche said. "I'm in the car with a madman."

"Yea, a madman that you married," Danielle said.

"Oh, will you two relax. I've got this." He took another left, to the tune of several car horns sounding a choir. Blanche flinched as one of the cars came close to smashing into the passenger side door. "I totally got this," Hank said, again, as he pulled straight onto the road.

"Are you sure?" Blanche asked.

Three seconds later, the black sedan, still sporting the broken rear window, spun out onto the road right in front of them. They were so close that Hank could make out the shocked expression on the gunwoman's face in the rearview mirror. Hank pressed on the gas, pushing his front bumper into the sedan's rear one. The sedan bumped off of it, pushing it forward on the road. But the driver managed to maintain control of the vehicle. Hank couldn't get a good look at whoever was behind the wheel. He tried to pull into the other lane, to get up next to them, but the oncoming traffic was too thick to allow it.

"We need to force them onto a less busy road," Hank suggested. His hand itched towards the GPS, but he kept it on the wheel where it belonged. "Blanche?"

But, suddenly, before she could try to put anything into the GPS, her attention was required elsewhere. The gunwoman, a smile replacing the shocked expression, flipped around in her seat, her namesake once again in her hand. She pointed the gun straight at the windshield of the crown vic, quickly emptying the clip at them. Blanche ducked behind the dashboard, trying to get out of the line of fire, but Hank didn't so much as flinch.

He just smiled as the bullets bounced off the glass of the windshield.

"This entire car is bulletproof," he told Blanche. "Why don't you roll down the window over there and show them that their car isn't?"

"Because there are still other cars on the road," Blanche said. "I might hit someone else."

"You? Miss what you're aiming at? Impossible. It's just as unlikely as--" Hank broke off, mid-gloat, as the sedan swerved around the next corner. Hank didn't react fast enough, blowing through the intersection to another car horn choir.

"You were saying?" Blanche asked.

Hank glanced down at the GPS, tracking where the red arrow was fleeing. He took the next right, onto the road parallel to the one the sedan was on. He pumped on the gas, trying to catch up to the other car.

"There is a speed limit, you know," Blanche said. "I think we left that about twenty minutes ago."

"Do you want to catch them or do you want to obey the speed limit?"

"I'd like to catch them while we're still alive to do something about it."

"Don't worry. I haven't crashed a car yet, and I don't plan on starting now."

"Guys, I have an idea," Danielle said. "Try to get them here." The GPS's display changed again, zooming out once more. A black square marked an intersection, several blocks further ahead in the city, on the street that the sedan was already on. If they didn't change direction, they would head straight for it without interference from them. "I've got a little surprise for this bitch."

"We're a little off their path, if you hadn't noticed," Blanche said.

"Not for long," Hank said. He barely let his foot off the gas as he took another right turn. They buzzed by a car that was sitting in the middle of the intersection, waiting for a chance to turn left. Hank eyed the GPS once more, making sure that he had timed it properly, as he drove the entire distance of the block in only a couple of seconds. He quickly turned back towards the left at the next intersection. Horns blared at them from every direction as he settled into the right lane. He looked all around, through the cars that surrounded him, trying to reacquire the black sedan, only to realize that he had overshot. The black sedan was right behind them, on his tail.

"Uh, Hank? Don't turn around," Blanche said, her focus on the car behind them. "Just focus on the road."

"Yes, dear," he said, half sarcastic. "Are they shooting at us yet, or did they learn their lesson the first time around?"

"Well... they're not firing at us, but I'm not sure how much they actually learned from their first attempt."

"What?" Hank asked. When Blanche noticed him trying to look back there, to see better than what the reflection in the rearview mirror could provide, she forced his gaze back towards the road in front of them. "What's going on?"

"Nothing," she insisted. However, despite her insistence, she rolled down the window next to her, reaching out with both guns in hand. As she half hung outside of the window, she let off shot after shot. From what Hank could see in the rearview mirror, most of the bullets went wide. They took out the windshield, but the shattered glass did more damage to the gunwoman and driver than the bullets would have. Knowing how good of a marksman his wife was, he had no doubt that her intention was not to hurt anyone in the other car.

"Where's that surprise of yours?" Hank asked. The black box on the screen was getting much closer to them, as the view continued to zoom in. Despite this, he couldn't see anything out in front of them that would constitute a surprise. It was just more people, watching the car chase as it played out right in front of them. A few of the spectators were even filming it on their phones, though not even that seemed that surprising to Hank.

"It's coming," Danielle promised. "It wouldn't be much of a surprise if you could see it coming. Don't worry, they know to expect you to be coming in first. They're prepared for that."

"They?" Hank asked.

Immediately after asking it, he drove through the targeted intersection. The black sedan was still hot on his tail. Yet, suddenly, he heard a low bang behind them, followed by the screeching of brakes. As he looked back there, two police cruisers pulled up into the intersection. Lights ticked on all over the place, lighting the evening up like midday. He could just make out the black sedan, blocked off in a circle of cop cars.

Hank slowed down once he knew that his quarry was caught. He took a circle around the block, his victory lap, coming back around to the intersection from another direction. The police cars were suddenly two, even three thick in certain places, effectively trapping the gunwoman and her compatriot within. Hank had an unsettling sense of deja vu as he pulled the crown vic as close as he could to the police cars. However, this time, instead of coming up on a murder scene, this one was still quite active.

"Stay here," Hank said, knowing that Blanche wouldn't listen. He left the car running as he popped out, walking the rest of the way through the blockade of police cars. When he got through to the inner circle, he saw that inside the line of cars was another line. This one was made up of men and women in blue, all aiming their guns straight at the woman in the car. She and her driver were still inside the black sedan, looking as stunned as could be at the force aligned against them.

"No one goes after one of our own," the detective from the murder scene said, when he noticed Hank's approach.

Hank barely registered the words as he said them. His focus was on something else entirely. As shocked as the gunwoman and the driver were at the police presence on the scene, Hank was double shocked to recognize the man sitting behind the wheel.

No matter how suspicious Hank had been of Jack, he never would have thought he would be driving the gunwoman around in a car chase against him.

Chapter Thirty-Seven
The Return of Jack

"Isn't that his partner?" another one of the officers asked.

"Yea, I wasn't going to say anything," the detective said.

"No, it's okay. I did arrest him before the assault on our offices," Hank said.

"Oh, well, then you saw it coming at least."

"Not exactly. Not this. Something, sure, but... well, his aunt is a member of Remember Sami, so I guess it makes sense that he'd be tied up with them, just not against us is all."

"Hey, Hank," Jack called out. He waved his hand gently over the steering wheel. He looked a bit sheepish, sitting there, right next to the woman that had led the assault. It was like he was caught with his hand in the cookie jar, rather than caught aiding and abetting a known terrorist.

"Jack," Hank said, simply, nodding in the direction of his former partner.

"Well, isn't this awkward," Jack said.

"Shut up," the gunwoman said.

"This isn't what it looks like," Jack insisted.

"I said, shut up."

"Yea, Jack. You should really listen to her," Hank said.

"Shut up. No sense in digging yourself in any further."

"Digging myself... She kidnapped me, out of the cell you put me in, and forced me to help her."

"He really has been quite useful," the gunwoman said.

"She didn't seem like she had you at gunpoint while you waited for her outside the Judd building."

"I... That... She had me cuffed to the steering wheel."

"Yea, with the engine running," Blanche said. "I saw her jump in and the both of you drive off within seconds."

"Duh. Autostart. Seriously." He pulled up his hands, which were still cuffed to the wheel. "I mean, come on, she's a nut job."

"Shut up," the gunwoman said, again.

"Hey, bitch," Blanche yelled. "You don't get to tell him to shut up. We get to tell him to shut up. He's one of us."

"Thank you, Blanche," Jack said.

"Shut up, Jack," Hank and Blanche said together.

"Out of the car, now," the detective yelled.

"Bitch," Hank and Blanche said together.

"She has a gun on her," Jack said.

"Well, of course she does," Hank said. "She's the gunwoman."

"That's what you've been calling her all this time?" Blanche asked, barely taking her eyes off the gunwoman to look Hank's way. "I've just been calling her Bitch."

"Well... she has a gun, and she's a woman," Hank said. "So, the gunwoman. Seemed rather obvious to me."

"God, I'm right here," the gunwoman said. "My name is Cindy."

"No, I think Bitch works better," Blanche said.

"Yea. Cindy sounds too bubbly," Hank said. "Who in their right mind would name you Cindy?"

"To be fair, she probably wasn't a bitch when she was named."

"Yes, I guess that's true. Still, with a name like Cindy, you would think something bubbly would rub off on her."

"Are you two done teasing the suspect?" the detective asked.

"No," Hank said.

"But we can stop," Blanche said.

"For now," Hank added.

"Out of the car, Cindy," the detective yelled.

"Fine," Cindy said, with a huff. She pulled open the door, stepping out into the evening. All guns followed her as she did so. No one missed the glint of silver still in her hand. As she closed the car door, a single bullet went off. No one knew who fired that first bullet, but it wasn't the last. When the gunfire was over, Cindy was on the ground, her blood seeping out into the street.

"Damn it," Hank shouted. "We wanted her alive."

"Did we?" Blanche asked. "I just wanted her dead."

"Okay, then I wanted her alive. We still don't have any answers. About the group. Their ties to Jered's murder. To Judd. We don't even know who she was working for, or with. There's no way she hit the prison all by herself."

"Jack will know some of those answers already. Assuming I do all the questioning, we might even get those answers."

"What's that supposed to mean?" Hank asked.

"Hank, you locked him up for being related to an old woman who owned the car that hit Jared. You're not exactly unbiased when it comes to him."

"Uh, can someone unlock me, please?" Jack asked, drawing the attention of everyone there. He had ducked down behind the steering wheel when the gun fire had started. But there was only so much one can do, so much one can hide, when they're cuffed to the wheel. He held up his hands, straining the cuffs that still bound them. "I kind of need a new pair of pants... and a shower... and a cheese burger."

Blanche smiled over at him. "I think we can manage at least some of that."

Several people started laughing at the pseudo joke, as the tension began to fade. Blanche, Hank, and the detective headed over to Jack, while a pair of paramedics went over to Cindy's body. Hank doubted there was anything that the two of them would be able to do, not with half the police force opening fire on her. It would be interesting to see which one of them would be required to see a shrink about using their weapon on the job. After everything that had been going on lately, Hank almost wished their department had similar regulations. All he knew was that, when the guns all went off, his was never used.

"So, what can you tell us?" Blanche prompted. The detective knelt in front of Jack, fumbling around with his own set of handcuff keys.

"Not much," Jack said. He eyed Hank, as if to indicate that he wasn't going to talk with him there.

"Fine, I'm sorry," Hank said, exasperated. "Really. I overreacted. Everything seems to have worked out in the end, though."

"Worked out in the end? Seriously? I'm handcuffed to the stupid steering wheel. I've been a hostage for a day and a half now, with no one trying to rescue me. I'll bet you even thought I was a member of Remember Sami this whole time."

"Worse," Blanche said. "He thought you were a part of the terrorist arm."

"All because I have an aunt that I didn't know about who is involved with the group. Besides, you've never treated me like a real agent."

"Because you're not a real agent," Hank snapped. "If it wasn't for... the incident, you'd be in prison right now."

"Oh, please. The case was completely circumstantial, and you know it. Why do you think it was a clandestine group that arrested me, rather than the actual police?"

"Ah, there we go," the detective said, once he found the right key. The cuffs opened up with several clicking sounds. Jack rubbed his sensitive wrist as the detective popped open the other cuff. "Why don't I leave you three to it, then. We'll close down the scene. We just need some statements from all of you, but that can wait till tomorrow. It's been a stressful week for all of you. Why don't you guys head home and rest up. You know, before you say something you'll regret?"

The detective shook his head as he left them to organize the officers. The paramedics were already zipping up Cindy in a body bag, though neither seemed the least bit sympathetic to the woman. More cops were already arriving on the scene, and each of the officers that had been there when the shooting had started were turning in their weapons to be tested. It was a not so subtle reminder of the bureaucracy that those other organizations had to put up with, that the HPS had managed to avoid so far.

"Yea, he's right," Blanche said. "Let's head home. We can review everything tomorrow."

"Just tell us one thing," Hank said. "Well, two things. How did they find the prison?"

"I didn't tell them, if that's what you were suggesting," Jack said. "They probably got it off your phone."

"So, she did take his phone?" Blanche asked.

"Yea. What's the second thing?"

"What happened to the team that hit the prison?"

"I don't know," Jack said. "They kept me near the highway the entire time. A team went in, sure, but only the madwoman came out. I saw a few demons running out of the woods, but, other than that, nothing. Maybe you should ask your pet demon about what happened to them."

"You mean Phil?" Hank asked. "Seriously, why is everyone becoming so demonophobic all of a sudden? It was the humans that attacked us, not the demons."

"Yea, they attacked us because we were standing between them and the demons," Jack said. "If the demons weren't here, they wouldn't have come after us. They still wouldn't have even known that we existed."

"Exactly what I was saying," Blanche said.

"Alright, alright. Let's just get home," Hank said.

He led the way back to the crown vic. As they passed the officers that were still standing around, they each would nod in their direction. A silent acknowledgement that they were on their side. That they had their back. It seemed weird to Hank, almost a contradiction to the friction that he had been experiencing from all the local police departments that entire year. But, despite all the problems they had been having, despite the HPS's tendency to come swooping in to claim credit for cases involving demons, they were all on the same team. They were all working towards creating a safer world for their children to grow up in. By the time they were back at the car, Hank was glowing with pride over the camaraderie forged there.

"Hello?" Danielle's voice said. She was practically screaming through the phone, still coming out of the GPS system's speakers. But no one had heard a thing until Hank had opened the driver's door. "Hello. Is anyone alive out there?"

"Oh, sorry, Danielle," Hank said. "I... I forgot you were on the line, actually."

"Hey, Danielle," Jack said.

"Jack? Is that you? Did Hank arrest you again?"

"Not yet," Hank said.

"No, he rescued me. I'm thinking he's still a little annoyed about it, so we would do well not to bug him."

"Uh huh. It's unlocked," Hank said. He slammed the driver's side door, trying to blot out the fact that Jack was back.

"So, Bitch had you this whole time?" Danielle asked.

"Bitch?" Jack asked, as he climbed in the back. He settled in behind Hank, figuring it would be the best place to hide from his view.

"Cindy," Hank supplied. "Her name was Cindy."

"Was?" Danielle asked.

"Seriously, you have access to those satellites. Why weren't you watching us the whole time?"

"Huey was bogarting it the whole time."

"I was not," Dr. Howard said. "I was just watching until the cars went through the intersection. We lost the angle from that satellite, and there wasn't another one in range after that. We really got to get better coverage than this."

"Well, it's a good thing we didn't need your help out there, then," Hank said.

"Hey, I got you like fifty cops. What more help do you need?"

"How did you get so many cops together like that?" Hank asked. "It looked like every cop in the city was there."

"It's a big city. There are more cops than that. But, no, they heard about your driving and called me to see if they could help. It was interesting trying to coordinate between the two systems."

"She was typing on two different keyboards at the same time," Dr. Howard said. "It was really quite impressive."

"That's our Danielle," Jack said, with pride.

"Are we ready to go?" Hank asked. He was looking pointedly at Blanche and ignoring Jack as best as he could.

"I imagine so," Blanche said. She flicked a lock of hair behind her ear, a move that seemed to be meant to hide her glance back towards Jack. It didn't work though, and Hank fumed as he started flipping off the full chase mode systems. The last to go was the full screen GPS, though the connection with the phone still stayed live.

"What happened to your fitness band?" Jack asked, pointing at Blanche's band. "There are only two lights lit. Did you two break up?"

"No, you idiot," Hank snapped. "That... Cindy stole my fitness band. Remember? She used it to unlock my phone."

"Wait, that's how she did it? I just thought you left it unlocked or something. No, I hadn't seen her using your band at all. Granted, I was a little preoccupied, what with being pulled out of a cell by a madwoman and put in handcuffs. Seriously, if you guys hadn't killed half her team, she probably would have killed me, too."

"Wait, half her team?" Hank asked. "I thought we killed her whole team."

"We?" Blanche asked.

"I thought Blanche killed half her team and the kill bot killed the other half," Hank clarified, sensing a similar reaction forthcoming from the scientists on the phone.

"I think she had the team that she went into the prison with at the office as well. There were two big, white vans parked outside, along with a black SUV. The madwoman forced me to drive the SUV out of there."

"Wait, black SUV? Was it--"

"No, it wasn't the same one that ran down Jared," Jack said, cutting off Hank's question. "I actually asked her about Jared's murder last night, back when she still had me outnumbered ten to one. She said she had no idea what I was talking about. And, I have to admit, I actually believed her."

"I thought you said you hadn't seen the other team," Hank said.

"What?"

"Before, when I asked about the attack on the prison, you said you didn't know who attacked it with her."

"Yea, I never actually saw the team. They were in the vans when I came out of the office. I never actually saw them. The madwoman kept me apart from them. I think we split up after the office. Anyway, the vans were out front at the office, and we came out the back. She was on the phone with them and told them to take off, that we'd be going in the SUV. That was when she dumped your phone onto a thumb drive and then... well... dumped your phone in the trash. I never saw a fitness band in all of that, though."

"Damn," Hank said. "I was kind of hoping to get that back. Those aren't cheap, you know."

"Why don't you just have Danielle track down the GPS signature?" Jack asked. "I'm sure she could do that easily, especially given all the awesome stuff she does for us on a daily basis."

"Aw, shucks," Danielle said.

"It doesn't have onboard GPS," Hank said. "It just logs into local hubs and phones that are synced to it. Unless it's near a hub--"

"It's near a hub," Danielle said. "Or, well, it was, about fifteen minutes ago."

"Wait? It was? Where?"

Chapter Thirty-Eight
An Abandoned Building Somewhere

"Are you sure this is where it was?" Hank asked. He was looking up at the infamous abandoned apartment complex as he leaned against the crown vic. It looked haunted even from outside.

"It's the only place that it could be," Danielle said, over the phone. "The hub that registered the fitness band is across the street from you right now."

"But... I mean, it only registered the band for a moment, thirty minutes ago. It's not like it was getting a constant feed from it."

"Right, but I've been going over the logs, and it's been showing up here a lot over the past day or so. Whoever had the band must be camped out in there."

"What? Are you scared of a few ghosts?" Jack asked, snickering under his breath.

"There are no such things as ghosts," Blanche said.

"Tell that to your husband."

"I just did."

"No, I'm not scared of ghosts," Hank said. "I'm scared of what else has been going on in there since the invasion."

"Nothing's been going on in there since the invasion," Blanche said. "No one has been in there since. That's why they call it the abandoned apartment complex."

"I'm sure someone has been in there, at some point," Jack said. "I mean, come on. There are three other complexes within walking distance of this place. If there was somewhere that was supposed to be haunted just a couple blocks over from my house in Jersey growing up, I would have been in there every day trying to find ghosts."

"There are no such things as ghosts," Blanche said, again. This time, it sounded like she was trying to convince herself of that.

"I'm saying that it hasn't been maintained since the invasion," Hank said. "I know that no one has lived here since the invasion, since everyone inside was slaughtered by those five wrath demons--"

"All of whom are now at large, thanks to that attack on the prison," Blanche said.

"Not my fault," Jack said.

"But that means that anything that needed repairs, a support beam here or there, a leaking faucet or toilet, all of that would have gone unattended. For all we know, the whole place is going to fall down on our heads if we so much as sneeze inside of it."

"So, don't sneeze," Jack said.

"It still sounds like you're afraid of ghosts," Blanche said. "Why don't I stay here, in case you need backup."

"How will that help?" Jack asked. "If we need backup, shouldn't you come along with us?"

"No, it's alright," Hank said. He looked over at his wife, who wasn't so much leaning against the car as using it to support her weight. Her face was starting to look more like she had already seen a ghost than that she was afraid of seeing one. "If the roof falls in on us, it will help to have someone out here to call for help. No sense in all of us being trapped in there."

"God, you two are just big scaredy cats," Jack said. "I'll go first, if that'll make you two feel better. I'll be able to see if the structure is compromised in any way."

"Yea, let the arsonist go first," Blanche said.

"Fine. Lead the way," Hank said.

Jack shook his head, rolling his eyes at the two of them, before heading off away from the crown vic. They had parked in the huge parking lot that had stood outside one of the three apartment buildings that made up the complex. No one else was parked there, the entire lot was as abandoned as the buildings themselves. But Hank knew that was no indication that no one else was inside. And, if Danielle was right, if his fitness band was in there somewhere, it was likely that at least one person was inside with it.

"Maybe I should just buy a new one," Hank said. Fear held him in place against the crown vic, as he watched Jack head off.

"It does seem like an awfully lot of work over something so simple," Blanche said. "It's only a couple hundred dollars to replace. No big deal."

"Exactly," Hank agreed.

"Oh, no," Jack yelled back at them. "Remember, whoever has your band got it out of the office. They could have had a hand in the attack. Besides, I sure as hell am not going in there on my own. It's your fitness band."

"He's got a point," Blanche said, though she still didn't look the least bit interested in heading inside.

"Damn it," Hank mumbled. "Alright, I'm coming."

"Good," Jack said.

By the time Jack made the door to the closest of the three buildings, Hank had caught up with him. The front door was wide open; whatever locking mechanism that had been in place when the apartments were in use had been broken by the authorities during the attack. Other than Sami's murder, the battle that took place at that apartment complex was the most well-known incident that happened that night. It had been the beginning of the end of the carnage that the demons had been causing. While most of the demons had just come along for the ride, there had been a large group of wrath demons that had come there with a purpose. To kill off as many of the humans as they could. They had not been expecting the response they had gotten there that night. Half of the demons were taken down by bullets. However, even those gunned down had recovered, no matter how mortal the wounds should have been. It had given many the impression that the demons couldn't be killed at all, though it had more to do with the mana that hadn't faded from their systems. After that night, and the rumors of hauntings to follow, no one wanted to move into any of the units. So, the buildings had been held as a memorial to those lives lost during the invasion. There were plans on placing a plaque, listing all the names of the people that had died there and all over the area, on the first anniversary of the invasion.

Once they were inside, Hank took his phone out to use the flashlight again. Most of the lights that still hung along the hallway were burnt out. The rest were flickering intermittently, giving off a low, ambient buzzing sound, but little in the light department. The hallways stunk of the blood that had once flooded the place, even after all those months. It had the feeling of a bad horror movie, one where everyone knew that the monster was about to jump out at any moment. Hank did his best to convince himself that there was no monster. That the monsters had been cleared out long before. But, with those same monsters on the loose, he couldn't help but think that a few of them had come back to the scene of their capture.

"So, where do you think we should look first?" Jack asked.

"We're in a big abandoned apartment building," Hank said. "Any sign of someone here would lead us in the right direction. But... well, it is big."

"Yes. And?"

"And, it'll take us a while to search it. Maybe we should split up?" Hank looked down the hallway, leading off in both directions away from the lobby. There were two elevators against the far wall, but neither agent seemed inclined to trust them. Each of the two hallways seemed equally eerie, like one of those haunted forest paths that would obviously lead to nothing but trouble. Hank was tired of trouble. "Or... maybe we should just stick together."

"Maybe we should ask Danielle," Jack suggested.

"What do I know?" Danielle asked. Hank practically jumped when her voice came from his phone, having forgotten that she was still on the line. "I'm not even there. I can't see what you're looking at."

"Perhaps you should try to find a place in the building where the band is syncing to your phone," Dr. Howard suggested.

"Oh, uh, yea," Hank said. "I think I need to hang up for that."

"Alright," Danielle said. "Keep us posted, though, alright? I'm not sure I can get you any backup, now that the cops are all stuck at the scene of the shootout, but we can lend some moral support."

"And some much-needed intelligence," Dr. Davidson added.

"Yea, if we find ourselves in need of... either of those, we'll call," Hank said, rolling his eyes. Jack snickered a little when he saw that. "Talk to you later." He hung up the phone, instantly switching over to the family tracker app. The Angel Corp symbol seemed to take a lot longer than it should have to go away. But, once it did, the usual interface popped up instantly. Blanche and Marissa were listed as being updated within the last minute, with GPS coordinates and their usual biometric readouts. Hank's entry, at the top of the list, showed that it was last synced half an hour ago, though the biometric readout read as an error message. The GPS coordinates were the same as before, with the description of the hub at the grocery store across the street. "Well, it's not syncing yet."

"So, we're in the wrong part of the building?" Jack asked.

"Or we're in the wrong building or we're just too low in the building for it to reach through the floors. Maybe we should just walk along each floor from one end to the next, heading up a floor at a time, until we get something?"

Jack just shrugged his agreement, before heading off down the left hallway. With only the one phone between them, Hank liked the excuse to not split up. He followed closely behind Jack as they slowly made their way down the hall. Hank eyed each of the doors they came to, though most of them were closed. As they started passing those doors, Hank started to get the feeling like the danger he had been expecting was behind them, rather than ahead. It made him look back down the hallway as often as not.

"I don't like this," Hank said, before they made it down the first hallway. "Let's just go back."

"Fine, then give me the phone and I'll do it," Jack said.

"What?"

"If you're going to be all scared about walking down a dark and smelly hallway, let me do it."

"But..." Hank looked backward, down the dark hallway, back towards the front of the building. They had gotten far enough that, without the light from the phone, he wouldn't be able to see anything before making it back to the lobby. He somehow doubted that Jack would bother to light his way back there with the phone before heading onward. "Well, if you're not scared, then why are you walking so slowly?"

"To give the band time to sync with the phone," Jack said. "I don't know how large the radius is, and I don't want to miss it by walking too quickly."

"The radius isn't that small. As long as we're not running, it shouldn't be a problem."

"Oh, good. That'll speed things along nicely." Jack grabbed up the phone out of Hank's hands before he could stop him. He lifted the phone up, letting the flashlight extend all the way down the hall to the stairwell door at the end. "Try to keep up, will you?" he said, grinning back at Hank maliciously, before rushing off down the hall.

"That would be running," Hank said, as he hurried to keep up.

Jack laughed back at him, but didn't slow the pace any. He ran right into the stairwell, using his momentum to open the door. They didn't have to go much further, though. The phone let off a sound halfway up to the second floor. Jack stopped in mid-step, and Hank had to jump to the side to avoid slamming into him from behind.

"What was that?" Hank asked, hoping that he already knew what the answer was.

"It's syncing," Jack said. "I have coordinates. Shall we call up the brain trust to narrow it down?"

"Those coordinates will be for the phone," Hank said. "Why don't we just keep going up the stairs until it loses the connection. That will at least narrow down which floor it's on."

Jack shrugged, before continuing onward, heading up the stairwell. Hank followed until the landing on the second floor. When he turned to follow Jack further up, he saw something, some kind of flash out of the corner of his eye. It was coming from the window in the door to the second floor. Curious, Hank walked over to the window, trying to see through the dark glass. As the light from the phone faded behind him, his eyes adjusted to the darkness, and he could see the low glow that came through the hallway on the other side. Like on the ground floor, the hallway was mostly dark, with the occasional flickering from the lights on the ceiling. However, as he stared through the window, he could see much better than he should have been able to.

"What are you looking at?" came Jack's voice right behind him.

"Damn it, Jack," Hank said, jumping at the man's voice. "Don't do that."

"Sorry. I thought you were right behind me."

"I thought I saw something. Let's go."

"No need. I got up halfway to the third floor and the band disconnected again. It's somewhere on this floor."

"Oh... Great."

"What? Did you see a ghost?"

"There's no such things as ghosts," Hank said, more to himself than to Jack. "Come on."

Hank pulled open the door to the hallway. It squeaked on its hinges, the sound echoing off the hallway walls. Hank glared at the door and its unexpected betrayal, but continued forward onto the floor, knowing that whoever had his band would no doubt know that they were coming for them.

"So, do we just check each of these apartments one at a time now?" Jack whispered.

"No," Hank said, in a normal tone. "Let's see how far down the hallway we get before losing connection with the band. The right apartment should be somewhere in the middle."

"Or, maybe we just go to the one with the candlelight flickering out from under the door," Jack whispered. He pointed into the distance, covering the light from the phone so that it no longer hid the feint light. It was only three doors down from the stairwell, on their right, about halfway to the elevators.

"Let's go meet the mystery guest, then," Hank said. He pulled out his gun, relying on the secure, familiar feel of the metal in his hand.

"Can I get one of those?" Jack asked.

"Just keep the light behind me," Hank said, ignoring his question.

The gun led the way down the hallway. Hank pointed it each way when he hit one of the pairs of doors, making sure that no one was hiding in wait to jump out at them. The candlelight in the distance could just as easily be a ploy, bait for the two agents coming for the thief that took his fitness band. It was such a silly thing, for them to go to such lengths for something so easily replaced. But after everything that had happened that week, after everything that Hank had gone through, it was just this one last thing that he could have some control over.

He needed control. Wanted it back so badly he could taste it. And, with his quarry close at hand, he wasn't about to leave empty handed.

As they came to the third pair of doors, Hank checked the one on the left, even going so far as testing the lock, before turning his full attention to the door in question. He placed his back against the secure door, using it as leverage as he sprang forward, kicking open the door across from it. The candlelight spilled out into the hall, but Hank was no longer there. He burst forward, into the apartment, his gun flitting every which way. Searching for a target. Searching for the thief. Searching for something to kill.

A whimper directed his attention to the far corner where a person sat on the floor, huddled in on himself, his head on his knees as if hiding from the agents. The hardwood floors of the apartment were a mess, covered in dirt, dust, and other material that was less identifiable. A path had been made in the dust, one going directly between the door and where the huddled person sat. The person seemed just as messy as the floor, as if he had been rolling around in it for days, though no such disturbance seemed apparent on the floor anywhere.

Hank focused on that one person, the only one in sight, taking three steps towards him across the wide-open space. His footsteps boomed against the hardwood. The man in the corner seemed to flinch at each of them, until he finally looked up from his knees.

Hank stopped right there, still a few paces away from the man, when he recognized who he was.

Chapter Thirty-Nine
Doppelganger

"Jared?" Hank asked.

"No," Jared said. "No, no, no. My name isn't Jared. I'm not that demon."

"Yea, right," Jack said. "You're just trying to get out of being flagged a demon."

"Wait a minute," Hank said. He took two steps towards the hunched figure. When he was within reach, he grabbed him by the ear that was just barely visible behind his crossed arm. He pulled the ear up and away from his crossed arms, pulling the man's face into full view. The man squirmed a little at the invasion of his personal space, but otherwise didn't respond. Hank glared down at his eyes, watching, waiting. It was the only surefire way to detect a demon. Pulling on their ears causes their eyes to flash yellow with demon sign. When they didn't turn yellow, when they stayed their normal brown, Hank's eyes went wide with shock. "This isn't Jared," he confirmed. "This is... are you the man that Jared took the place of?"

"Well, wait, wouldn't his name still be Jared?" Jack asked.

"No, Jared was the demon's name."

"That's an awfully human name for a demon."

"How many times do I have to tell you, demons were human once, too."

"I'm not a demon," Jared's doppelganger yelled.

"Hey, it's alright. It's okay. I know you're not a demon," Hank said, trying to calm the man. "What's your name?"

"Mike," he said. "My name is Mike. Mike Caraway."

"Nice to meet you, Mike. I'm Hank. I'm... well, we're kind of police." He didn't want to mention that they were HPS. The man seemed traumatized enough, and hung up on being associated with Jared.

"Police?" Mike asked. His eyes went wide as he tried to back further away from them, back into the wall behind them. "No, no, no. No police."

"No, it's alright, it's okay. We're here to help you."

"No, it's a trick. You're just here to arrest me."

"Why would we be here to arrest you?"

"I heard you talking out there," he said, in a harsh whisper. His finger pointed towards the door behind them. "You're here because I took this." He pulled something out of his pocket, cradling it tenderly as if it were precious to him. Despite that, the object was covered in grime and soot. "I found it. I didn't steal it."

"It's okay. It's alright," Hank said, again. "May I?" Slowly, he reached towards the object, taking it out of Mike's hands.

The fitness band leapt alive in his hand, as if greeting an old friend. It let out three long beeps as the status lights lit up along the side, one by one along with the beeps. His blinked green a few times before turning more solid. Even without it on his wrist, it was able to detect his heart beat, detect that it was him. Hank smoothed out the display, cleaning it off a little as he did so, trying to get it back to the like new state he had always kept it in.

He smiled down at Mike. "Thanks," he said. "I've been looking for this."

"I... but..." Mike stuttered.

"I'm not stealing it, and neither did you," Hank said. "It belongs to me. You just found it, right?"

"Um... Right."

"And you returned it to its rightful owner."

"Right," Mike said again, though he sounded close to tears.

"Why don't I return the favor then? I can help you get back on your feet. Surely you don't want to live here--"

"This is my apartment," he said.

"No, I know," Hank said, placating him. "You've lived here for a while. But it's not safe here. Wouldn't you like to live in a place with actual people... and maybe some furniture?"

"No, this is my apartment. I live here. My name is on the lease. I've been here for years."

"Wait, you lived here before the invasion?" Jack asked.

"I've lived here for years," he said again.

"Were you out of town during the invasion?" Hank asked. "Did you... Don't you know what happened here?"

"I... No, I... I went somewhere, somewhere awful."

"Canada?" Jack asked. "Sounds like Canada."

"No, not Canada," Mike said. "I've been to Canada. Canada is beautiful. This place... It was awful, dark and scary. I... I don't know where I was. I don't know how I got back. But, when I got back, everything was different. Everything and nothing. Everyone I knew was dead. My neighbors. My... my w-wife. All dead. I... I think I was... in hell. Is that possible? Could I have been in hell? Am I still in hell? Is that why there are demons everywhere? Why a demon stole my face? Is this hell?"

"No, this is Seattle," Jack said. "But I can understand the confusion."

"Oh, shut up, Jack," Hank snapped. "Can't you see this is no time for jokes?"

"What are you talking about? It's always time for jokes. Jokes make the world go 'round and turns frowns upside down. Without jokes, life would be hell." Mike flinched away from the word, as if he was afraid that the word alone would be enough to send him back there.

"It's alright," Hank said, soothingly. He placed his hand gingerly on Mike's arm, trying to reassure him that he was safe. "It's alright. You're home."

"But, not," Mike said.

"Yea," Hank agreed. "How long have you been back from hell?"

"I-I don't know. Three, four days maybe? It's all so..."

"How long were you there for?"

"I... I don't... I can't..."

"No, it's alright. It's alright. Let's take it from another angle, alright? When did you leave? What day was it before you went to hell?"

"It was... December... I think."

Hank gave a heavy sigh. He sat down on the floor next to Mike, scooting around so that he was sitting next to him, against the wall across from the door. "That must have been rough, being in hell for all that time, alone."

"Oh, come on," Jack huffed. "You can't honestly be buying this."

"What?" Hank asked, surprised. "What are you talking about?"

"Everyone knows you can't just go to hell. If we could go there, we'd have sent the demons back months ago."

"Months?" Mike asked. "It's been months since they've been here?"

"It's September," Jack snapped. "He's just some crazy person. Let's just arrest him, put him in a cell so he can get a decent bed and some warm meals and let's be done with it already. I haven't slept since before the office was hit. I'd like to go home, take a long, hot shower, and sleep until Monday."

"Tomorrow is Friday," Hank said.

"I'm taking a personal day."

"Fine, whatever. Except, well, I don't think he's crazy. Or, well, not about that. I mean, spending months alone in hell should be enough to drive anyone crazy."

"God, even if he was in hell, he wouldn't be alone, right?" Jack said. "I mean, there were other demons there, right? The ones that hadn't come with the invasion. I mean, there are only a few thousand demons here right now. How could that have been all of them that had been in hell?"

"There was no one there," Mike said. "No one and nothing but dark, empty, vacant rooms, stone hallways, ashen planes, and grassy fields."

"Now, see, you had me right up to the grassy fields," Jack said.

"I don't know," Mike said, folding his head into his hands. "I don't know. There was grass, but it was like... like a football field, except it went on for forever. I tried... I looked everywhere, but there was no one there. I was all alone, with nothing and no one for all of eternity."

"Ha, but then how did you survive it? Huh? How did you survive without food and water if there was nothing there?"

"There was... a tree... Some kind of tree that kept... I mean, there were apples."

"Apples?" Hank asked. "Like... could that have been the tree of knowledge?"

"I don't... I don't think so. There were no snakes, or..."

"Oh, come off it. Like I said before, you can't go to hell. No one can go to hell."

"Except hell came to us," Hank said.

"Yea. You can get from hell to here, but you can't go back to hell. You'd need like... magic or something. Like at the prison, only more of it."

"The prison?" Mike asked.

Hank glared over at Jack, pointedly. He didn't seem to notice, though. "And if he went there in December, well, that was before the source fell to earth, isn't it?"

"Except he probably went on the 21st," Hank said.

"The 21st?" Mike asked. "I... I guess so."

"Invasion day? But then..." Jack stopped mid-sentence, his face still stuck in an incredulous, smug expression as his mind caught up with Hank's own thoughts on the subject. "Oh," he said, simply.

"Those portals must have gone both ways," Hank said. "As the demons came here, he could have been sent there. Now that we know that it could have happened, I'm surprised it didn't happen more often. There could have been any number of people sent over to hell as the demons came here, maybe even as many as demons came over."

"No," Jack said. "We saw evidence of a good portion of the deaths that happened that day. They couldn't have all just gone to hell... well, at least not through the portals."

"But... no one was there; not humans, not demons."

"Hell is a big place, isn't it?"

"Well, it didn't seem like it," Mike said.

"But... still, there had to be other demons there, right?" Jack asked.

"The demons always said there was a reason they came here," Hank said. "It was just that only the higher ups knew what it was."

"Yea, and no one would ever cop to being one of those higher ups. But, seriously? Abandoning hell in its entirety? What the hell could have happened?"

"Well, how did you get back?" Hank asked.

Mike seemed a bit surprised by the question, and he just shook his head for a few seconds. "I-I don't know. I just... came back. I was walking to the tree again, to get some more food, and then, suddenly, I was back, I was here, and no one else was here."

"And you've just been hiding out here all this time?" Jack asked.

"Um... well... mostly," Mike said.

"Wait... You said... You mentioned Jared," Hank said. "How would you have known about Jared?"

"No, Hank, you brought up Jared," Jack said. "Because they look exactly alike."

"I said he looked just like Jared," Hank said. "But... I never said he was a demon."

"I saw that monster," Mike said. His face turned from the scared, tortured expression that had been there the entire time to something else, something darker. His eyes seemed to turn black, and the light from the phone faded a little. "I saw him, walking around with my face. How dare he? It's my face. Mine."

"Okay," Hank said, trying to placate the man. "You're right. It's your face. He had no right to use it without your permission."

"Yea, especially since he had his own," Jack muttered.

"What did you do when you spotted him?" Hank asked. "Where did you spot him?"

"I didn't steal the car," Mike practically shouted. Hank took a step away from him, trying to give the man some space. He seemed to be answering a question he hadn't asked yet. "It was like... what you said about the watch. I was just borrowing it. I know the owner. I know Jennifer. I don't know what she told you, but... I didn't steal the car."

"Oh, god," Jack said. He looked at Hank, looking more shocked than he had ever seen him.

"What?" Hank asked.

"She let me borrow it plenty of times before," Mike said. "I even knew where she kept the keys. I didn't steal it. I was going for groceries and there he was. He looked so smug coming out of that house, a house that I could have never afforded, not with what I make. But that job is probably long gone, too."

"Uh, yea," Jack said. "I'm sure Jennifer wouldn't have minded you borrowing her car. I mean, it's been a while since I had seen her last."

"Oh, please, you don't know Jennifer," Mike snapped. "You're just trying to placate me, to calm me down. It's not going to work."

"No," Jack said. "You don't understand. Jennifer was my cousin. Well, second cousin, or something. I don't know. That side of the family was much older than me and I lost touch of them over a decade ago. But I remember Jennifer. She was nice."

"Was? What, is she a bitch now?"

"No, she's dead. She died a few months back. I only found out about it a couple of days ago, when I ran into my aunt."

"Oh," Hank said, finally catching up with the conversation. "Oh," he said again, as he looked towards Mike.

Mike was no longer huddled in a ball in the corner. He was standing there, his back against the walls. His hands were solidly against them as if to spring off of it at the agents. He was like a cornered animal, and whatever happened to him in hell, or perhaps it was seeing that demon pretending to be him, was making him almost unrecognizable. His eyes darted back and forth between the two agents, darting around, looking for a way past them.

"You don't have anything on me," he shouted out, as he jumped forward.

Hank and Jack turned to the side, avoiding the sudden projectile that Mike had become, as the man darted towards the front door. He didn't get far, though, tripping on Hank's foot when he didn't get it out of the way in time. Hank fell back against the wall, but Mike face planted in the middle of the hardwood floor. Stunned, Mike just lay there, as the two agents moved around him.

"So, what do you think?" Jack asked.

"Honestly? Can you really blame a person for killing their doppelganger?"

"That sounds like something I would say. We're not just going to let him off the hook on this one, are we?"

"Of course, not. We're arresting him. But, given everything that's transpired over the last few days, we might want to hand him over to the local PD. Perhaps that detective that pulled the case to begin with. He would make a nice peace offering."

"I don't know. I think the guy has a pretty solid insanity plea going for him. I mean, spending months alone in hell is enough to drive anyone crazy."

"Well, besides, he's human," Hank pointed out.

"Yea? So?"

"When was the last time we arrested a human?"

"Last... November? That thing in Delaware?"

"Exactly. We were ICE for that mission. We just handed them over to the field office and let them handle it. We've never actually arrested a human as HPS before."

"So?"

"So, what do we even do with him? We can't process him through the usual process. I mean, if he were a demon, we'd have ways to handle it. We'd send him to the prison for a certain amount of years, or forever. Demon on human, even demon on demon, we can do. But, human on demon? I think we might want to pass the buck on this one, anyway."

"Huh," Jack said, pensively. He looked down at the prone form of Mike, who seemed to be crying into the wood floor. "That's kind of a dangerous precedent, isn't it?"

"Maybe," Hank said. "Or, maybe it'll be the start of a lot more cooperation between all the law enforcement agencies. Wouldn't it be nice to spread out the workload a bit more and let us get back to doing what we do best?"

"Hiding behind other agencies?"

"No, solving the unsolvable cases."

"You want cases harder to solve than this one?" Jack asked.

"I'm surprised you're not gloating right now," Hank said.

"What? Why?"

"Well, didn't you say we'd just find the murderer hiding out in some abandoned building somewhere?"

Chapter Forty
What to Do About a Boy Named Mike

"Is that really necessary?" Blanche called out to them, as they came out the front door of the building. "Arresting someone for what basically amounts to petty theft? I mean, it was only a couple hundred dollars to replace the thing."

"Oh, we're not arresting him for petty theft," Jack said, with a level of glee that Hank hadn't seen from him in months. "We caught Jared's killer."

"Oh, come off it," Blanche said. "You're not going to pin this on some random guy you found in an abandoned building. I know you want to close the case and everything, but..."

"No, really. He killed him. Doesn't he look familiar to you?"

"No. Should he?"

"Jared modeled his appearance off of him," Hank said. "It must have been off of a picture inside. Mike here used to live here, but he got pulled into hell when the demons came."

"Wait, seriously? That can happen?"

"Not anymore, I imagine, 'cause there's no one left in hell to do it," Jack said. "It certainly puts the invasion in a whole new light, doesn't it?"

"But... He had the fitness band, right? Or... I mean, why would he have taken the fitness band? How would he have gotten it?"

"I... I came by the HPS offices the other day," Mike said. "I was at a low point. I wanted to turn myself in."

"See? A killer with a conscience," Jack said. "He must have come by while we were under attack and found the band lying on the ground."

"It was a perfectly good watch, just lying there on the ground, forgotten. I thought it was a shame for something like that to go to waste, when all my possessions had been taken away from me. I didn't know it was anything more than that. What is a fitness band?"

"Originally, they were just to track a person's heart rate while exercising, to make sure they're keeping in the targeted zone or whatever," Blanche explained. "After the invasion, Angel Corp showed up with a supercharged version that could track a person's vitals well enough that no one would be able to pose as them. Suddenly, there was a huge need for something like it."

"Yea, but it doesn't help much in determining who is human and who is demon," Hank said. "For that, we need to tug on their ear a little. Works every time, though."

"Every time that we know about at least," Jack said.

"Anyway, watch your head," Hank said. He pushed Mike's head down as he slid him into the back seat of the crown vic, slamming the door behind him once he was in.

"I kind of feel sorry for him," Blanche said.

"Yea, we all do," Hank said. "He's having some mental issues right now."

"To say the least," Jack said.

"Nothing a long stay in a padded room won't help with."

"Well, Herb and Jenkins should be back tomorrow," Blanche said. "We can start rebuilding the offices."

"We're going to need some serious discussions about security," Hank said. "That can't happen again. We should try to go back to being covert, or at least our offices should. We're not going to do anyone any good if we get ourselves killed."

"And, Hank wants to start working with the local PD's," Jack said.

"Yea. Give them the credit. We'll just run support where needed. Have them all get a special task force for dealing with the demons. Even if we let on that there is some way for us to contain the demons, as long as we don't reveal just what that is, it's better than having all that knowledge condensed in one office. I mean, can you imagine if those gunmen had hit us when everyone was there, and we didn't have the kill bot to save us? No more HPS, no more prison, demons all out and about until they take over the world."

"Speaking of which, I'll be heading out first thing tomorrow to start rounding up those demons," Blanche said. "As soon as Jenkins is back."

"What about rebuilding?" Jack asked.

"Well, if we're not going to be rebuilding as is, it might be a better use of my time. We can't very well let them continue to run amok around the place, especially those more well-known demons. If people catch wind of their escape, not only will they know that we have a way to contain them, but the demons might spill the secrets themselves. It would probably work in their favor for the world to know that they had been held prisoner in a magic prison."

"So much for our family vacation," Hank said.

"If this works out, we'll be able to have one next September. We'll take the whole month off. Sound better?"

"Sure, but you're just saying that. Something is going to come up before that happens, and we'll have to drop everything again."

"What could possibly go wrong?" Blanche asked.

As if to answer her question, her phone started to ring. Hank gave a half smile, motioning towards the phone. "You might as well see what else has gone wrong."

Blanche rolled her eyes as she pulled out the phone. She fiddled around with the screen until she managed to answer it, putting it on speaker so the three of them could hear. "Hey, Danielle," she said. "What is it now?"

"Well, I'm not sure if this is a good thing or a bad thing, exactly," she said. "I just... well, it's going to be headline news tomorrow, obviously."

"What is it, Danielle?" Hank asked.

"It's about Randolph Judd."

"Oh, him," Hank said. "Right. We still have one loose end on that end."

"Actually, you're not going to be able to get much out of him anymore," Danielle said.

"What? Did he run off to Mexico?" Jack asked. "Switzerland?"

"No... He's... He's dead. The helicopter he was in, it crashed down in Oregon."

"Yea, right," Hank said.

"No, it's true," Danielle said. "It's all over the news right now. They have pictures of the crash and everything."

"That doesn't mean that he was on the helicopter when it went down," Hank said. "He's just running from us, now that we know he's involved with Remember Sami. And, with that Cindy person showing up at his offices, minutes after he left, he was probably wrapped up in the terrorist cell as well."

"Yea, but without Cindy around to corroborate that," Blanche said. "Why would he run, though?"

"'Cause he didn't know that Cindy was dead," Jack said.

"Guys, will you please listen to me?" Danielle yelled. "They're showing them pulling his body out of the wreckage right now."

"Not his body," Hank said. "'Cause he's not dead."

"There was no one else on the helicopter."

"Exactly," Hank said. "It was the pilot."

"He was the pilot," Danielle said. "I verified it with our satellite network. One person, Judd, got on. The helicopter went straight south, heading for the state border. Just before it, the craft started drifting. Then it crashed. I didn't lose sight of the thing the entire time. There didn't even seem like there was any problem with it until it went down."

"Could he have crashed it on purpose?" Blanche asked.

"Uh... Sure, I guess. But what would be the point of that? Those choppers aren't designed to take a nose dive into hard ground. And he hit inside a parking lot. It's not even like he landed in some trees or something, somewhere that he had a chance to survive the fall. The thing crumpled in on itself, folding into a ball of metal. It didn't explode, but that would have been overkill at that point."

"Maybe he forgot to fill the tank," Jack suggested. "He was in a bit of a hurry, trying to get away from you when he did."

"Except he needn't have been," Hank said. "He knew we were coming. He knew why we were coming. He probably knew about the attack on our office. Cindy showing up might have thrown him, but he could have hidden her until we left. The building was certainly big enough, and it wasn't like we were looking for her there."

"Well, crap, he's really dead, isn't he?" Blanche said. "That certainly makes things more complicated."

"Maybe for the hate group," Jack said. "They lost their leader."

"No, I mean us tracking down that terrorist cell. Judd was our only lead on their leadership."

"Well, we saw plenty of people up on that stage at the rally," Jack said. "One of them is probably going to take over as leader of the hate group, maybe even the terrorist cell while they're at it."

"Oh, right, and I have video of it, don't I?" Hank said, remembering. "I just have to..." He pulled out his phone and started flipping through the files. It took him a few moments to find the right location, but there wasn't anything in it. Confused, he recorded a sample video for a few seconds. But, when that file showed up where he expected, he realized what must have happened to the video. "Damn it, I think Cindy deleted it."

"Are you sure you even saved it to begin with?" Jack asked.

"Yes, I'm sure."

"Well, we can find out where the next rally is," Jack suggested. "Onward and upward, right?"

"No," Blanche said, raining on his parade. "I'm going to find the next rally. Jenkins and I. You two are going back to playing with the nice demons that need your help."

"But none of them need our help right now," Jack said.

"Actually, they do," Hank said. "It's been open season on them ever since the contact list got leaked. Hopefully, that will have stopped, what with Cindy out of the way. But there's no guarantee of that. We need to track down the group that's been--"

"Oh, no," Blanche interrupted. "Jenkins and I will--"

"But then what are we supposed to be doing?" Hank asked.

"How about go home," Blanche suggested. "Rest up. Take your vacation and turn it into more of a staycation. Or, better yet, head up to Canada and spend some time with our daughter. At least one of us should while we still can. Leave the dangerous stuff to the grownups."

"Either way, you guys," Danielle said, interrupting them. "It's been a long day, a long week. Jenkins isn't going to be back till tomorrow, and you have a case to put to bed. Why don't you bring your prisoner to central booking? They're better equipped than us to handle a human prisoner right now. Heck, they'd be better equipped to handle any prisoner right now. I'll make sure they know you're coming. Once he's safe and sound, everyone can go home and fill out the paperwork."

"Yea, and what about that whole task force idea?" Jack said. "You'll need to lead that up, at least until Herb gets back and can take credit for it. Focus on that while your wife heads back out into danger and kicks everyone's asses."

"It is what I do," Blanche said.

"Alright, fine," Hank said. "Danielle, reach out to the detective from earlier. In the spirit of inter-agency cooperation, and as a start to the task force we want to put together, we're going to be giving him the collar."

"Okay, uh... What exactly is this task force of yours?"

Hank smiled at Blanche and Jack. He nodded towards the car, moving around to the driver's side. Blanche wasn't about to give up the passenger seat, which left Jack stuck riding in the back with Mike. As they drove off towards central booking, which Danielle had to give them the address to, he explained his vision for the future of handling crime involving demons. Whether they were the perpetrator or the victim, or even both. With the prisoners from the penitentiary in the wind, and all the events they no doubt missed out on while they were on their little goose hunt, they were going to need all the help they could get.

###

About the Author

Cassandra Morphy is a Business Data Analyst, working with numbers by day, but words by night. She grew up escaping the world, into the other realities of books, TV shows, and movies, and now she writes about those same worlds. Her only hope in life is to reach one person with her work, the way so many others had reached her. As a TV addict and avid movie goer, her entire life is just one big research project, focused on generating innovative ideas for worlds that don't exist anywhere other than in her sick, twisted mind.

Other books by this author

Please visit your favorite ebook retailer to discover other books by Cassandra Morphy:

Crowbarland Chronicles
In Time for Prom
The Awakening
Demons Force
Angels Innocence
Crowbarland Prep
Light Through the Windows
Last Scientist
Missing Mars

The Delnadian Invasion
Alien Fireworks
Alien Life
Alien Death
Alien War

Desparian Legacies
The Prophecy
Mountain Princess

Doors of Despair
The Mind's Door
The Door in the Sky
Gates of the Inferno
Heaven's Door
Door to Victory

No One Can Hear You
Travel
Train
Thrive
Fly
Spy